DISCARDED

don't look back

Jennifer L. Armentrout

HYPERION

NEW YORK

Copyright © 2014 by Jennifer L. Armentrout

For information address Hyperion, 125 West End Avenue,
New York, New York 10023-6387.

First Edition
1 3 5 7 9 10 8 6 4 2
G475-5664-5-14015

Printed in the United States of America
This book is set in 12-pt. Griffo Classico
Designed by Tyler Nevins

Library of Congress Cataloging-in-Publication Data
Armentrout, Jennifer L.
    Don't look back/Jennifer L. Armentrout.—First edition.
        pages cm
    Summary: Seventeen-year-old Sam seems to have everything until
she and her best friend, Cassie, disappear one night and now Sam has
returned with amnesia, striving to be a much better person and aware
that her not remembering may be the only thing keeping Cassie alive.
    ISBN 978-1-4231-7512-4 (hardback)—ISBN 1-4231-7512-3
[1. Missing persons—Fiction.   2. Amnesia—Fiction.   3. Identity—
Fiction.   4. Interpersonal relations—Fiction.   5. Dating (Social
customs)—Fiction.   6. Family life—Fiction.   7. Mystery and
detective stories.]   I. Title.   II. Title: Do not look back.
    PZ7.A699Don 2014
    [Fic]—dc23   2013047574

Reinforced binding

Visit www.hyperionteens.com

SUSTAINABLE FORESTRY INITIATIVE   Certified Sourcing
www.sfiprogram.org
SFI-00993

THIS LABEL APPLIES TO TEXT STOCK

*Dedicated to every reader and every blogger,
big and small, new and old.*

don't look back

chapter one

I didn't recognize the name on the street sign. Nothing about the rural road looked familiar or friendly. Tall, imposing trees and overgrown weeds choked the front of the dilapidated home. Windows were boarded up. There was a gaping hole where the front door had been. I shivered, wanting to be far away from here . . . wherever here was.

Walking felt harder than it should be, and I stumbled off the chilly asphalt, wincing as sharp gravel dug into my feet.

My *bare* feet?

I stopped and looked down. Chipped pink nail polish peeked through the dirt . . . and blood. Mud caked the legs of my pants, leaving the hems stiff. It made sense, seeing as how I wasn't wearing any shoes, but the blood . . . I didn't understand why there was blood staining the knees of my jeans.

My vision clouded and dulled, as if a gray film had been dropped over my eyes. As I stared at the weathered asphalt under my feet, large, smooth rocks replaced the tiny stones. Something dark and oily seeped over the rocks, slipping through the cracks.

Sucking in a sharp gasp, I blinked and the image was gone.

Hands trembling, I raised them. They were covered with dirt and scratches. My nails were broken, bloodied. A silver ring, encased in soil, wrapped around my thumb. Air froze in my chest as my gaze crawled over my arms. The sleeves of my sweater were torn, revealing pale flesh covered in bruises and gashes. My legs started to shake as I swayed forward. I tried to remember how this had happened, but my head was empty—a black void where nothing existed.

A car drove by, coasting to a stop a few feet in front of me. Somewhere in the trenches of my subconscious, I recognized the flashing red and blue lights as a source of safety. Elegantly scrawled along the black-and-gray side of the cruiser were the words ADAMS COUNTY SHERIFF'S DEPARTMENT.

Adams County? A flash of familiarity came and went.

The driver's door opened, and a deputy stepped out. He said something into the radio on his shoulder before he looked at me.

"Miss?" He started around the cruiser, taking tentative steps. He looked young for a deputy. Being barely out of high school and able to carry a gun seemed wrong somehow. Was I in high school? I didn't know. "We've received some calls into dispatch concerning you," he said gently. "Are you okay?"

I tried to respond, but only a hoarse squeak came out. Clearing my throat, I winced as the motion scratched and pulled. "I . . . I don't know."

"Okay." The deputy held up his hands as he approached me, as if I were a skittish deer about to bolt. "My name is Deputy Rhode. I'm here to help you. Do you know what you're doing out here?"

"No." Knots formed in my belly. I didn't even know where *here* was.

His smile strained. "What's your name?"

My name? Everyone knew their name, but as I stared at the deputy, I couldn't answer his question. The knots started twisting more. "I don't . . . I don't know what my name is."

He blinked, and the smile was completely gone. "You don't remember anything?"

I tried again, concentrating on the empty space between my ears. That was how it felt. And I knew that wasn't good. My eyes started to tear up.

"Miss, it's okay. We'll get you taken care of." He reached out, lightly taking hold of my arm. "We'll get this sorted."

Deputy Rhode led me around the back of his cruiser. I didn't want to sit behind the Plexiglas. Only bad people sat behind the glass in police cruisers. I knew that much. I wanted to object, but before I could say anything, he settled me into the seat and wrapped a coarse blanket around my shoulders.

Before he locked me in the bad part of the car, he knelt and smiled reassuringly. "Everything's going to be okay."

But I knew he was lying, trying to make me feel better. It didn't work. How could everything be okay when I didn't know my own name?

5

jennifer l. armentrout

* * *

I didn't know my name, but I knew I hated hospitals. They were cold and sterile, smelling like disinfectant and desperation. Deputy Rhode left me once the doctors started a battery of tests. My pupils were checked, X-rays were done, and my blood was taken. The nurses bandaged the side of my head and cleaned the numerous wounds. They'd given me a private room, hooking me up to an IV that pumped "fluids that will help you feel better" into me, and left.

A nurse eventually wheeled in a cart laden with a set of ominous-looking instruments and a camera. Why was there a camera?

She silently bagged my clothes after giving me a scratchy hospital gown to change into. She smiled when she looked at me, just as the deputy had. False and well practiced.

I learned I didn't like those kinds of smiles. They gave me the creeps.

"We need to do some more tests on you while the X-rays are being run, sweetie." She gently pushed my shoulders down on the hard mattress. "We also need to take some pictures of your injuries."

Staring at the white ceiling, I found it hard to pull enough air into my lungs. It was even worse when she made me scoot down. A surge of embarrassment shocked me. *This is so awkward.* My breath caught. That thought wasn't from now, but before . . . before what?

"Relax, sweetie." The nurse moved to stand beside the cart. "The police are contacting neighboring counties for missing

6

person reports. They'll find your family soon." She picked up something long and thin that gleamed under the bright, impersonal light.

After a couple of minutes, tears streaked my cheeks. The nurse seemed used to it because she did her thing and left without saying another word. I curled up under the thin blanket, pulling my knees to my chest. I stayed like that, with my empty thoughts, until I fell asleep.

I dreamed of falling—falling endlessly into the darkness, over and over again. There were screams—shrill sounds that raised the tiny hairs on my body—and then nothing but a soft, lulling sound I found comforting.

Upon waking the following morning, I decided to start small. What was my name? I had to have one, but there was nothing I could grasp on to. Rolling onto my back, I yelped as the IV pulled on my hand. Beside me, there was a plastic cup of water. I sat up slowly and grabbed the cup. It shook in my hand, sloshing water over the blanket.

Water—there was something about water. Dark, oily water.

The door opened, and the nurse entered with the doctor who'd examined me the night before. I liked him. His smile was genuine, fatherly. "Do you remember my name?" When I didn't answer immediately, his smile didn't falter. "I'm Dr. Weston. I just want to ask you a few questions."

He asked the same questions everyone else had. Did I remember my name? Did I know how I'd gotten on the road or what I'd been doing before the deputy picked me up? The answer to all his questions was the same: no.

7

But when he moved on to other questions, I had answers. "Have you ever read *To Kill a Mockingbird*?"

My dry lips cracked when I smiled. I knew that answer! "Yeah, it's about racial injustice and different kinds of courage."

Dr. Weston nodded approvingly. "Good. Do you know what year it is?"

I arched an eyebrow. "It's 2014."

"Do you know what month it is?" When I didn't answer immediately, his smile slipped.

"It's March." I moistened my lips, starting to get nervous. "But I don't know what day."

"Today is March twelfth. It's Wednesday. What is the last day you remember?"

I picked at the edge of the blanket and took a guess. "Tuesday?"

Dr. Weston's lips once more curved into a smile. "It had to be longer than that. You were dehydrated when they brought you in. Can you try again?"

I could, but what would be the point? "I don't know."

He asked some more questions, and when an orderly brought in lunch, I discovered I hated mashed potatoes. Dragging the IV behind me like baggage, I stared at a stranger in the bathroom mirror.

I'd never seen her face before.

But it was mine. I leaned forward, inspecting the reflection. Coppery hair hung in clumps around a slightly sharp chin. My cheekbones were high, and my eyes were a cross between brown and green. I had a small nose. That was good news. And

I guessed I'd be pretty if it weren't for the purplish bruise spreading from my hairline and covering my entire right eye. The skin was scuffed on my chin. Like a giant raspberry stain.

I pushed away from the sink, pulling my IV back into the tiny room. Raised voices outside the closed door halted my attempts to get into the bed.

"What do you mean, she has no memory of anything?" a woman's thin voice demanded.

"She has a complex concussion, which has affected her memory," Dr. Weston explained patiently. "The memory loss should be temporary, but—"

"But what, Doctor?" asked a man.

At the sound of the stranger's voice, a conversation floated out of the cloudy recesses of my thoughts, like a distant television show you could hear but not see.

I really wish you wouldn't spend so much time with that girl. She's nothing but trouble, and I don't like the way you act around her.

It was his voice—the man outside—but I didn't recognize the tenor and there was nothing else associated with it.

"The memory loss *could* be permanent. These things are hard to predict. Right now, we just don't know." Dr. Weston cleared his throat. "The good news is that the rest of her injuries are superficial. And from what we can gather from additional exams, she wasn't assaulted."

"Oh my god," cried the woman. "Assaulted? Like in—"

"Joanna, the doctor said she wasn't assaulted. You need to calm down."

"I have a right to be upset," she snapped. "Steven, she's been missing for four days."

"The county boys picked her up outside Michaux State Forest." Dr. Weston paused. "Do you know why she'd be there?"

"We have a summer home there, but it hasn't been opened since September. And we checked there. Right, Steven?"

"But she's okay, right?" asked the man. "It's just her memory that's a problem?"

"Yes, but it's not a simple case of amnesia," the doctor said.

I backed away from the door and climbed into the bed. My heart was pounding again. Who were these people, and why were they here? I pulled the blanket up to my shoulders. I caught bits and pieces of what the doctor was saying. Something about suffering an extreme shock combined with dehydration and the concussion—a medical perfect storm, where my brain had dissociated from my personal identity. Sounded complicated.

"I don't understand," I heard the woman say.

"It's like writing something on your computer and then you save the file, but you can't remember where you saved it," the doctor explained. "The file is in there, but you just have to find it. She still has her personal memories. They're in there, but she can't access them. She may never find them."

I sat back, dismayed. Where did I put the file?

Then the door swung open, and I shrank back as this woman—this force to be reckoned with—stormed into my room. Her deep russet-colored hair was pulled into an elegant twist, exposing an angular but beautiful face.

She came to a complete stop, her eyes darting all over me. "Oh, Samantha..."

I stared. *Samantha?* The name didn't do anything for me. I glanced at the doctor. He nodded reassuringly. *Sa-man-tha...* Nope, still nothing.

The woman came closer. There wasn't a single wrinkle in her linen pants or her white blouse. Golden bangles hung from each of her slender wrists, and she reached out, wrapping her arms around me. She smelled like freesia.

"Baby girl," she said, her hand smoothing my hair as she looked me in the eyes. "God, I'm so happy you're okay."

I pulled back, clamping my arms to my sides.

The woman glanced over her shoulder. The strange man looked pale, shaken. His dark hair was a mess. Thick stubble covered his handsome face. Compared to this woman, he was a barely contained disaster. I stared until he turned away, rubbing a shaky hand down his cheek.

Dr. Weston came to the bedside. "This is Joanna Franco—your mother. And this is Steven Franco, your father."

A pressure started building in my chest. "My...my name is Samantha?"

"Yes," the woman answered. "Samantha Jo Franco."

My middle name was *Jo*? Seriously? My gaze darted between the people. I took a deep breath, but it got stuck.

Joanna—*my mom*—whoever she was—placed a hand over her mouth as she glanced at the messy man, who was apparently my dad. Then her gaze settled on me. "You really don't recognize us?"

I shook my head. "No. I'm . . . I'm sorry."

She stood, backing away from the bed as she looked at Dr. Weston. "How can she not know us?"

"Mrs. Franco, you just need to give her some time." Then to me, "You're doing great."

It didn't seem that way.

He'd turned back to them—my parents. "We want to keep her under observation for an extra day. Right now, she needs to get a lot of rest and reassurance."

I looked at the man again. He was staring at me, sort of dazed-looking. Dad. Father. Complete stranger.

"Do you really think this could be permanent?" the man asked, rubbing his chin.

"It's too soon to tell," Dr. Weston responded. "But she's young and otherwise healthy, so the outlook is great." He started out of the room, stopping by the door. "Remember, she needs to take it easy."

My mom turned back to the bed, visibly pulling herself together as she sat down on the edge and took my hand. She turned it over, brushing her fingers over my wrist. "I remember the first and last time we had to take you to the hospital. You were ten. See this?"

I looked down at my wrist. There was a faint white scar running right under the palm of my hand. Huh. I hadn't noticed that before.

"You broke your wrist during gymnastics practice." She swallowed, looking up. Nothing about her hazel eyes, which were so much like my own, or the perfectly painted lips triggered anything inside me. There was just a vast, empty hole where all my memories, my emotions should've been. "It was a pretty bad break. You had to have surgery. Scared the living daylights out of us."

"You were showing off on the balance beam," my father added gruffly. "The instructor told you not to do—what was it?"

"A back handspring," my mom said quietly, keeping her gaze trained on me.

"Yes." He nodded. "But you did it anyway." He met my stare then. "Angel, you don't remember anything?"

Heaviness spread from my chest to my stomach. "I want to remember—really, I do. But I . . ." My voice cracked. I pulled my hand free, holding it to my chest. "I don't remember."

My mom forced a smile, clasping her hands together in her lap. "It's okay. Scott has been really worried. Your brother," she added when she saw my blank look. "He's at home right now."

I had a brother?

"And all your friends have been helping with the search party, hanging flyers and holding candlelight vigils," she continued. "Isn't that right, Steven?"

My father nodded, but the look on his face said he was a thousand miles from here. Maybe he was wherever this Samantha Jo was.

"Del has been beside himself, spending day and night looking for you." She smoothed back a piece of hair that had escaped her twist. "He wanted to come up with us, but we thought it would be best if he stayed behind."

I frowned. "Del?"

My father cleared his throat, refocusing on us. "Del Leonard. Your boyfriend, angel."

"My boyfriend?" Oh, sweet baby Jesus. Parents. Brother. And now a boyfriend?

My mom nodded. "Yes. You two have been together since, well, forever, it seems. You're planning to go to Yale in the fall with Del, like your fathers."

"Yale," I whispered. I knew what Yale was. "That sounds nice."

She glanced at my father pleadingly. He stepped forward, but two deputies entered the room. My mom stood, smoothing out her pants. "Gentlemen?"

I recognized Deputy Rhode, but the older officer was new to me. No big surprise there. He stepped forward, nodding at my parents. "We need to ask Samantha some questions."

"Can it wait?" asked my father, suddenly coming out of his slouch. An air of unmistakable authority surrounded him. "I'm sure there's a better time."

The older officer smiled tightly. "We're happy that your daughter appears to be in one piece, but unfortunately, there's another family who's still hoping for news on their daughter."

I sat up straighter, looking between my parents. "What?"

My mom came to my side, taking my hand once more. "They're talking about Cassie, honey."

"Cassie?"

She smiled, but it looked more like a grimace. "Cassie Winchester is your best friend. She disappeared with you."

chapter two

assie Winchester. *Best friend.* That was an important term, but just like *mother* or *father*, there were no memories or emotions tied to it. I stared at the officers, feeling as if I should show some sort of emotion, but I didn't know this girl—this Cassie.

The older cop introduced himself as Detective Ramirez, and he proceeded to ask the same questions that everyone had. "Do you know what happened?"

"No." I watched the liquid in the IV drip into my hand.

"What is the last thing you remember?" Deputy Rhode asked.

I lifted my eyes. He had his hands clasped behind his back, and he nodded when my eyes met his. It was such a simple question, and I really wanted to answer it correctly. I needed to. I glanced at my mom. The cool facade was starting to crumble. Her eyes were glistening, lower lip thin and trembling.

My dad cleared his throat. "Gentlemen, can this please wait?

She's been through a lot. And if she knew anything right now, she'd tell you."

"Anything," Detective Ramirez said, ignoring my father. "What is the last thing you remember?"

I squeezed my eyes shut. There had to be something. I knew I'd read *To Kill a Mockingbird*. More than likely, I must've done so in class, but I couldn't picture the school or the teacher. I didn't even know what grade I was in. This sucked.

Deputy Rhode moved closer, earning a disgruntled look from his partner. He reached into his breast pocket and pulled out a photo, showing it to me. It was a girl. She actually *looked* like me. Her hair wasn't as red as mine, though. It was browner, and her eyes were a startling, beautiful green—much more stunning than my own...but we could have passed as sisters. "Do you recognize her?"

Frustrated, I shook my head.

"It's okay if you don't. The doctor told us it may take a while to come back, and when—"

"Wait!" I jerked forward, forgetting that damn IV. It tugged at my hand, nearly coming loose. "Wait, I remember something."

My father stepped forward, but the detective warned him off by saying, "What do you remember?"

I swallowed, throat suddenly dry. It was nothing, but I felt as if it was some kind of huge achievement. "I remember rocks—like boulders—and they were smooth. Flat. Colored like sand." And there was blood, but I didn't say that, because I wasn't sure if that was true.

My parents exchanged looks, and Detective Ramirez sighed. My shoulders slumped. Obviously that was a fail.

The deputy patted my arm. "That's good. That's really good. We think you were in Michaux State Forest, and that would make sense."

Didn't feel good. I stared at my dirty nails, wishing everyone would all go away. But the officers lingered, talking to my parents as if I weren't capable of comprehending anything they were saying. Cassie's continued disappearance was major. I got that. And I *did* feel bad. I wanted to help them find her, but I didn't know how I could.

I sneaked a peek at them. Detective Ramirez watched me with eyes narrowed in intense, distrustful scrutiny. A shudder rolled down my spine, and I hastily looked away, feeling as if I deserved that look he was giving me.

Like I was guilty of something—something terrible.

Tendrils of fear coated in confusion crawled through me when the strangers—er, my parents—checked me out of the hospital the next day. I couldn't believe the authorities were just letting me leave with them. What if they weren't really my parents? What if they were psychos kidnapping me?

I was being ridiculous.

It wasn't as if random people would claim a seventeen-year-old girl for no reason, which is exactly how old I was. Discovered that when I peeked at my chart at the end of my bed that morning.

My gaze slid to my father's head of dark hair. An air of

influence coated his skin, seeped into everything he touched. I didn't need to know anything about him to realize that he was powerful.

Tall trees and rolling green hills that were as well manicured as the golf course I'd seen on the TV in my hospital room surrounded the road leading up to their house. We went over one dip in the road, and I saw a cluster of small houses that were cozy.

We drove past them . . . in our Bentley.

Quickly, I learned that they were rich. Sickeningly rich. It was funny how I didn't remember squat, but I knew what money *looked* like.

I kept rubbing the palm of my hand over the supple leather. The car had to be new because it had that crisp, just-manufactured scent.

Then I saw our house. Holy crap, it was the size of a small hotel. An intimidating structure with thick marble columns in the front, rising four or five stories into the sky, and the garage to the left was the size of the houses we'd passed a few moments ago.

"Is this really our house?" I asked when the car rounded a fountain—kind of gaudy—surrounded by foliage in the middle of the wraparound driveway.

Mom glanced back, smiling tightly. "Of course it is, sweetie. You've lived here your whole life. So have I. This was my parents' home."

"Was?" I asked, curious.

"They've moved to Coral Gables." She paused and took a little breath. "They're in Florida, honey. This is their family estate."

Estate. That was a fancy word. My gaze shifted to my dad

again, and I realized that Mom had said *their* and not *our*. As if the house wasn't Dad's home, but it was *her* family's.

Pushing that thought aside, I took a deep breath and then planted my face in the window again. Dear god, I lived in this place. Once I got inside the opulent foyer and saw the crystal chandelier that was probably worth more than my life, I suddenly didn't want to move. Expensive stuff was everywhere. The rug near the grand staircase looked soft. Oil paintings of foreign landscapes graced the buttercream walls. There were so many doors, so many rooms.

My breath was coming out in short, raspy bursts. I couldn't move.

Dad placed his hand on my shoulder, squeezing gently. "It's okay, Sammy, just take it easy."

I stared into the face of the man I should know. His dark eyes; handsome smile; tough, hard jaw ... There was nothing. My dad was a stranger. "Where is my room?"

He dropped his hand. "Joanna, why don't you take her upstairs?"

Mom came forward at a slow, measured pace, wrapping her cool hand around my arm. She led me upstairs, chattering about who'd helped search for me. The mayor had taken part, which apparently was a big deal to her, and then the governor had sent our family his prayers.

"Governor?" I whispered.

She nodded and a slight smile pulled at her lips. "Your great-grandfather used to be a senator. Governor Anderson is a friend of the family."

I had no idea what to say to that.

My bedroom was on the third floor, at the end of a long hall lit by several wall sconces. My mom stopped in front of a door with a sticker that read THIS BITCH BITES.

I started to smile, but then she opened the door and stepped aside. Tentatively, I entered the unfamiliar room, which smelled of peaches, stopping a few feet in.

"I'll give you a few minutes," she said, clearing her throat. "I had Scott lay out some of your yearbooks. They're on your desk when you're ready. Dr. Weston said they could help."

Help with finding my file of memories. I nodded, pressing my lips together as I scanned the room. It was big. Like, twenty times bigger than the hospital room. There was a bed in the middle of the room. A pristine white down comforter was tucked in neatly. Several gold-trimmed pillows were placed at the top. A brown teddy bear rested on them, looking out of place in the otherwise sophisticated bedroom.

Mom cleared her throat. I'd forgotten about her. Turning around, I waited. Her smile was pained, awkward. "I'll be downstairs if you need me."

"Okay."

With a curt nod, she left, and I started to investigate the room. The yearbooks were on my desk, but I avoided them. Part of me wasn't ready for the weird walk down nonmemory lane. There was an Apple laptop next to several smaller devices. I recognized one as an iPod. A flat-screen TV hung from the wall above the desk. I assumed that was what the remote control belonged to.

I made my way to the closet, throwing open the double doors. It was a walk-in. A tiny part of me was curious. Clothes weren't a big deal to me. I *knew* that. Then I saw the racks in the back, and I almost squealed.

Shoes and purses *were* a big deal.

Could that be a part of the old me, or was it just because I was a girl? I wasn't sure as I ran my fingers over the dresses. They felt like quality.

Back in my bedroom, I discovered there was a balcony, and I had my own bathroom stocked with products I couldn't wait to try out. Near the bed, there was a corkboard full of pictures. Huh. I had a lot of friends, and they were . . . dressed like me. Frowning, I inspected the collage of pictures closer.

In one photo, there were five girls. I was in the middle, and all of us wore the same tube dress in different colors. Oh dear god. Matching dresses? I smirked as my eyes drifted over the images. One was of me and two other girls, smiling on a golf course. In another the same group from the first picture stood together on a dock, posing in really skimpy bathing suits in front of a boat named *Angel*. Mine was black. I was starting to see a trend.

I ran my hands over my hips and stomach, pleased to discover that the body in that picture was actually mine. There were a few more photos at school, a group of us clustered around an oversize table, surrounded by boys.

I was always smiling in the pictures, but the smile was . . . off, reminding me how everyone had smiled at me in the hospital. Like a doll's smile, fake and painted on. But my smile was also cold. Calculating.

And in every picture, the same girl was always beside me. In some, we had our arms around each other or were puckering our lips for the camera. She always wore red—red like fresh blood.

Her smile was like mine, and she was the girl in the photo the deputy had shown me in the hospital. A hot feeling sparked in my stomach. Jealousy? Was I jealous of her? That couldn't be right. She was my friend. My *best friend*, if what they'd been telling me was true.

I wanted to know more about her.

Carefully, I peeled one picture of us together off the board and held it close to my face. Her smile made me shiver, and my gaze flicked up from the photo. Color bleached from the room, replaced by dull shades of gray. Goose bumps spread across my flesh. *Cold. So cold here, and dark, with only the rushing sound . . . in and out, in and out. . . .*

I closed my eyes and shook my head to clear it of the dank, earthy feel that had suddenly come out of nowhere. I forced my eyes open, and the room was back in vivid color. My gaze settled on the pictures tacked to the board again. The images all blurred, and there was a flash, a quick glimpse. A tall, blond girl with a wide smile and a floppy red hat stretched out her arms to me.

The image of the girl faded as if it had never been there. Confused, I peered at the photos, hoping to find the girl in one of them. She looked as if she was only ten or so in my head, but there was no child who looked like her on the board or an older version of her. My shoulders slumped as I stepped back. I was disappointed. Something about that smiling girl was warm and real, unlike all the rest. I would've been happy to see that she was on my wall of friends.

"Look who's back."

Startled, I jumped at the sound of the deep voice and dropped the picture on the floor. Shaky and disoriented, I turned around.

A boy stood in the doorway, tall and slender. Hazel eyes peeked through messy auburn hair. There was a mischievous, quirky look on his face. I was going to make a guesstimate here and say he was my brother. We shared some of the same features. This was Scott. We were fraternal twins. At least, that was what Mom had explained on the way home.

He tipped his head back, eyeing me curiously. "Are you going to cut the bull and fess up to me?"

Pushing the picture under the bed with my toes, I ran clammy hands down my hips. "What . . . what do you mean?"

He sauntered into the room, stopping a few feet in front of me. We were the same height. "Where have you really been, Sam?"

"I don't know."

"You don't?" He laughed, and the skin crinkled around his eyes. "Come on. What did you and Cassie get yourselves into this time?"

"Cassie's missing," I mumbled, glancing down at the floor. She hadn't really looked like the girl the deputy had shown me. I bent down, grabbing the picture from underneath the bed. "This is Cassie, right?"

He frowned as he glanced at the picture. "Yeah, that's Cassie."

I quickly placed the picture on the bedside table. "I don't know where she is."

"I have theories."

Interest piqued, I rocked back on my heels. "You do?"

Scott flopped on my bed and stretched out lazily. "Shit, you probably killed her and stashed her body somewhere." He laughed. "That's my main theory."

Blood drained out of my face, and I gasped.

The smile on his face faded as he watched me. "Sam, dude, I was *kidding*."

"Oh." Sweet relief shot through me, and I sat on the edge of the bed, staring at my chipped nails. In an instant, everything turned gray and white. The only color was red—vibrant, garish red under my fingernails. *Soft whimpers—someone was crying.*

Scott grabbed my arm. "Hey, you okay?"

I blinked, and the vision, the sounds faded away. Shoving my hands under my legs, I nodded. "Yeah, I'm okay."

He sat up, staring at me. "Holy shit, you're not faking it."

"Faking what?"

"The whole amnesia thing—because I was betting money you were off partying somewhere, got trashed for days, and couldn't come home until you sobered up."

Damn. "Did I do that often?"

Scott barked out a laugh. "Yeah . . . this is weird. You're definitely not faking."

Now I felt even more confused. "How can you tell?"

"Well, for starters, you haven't kicked me out of your room or threatened to ruin my life yet."

"I'd do that?"

He stared at me, his eyes wide. "Yeah, and sometimes you'd even hit me. Once, I hit you back, and, well, that didn't go over well. Dad got pissed. Mom was *mortified*."

My brows pinched. "We...hit each other?"

Shaking his head, Scott leaned back. "Man, this is bizarre."

No doubt. I pulled my hands out from under my legs and sighed. "Back to the whole killing-Cassie-and-hiding-her-body thing. Why did you say that?"

"I was kidding. You two have been best friends *foreva*." He smirked. "Actually, you guys were more like frenemies in the last couple of years. There was some kind of unspoken rivalry going on between you two. It started when you made homecoming queen during sophomore year and she made court. At least that's what you tell everyone, but I'm thinking it started when you two were freshmen and you started dating Del the Dick."

"Del the *Dick*?" I tucked a strand of hair back. "That's my boyfriend."

"*That's* your whole world."

Not liking the sound of that, I made a face. "I don't remember...him, either."

"That's going to be a blow to his confidence." He grinned. "You know, this is possibly the best thing that has ever happened."

"Me losing my memory and not knowing what happened to me?" Anger sparked deep inside me, familiar and powerful. "Yeah, I'm glad that's so great for you."

"That's not what I mean." Scott sat up, looking me straight

in the eyes. "You were a terror to everyone who knew you. And this"—he waved his hand around me—"is an improvement."

That icky feeling was back, coiling around my insides. I was a terror? I bit my lip, frustrated that there was nothing in my head confirming or denying what he'd said.

Someone cleared his throat.

We twisted around and . . . wow, just wow. My jaw hit the bedspread. There was a tall *boy* standing in the doorway to *my* bedroom. Dark brown hair fell over his forehead and curled around his ears. His skin was deep, almost olive in comparison to my paler skin, hinting at a Native American or Hispanic ancestry. His cheekbones were broad, giving him an exotic look, and his jaw was strong, clenched tight. The long-sleeved shirt he wore stretched over his broad shoulders and biceps. His body was purely athletic, slender and yet muscular.

A black baseball cap dangled off the tips of his fingers, forgotten. Our eyes locked, and I felt a stirring in my chest. His were a magnetic, intense blue. The color of the sky right before the day ended and night took hold—the color of dusk. There was stark relief in his gaze, and also a wariness I didn't understand.

"Is that my boyfriend?" I whispered, hopeful and scared all at once. If he was my boyfriend, I had no idea what to do with him. Well, I did—I suddenly had lots of ideas that involved kissing, touching, and all sorts of fun things, but he was . . . mouthwateringly *gorgeous*, and that intimidated the hell out of me.

Scott choked on his laugh.

The boy in the doorway glanced at my brother and then at me. Heat crept across my cheeks. The relief was still in his eyes, and my lips split in a hesitant smile. He was happy to see me, but . . . but then his eyes hardened into chips of ice.

"Boyfriend? Yeah," he said slowly, voice deep and smooth. "Not even if you paid my tuition to Penn State next year."

Stung and embarrassed, I jerked back, and the question came out before I could stop it. "And why not?"

He stared at me as if I had an arm sticking out of my head and waving around. He turned to my brother, brows raised. "I'll be waiting outside."

"Sure, man, be there in a sec, Car."

"His name is *Car*?" I said, folding my arms.

Vehicle Boy stopped and turned back around. "Car, as in Carson Ortiz."

Oh. That made sense. I lowered my arms, feeling about nine kinds of stupid.

Carson's eyes narrowed. "She really has no clue about . . . about anything?"

"Yep," Scott replied, lips pursed.

Carson started to leave again but stopped once more. Muttering under his breath, he looked at me. "I'm glad you're okay, Sam."

Before I could even respond to that, he was gone. I turned back to Scott. "He doesn't like me."

Scott looked like he wanted to laugh again. "Yeah, he doesn't."

A weird, twisty feeling sprang in my chest. "Why?"

Pushing off the bed, he sighed. "You don't like him."

I didn't? Did I not have taste? He was baby-making material.

Then I frowned. How did I know who was baby-making material? "I don't get it."

"You were kind of a bitch to him . . . in the last couple of years."

"Why?"

The look on his face told me he was getting tired of the question *Why?* "Because his dad is hired help, and you're not a fan of the hired help. Hell, or their offspring and anyone who associates with them."

I dropped my hands into my lap, unsure of how to respond to that. He had to be kidding. "We have hired help?"

Scott rolled his eyes. "Dad and Mom do, which is funny because Mom hasn't worked a day in her life." When he saw my expression, he cursed. "Jeez, this is like talking to a toddler."

Anger pricked my skin, and so did hurt. "Sorry. You can go talk to Car, who apparently doesn't suffer from an impaired IQ."

Regret flickered in his eyes, and he sighed again. "Look, I'm sorry. I didn't mean that, but, Sam, this is weird. It's like *Invasion of the Body Snatchers* or something."

It *was* weird. I glanced at the empty doorway, anxious and even a little afraid. I suddenly realized I didn't want to be left alone. "Where are you guys going?"

He glanced down at his sweats, one brow raised. "We have baseball practice."

"Can I go?"

Surprise shone on his face. "You hate going to baseball games. The only reason you do go is because of Del."

"I don't know who Del is!" My hands balled into useless

fists. "I don't know what I hate. Or what I like. Or what I'm supposed to do or say. I don't recognize *any* of this. To make things worse, now I find out that everyone apparently hates me—including my best friend, who disappeared at the same time I did—and I can't even remember *why*." I looked around the room, close to tears. "And my middle name is Jo. Who gives their kid a middle name like *Jo*?"

Scott didn't say anything for several seconds, and then he knelt in front of me. It was strange looking at his face, seeing my own face—but more masculine and hard—staring back. "Sam, it's going to be okay."

A tremble started in my lower lips. "Everyone keeps saying that, but what if it's not?"

He didn't answer.

Because it wasn't okay—it was never going to be okay. I was stuck in this life I didn't remember, squeezed into the shell of this girl—this Samantha *Jo* Franco—and the more I learned about her, the more I was starting to hate her.

chapter three

On Saturday I met my friends...for the first time. They talked. A lot. And they sounded and looked the same. Hair with brighter streaks strategically pieced throughout. Each of them looked as if they could use some of the doughnuts I was scarfing down.

They crowded around me, hugging and crying. My mom lingered in the kitchen, sipping wine at eleven in the morning. One of the three girls stood out from the rest. Her name I learned pretty quickly.

Veronica Hodges.

Blond. Tan. Skinny. Perfect. The type of girl who could do tanning-bed commercials and be crowned homecoming queen in a bikini.

Smoothing her manicured hand over her white cashmere sweater, Veronica curled her red-painted lips at the package of doughnuts and croissants as if they were infested with cockroaches. "We are so glad you're okay, Sammy. All of us have been so worried."

I brushed white crumbs off my hands. "Thanks."

Veronica glanced over her shoulder at my mom and then leaned forward and spoke in a hushed voice. "And we're really hoping that Cassie will show up, too."

Curious as to why she was whispering that, I looked at the other girls. They all nodded like good little dogs. I picked up a croissant. "Me too."

She frowned. "But . . . your mom says you don't remember her."

"Or us," chimed in Candy Alderman. She, too, eyed the box of goodies. "It's good to see that your appetite is the same."

I paused, a croissant halfway to my mouth. "It is?"

Candy nodded. "You've always eaten like a guy."

"That is so true," Mom murmured over the rim of her wineglass, eyes focused on the ceiling.

Lowering the croissant, I wasn't sure if it was a good thing or a bad thing that I'd retained my manly appetite. I glanced around the room, and all I could think about was the girl I'd seen in my thoughts, the natural blonde who had been so happy and so real. I wanted to know who she was.

"So," Candy said, drawing the word out. "You don't remember anything?"

Just like that, my appetite vanished. I tossed the croissant back into the box and glanced at my mom. Now she was paying attention. "I don't remember, but the doc thinks it will come back to me soon."

The girls looked relieved, and then they started talking about school, the upcoming start of the baseball season, which appeared to be a big deal around these parts, and where they were going tonight. I was invited, but my mom kindly advised them that I wasn't stepping foot out of this house anytime soon. *Fabulous.* They moved on to the boyfriend I didn't remember.

"He's so hot," Candy squealed. "And so, so perfect."

"Totally." Veronica nodded, holding her hands out in front of her chest. "You guys have this perfect relationship."

I glanced at the quiet one with brown hair and blond streaks. She said nothing as she picked at a small napkin.

"He's been worried about you." Candy tipped her head to the side, grinning. "You're luckier than you realize."

Lucky to be alive, or lucky to have such a great boyfriend?

Oddly enough, except for what Veronica said, no one talked about Cassie. I was sure they were avoiding the topic so I wouldn't freak out. I appreciated that, especially considering I'd spent the bulk of last night going over all the terrible things that could've happened to us, but I wanted to know more about her.

When there was a lull in the conversation, I cleared my throat. "Did Cassie say anything before we . . . we went missing? Did she talk about plans?"

Veronica glanced down, sucking in her lip. "She really didn't—"

"I think that's enough for today, girls." Mom appeared behind Veronica, smiling without showing any teeth. "Samantha needs her rest."

"Mom," I snapped, embarrassed to be treated like a small

child. I pushed back, toppling over the bar stool, and stood. My knees shook, and my voice came out in just a whisper. "Mom . . ."

She shot a look around at the group of girls, who had paled under their fake bakes, and then grasped my hands, eyes wide. "What is it?"

My heart pounded irregularly. How could I explain it? I knew I'd snapped at my mom before like that. I'd *felt* that way before—frustrated, annoyed, and angry *at her*. The wash of familiarity when there'd been virtually nothing was dizzying. It wouldn't be a big deal to anyone else, but to my empty brain it was epic.

"Samantha?"

Everyone was staring at me. Each face belonged to a stranger. There was no rushing flood of memories or even a spark of familiarity as Google and WebMD said there would be. I'd thoroughly searched the Internet on dissociative amnesia last night, and other than the fact that it was linked to traumatic events and mental illness—*sweet*—there was little information on how, or if, I'd get my memories back.

Hands shaking, I pulled them free of my mom's and brushed my hair from my flaming cheeks. "It's nothing. I'm just tired."

My unofficial welcome-back get-together was coming to a close. The girls gave me quick hugs and pecks on the cheek before filing outside to their respective BMWs. I wondered what kind of car I drove.

"What really happened?" Mom asked, following me through the many rooms to the smallest one on the main level—the family room. "Samantha, answer me."

I sat down on the overstuffed couch. "It wasn't a big deal. I just remembered getting...mad at you before, snapping at you. It caught me off guard."

She stared at me for a moment, then knelt in front of me. I was surprised that she'd risk getting her linen pants dirty, but then she clasped my cheeks. Her hands were shaking. Tears built in her eyes. "I never thought I'd be happy to hear you remember being upset with me, but I am."

My smile was wobbly. "Lame, huh?"

"No, it's not lame, honey. It is progress." She stood, brushing off her slacks. "But I do think you should take it easy this weekend."

I arched a brow. "I was reading about it last night, and the articles said I should be around things that are familiar. That will spark my memory."

"I don't know. All of this is a lot to deal with."

I took a deep breath, already knowing this was going to be a problem. "I want to go to school Monday. I have to. I need to."

"It's too soon."

"I have to do something normal. Maybe it will help with my memories."

She looked even more concerned. "Dr. Weston said you need to take things slow. It could be too much."

"What damage could it do?" I threw up my arms, frustrated to my core. "Am I going to forget more? There isn't anything else I can forget!"

"I don't know." Mom turned away, fiddling with the gold bangles on her wrists. "I've already spoken with the school. They said it's okay if you stay home a week or so."

In that moment, I learned something new about myself. I didn't have any patience. Jumping to my feet, I planted my hands on my hips. "I'm going to school on Monday."

"Samantha, I really—"

"What's going on in here?" Dad walked in, pulling off white golfing gloves as he bent and kissed my cheek. "It sounds like old times."

I tried not to be skeeved by the chaste kiss. He was my dad. No reason to be freaked out. Mom turned on him, and the blood drained from her pretty face. Okay, maybe I should be skeeved out. I stepped to the side, nervous and unsure.

"What are you doing wearing those shoes in the house?" Her voice was shrill, hurting my ears. "You'll scratch the floors. Again!"

Dad laughed. "The floors will be fine. No one cares if they're scratched or not."

"I do!" Mom protested. "What would our friends think if they saw them?"

He rolled his eyes. "I think you are the only person I know who'd be ashamed over the condition of their floors. Anyway, what's going on?"

She huffed as she eyed him. "Your daughter wants to go to school on Monday."

He slapped his gloves into one hand, causing me to jump a

little. "Joanna, if that's what she wants to do, then we shouldn't stop her."

"But—"

"So I can?" I rushed on, hopeful.

She looked between the two of us and sighed heavily. "Two against one, I see. Some things never change." And with that, she turned on her heel and stormed out of the room.

"Don't worry, honey. Your mother is just concerned about everything." He sat, patting the space beside him. I followed suit, clasping my hands together. "She's been beside herself with worry. We thought . . ."

"That I was dead?"

He blanched and swallowed. "At first your mother thought you might have run away, and she was so upset. You know how she is." A puzzled look crossed his face, and then he shook his head. "Actually, you don't. She was worried that Cassie might've talked you into doing something like that, and if so, gossip would spread all over the place. I just wanted my little girl back, especially after we began to think the worse."

Was Mom more concerned about what her friends might think? Either way, I still couldn't imagine what my parents must've thought. "I want to remember."

"I know." He patted my knee.

"No. See." I dug out the photo of Cassie and me from my jean pocket. "I *need* to remember."

My dad swallowed again. "Do you . . . do you remember her?"

I shook my head. Nothing about her face or how she draped her arm over my shoulders was familiar. Hell, my own face in the picture was strange to me, even the freckles spotting my nose. Cassie had freckles, too, but on her cheeks.

"But she could still be out there, wherever I was. She could be hurt or . . ." I turned the picture over, looking up, meeting his eyes. "If I remember, I could find her."

"Honey, the police searched most of the state park and haven't found anything."

"Maybe she's somewhere else. No one knows if I . . . walked there. That's the first thing I remember. Walking," I told him. "Maybe I walked from somewhere else."

"That's a good point, but don't force yourself." He smiled as he stood, gloves dangling from his hand. "And if you don't ever remember, then it's not your fault. Okay?"

I nodded absently. Dad left after that. I went up the flights of stairs and placed the picture on my desk. Going into the bathroom, I reached to turn the faucet on but had forgotten it was one of those hand-motion-activated ones. Rolling my eyes, I waved my hand under the tap, and the water kicked on. After washing my face, I examined it again. I'd been doing that a lot, hoping that something would click. It hadn't yet.

I took several deep breaths and closed my eyes. I blinked twice when I reopened them. The bathroom light was off. Had I accidentally done that? I didn't remember hitting the switch on the wall. Backing up, I glanced out into my bedroom and swallowed hard.

I was under stress, and stress could make you do things absently. That sounded like a good theory, and I was going to go with it.

Heart pounding in my chest, I dropped onto my bed and stared at the plastic stars lining the ceiling. Last night I had learned they glowed.

I liked that.

Did I like them before, or did I think they were stupid? There was no answer. Nothing had an answer. I rolled onto my side and pulled my legs up, tucking them against my chest. *Cassie.* Her name had haunted me like a sad, strange melody ever since those officers left the hospital room. Could she be out there, not knowing who she was and in a different hospital? Scott had said Cassie and I fought a lot, but that was what friends did . . . or at least I thought they did. And I sounded like a real tyrant anyway—so bitchy that even Carson didn't like me. Hell, my own brother seemed afraid of me.

Squeezing my eyes shut, I forced my mind to go blank. Which shouldn't have been that hard, but I kept seeing this set of vibrant blue eyes rimmed in black. Ridiculous. I took a deep, calming breath and pictured Cassie's face. Obviously she was the last person I was with. What had we been doing? Movies? Partying? Just hanging out and talking?

I wasn't sure how long I lay there, staring at the delicate music box with a little ballerina curved to the side, one leg bent at a ninety-degree angle. Was I a ballerina? Somehow I doubted that. Sighing, I rolled over, shoving my face into the pillow.

Something crinkled underneath it.

Pushing up, I tugged the pillow away. Tucked halfway under the blanket was a piece of yellow paper folded into a triangle.

Positive that it hadn't been there this morning, I pulled the slip of paper out and slowly unfolded it.

My breath caught and I dropped the letter, scuttling back on the bed. Pulse racing, I closed my eyes, but I could still see the words.

Don't look back. You won't like what you find.

chapter four

Jumping off the bed, I raced into the hallway and smacked right into my brother.

"Whoa!" Scott grabbed my shoulders, steadying me before I toppled over. He grinned. "Slow down."

I gasped as I stared up at him, trying to catch my breath. "There's . . . there's this . . ."

The grin faded from his face. "There's what, Sam?" When I didn't answer, he shook me gently. "What are you trying to say?"

Snapping out of my panic, I pulled free from his grasp. "There's a note under my pillow!"

"What?" He brushed past me, heading for my bedroom.

I trailed behind him, stopping at the door as he approached my bed and picked up the note as if it were a venomous snake.

"'Don't look back. You won't like what you find.' Are you shitting me?" He turned, holding the letter up. "Who's been up here, Sam?"

"I don't know. No one that I know . . ." I stopped. I didn't know anyone.

"Maybe one of your friends roamed off or something?"

A horrible thought struck me. "My . . . my friends stopped over this morning. A couple of them left the kitchen to use the bathroom." I frowned. "Veronica left, like, three times."

"They were the only ones in the house." A muscle ticked in his jaw as he stared at the childish writing. "This looks . . . I don't know. It had to be one of them."

I didn't like the sound of that. They were supposed to be my friends, and even though I didn't remember them, I didn't want to believe one of them had left that note. "But based on that theory, you've been home, too. You could've done it."

He rolled his eyes. "Good point, but come on. It's a stupid joke." Stalking to the desk, he balled the paper up.

"What are you doing?" I moved to intercept him, but he tossed it in the trash. "Why did you throw it away? It's . . . like, evidence."

"Evidence? Someone is messing with you." He folded his arms, scowling. "And I'd be more than willing to bet that it's one of your stupid friends."

"My friends aren't stupid."

He cocked his head to the side. "You don't remember your friends."

"Good point." I plopped down on the edge of my bed. "But why would someone leave a note like that? I mean, it isn't funny. It's . . . it's more like a warning."

Scott hesitated. "Sam . . . it's a joke."

I glanced at the trash bin. It didn't feel like a joke. A shiver rolled through me. From my perspective, it was a clear warning. A *threat*, a voice whispered in the back of my mind.

"Look, you've been through a lot." Scott cleared his throat, looking away when I turned to him. "I honestly can't even imagine how it feels to not have a freaking clue who you are, but don't let those girls mess with you."

"I'm not." I felt the need to defend myself.

"And I really don't think you should tell Mom and Dad about this. They'd freak and never let you out of this house."

Ah, damn it. He had another good point. "But what if one of those girls knows what happened? Cassie is still missing and—"

"And what, Sam? You're going to question them based on a note you found? Hold them down and demand answers?"

I folded my arms. "Maybe."

Shaking his head, he headed for the door. "Let it go, Sam. It's a joke. And honestly, when it comes to Cassie, out of sight, out of mind."

Twisting around, I stared at him. "What do you mean?"

His jaw worked. "All I am saying is that . . . thank god it's not a nice person who's gone missing. Like Julie."

"Julie?"

Scott sighed. "My girlfriend—you used to be friends with her, but she wore the color purple on the wrong day or some bullshit like that."

"I wouldn't have stopped being friends with someone because they wore the color purple on the wrong day!"

He arched a brow and a moment passed. "*Anyway*, Cassie was worse... worse than you. And that's saying something. You became a different person when you started hanging out with her. Most of the people who knew her... they're probably glad she's gone. Including her friends."

My brother's words haunted me the rest of Saturday and into Sunday. It was one thing finding out you acted like a total bitch to most people, but to discover that your missing best friend was just as bad was overwhelming. If we were such douches, why did people even bother looking for us?

"Fear and popularity go hand in hand," I muttered, turning off my hair dryer.

I froze, staring at my reflection. Where in the hell had that come from? *The Bitches' Handbook to High School Survival*? Leaning forward, I dabbed on some lip gloss and took a deep breath.

This would not be awkward.

Leaving the bathroom, I grabbed the shiny new phone Dad had picked up the night before. My old one was wherever my memories were.

This would not be awkward.

I slid the photo of Cassie and me into a back pocket of my übertight jeans and headed downstairs. My pulse was all over the place. I was going to meet Del today—my boyfriend.

This was going to be so awkward.

I wandered around the massive rooms downstairs, ending up in the pantry on three different routes, until my mom yelled my name.

He was here.

All thoughts of the strange note I'd found vanished as I slowly made my way back to the foyer, which could've housed a small tribe. Stopping just outside the archway, I peeked around the corner.

Del stood beside my mom. Taller than her but not as tall as Carson, I realized. He was lanky, had artfully messy brown hair with faint blond highlights. His skin was tan, eyes the color of milk chocolate. He was handsome. Not bad at all, I thought. The V-neck sweater he wore was rolled up to his elbows, revealing powerful forearms. His hands were shoved into his faded jeans.

"Sammy," he said. Del had a megawatt smile, the kind on celebrity magazines—perfect, too perfect. He glanced at my mom, who nodded, and then started toward me. "I am so happy to see you, babe. You have no idea."

I froze.

His expression washed out, and I felt like I was being thrown out of the room and into a weird time loop. Everything went gray and white.

Del was pleading with me, begging with his eyes as he was coming forward. Desperation poured from him, but he was also angry—so very angry. My heart was pounding as rage swelled inside me, matching and overshadowing his anger.

Gasping, I blinked and took a step back. The look—the vision—was gone. I didn't know if it was a memory or if I was just seeing things.

"You okay, Sammy?" Del asked, stopping short.

I felt dizzy. Mom had that look on her face, the same from the day before. Pained. Worried.

"I'm okay."

The smile returned to Del's face, and he crossed the remaining distance, sweeping his arms around me and lifting me up. A sliver of panic clawed its way through me as he held me tight against him. My fingers dug into his shoulders, and I desperately tried to find something familiar in his suffocating embrace.

Del made a deep sound in his throat as he buried his head in my hair. "Damn it, Sammy, don't you ever scare me like that again."

I couldn't respond or breathe. My thoughts were on a loop. *I don't know you. I don't know you.* Over and over . . . *I don't know you.*

When he put me down, I had to fight the urge to run away. Over his shoulder, my mom watched us, squeezing the gold around her wrists.

The front door opened behind her, and my brother strolled in. Sweat plastered his hair to his cheeks. An iPod hung from his fingers. Behind him was Carson. My chest did a weird leap, and I stepped back, tripping over my own feet.

Del caught my arm, steadying me with a rich laugh. "You're so jumpy."

"I wonder why," muttered Scott, eyeing us.

Carson had his baseball cap pulled down low, shielding his extraordinary eyes. All I could see was the tight-lipped smile he gave my mom. "Hey, Del," Carson said.

Del gave him a curt nod.

"Boys, why don't you go down to the basement?" Mom shooed them toward the stairs. "I don't care what you sweat on down there."

My gaze was fixed on Carson, even as Del dropped an arm around my shoulders. Scott bumped his best friend as they shuffled past us. I lowered my eyes, unable to shake the feeling I'd been caught doing something bad.

"Carson, can you tell your father I need to see him first thing Monday morning?" Mom's voice carried through the large house. "The trees around the pool house need to be cut back...."

Del laughed, shaking his head. "I don't know why your brother hangs out with Carson."

I lifted my head, frowning. "I guess he likes him."

"They have nothing in common." Del took my hand, leading me through the archway toward the small rec room that I liked. Maybe I had liked that room before, and he knew that. Hope sparked. He sent a devilish grin over his shoulder.

I started to smile back, thinking I liked his grin.

"Has Carson been hanging around here a lot?" he asked, pulling me down on the couch beside him, holding my hand.

"I really don't know." I glanced down at our joined hands. His was so much larger. "He was here on Friday, but..."

"You don't remember. Right." He squeezed my hand. "I keep forgetting that. Oh, I almost forgot *this*." He let go of my hand and stood, reaching into his pocket. He pulled out a tiny, flat blue box. "I wanted to give this back to you."

"Back to me?" I took the gift box, sliding my finger under the lid.

"Yeah, you...you left it at my place before you...well, before everything happened." He looked away, swallowing. "I put it back in the box for you."

Removing the lid, I picked up the piece of cotton. A silver chain peeked out, and at the end was a crooked heart. Tiffany's. I knew a damn Tiffany's box when I saw one, but I didn't know the boy who'd given it to me. "I've worn this?"

Del nodded, taking the box and setting it aside. "Nothing about this necklace seems familiar?"

I shook my head. "Why did I take it off?"

His lashes lowered, shielding his eyes. A long second passed before he responded. "You wanted...to take a shower."

"Why did I want to take a shower at your place?"

Del's brows pinched, and a flush stained his cheeks. "You didn't want to go back to your house without showering, because we'd..."

My gaze dropped to the heart, and understanding slowly crept in. "We've had...sex?"

He rubbed the bridge of his nose and nodded.

Heat swept over my cheeks and down my neck. We'd had sex, and I didn't even remember. "Was that my first time?"

Del shook his head, blowing a little breath. "No. We've been dating for several years, Sammy."

I wasn't sure what was worse: having this epically awkward conversation or not even remembering my first time with him. Hands shaking, I clasped the silver chain around my neck. The slight weight felt unbearably heavy for some reason. A tide of frustration rolled over me, itching under my skin. How could I not remember any of this? Tears built behind my eyes, and the urge to run kicked me in the stomach again.

"It's okay." Del forced a smile. "Your parents warned me that you wouldn't remember anything. And you don't, right? Not even the night you disappeared?"

My knees felt weak as I stood. "I don't remember anything. I had to ask my mom yesterday when *my birthday* was." I let out a choked laugh as I faced him. "The doctor says I might get my memories back, though."

He shifted on the couch, his eyes deepening until they were almost as dark as his pupils. "Is there anything I can do to help?" His voice turned serious. "Because I've always had your back, Sammy, and I always will."

I frowned, thinking that was a strange way to put things.

"Anything?" he prodded again.

Doubtful. But as I stared at him longer, I realized that maybe he could. "I saw you the night I disappeared?" When he nodded, excitement hummed like that rapid beat of hummingbird wings. This was a start. "What were we doing besides . . . ?"

"It was late Saturday night, and we were just hanging out and talking. Among other things," he added with a grin, "we were watching old videos of my baseball games."

Stimulating. "Do you know when I left?"

"It was around nine. I wanted us to go hang out with Trey, but you got this text."

"Wait. Who's Trey?"

Del leaned back, kicking his feet up on the coffee table. I didn't even have to remember my mom to know she'd freak if she saw that. "Trey is a good friend of mine. He was Cassie's boyfriend, but they broke up a few days before . . . she went missing."

"She had a boyfriend?" I sat beside him, eager to learn more. He nodded. "They fought. A lot. Their arguments were pretty much a source of entertainment to everyone."

"Did we fight?"

"No. *Never,*" he said quickly. "We had—have a perfect relationship." He leaned over, brushing his lips over my cheek. "Just like our parents."

Warning bells went off. From what I'd seen, my parents did *not* have a perfect relationship. Since I came . . . came home, I hadn't even seen them touch or even be in the same room together longer than a few minutes. I fiddled with the silver heart. "So . . . I got a text, and I left?"

"Yeah." He sat back. Disappointment pulled at his lips, and I felt as if I'd done something wrong. "I think it was from Cassie, but you didn't say. You left my house mad."

"Mad at Cassie?"

He shook his head. "I don't know. You and Cassie had this—"

"Rivalry? That's what my brother said."

"He's not lying. Cassie . . . wow, how do I say this without sounding like a dick?" He exhaled slowly. "Cassie wanted to be like you. She always has. In her eyes, you had it all. She copied *everything* you did. If you didn't like someone, she didn't like them. If you wanted someone, she wanted them. Everyone knew it."

I arched a brow. "Okay . . ."

"I'm not trying to talk bad about her—especially under the

circumstances. God, she could be dead." He saw me wince and immediately apologized. "Sorry, but you know what I mean. Cassie caused problems. Even with us."

"I thought we didn't fight." Unease started to form hard little balls in my stomach.

He looked away. "We didn't *fight* fight. Like I said, I have your back. But sometimes Cassie could be . . . inappropriate when you weren't around."

"What do you mean?"

His gaze flicked to mine, then focused on the massive deer head on the wall. "She'd come on to me, even though we were together and Trey's my bud."

I expected to feel a rush of jealousy, but I felt nothing. "Did you like Cassie?"

Surprise shone on his face. "Yeah, I mean, she could be cool." And then his eyes narrowed and lips thinned. "Why are you asking?"

My mouth opened, but nothing came out. I had this impression of having asked the same question before, only with a lot more emotion behind it. Anger was there. Disappointment, too. But there was nothing else attached to those emotions. It was as if my feelings were balloons floating away with nothing to tether them down.

I shrugged. "You just sound like you didn't like her. I don't think Scott liked her, either."

"Cassie could be hard to get along with." He shifted closer, placing a hand on my bent knee. Instantly, my muscles locked up. "I don't know what happened the night you two disappeared.

I don't even know if you guys were really even together. And I don't want to talk about her. I want to talk about us."

"Us?" I squeaked.

He held his free hand out to me. "Come here."

My pulse shot way up, and I didn't want to *come here*. But he was waiting with this patient smile on his handsome face, and I didn't want to hurt his feelings. This had to be hard for him. I was his girlfriend, and I couldn't recall a single detail about him or our relationship. I scooted over until my legs were pressed against his.

His hand found the back of my neck, guiding my head to his chest. He let out a ragged sigh, brushing his lips over my forehead. "I really didn't think I was going to be able to do this again. It's like getting a second chance."

"It is?" I whispered, confused.

"Yeah." He pressed a kiss on my temple.

We spent the entire afternoon talking, which helped me get to know him again. Evidently, we had started dating at the beginning of freshman year and, according to Del, all my friends were jealous. Our fathers were in business together, working in Philadelphia while our mothers stayed at home. Supposedly, there was this huge deal between our fathers' businesses. Something to do with stock trade and company transfer—nothing I knew anything about.

We spent the holidays each year in the Catskills with our families and summers on various vacations. Last year, we were prom king and queen, and the two of us were expected to win again this year—something Del was proud of. At school, we left when we wanted to, ate lunch off campus, and skipped classes together, and no one apparently stopped us. Yale was in our future, and I got this feeling that people expected us to stay together. As in forever. Second- or third-generation rich kids, like royalty. That was what it seemed like to me.

There was this whole life with him that I was completely detached from. Even though I tried as hard as I could, I couldn't see or feel any of it. So I let him talk about himself, which he *excelled* at. He played shortstop on the high school baseball team and was on his second BMW, and his favorite team was the Yankees. At home, he had an entire floor to himself. No brothers or sisters. There were a couple of cousins and a grandfather who had run one of the largest stock-trading firms in New York.

"Our dads could buy and sell this town," he said, twirling a strand of my hair around his finger. "Well, your mom could, actually."

"Why?" I said, probably for the hundredth time.

"Money is on my dad's side of the family," he explained proudly. "And it's on your mom's side. Her family invested in the railroad before it took off or something. She's not a billionaire, nowhere close to the kind of capital my father brings in, but she's old money."

I struggled to not roll my eyes. "Do you know what my dad did before he met my mom?"

He shrugged. "He went to Yale, obviously, on a scholarship. I think his mom was a schoolteacher and his dad a construction worker. Both of them passed away a few years back. Sorry."

I took a moment to mull over the dead grandparents I had no recollection of. That sucked. "Well, I guess he got lucky when he met Mom."

"Hells yeah, he was." Del laughed. "He didn't have anything before he met her. Her father got him in the business. If it wasn't for your mom, I'm not sure how far your dad would've gotten. But my dad was groomed to run the firm—just like I am." He kissed my cheek again. "And my son will be."

My eyes widened. *His son?* Blech. I felt nauseated, allergic to the very idea.

There was a lull in the conversation, and my arm was tingling from being squeezed between our bodies. I briefly considered telling him about the note I'd found but decided against it. "What did I like?"

Del pulled his head back, searching my eyes. "Besides me?"

Okay, not funny. With narrowed eyes, I nodded.

"You like to shop." Del laughed, running his fingers over my cheek. "Your favorite drink is anything fruity mixed with vodka. You're a hell of a girl to party with. You're wild." This time, when he leaned in, his lips met mine. The kiss was brief. "Okay, usually a lot wilder than that."

"Sorry." I flushed. "What I meant was, did I have any hobbies?"

Confusion flickered in his eyes. "Does shopping count as a hobby?"

"I don't think so."

"You always liked to visit the old battlefield area," he said after a few moments. "You used to go with that chick Julie, and you guys would spend all day there. I think you had a thing for history. Or maybe just the macabre."

Wow. The only nonshallow thing I did was hang out in a giant graveyard with a girl who wasn't even my friend anymore. I was really beginning to hate myself. Del talked about the upcoming baseball season for a little while, bitching about Carson's throwing arm. He was the pitcher, and there was no love between them.

When my mom stopped in and asked if Del would be joining us for dinner, he politely refused. Family was in town. Before he left, I pulled out the picture in my pocket and showed it to him. "Do you know where this was taken?"

Del stared at the picture for several seconds, then turned away. A distant look crept into his eyes, hardening them. "It was actually a couple of months ago, on New Year's Eve. You guys were freezing in those dresses. Hot, but freezing." He gave a short laugh. "We were in Philly. You passed out before midnight."

The more I heard about myself, the more I wanted to slam my head into the coffee table. "Who was with us?"

"Trey, but he passed out, too."

"So that left just you and Cassie?"

His lips thinned. "Yeah, that night sucked."

What was strange to me was that he sounded like he couldn't stand Cassie, but the three or four of us obviously hung out a lot. Did he tolerate her because she was my friend? I sighed. "I wish I could remember something. She's still out there, and I feel like I'm the only person who can find her."

Del pulled his arm away and stood. "This is going to sound cruel, but she's not your problem right now."

Damn, that *was* cruel. "But—"

"But you need to focus on getting better and moving on with your life." He ran a hand through his hair, frowning. "I think it's best if you just let it go for right now. People are looking for her. You need to take care of yourself."

My gaze fell to the picture of me and Cassie. I'd thought we looked so happy in this picture, like real best friends, but the more I studied it, the more I saw—the razor-sharp edge to our smiles, the coldness in our near-identical features.

Everyone wanted me to forget about her, to move on. As if this girl wasn't missing. Like she never existed in the first place. And as I ran my thumb over her side of the picture, I realized I couldn't do that. Just like I couldn't be the person I was before. That Samantha was still missing, stuck wherever Cassie was, and maybe she would've been able to let Cassie drop, but I couldn't.

chapter five

Going back to school so soon had sounded like a bright idea a few days ago, but as I paced my bedroom Monday morning, I was terrified. The yearbooks remained unopened on my desk, and while I should've been reacquainting myself with the names and faces of my fellow students, I sucked up time by trying to access my e-mail and Facebook account. No such luck there. Each of the websites showed too many failed log-in attempts, and I couldn't answer the personal questions to retrieve my information. Was it possible that someone else had been trying to access those accounts? Probably when I was missing. That made sense.

When Scott popped in my bedroom, he handed me a printout of my class schedule. Grateful, I thanked him.

"You gonna wear that?"

Confused, I glanced down. I had on jeans and a heather-gray cardigan over my shirt. "What's wrong with it?"

"Nothing." His brows were arched. "But you usually dress

like you're going to a fashion show instead of school. Well, not always. Like, before Cassie, you dressed like this, but after her, not so much."

"Oh." Uncomfortable, I glanced at my closet. According to Del, Cassie did everything I did, but it seemed like the other way around sometimes. "Should I change?"

"Nah, come on. We're going to be late if we don't hurry."

I grabbed my messenger bag and followed him through the house and into the garage. The Bentley was gone, but there were a red Porsche and a newish white Audi.

"Mom wanted me to tell you that you'll be meeting with the guidance counselor during homeroom," Scott said, coming to a stop in front of the Audi. He opened the back door, throwing his bag in. "I think she said something about you meeting with her three times a week."

"What?" I gaped at him.

He grimaced. "Yep. When you get there, you need to go to the front office."

I slid into the passenger seat, clutching my bag to my chest. "Are you serious? Everyone is already going to stare at me like I'm a freak. And now I have to meet with a therapist?"

"I don't think she's a real therapist, Sam." He pushed a button on the sun visor. A second later the garage door groaned and rattled, sliding open. Bright sunlight filtered through the windows. "And you always liked it when people stared at you before, good or bad."

"Well, I'm not the same person," I snapped.

He glanced at me. "Yeah, I'm beginning to see that."

Sighing, I stared straight ahead as he backed out. "I don't have a car?"

Scott laughed as he spun the car around. "You did. A really nice one, too, but you wrecked it."

"I did?"

He nodded, easing the car down our long driveway. "You and Cassie got drunk one night. Drove it into a tree, and Dad had to pull all kinds of strings for the police to label it an accident due to road conditions. He was pretty pissed for a while."

My mouth dropped open. Several seconds passed before I could even think of something to say. "I don't think I want to know anymore about myself."

Another strange look was shot in my direction, and then he shook his head. "So weird."

I didn't say anything until I realized he was slowing down near the main road and pulled off to the side. "Why are we stopping?"

"I always give Car a ride. He drives a motorcycle, and school admins don't want him driving it there."

Carson on a motorcycle? Seriously, what could be hotter than that? I craned my neck, spotting a two-story brick home three houses in. There was a covered bike sitting in the small driveway. "He lives on our property?"

"He and his dad live in our guesthouses," Scott explained. "His father works for rent and what crap money Dad pays him. Something you loved reminding him of."

I winced. "Where's his mom?"

"Dead. Cancer. No health insurance—the trinity of shittiness."

Before I could respond to that observation, I saw Carson trotting across the driveway, a backpack slung over one shoulder and a gym bag on the other. I wet my lips nervously as he approached the car. He wore faded jeans and a short-sleeve shirt over a white thermal. His hair was still damp, curling on his forehead.

He looked good—really good.

Carson stopped in front of the passenger door and then realized I was already there, gaping at him like an idiot. Frowning, he darted around the front and slid into the seat behind Scott. He didn't look at me. "What's she doing here?"

Scott glanced in the rearview mirror. "She used to ride with Cassie, dude."

"Oh, yeah, that's right." His ultrabright gaze touched my face for a second, and I felt my skin burn in a pleasant, heady way. He settled back, throwing his arm over the backseat in a lazy, arrogant sprawl.

The car had started moving, and I was still staring at him. Carson's dark, fathomless blue eyes finally made it back to mine. His gaze dropped, and I realized he was looking at my necklace. A smirk pulled at his lips. "What's up, Sam?"

"Nothing," I sputtered. Why couldn't I pull my eyes away? It was like an old part of me was bold, knew it saw something she liked, and refused to let me turn away.

Scott cleared his throat but didn't say anything.

A muscle started to tick in Carson's jaw. "It's early, and I'm really not up to trading insults with you, so can we just get this out of the way? Yeah, I don't have a car. Uncool. My clothes didn't cost me a house payment, and my dad works for your dad. Oh, burn."

My eyes widened, and I flushed with shame. "I said things like that?"

He shot me a pointed look.

Feeling like the biggest tool ever, I turned around and stared out the window. My stomach was twisting again as I fiddled with the strap on my bag. The back of my throat burned. I couldn't imagine saying those things to someone else, but I had. After several strained minutes, Scott coaxed Carson into a conversation about baseball practice and I kept to myself. Both of them seemed to appreciate that.

We stopped to get coffee because we apparently weren't running that late and Scott felt as if he was going to pass out behind the wheel and "pull a Samantha." Carson ordered straight black, Scott was over at the counter, adding more milk than coffee in his plastic cup, and I stood there, hands twitching at my sides, staring at the menu. The middle-aged woman behind the counter sighed loudly.

Chewing on my lip, I read the entire menu three times. Coffee—my choice of coffee— should be simple, but it wasn't. I felt . . . lost.

"Hey," Carson said from behind me, his breath warm on my cheek, causing me to jump. "You doing okay?"

Feeling my cheeks burn, I nodded.

A man behind me sighed, muttering. I heard the words *stupid* and *rich* tossed about. My mortification level soared to new heights.

Carson pulled me out of line, shooting the guy a dark look of warning. "What's your deal?" he asked.

I glanced down at where his hand wrapped around mine. How could such a simple touch feel sweet as sin? Probably not the best thing to be thinking about given I couldn't place an order for coffee.

"Sam," he said, impatient.

Lifting my gaze, I was horrified to feel tears building. "I don't know what to order." My voice cracked. "I don't know . . . what I like."

Understanding softened his jaw, and he nodded. "You usually drink a latte—vanilla." He paused, dropping his hand. "I've seen you drink them. Stay here and I'll order."

I waited off to the side while he placed the order. People were staring at me. I felt like a child, unable to complete the simplest task. I wanted to crawl into a hole somewhere. There was no doubt in my mind that Carson thought I was an idiot.

When he returned with my drink, he popped the lid on the cup. "Careful. It's hot."

"Thank you." I wrapped my hands around it, welcoming the warmth slipping through the java sleeve.

I didn't talk the rest of the way to school but took in the unfamiliar scenery. A lot of rolling hills, old estates, and very few subdivisions smack-dab in the middle of signs for the battlefield. The town had been around for a long time, and there was a lot of old money by the looks of it.

There was no spark of recognition when I laid eyes on Gettysburg High. It was a large brick building that reminded me of several dorms strung together, surrounded by trees and a sprawling pavilion.

With my heart in my throat, I followed the guys across the parking lot. There was a maroon-and-white banner hanging over the front entrance. HOME OF THE BATTLERS. It had a picture of a demented-looking Easter bunny on it.

The hallways weren't too crowded yet, but *everyone* stopped when they saw me. Just stopped and stared. Within seconds, the whispers started. Tipping my head down, I let my hair fall forward and shield my face, but I could still feel them. Eyes filled with curiosity and morbid fascination.

My heart pounded and I clutched the coffee cup. I couldn't do this. Not when everyone was staring. It would only get worse. Did they know I didn't remember *anything*? Maybe Mom was right. I should've waited.

Scott fell in step beside me, his back stiff. When I peeked at him, he was shooting death glares at everyone. Kids promptly turned away, but it didn't stop them from talking. On my other side, Carson kept watch quietly. I had no idea what he was thinking. Was he embarrassed to be seen with me? I couldn't blame him.

They dropped me off in a lobby surrounded by glass windows. The plump secretary's smile was full of pity as she ordered me to sit in one of the uncomfortable chairs. Each time I glanced over my shoulder, it seemed as if the group of kids gathering outside the room grew. I was like this gruesome car accident, and everyone had to stop and look.

A neatly dressed woman appeared in the narrow hallway, finally ending my torment. She straightened her glasses. "Miss Franco, are you ready?"

Standing, I grabbed my bag and followed her back to a cramped office. The first thing I did when I sat was search for her name. Judith Messer, counselor extraordinaire.

She took off her glasses, folded them, and placed them aside. The light from the lamp on her desk reflected off her diamond-encrusted wedding band. "How are you feeling, Samantha?"

That seemed like an incredibly stupid question. "Good."

Mrs. Messer smiled. "I'll admit we're a little surprised that you're joining us so soon. We thought you'd take some time to . . . recover from everything."

My grip tightened on the cup, and I was ready for this to be over. "I feel perfectly fine."

"I'm sure you do physically, but emotionally and mentally you have gone through a terribly traumatic experience, and adding that on top of the memory loss, this has to be hard on you."

"Well, it hasn't been easy." I glanced up, finding her studying me closely. I sighed. "Okay, it sucks. I couldn't even order coffee this morning, but I need to get back to doing things. I can't hide in my house forever."

She tilted her head to the side. "When the principal informed me you were coming back today, I spoke with a colleague who works with people suffering from amnesia. He did tell me that it's best that you surround yourself with things that are familiar. Coming back to school isn't a bad idea, but emotionally, the cost may be too high."

"And what happens if it is?"

Her smile tightened, and she didn't elaborate, which irked me. "I don't think your classwork will suffer. Dissociative amnesia rarely affects that sort of thing, but we'll be monitoring your progress to make sure that the general curriculum is still the right avenue to take."

My teeth gnashed together at the unspoken warning. If my grades sucked, I was out of school. Nice. No pressure or anything with my *fragile emotional state*.

"Have you been able to remember anything?" She leaned back, crossing her legs.

I considered lying, but that wouldn't help. "Sometimes I have these thoughts or feelings that feel familiar, but they don't make sense." When she nodded, I took a deep breath. "A few times I've seen things, flashes, but . . . those don't make any sense, either."

She nodded. "Your memory could come back in disjointed images or all at once. All it takes is something to trigger it."

The Internet already told me that. I thought about the note, but I was afraid she'd tell my parents. "I haven't really remembered anything else. It's like I'm a . . . blank slate. When I met my friends, my boyfriend, I didn't . . . feel anything for them, like I didn't care at all." I felt bad for saying that, but a little of the pressure lifted off my chest. "That's terrible, isn't it?"

"No, it's not terrible. Right now, you have no bonds formed with them." She smiled reassuringly. "Don't be shocked if you find yourself making new friends or trying things that surprise those around you. It's almost like being born again, but with the necessary survival skills already in place."

Nice way of looking at it. Mrs. Messer asked a few more questions, and then she briefly touched on the subject of Cassie. "How are you handling that? Knowing that a friend of yours is missing?"

I hesitated. "I don't know. It's weird. I don't remember her at all, and from what everyone is telling me, we weren't the greatest of friends, but if she was with me, then I feel responsible. Like I need to remember so that people can find her, but no one really wants to talk about her."

She nodded again. "You do understand that even if you never gain your memories, finding her isn't your responsibility."

The guilt chewing on my stomach told me differently. If I could just get my brain to work, then I'd bet I could lead everyone right to her.

Mrs. Messer slid a slip of paper toward me. My locker number and combination were on it. Our little counseling session was over, and it took me freaking *forever* to find my locker. I had to refer to my schedule to figure out which books to shove into my bag while ignoring the stares and whispers of the people around me. Closing my locker door, I took a deep breath and faced a crowded hallway filled with kids going to first period.

A wave of strange faces greeted me. Not a single one looked familiar. Squeezing the strap on my bag, I pushed through the throng of people. It could be worse, this whole memory thing. I could still be missing.

Or you could be dead, a voice whispered in the back of my mind.

chapter six

On each class, I had to wait for the teacher to tell me where to sit. Once everyone got over the initial shock of seeing my face, they made small talk with me. Asking questions like, "How are you?" and saying things like, "I'm so glad you're back."

Only half of them sounded sincere.

School didn't turn out to be a problem. It took me a couple of minutes to figure out where we were in each class, but the material wasn't outside the realm of my understanding. Veronica was in my English class, and she tugged me into the seat beside her.

Leaning across the tiny aisle, she plucked at the sleeve on my cardigan. "Did you wake up late this morning?"

"No. Why?"

Her eyes drifted over me. "It's just what you're wearing isn't really..."

"Cute," suggested Candy, tossing her bleached hair over one

shoulder. "I mean, it's great for the weekend, but I know for a fact you have cuter clothes in your closet."

"We totally covet your closet, actually." Veronica giggled as she rapped her nails on her desk. "Okay, we also covet Del."

"Oh, girl, don't we ever." Candy fanned her cheeks. "He said he was coming over yesterday. Did he?"

"Yeah, he stopped over." I dug out my necklace, showing them. "He gave this back to me. I left it at his house."

Veronica's lips twitched before she plastered a huge smile on her face. "Was it hard? Seeing him when you . . . don't remember him?"

I nodded. "It was different, but we got . . . caught up."

Candy glanced at Veronica knowingly. "I bet you guys did."

My brows shot up. "Not in that way. Jeez, he's kind of like a stranger to me."

Veronica didn't miss a beat. "I was talking to Trey this morning, and he said Del was pretty happy after seeing you. That's good news, right?"

"Yeah, about . . . Trey, how is he doing?"

Like a switch being thrown, both girls' faces went blank. "What do you mean?" asked Veronica.

"He's dating Cassie, right? Is he doing okay?"

Two seats ahead, a boy with black hair snorted and twisted around. His face was ghastly pale. Thick black eyeliner curved around slanted eyes. "Trey is doing great. He practically had his tongue down her throat in homeroom." He pointed at Candy with one nail coated in black fingernail polish. "That must be his coping mechanism."

Candy's tanned cheeks turned a mottled shade of red, but Veronica leaned forward. Her chest nearly spilled out of her low-cut sweater. It had no effect on Goth Boy.

"Look, Pham or Long Duck, whatever your name is, turn around. This conversation doesn't involve you. And maybe you're just jealous." Her eyes were locked on him like lasers set to destroy. "Maybe you wish Trey had his tongue down *your* throat."

"Veronica," I gasped, embarrassed for the kid *and* her.

Without another word, the boy flipped in his seat. The back of his neck turned bloodred. I twisted toward Veronica, but she was smiling at Candy.

"It's not my fault that he wants to *be* me," she said, winking.

Candy giggled.

Anger whipped through me, but the teacher ambled in, starting class. I might not have known who I was, but I knew what Veronica had done was wrong. When the bell rang, I grabbed my belongings and hurried out of the class, ignoring Veronica's and Candy's attempts to get my attention.

I caught up to the boy, grabbing his arm. "Look, I'm really sorry about that."

Goth Boy was shorter than me, and he had to tip his head back to meet my gaze. Even then, I could barely see his eyes through the dyed hair. "Excuse me?"

"I said, I'm sorry about the way they acted. That wasn't right."

His rounded cheeks turned ruddy as he jerked his arm back. "Seriously?" He laughed. Kids moved past us. Some stopped and stared, openmouthed. "This is priceless. The queen bitch is apologizing for her baby bitches. Whatever. *Don't* talk to me."

He left me standing in the middle of the hall, mouth hanging open. A high-pitched snicker cut through the haze. A shiver of awareness whispered its way down my spine. I turned to the right, the source of the sound blocked by a chorus of shifting, moving bodies.

Catching a glimpse of a satiny red dress and black tights and deep auburn hair, I felt my heart stutter in my chest. A mocking laugh raised the hairs on my arms.

Then I saw her. She stood beside the water fountain, her pouty lips painted to match her dress—not the same dress as in the picture I carried with me. Something—*something* was wrong with the dress.

I took a step forward, right into the path of a bulky guy. He laughed, catching my shoulders before I toppled over backward. "Watch out, Sammy. Don't want to send you back to the hospital."

"Sorry," I murmured, darting around him.

The space beside the fountain was empty.

Smoothing a hand over my forehead and through my hair, I spun around and hurried toward my bio class. Aiming for a table in the back, I took my seat and started rummaging around in my bag as my breath came out in short gasps.

Had I really just seen Cassie? The vision was nothing like the others. Hands shaking, I set my notebook down and dug around for a pen. I closed my eyes for a few seconds, got control of my breathing, and then opened my eyes.

A loose piece of paper folded in the shape of a triangle was right in front of my open bag. It could've been inside it and fallen out or . . .

I glanced around quickly, but no one was near me.

Part of me didn't want to read it, didn't even want to begin to figure out how it had gotten into my messenger bag or if it had dropped out of the sky. There had been chances, opportunities during the first three classes. Someone could've slipped it in there. Drawing in a shallow breath, I unfolded the slip of paper.

There was blood on the rocks. Her blood. Your blood.

I stared at the words until they blurred on the yellow paper. Cassie's blood—my blood on the rocks? Waves of nausea rolled through me.

"What are you looking at?"

Jumping at the unexpected voice, I slapped my hand over the note and looked up. Two vibrant blue eyes, the color of polished sapphires, locked onto mine. Carson was sliding into the seat next to me.

"Why are you sitting here?" I asked, quickly folding up the paper.

He arched a brow. "I sit here."

I shoved the note in my bag. "You do?"

"Yeah, I'm your lab partner. Have been all year, Sam." Carson propped his elbow on the table, resting his cheek on a closed fist. "So, what are you doing?"

"I'm...I can't find my pen."

He offered me his.

"What about you?"

One side of his lips curved up. "I have many, many more. I have a pen fetish. I just keep collecting them."

I couldn't tell if he was joking, but I smiled and took the pen. Our fingers brushed, and a jolt traveled up my hand. I looked up, my eyes meeting his. He still held the pen, but his gaze was wary. "Thanks?" I said, tugging gently.

Carson let go. "How's your first day back?"

I laughed under my breath. "It's been great."

"Care to elaborate?"

"I'm kind of surprised you're curious."

He watched me for a moment and then pulled back, folding his arms over his broad chest. "Well, I was just trying to be nice and make small talk. Usually, we just glare at each other and trade insults. We could go back to that if you want?"

"No." My voice sounded sad. "I don't want that."

Carson tried to hide the flicker of surprise with a short laugh, but I saw it. "Oh, well . . ."

Swirling emotions rose to the surface—hurt, anger, confusion. "I'm sorry for being such a bitch to you since . . . well, since whenever. Really, I am. But can we just start over?"

He stared at me, eyes wide and dilated. His expression was unreadable.

Shaking my head, I faced the front of the class. Why had I even bothered? It wasn't as if a simple apology was going to repair years of me being mean. And coming to my rescue this morning at the coffee shop didn't constitute Carson waving a white flag of friendship. "Guess not."

"Sam—"

"Just forget it," I grumbled. Flipping the notebook open, I attempted to read the biology notes that I couldn't seem to remember taking when I saw Candy in the front of the classroom.

She stared back at me, her gaze darting between Carson and me. When she caught my eyes, her brows rose. I shrugged and went back to reading the notes that I obviously hadn't put much effort into. I didn't look once in Carson's direction during the entire class, but his presence was overwhelming anyway. Every part of my body was aware of his movements. When he scribbled down notes, or when he rubbed his hand over his chest or flexed his right wrist. My nerves were stretched thin by the time the bell rang. I bolted from the classroom like a scared, caged animal.

Lunch wasn't much different.

I had to go through the line alone, and nothing looked edible. Settling on pizza, I grabbed a bottle of water and searched the tables. Veronica was in the back, waving her hand like an air traffic controller. Getting used to the stares, I headed in their direction.

"I heard she doesn't remember a *thing*," whispered a girl. "Like she had to be told what her name was. How insane is that?"

"Well, she certainly forgot who she was friends with," replied another girl, much louder. "I saw her talking to Louis in the hallway today. Hell froze over."

Passing another table, I heard a guy say, "I'm not sure which one I wanted to come back. Both have the tightest . . ."

I hurried up, not wanting to hear the rest of that. I passed my brother, who was sitting next to a pretty blonde. They didn't seem to notice me, as their mouths were attached to each other.

Sitting down beside Veronica, I forced my muscles to relax. The girls were talking about what happened on a TV show they watched last night, and I was able to eat half of my pizza in silence. A few minutes later, a guy with short dark hair and a supermuscular build joined us. He sat beside Candy.

"Trey." He shoved his hand out, grinning. He had a slight accent—British? "Nice to meet you."

Veronica knocked his hand away. "Don't be stupid."

"What?" He winked at me. "Del said she doesn't remember any of this. Figured I'd introduce myself."

"Samantha." I held my hand out, going along with it. He laughed, shook my hand, and settled back, throwing an arm over the back of Candy's chair. "Damn, you really don't remember a thing?"

Damn, I was really getting tired of people asking if I remembered anything. "Not a thing."

His eyes narrowed. "So you have no clue about what happened to Cassie?"

Silence descended on the table like a thick, itchy blanket. A fist-size ball of unease formed under my ribs as I met Trey's stare. "No. Do you?"

"No." Trey laughed. "I hadn't seen her that whole weekend. We broke up."

Veronica cleared her throat. "Guys, can we talk about something else? This creeps me out."

He ignored her. "Have you asked Del if *he* saw her that weekend?"

The ball grew larger, heavier. Had I asked Del? I didn't think so, not in so many words. "He didn't mention seeing her."

Trey's look of innocence didn't fool me. "You might want to ask again. Just saying."

"What does that mean?" I demanded.

"It doesn't mean anything," Veronica said, pushing a piece of lettuce around on her plate. "Trey's missing a few brain cells. Anyway, Lauren and I were planning on going to Philly this weekend to get new dresses for the party Del's throwing after prom."

Lauren was the brunette with blond streaks, the quietest one of the bunch. She smiled at me.

"Del's having a party?" I asked.

She shook her head at me and then laughed. "Oh, yes, I'm stupid. He throws one every year. Everyone goes. And some people who shouldn't be there go, but there's no way to control the population."

"Yeah, like if she shows up, we're going to have to hide the food," Candy said, her lip curled. "And lock the fridge."

The words were so loud I didn't have to guess at whom she was talking about. The girl was sitting down at a table in front of us. Her curly hair was pulled up, and the back of her neck was beet red.

"Oink. Oink," said Veronica, brows puckered together.

I stared at them. "That girl isn't even big," I said in a hushed voice. She wasn't as skinny as Veronica and Candy, but hell, people in Third World countries were heavier than they were.

Candy glanced over her shoulder and snorted. "What is she? A size ten?"

My mouth dropped open. "Yeah, wow, call Jenny Craig. You guys are joking, right?"

Trey leaned back farther, amusement dripping from his pores. The table of girls stared at me as if I'd stripped naked and done a little jig. I gripped my bottle, wanting to throw it at one of their heads.

"Jeez, that's rude on so many levels."

Veronica jerked her head back. "Okay, that's coming from you?"

"So?" I said.

She bit down on her lower lip as she scanned the cafeteria. "Okay. Do you see her?" She pointed out a pretty girl with mocha-colored skin and kick-ass boots. "Just a couple weeks ago, you called her"—she lowered her voice—"a fat bitch whose thighs were capable of setting the world on fire. So you have no room to talk."

My jaw hit the floor. "I . . . I wouldn't say that."

Lauren nodded slowly, her eyes focused on her plate. "You did."

"And a week before that, you actually offered a salad to some chick and suggested that she eat that instead of her pizza." Trey laughed. "I really thought you were going to get your butt kicked."

A horrible feeling surged through my veins as I stared at my friends, the same combination of shame and confusion I'd felt when I tried to apologize to the boy in the hall. I couldn't decide which was worse: that I had said and done things like that, or that my friends all seemed to think it was okay. Disgusted with them and myself, I grabbed my tray and stood. "I'll see you guys later."

Veronica's mouth snapped open. "Sammy!"

I ignored her, blinking back the angry rush of tears. More than anything, I wanted to get away from myself—from any reminder of who I used to be. And I knew exactly where to sit.

I stopped in front of my brother's table, my eyes fixed on him. "Can I sit here?"

He looked surprised but nodded. "Sure. Have a seat."

With my cheeks blazing and a sob stuck in my throat, I sat down. Several moments passed before I realized that Carson was at the table, and he was watching me through narrowed eyes. When I glanced up, my eyes met those of the girl sitting beside my brother.

In an instant, I knew who she was—the girl I had a brief memory of; the one with the red floppy hat. Excitement hummed through me as I realized I knew someone. "You're Julie!"

She glanced at my brother and then back, blinking rapidly. Scott placed his fork down. "Do you remember her, Sam?" he asked.

I nodded eagerly, kind of like a puppy in the dog treats commercial I'd seen the day before. "Yes. I mean, I remember a younger version of her. You were wearing a red hat, but I couldn't find a picture of you on my wall, but I think we used to be friends." I glanced at Scott, who was staring at me with wide eyes. Actually, half the table was gawking at me. My cheeks flushed as I trailed off.

Julie cleared her throat. "I used to wear this really big hat when I was younger. It belonged to my mom. We—you and I—thought it was the coolest thing ever, but that was a long time ago."

Back before I turned into an überbitch or one who had an entire table enthralled for all the wrong reasons. I shoved a piece of pizza in my mouth.

Carson shook his head. "You're right, Scott. This is really bizarre."

I pressed my lips together and glanced around the jammed cafeteria. *I will not break down. I will not break down.* The lump was almost in my mouth, stuck around the pizza. Del strolled in through the double doors, talking to a boy in a neon-green polo.

Horrible shirt.

Del's gaze drifted over me and then shot back. His eyes widened. The look on his face was almost comical. He said something to his friend and then started toward me.

"Great," muttered Carson, screwing the lid back on his drink. "I can tolerate her sitting here, but not Del the Dick."

My laugh bubbled up before I could stop it, and I started to turn toward Carson when something red caught my attention.

At once, everything froze around me. A second later, the lunchroom crumbled away, flaking off in chunks of ash and broken stone. The sounds of people talking, laughing, and eating vanished. A film settled over my eyes, fading everything to a lifeless gray with the exception of one color.

Red.

The only color in the whole room was the red ripped dress hanging from her body.

Cassie stood at the end of our table.

chapter seven

She stared at me, eyes narrowed and fists clenched at her sides. Her hair was all over the place, darker at the top of her head, plastered there. A dark stain spread over her hairline, leaking down her face like a ghoulish, insidious river.

"You think you're so perfect," she said, her voice eerily flat as blood ran into her unblinking eyes. "You're not! You have no idea! Your life is so messed up, and you have no idea."

I jerked back. "Cassie?"

A warm hand wrapped around mine, and Cassie vanished. Dazed, I met Scott's worried stare. "What did you say?" he asked.

"You didn't see . . ."

"See what?" Scott's grip tightened.

"Nothing." I pulled my hand free, heart racing.

"You said Cassie's name," Julie said, pale and visibly shaken. "God, Sam, you look like you saw a ghost."

I was beginning to think I had. Or I was certifiable. All of them were staring at me. Carson's eyes were wide and had that dilated look again. There wasn't enough air coming into my lungs. They were contracting painfully. Legs trembling, I stood and grabbed my bag. "I have to go," I rasped.

"Sam." Scott stood.

I hurried away from the table. A confused Del reached for me, but I dodged him. Out in the hallway, I started running and I didn't stop as I pushed open the doors leading outside. My feet slapped off the concrete and then the asphalt. Reaching my brother's car, I dropped down beside it and pulled my knees up to my chest, dragging in air in painful gulps.

Now I understood what everyone had warned me about—it was all too much.

Mom picked me up from school early. The ride home was tense, and I kept getting the impression that she wanted to say something but didn't know what. And honestly, what could she say? Something like this couldn't be fixed with a few simple words.

"Honey," she said when we pulled into the driveway. "There's a doctor your father knows—"

"What kind of doctor?" I twisted toward her, clutching my bag.

She grimaced as she killed the engine. "He's a psychologist."

Anger and embarrassment warred inside me. I should've never told her what had happened over the phone. "I'm not crazy."

"Honey, I'm not saying you're . . . crazy." She looked at me, her smile pained. "But you said you saw Cassie in the lunchroom and—"

"That doesn't mean I have to see a therapist. You already

have me seeing the guidance counselor." I climbed out of the car, slamming the door. "I don't want to see a therapist."

"You might not have a choice," she said quietly.

I whipped around, and the next words came from a place hidden deep inside me. "What would your friends think, Mom? Having a daughter who needs to see a therapist?"

Mom blanched. "The same thing they thought when my daughter got drunk and drove her *brand-new* car into a tree. Or when my daughter was in those pictures for everyone to see! Or when—"

"Wait. What pictures?"

She gave me a pointed look, one that said she wouldn't disgrace herself by repeating what *those pictures* were.

"What pictures?" I screamed.

Mom didn't answer.

The moment we stepped inside the house, she went straight to the liquor cabinet and poured herself bourbon. She downed it in one gulp and then poured another. "Honey, I want you to get better. Not because of what my friends think, but because you are my daughter. Seeing a therapist isn't—"

"No," I cut her off. "I'm not going to a therapist."

She looked away, taking a healthy drink of the bourbon. I left the room, having nothing else to say.

I spent a couple of hours in my bedroom, pacing back and forth. Every so often, I stopped and looked at the music box and then at Cassie's picture. When I heard the garage door open, I panicked. I didn't want to be in the same house with the woman I was driving to drink and the brother who surely thought I was crazy. Slipping out the back door, I started walking beyond the pool and the little bungalow surrounded by trees. A man was working on them, carrying thick branches to the back of a pickup truck. Sweat glistened off his dark skin.

He didn't even look up. I was invisible to him, and I liked that.

Moving toward the end of the property, I climbed over a stone wall surrounding the yard. There was a path carved through the grass and rocky soil, splitting between trees. Up ahead was a tree house built into a large maple.

I stopped under it, wondering if my subconscious had led me here. There had to be a reason why I found this.

There wasn't anything special about the tree house. It was more like a hut in a tree, with an open side that allowed you to look out over the grounds. It took several tries to get into the main part. From there, I crawled through a small opening and into a space big enough for me to lie down in but not stand. I seriously hoped the wood wasn't rotten.

A cool breeze picked up a few strands of my hair, tossing them across my face. I shivered and hunkered down in my sweater.

I'm not crazy.

Didn't Mrs. Messer say that the memories could come back in the form of disjointed images? Images that screamed at me— *that bled?* A horrible thought struck me. What if the image of Cassie bleeding had been a recollection of something I saw that night? But why would she yell those things at me? There was no answer to that, because I didn't know what my life was like before Wednesday. And then there were the two notes. The last one talked about blood . . . and then I saw a bleeding Cassie? I knew the notes weren't imaginary. Scott had read one. Someone had to be placing them there. To scare me? To warn me?

What pictures?

Surrounded by birds chirping and the dragging swoosh of bare branches rubbing together, I realized another terrible thing. Missing best friend or not, I didn't want any part of my old life back. I didn't want to remember the terrible things I'd said and done, but I suppose it didn't matter. Even if I couldn't remember who I was, everyone else would never forget. No matter how badly I wanted to ignore the person I used to be, I couldn't escape a past I didn't remember.

I must've been so lost in my thoughts that I didn't realize someone had joined me in the little tree hut until I heard the wood creak and groan behind me.

My heart jumped in my throat, then skipped a beat when I turned and saw him sit down beside me. "Carson?"

"You know, you could've picked a more comfortable place to hang out. I doubt this place is entirely safe."

Several moments passed before I could find the ability to say something other than his name. "I didn't mean to be up here so long."

"I figured as much." He tilted his head toward me, eyes shadowed.

I scrubbed my eyes, fighting a yawn. "What time is it?"

"Almost nine thirty." Carson paused. "Everyone is looking for you. Your parents—Scott and Del. They're combing the whole town."

"And *you* found me?"

Carson laughed. The sound was nice, deep, and warming. I had this impression that I didn't get to hear him laugh a lot. "I know. It's a shocker, huh? I was kind of surprised you were in the tree house. No one would have thought to check here. And it was really a last-ditch effort on my part."

Warmth crept through me as I stared at his half-shadowed face. Our gazes locked, and the heady rush of heat spread lower. "Why were you looking for me? You don't even..."

"Like you?" he supplied, grinning.

"You hate me."

His brows shot up. "I don't hate you. I've never hated you. You were... just really hard to like sometimes." He turned back to the night sky, letting out a soft breath. "Why did you come here? Did you remember this place?"

I twisted my chilled fingers together, pleased that at least he never hated me. It was probably the best news I'd heard all day. "I don't know. I don't remember it, but I ended up here anyway."

"The three of us used to play here when we were little," he explained. "And when you would get in trouble for not going to piano class or dance class, you'd hide here. I bet you haven't stepped foot in this tree house since you were eleven, though."

Piano and dance classes? That explained the music box, but that wasn't what was important. I thought about the coffee trip this morning. "You know a lot about me."

"We grew up together." He was quiet for a moment. "You spent a lot of time here. Scott used to dangle you off the ledge."

I laughed. "That sounds like fun."

Carson nudged me with his arm. "You loved it. You had this thing about flying. Once you actually jumped out of this thing. Your brother broke your fall. And he broke his arm." My lips kept spreading as I stretched out my legs, wiggling my toes in my sneakers. "Was he mad at me?"

"No." Carson laughed. "He was scared to death you were going to break your neck. Don't even get me started on the things you used to do on top of the pool shed. Like I said, you had this thing with flying and a daredevil streak. You still kind of do, actually. Scott was telling me a few weeks ago you went bungee jumping, and apparently Del almost pissed himself."

Instead of laughing, I felt something heavy pressed down on my chest. I turned away. The sky was dark, full of clouds. No stars, and just a glimpse of the moon.

Carson sat up, his shoulder resting against my back. "What is it?"

I glanced over my shoulder, finding our faces inches apart. A sudden wild curiosity consumed me. I wanted to know if his lips felt as soft as they looked. I bet they were firm, sensual. Dispelling the desire, I lowered my gaze. Not hating me didn't equal wanting to make out with me. "I asked Del what I was like."

"And?" His breath was warm, tantalizing on my cheek.

"And all he could tell me was that I liked to shop and party." I sighed. "But after ten minutes with you, now I know I was sort of an adrenaline junkie. That's better than being the party girl, right?"

He leaned back, putting some distance between us. "You're more than a party girl, Sam. You're smart—incredibly smart. I'd be failing bio if you weren't my partner. And I can't fail if I want that scholarship, but anyway, you're also strong. I mean, come on, how many people who have a complete loss of memory would jump right back into their life? You're tenacious."

I flushed. "Tenacious?"

"Yeah, it's my word of the day."

Twisting around, I grinned at him. "Your scholarship? Where do you want to go?"

"Penn State," he responded. "If I can keep my grades up, I'll get a full ride."

"That's awesome."

Carson stared at me, then laughed and shook his head. "You're planning on going to Yale. *That's* pretty awesome."

My grin faded. "What if I don't want to go to Yale now?"

He laughed again. "Your parents would freak out, Sam. And seriously, that's an opportunity you shouldn't just give up because things . . . are different now."

I tucked my feet under me and sat back. He had a point, but I wondered if Yale was ever my dream or more of my parents' heritage. "Do you still come to the tree house?"

"Yeah, it's a good place to get away and think."

"Maybe that's why I came here." I shrugged.

"Can I ask you a question?" he said. When I lifted my eyes, he was close again. I nodded, and he reached out, catching a piece of my hair the wind had blown across my face and tucking it back behind my ear. His hand lingered for maybe a second, but I felt it in every cell of my body. "What happened at lunch?"

Spell broken, I moved to the edge of the observation deck. "Nothing."

Carson scooted forward, giving me no place to go. "Something happened."

There was no way I was going to tell him what I'd seen. Having my mom think I was crazy was one thing, but a boy this incredibly hot? Yeah, not going to happen. I shook my head. "Nothing happened. I was...tired."

He looked doubtful. "I'm just trying to help, Sam."

I started to tell him that I didn't need his help, but then I had an idea. And once it took hold, it wouldn't let me go. "You really want to help me?"

"I wouldn't offer if I didn't."

"Okay." I took a deep breath. "Do you know where Cassie lives?"

"Yeah," he said. "Why?"

"I think seeing her stuff might help me remember." It was a long shot, but it was something. "Can you take me there?"

Carson stared at me for a long moment and then nodded. "I can do it. Next Saturday, if you can wait that long? I have practice almost every day until then."

I didn't want to wait that long, but I also didn't want to ask anyone else. "I can wait."

Mom and Dad read me the riot act when I returned to the house, and I did feel bad. Considering that I was gone for four days, the last thing I should've done was to disappear without any warning. I apologized and meant it.

Dad looked so surprised I was worried he was going to have a heart attack.

There were several missed calls and texts from my friends and Del. I sent a mass text, telling them that I was okay. When Del responded with a phone call, I felt terrible for vanishing. The concern that tainted his voice pulled at my heart.

"I want to come over," he said, and I could hear a door shutting behind him. "I have to see you."

I dropped down on the edge of my bed, staring at the music box. "I don't know if that's a good idea. My parents are pissed."

A heavy sigh came through the phone. "But your parents love me."

"I'm not sure they love *me* right now." I chewed on my lip. "Can you come over tomorrow after school?"

"Yeah, of course." There was a pause, and then the sound of a can popping open. "What happened today at lunch? Veronica said you were acting really weird, and then you got up and sat with your brother. A few minutes later, you just ran out of there without saying anything."

"I was just tired." I flopped onto my back. The stars were glowing. "Do my friends hate me now?"

"No." Del laughed. "Don't be stupid, Sammy. They know you're going through a lot."

Don't be stupid? I frowned.

"And you'll be back to your old self in no time. They understand," he said. Another door shut. "Look, I've got to get off here. I'll see you tomorrow at school."

"Hey, wait a sec." I sat up and swung my legs off the bed. "Mom said something today about pictures of me. Do you know what she was talking about?"

He was quiet so long I thought he'd hung up. "Who knows? You probably weren't wearing any makeup or something. You know your mom."

Not really, but it sounded like her. I let him go after that, and even though it was late, I opened my laptop and tried again to access my e-mail. There had to be personal stuff in there. Something that could help me remember. Mrs. Messer said there'd be triggers.

I needed a trigger.

But I couldn't answer the damn personal-verification question. *Who is your childhood friend?* I'd already typed *Cassie*. Didn't work. *Veronica.* Nope. *Lauren.* No chance. I then tried *Julie* and still couldn't get in. Frustrated, I got up and went to my brother's bedroom door. I knocked on the door.

Bedsprings creaked, followed by the sound of clothing being hastily dragged on. *Oh no* . . . I started to step back from the door, but it swung open.

Scott was pulling his shirt down his flat stomach. Over his shoulder, Julie sat on his bed with a book in her lap. The book was upside down, and I grinned. He cleared his throat, cheeks flushed. "Are you okay, Sam?"

"Uh, yeah." I averted my gaze to the poster of the Phillies above his bed. "I was wondering if you can answer a question for me."

Julie looked up, a curious expression on her pretty face. I smiled at her, and she responded with a tentative smile.

"Sure." Scott leaned across the door frame, crossing his arms. "I'm a fountain of knowledge. Ask away."

I felt really stupid for asking this. "Who was my childhood friend?"

Scott stared at me.

My cheeks burned. "I'm trying to change my password so I can check my e-mail."

"Oh, that makes sense. Try Carson."

Shock immobilized me. "Carson?"

Scott nodded. "You guys were closer than he and I were growing up. He'd be my best bet."

Carson was my best childhood friend? I couldn't believe it, given the initial animosity he showed toward me. "Why aren't we friends anymore?"

"Cassie and Del," Julie answered, closing the textbook in her lap. "You started hanging out more and more with them, and, well, your old friends just didn't make the cut."

"Including you?" I asked, remembering what Scott had said.

"Oh god," Scott muttered, rubbing the heel of his palm down his face. "Sam, after today, maybe you . . ."

"I should what?"

Julie set the book aside. "We were friends up until the beginning of junior year."

"What happened then?"

She hesitated. "I wanted to start dating your brother, and you told me we couldn't be friends if I did. And I put it to the test. You weren't joking."

Wow. I was seriously starting to believe I was the Antichrist. "I'm sorry," I said. Then I spun around and speed-walked down the hall. I made it halfway before I heard Julie's voice.

"Sam, wait a sec."

I turned back to the taller girl and braced myself. Whatever she was going to say was something I most definitely deserved.

She stopped in front of me, smoothing her hands over the studded belt around her hips. "I wanted to talk to you more today, but..."

Surprised that she wasn't cursing me up and down, I felt the muscles in my back ease up a little. "But I ran off like a freak."

"I wouldn't say it was like a freak." She gave me a tentative smile. "Are you okay?"

There was a moment when I wanted to spew everything that I'd been seeing, because there was a part of me that recognized Julie on some kind of internal level, but the last thing I wanted to do was come off as someone crazy. "Yeah, I'm fine. It was... it was just a lot today."

"I can imagine." A sympathetic look crept across her face, and then she took a deep breath. "You really did remember me? Briefly?"

I nodded. "It wasn't much. I just remembered you when we were—"

"We were probably ten," she cut in, biting down on her bottom lip. "We hung out every day after school and on the weekends. We were practically inseparable."

A yearning to go back to that time filled me. "Did I really stop talking to you because you started dating Scott? Because he said I stopped talking to you because you wore something I didn't like, but I... I don't think I was that big on fashion."

"You've always had really nice clothes and dressed like a

socialite, but you've never cared about clothes. Not like the other girls." Julie's lips pursed as she brushed a strand of hair off her forehead. "I don't know what the real reason was. Who knows if it was Scott? That's what you told me, but it didn't make sense. And Cassie didn't like me, Sam. She was epically jealous over our friendship, and I'm pretty sure she had something to do with it."

Everything came back to Cassie. Did the girl have that much control over my life? Or was it something more than that?

"I should get back. We're busy studying." She winked at the look that crossed my face. "I really would like to hang out if you want."

"That would be nice," I said quickly. "I mean, I really would like that."

She laughed softly. "I got it. See you later?"

I gave her a quick, majorly awkward wave and then headed to my bedroom. Closing the door behind me, I let out a ragged breath and sat in front of my laptop. Very slowly, almost reluctantly, I typed in Carson's name. As I clicked on NEXT, I squeezed my eyes shut.

I pried opened one eye.

The space to enter my new password greeted me.

Confusion bulldozed over me, but behind the question of why I would've picked him as a secret answer when I seemed to have hated him, there was a thrilling, humming excitement that brought a giddy smile to my face. A smile I didn't understand, because I had a boyfriend who I'd apparently been really into.

But Carson had been so close to me in the tree house.

Pushing thoughts of Carson aside, I picked a new password

and finally logged in to my account. All the e-mail in my in-box before last Wednesday had been deleted.

Huh . . . Now that was odd—there wasn't a single e-mail from Cassie. Not one saved or even in my sent file. Nothing. Someone had been in my e-mail account. That would explain why the password had been goofed up, but the thought made me feel paranoid.

Opening a message from Veronica, I read that she was sorry about lunch and she still loved me. Rolling my eyes, I started to delete it but responded back and told her it was okay. My friends might be jackasses of the highest order, but I needed to give them a chance. Before I shut the computer down, I opened up a new message and typed *C* in the address bar.

CASSIEBLIVELY@LIVE.COM autofilled.

Seeing the e-mail address stole my breath. I didn't know why I did what I did next, but I typed two short sentences. *Where are you?* And then, *Who are you?*

I hit SEND.

chapter eight

The rest of the week was sort of normal. I went back to school, and I tried to fit back into this life that was so unfamiliar to me. I learned the hierarchy of my school pretty quickly and how it all worked. There were three groups, it seemed: those at the top, those who managed to become friends with the ones at the top, and then everyone who didn't.

My friends were clearly part of the first group. Each of our families had strong roots in Gettysburg or in the surrounding towns. All the sprawling estates we passed from our home to school were owned by one of them or their extended family.

And our families ruled the county.

Lauren's father was involved in investment, like mine. Candy's father owned the largest realty company in the state. Veronica's father was a state supreme court judge. Trey's father worked in New York City at the British Embassy. And we were just like our parents—we ruled the school.

I quickly realized that our actions were rarely questioned, mainly because of who our parents were. Old blood. Old money. I had a feeling it wasn't like this in other places. Sure, there was always one group that ran the school, but everything was so stratified here. I thought maybe it had to do with how tight-knit the community was. Well, the rich portion of it. They—er, we—were tight-knit. Everyone else was an interloper or whatever.

Something didn't fit in the equation, though, and that was Cassie. I don't know how I knew that or if it was one of the weird feelings I got that I knew was linked to my life before, but I had this distinct impression that Cassie had been an interloper and I had been fiercely protective of that.

None of that made sense. Hell, my life didn't make much sense.

At lunch, I ate with the girls. Twice they invited me to go dress shopping with them, but I refused. Planning for prom just seemed inappropriate given everything. And as much as I tried to make things normal, there was this huge gulf between my friends and me. I didn't join in when they made fun of other people or laugh at their jokes. With each day, their looks became longer and darker, their comments more snide. I couldn't help but feel as if I'd ended up on the wrong side of special with them.

I hung out with Del after baseball practice. Once I went to his home, which made my house look like one of the seedy motels alongside highways. Money was clearly one of the most important factors in his family's life, much like in mine. He was patient with me and the whole getting-to-know-you-again thing, but I could tell he was waiting for me to snap out of it, to become this girl he'd fallen in love with, and so was I. Their expectations—my parents', friends', and Del's—all weighed on me, and at the end of the day I always resurfaced feeling as if I was lacking... *something*. The only part of the day I really, truly enjoyed was the ride to school in the morning and bio.

Both involved Carson.

I hadn't had any more hallucinations or found notes.

And Cassie was still missing.

Hope that she'd suddenly reappear like I had dwindled a little more each day. There was no mistaking the looks I got in class or in the hallway. Suspicious, accusing looks. When I said something about it one morning on the way to school, Scott and Carson told me I was being paranoid.

I wasn't so sure.

Chances were my reputation was scary enough that people believed I was capable of doing something heinous to Cassie. I didn't want to think that, but there was a teeny, tiny part of me that was afraid.

Detective Ramirez showed up Thursday after school. He must've contacted Dad first, because Dad was home and he didn't leave my side as Ramirez interrogated me. The detective asked the same questions over and over again. Unfortunately, my answers weren't any different. After half an hour of going in circles, Ramirez gave up and left, empty-handed and disappointed.

Not as disappointed as I was.

Mom had stayed quiet through the whole event, drinking out of a coffee cup that I suspected wasn't full of coffee. After the detective left, she headed out of the kitchen. Dad reached for her, but she sidestepped him with the agility of an alley cat. There was a flash of frustration in my father's eyes, but it was gone when his gaze met mine.

"It's okay." Dad placed his hand over mine and squeezed. His lips twitched into a smile. "I know you're trying to remember and help, princess."

"Princess?" I whispered. "You haven't called me that in . . ." I trailed off, frowning.

Dad became very still. "Since when?"

My mouth worked, and I swore the answer was right there, at the edge of my thoughts, but when I grasped for it, the knowledge simply evaporated like smoke in the wind. I shook my head. "I don't know."

He didn't say anything immediately. And then, "I haven't called you that since you were eleven or so."

"Why did you start again?"

"Lately, it's like I have my little princess back. The way you were before . . ." He leaned back, slipping his hand off mine. He folded his arms across his chest, his gaze switching to the large windows looking out into the back patio. "You didn't want me calling you that anymore, and I know you're going to ask why." A fleeting grin graced his lips, and it looked tired. "The last time I called you that was the day you brought Cassie over here for the first time. You made a point of asking me not to later that night."

My brows knitted as I watched him blow out a low breath. "Why would she have anything to do with you calling me that?"

His gaze shifted to me. "I don't know. Only you know the answer to that."

* * *

"We still on for tomorrow?" Carson asked as soon as he sat down in bio.

I nodded. "As long as you still want to help."

Again, he got that look on his face, like he was confused and then wary. The same look that crossed his striking features during every conversation with me. "Yeah, I do. I have practice in the morning."

"That's okay." I kept my gaze just above his eyes. Looking directly into them or at his lips was just asking for a return of confusing, frustrating emotions.

Scooting his chair closer to mine, he leaned over my shoulder and laughed. Shivers danced down my spine. "What are you drawing? Bigfoot?"

My fingers stilled around the pen, and I frowned at my drawing. It was a poorly drawn sketch of a guy. "I think that's supposed to be shadows surrounding him, not hair."

"Oh, I kind of see it now."

"I honestly don't know why I'm drawing this." Laughing self-consciously, I put my pen down and looked at him. He was so, so intoxicatingly close. "Well, I've learned I'm not an artist."

"I'm going to have to agree with you on that." Sitting back, he studied my drawing. It was really just an outline of a guy, shaded in with my pen. I hadn't stayed in the lines. Guess that explained the whole hair thing. "There may be hope for you, though."

Right then, I decided I liked the way one side of his lip

curved up. Crooked but perfect. "You were quiet on the way to school today."

Carson brushed an unruly lock of hair off his forehead. "Big test in history."

"Do tests bother you?"

He laughed softly, stretching out his long, lean legs under the white table. "Any test bothers me because if I fail one, it kills my GPA."

"You'll do fine. You're kind of great, so—" I smacked my hand over my mouth, horrified and unsure of where those words came from.

Carson stared at me, a slow smile pulling at his lips. "Well, I'm going to have to agree with you again."

Cheeks blazing like I'd been out in the sun for too long, I lowered my hand. "I can't believe I just said that."

"It's okay." He chuckled. "I can pretend I didn't hear you."

"That would be great."

A sly, mischievous look crept into his dark blue eyes. "But I won't forget."

Mrs. Cleo rolled into bio then, carrying a stack of paper. The heavy bracelets around her thick arms jangled with every step. I faced the class, fighting off a stupid grin, and locked eyes with Candy. She arched a brow and mouthed, *"Carson?"* The way her lip curled around his name was a work of art. Glancing at Carson, I was happy to see he hadn't noticed.

After class, Candy all but dragged me into the nearest bathroom and stood in front of the door, arms folded across the chest of her sweater dress. The lingering scent of cigarettes and disinfectant rushed over me. The graffiti on the walls looked completely unintelligible. "Okay, Sammy, what the hell is up with you and Española?"

Anger blasted through me like a gunshot. "He has a name. And that was freaking rude, like, on a disgusting level."

Her thick lashes batted. *"Sorry."* She threw up her hands. "God, you are so *sensitive* now. Yes, Carson is hot. No one can take that from him, and he's good for some fun, but he's the son of your *groundskeeper.*"

My hands balled into fists. "He's also really smart, a kick-ass pitcher from what I hear, and he's nice."

Candy's mouth dropped open. "Oooh-kay, what about Del? You guys have this epic romance that everyone wants—especially Veronica—but anyway, have you, like, forgotten about him?"

Oh…oh crap. I *had* forgotten about Del. "This has nothing to do with Del."

"It doesn't?"

The bathroom door opened, and Candy swung around, slamming her hand on the door.

"What the hell?" came a startled voice from the other side.

"This bathroom is in use," Candy shot back. "Go find another." Facing me, she tossed her hair over her shoulder. "How do you think Del would feel if he knew his girlfriend was making screw-me eyes at another dude?"

"I was not." I took a step forward, feeling my cheeks flame. "Carson and I are just friends."

"Since when? I get that you don't remember anything, but you and Carson are from two different worlds. He *hated* you. And the feeling was mutual."

Those three words hit me in the chest harder than they should have. "He hated me?"

She smiled at me like I was a small child who'd just tried to stick my finger in an electric socket. "Do you like him?"

"What?" I shouldered my bag and stalked over to the mirror above the sink, pretending to be engrossed in applying lip gloss. "I already told you I like him as a friend."

Her face appeared over my shoulder, her eyes catlike. "That's reassuring, because it would be really awkward if you did."

"Why?" I snapped the lip gloss shut, fighting the urge to throw it in her face. "Because he's not rich?"

She scrunched up her nose. "No. Because he totally got with Cassie last summer at a party, and he did the same with Lauren. Carson's a player."

Later that night, I had a boy on my bed. Mrs. Messer insisted that I do normal things every day, things that could trigger my memories. And considering my lack of virginity, having Del in my bedroom had to be something familiar.

Mom and Dad were at some kind of silent auction in Philly, and I had no idea where Scott was. He could be anywhere in the massive house, and I'd have no idea.

"Why didn't you go shopping with the girls?" Del asked, stretching out beside me.

I gave a lopsided shrug and turned my head toward him. His

eyes were like warm chocolate, but I had a feeling they could be colder, harder. "I wanted to spend time with you."

Del appeared to be happy with that, and it was the truth. Spending alone time with him could only help. Apparently we were the things fairy tales were made of, and I wanted to remember it—to *feel* it. Right now, I felt nothing. My breath didn't catch, there wasn't a flutter in my chest or the sweeping heat that—I wouldn't think of *him*, especially after what I'd learned about *him*.

He had slept with Lauren.

And he'd slept with Cassie.

Squeezing my eyes shut, I strung together an atrocity of curse words. I *wasn't* going to think about Carson. Seriously. Not when I was with Del. That was wrong on so many levels, and I didn't need my memories to know that.

I reached out, running the tips of my fingers over the curve of his jaw. His was smooth. I wondered how many times I'd done this in the past.

The simple brush of fingers hadn't triggered anything in me, but it must have been a sign for Del. His lashes lowered as he rose up on his elbow, hovering over me, not touching, but there, so close.

I swallowed, pulling my hand back to my chest. My breath did catch then, but not out of excitement. Fear and anxiety rode me hard. A questioning look appeared in his eyes, as if he wasn't sure he should be doing this.

But I wanted him to be doing this. It could help me remember. I needed to remember. Then maybe I'd remember what happened to Cassie.

I nodded and forced my lips into a smile, but I felt my lips tremble.

Del lowered his mouth to my neck, nuzzling the skin there. My fingers curled into the comforter as I pressed my lips together, holding back the word I wanted to scream. *Stop.*

How many times had we done this? Freaking a lot, I imagined. Why wouldn't I be kissing and doing all kinds of naughty things with someone who looked like him? And what he was doing was nothing in comparison to how far we'd already gone. Why in the hell couldn't I remember *that*?

I closed my eyes, willing my heart to stop racing. This thumping in my chest wasn't pleasant. Was I having a heart attack? God, that sounded stupid. I wasn't having a heart attack. Though I kind of wished I were. Then we'd have to stop.

And right then, with the worst timing known to man, I thought of Carson. Why couldn't Del have such brilliant blue eyes? Or be as goddamned patient as Carson had been at the coffee shop, in the tree house, and in class? No matter whom he'd slept with in the past, I doubted Carson would be fumbling with the buttons on my shirt. He would've at least noticed that my arms were shaking and that my fingers were digging into the comforter until my knuckles turned white. Okay. That wasn't exactly fair to Del. This had been my idea.

My heart jumped again, so I focused on the television. ESPN was on, playing a recording of a baseball game from last season. Go figure. Bottom of the third inning. Atlanta Braves were up to bat. Two strikes and one ball. The batter would have to swing. A dizzy feeling swept over me with the realization that I had such knowledge of baseball.

Del's hand drew me back to my own body. It rested just below my navel. His fingers brushed under the band on my jeans. I drew in a shallow breath and opened my eyes. "Del?"

His wet kisses moved down my neck, over my collarbone. And his damn hand was traveling farther south. Unable to stop myself, I clamped my thighs together and said his name again.

He lifted his head and stared down at me with muddled brown eyes. "What is it, babe?"

"I...I don't remember any of this," I whispered.

"Too fast?" When I nodded, Del stared at me for a moment, then kissed me gently. Just a sweep of his lips over mine, the slightest pressure, really.

I still flinched, and he saw it. Looking hurt, he pulled back a little and removed his hand. Now I felt like crap. "I'm sorry. Really, I am. I..." I didn't know him. That was the problem. It was like making out with a complete stranger.

He rolled off me and leaned onto his elbow. His eyes went to the television screen. The batter had struck out. "I thought that's why we were doing this. To help you remember? It was your idea."

"I know." I sat up, quickly buttoning my blouse. Hunched over my knees, I stared at the screen. "I really am sorry."

There was a pause, and I heard him sigh. "It's okay. No big deal. We'll...try again later."

The idea of trying again later kind of made me want to hurl.

"Okay?" Del dropped his heavy hand on my shoulder.

Unexpectedly, my vision went gray. The weight of his hand dragged me down, through the mattress, and without any warning, I was no longer in my bedroom.

But falling, over and over again, spinning through darkness. Cold, wet air rushed up, grabbing ahold of me, pulling me down, down. Falling so fast, I couldn't catch my breath. My lungs were frozen, my thoughts on repeat.

I'm going to die. I'm going to die. I'm going to die, like her.

My body stopped, not from impact, but just stopped. The black sky turned a milky, dull color. Above me there were trees painted gray. Bent over, snapped in half, their naked branches reached toward me, splaying like fingers sharpened to a point. Water rushed below me.

Everything was dead, dead, dead.

Something fell past me in a blur of red. Screams—screams that raised the hair on my body, howls that chilled my soul. And then there was nothing but silence.

Suddenly Del was leaning over me, eyes wide. He had a hold of my shoulders, shaking them. My head flopped around. "Sammy! Sammy, snap out of it!"

Feet pounded outside the room, and then my bedroom door swung open. Scott drew to a halt, his cheeks red and his eyes narrowed. "What's going on? Why was she screaming?"

Del jerked away from me. "I don't know. She was fine one second, and then she just got this look on her face and started screaming."

Scott hovered over me. "Sam, say something."

I blinked slowly, focusing on his face. "I'm going to die."

"What?" He sat beside me, pulling me up so that I was half sitting, half leaning on him. "Why would you say that, Sam?"

I stared into eyes that were identical to mine—brown with a splash of green around the irises. Concern drew harsh lines around his. "I remember thinking that," I said.

His eyes widened slightly, and I felt the bed dip under Del's weight. "Do you remember anything else? Do you have your memories back?" Scott asked.

"I remember falling." I scooted back a little and looked down. Half my shirt was buttoned wrong. Nice. There was no doubt Scott had noticed that. "And there was water, but that's all."

Scott's shoulders slumped in disappointment . . . or relief? "That's important, though. You should really tell that detective. Do you still have his number?"

"Why?" Del asked. "There's no way of knowing if what she remembers is actually a memory or just a hallucination. There's no need for her to embarrass herself like that."

"Why do you think it's a hallucination?" I asked, suspicious and fearful at once.

A sheepish look crept across his face. "Your mom mentioned you were . . . seeing things."

I was so going to kill her.

"She's not seeing things," Scott snapped, pushing off the bed. "The way you say that is like she's crazy or something. And she's not."

My cheeks burned. Del had a point. I didn't know if the things I had been seeing were really memories. They didn't make sense, and not all of them could be true. There was no way I could've stopped myself from falling in midair like that, and trees sure as hell weren't gray.

Out of the corner of my eye, I saw Scott give Del a look. "I don't know what you guys were doing up here, but try slowing it down, bud. She's been through a lot, you know."

Del's jaw popped, as if he was grinding his teeth to keep from responding.

Scott left after that, slamming the bedroom door shut behind him. Awkward silence descended. "Do you think I'm crazy?" I asked, my voice tiny.

"No, of course not...but I do think you're confused, and that's to be expected." He paused, and I could feel his eyes on me. "Look, I better get going. I'll call you tomorrow, okay?"

I nodded.

Del leaned in, kissing my cheek, and then he stood, bumping into the bedside table, jarring the music box. It kicked on, playing a note of the haunting melody. He stared at it, shaking his head. "I hate that thing."

"Why?"

He just shook his head again. "I'll talk to you tomorrow."

After he left, I went to my desk and picked up the card the detective had left me. It had his personal cell on it, and he'd left instructions for me to call at any hour if I remembered anything. I picked up my phone, debating. What if it wasn't real? I'd just look stupid.

And crazy.

Sitting down on my bed, I stared at his number. Stupid and crazy were worth the risk if it helped them find Cassie. I dialed his number.

Detective Ramirez answered on the third ring. "Hello?"

I cleared my throat, clenching the business card. "Hi. This is . . . this is Samantha Franco."

There was a pause, and it sounded like he muted a television or something. "Yes? Is everything okay?"

"Yeah, everything's fine." It was now or never. Closing my eyes, I prayed I wasn't making a mistake. "I remembered something, but I'm not sure if it will help."

"Anything at this point will help," he said gruffly.

I told him what I remembered—the darkness, falling, and the water rushing. At first he didn't respond, and then he did. And I suddenly felt so heavy, so weighted down by his words.

"Up at the state park, there's a lake that feeds into a waterfall. I'm assuming you don't remember either of those things, but we're dragging the lake on Sunday."

Cops didn't drag lakes looking for survivors. They dragged them looking for bodies.

chapter nine

$\mathcal{I}$ felt nauseated most of Saturday morning, having not slept much after the phone call with the detective. The rescue endeavors had turned to recovery. It was unspoken, but I knew it in my bones.

They didn't expect to find Cassie alive.

A little before one, I snuck out. Not hard to do when Mom was still in bed and Dad was off on a golf course somewhere. Shoving my hands into the pockets of this really cute military-style jacket I'd found in my closet, I headed down the winding road. Chances were this trip would be pointless. Cassie's parents might not even be home, but I couldn't bring myself to call them, especially because they hadn't contacted me once since I'd been back.

This could be bad.

Crossing the small yard, I stepped onto the tiny porch of the brick house and knocked on the front door. A crash sounded from inside, followed by a deep, husky laugh—Carson's laugh.

The door opened, and he was looking over his shoulder. "I got it, Dad! I'll be back in a little while." Turning, he gave me a lopsided grin and stepped outside, shutting the door behind him. "Hey."

"Hey," I repeated, stepping back.

Carson eased around me and then motioned me to follow him when I didn't move. Red and blond highlights appeared in his shaggy hair under the sun. "Since you didn't arrive in a car, I'm hoping you don't mind my method of transportation."

I'd figured he'd borrow his dad's truck or something, but he stopped in front of the motorcycle, pulling the blue tarp off it. My stomach dropped. "I'm not sure if I've ever been on a motorcycle."

"Not with me. And I seriously doubt pretty boy would risk his face to ride one."

I glanced at him. Del was a pretty boy, and while Carson was hotness incarnate, his features were rougher around the edges. Pulling out a hair tie, I wrangled my hair into a low ponytail. Shorter strands slipped free, curving around my cheeks.

Carson handed me a sleek black helmet. "It's really easy. Just hold on tight."

My gaze dropped to his narrow waist, and my insides turned to goo. I turned the helmet over slowly. "How...how do you know where Cassie lives? I never asked."

He squinted. "She used to throw a lot of parties."

I shifted from one foot to another, thinking about what Candy had said. "Did you guys...date or something?"

His eyebrows knitted. "Why are you asking?"

"One of the girls mentioned it. Said you two hooked up."

Unexpectedly, he laughed. "I'm kind of curious as to why I'd even come up in conversation, but whatever."

I couldn't let it go. "So did you?"

He looked away, squaring his shoulders. "Yeah, we did."

A red-hot feeling unfurled low in my belly, sliding through my veins like a snake. "Did we ever hook up?"

His head snapped back to me, and his brows shot up his forehead in astonishment. He choked out a "No."

"Why not?"

A heartbeat later he gave me a close-lipped smile, and his eyes lowered. "Good question. I'd have to go with the fact that we didn't get along."

Made sense, and I really needed to stop asking questions, but curiosity had its claws in me. "Then why did you hook up with Cassie?"

Carson moved closer, and I had to tilt my head back to meet his eyes. "Honestly? I really can't tell you why. I was at a party she was throwing. We both were drinking. You two had just gotten into an argument about something—I don't know what about—and she came on to me. End of story."

There was a name for what I was feeling. *Jealousy.* Something I had no ownership to, but it was there, boiling my blood. "So she came on to you, and you were all about it? Just like that?"

His eyes narrowed into lively, thin crescents. "That's how it happens. If it makes you feel better, I don't remember much of it. And she wasn't with Trey then."

I forced a laugh. "It doesn't make me feel anything. I was just curious."

"Sure you are."

"What about Lauren?" I asked before I could stop myself. Some of the amusement faded from his expression. "Lauren and I didn't hook up. We went out on one date, much to all of her friends' shock—including yours. She didn't want a second one." He grabbed the helmet out from under my hands. "Are you done with the personal Q-and-A?"

"Yeah," I said, embarrassed. Along with amnesia, I must've lost any and all filters. Worried that he'd changed his mind, I went for the helmet, but he stepped back. "What are you doing?"

He flipped it. "Helping you out."

I stood still and waited. Carson moved forward again, and with one hand, he tucked back the shorter strands of my hair. Tingles shot across my skin as his knuckles brushed my cheek. My lips parted as he did the same to the other side. His hands were large but incredibly gentle. I wondered if he'd touched Cassie like that, but I pushed that thought away.

Carson slid the helmet on, buckling the straps under my chin. Each time his fingers touched my skin, I shivered.

"There," he said, his gaze lingering below my eyes. "You're ready."

Before he could slip the shield down, I grasped his hand and had the worst case of verbal diarrhea known to man. "I had you listed as my security question."

Carson blinked and let out a tight laugh. "What?"

"On my e-mail account, it asked who my childhood friend was," I explained, nervous and wishing my mouth had a stop button. "It was you."

"Interesting," he said, pulling his hand free. Without further explanation, he moved the shield down. "Let's go."

Not the reaction I'd been hoping for, but then again, I had no idea what I'd wanted him to say. Confused, I watched as he climbed onto the bike and patted the seat. Swallowing, I swung a leg over and sat. When the motor roared to life, I tentatively placed my hands on his waist. Under the sweater, his muscles were hard and toned.

My mouth went dry.

Shoulders shaking with silent laughter, Carson reached down, grasped my hands, and pulled them so that they were clasped across his navel. The motion brought my breasts flat against his back and left very little room in other places. The scent of him—citrus and soap—seeped in under the helmet.

I squeezed my eyes shut. Not because of the jerk of the bike moving into gear or the fear of flying off when his tires moved onto asphalt, but because every cell in my body was responding to how close we were. It was wrong, the way I snuggled against his back as the wind beat upon us, especially when I hadn't even felt a smidgen of this with Del.

Cassie lived about five miles past the old battlefield, down a road obscured by large maples. As we passed the numerous monuments and old, wooden fences surrounding them, interest stirred inside me, and I almost wanted to ask Carson to stop. When we rode up to Cassie's house, it was like seeing another version of my own—sprawling and beautiful.

Carson came to a stop, and I slowly took off the helmet. So

many questions went through my head. What would I say when I saw her parents? Would they be welcoming or turn me away? Most of all, was I making a mistake by coming here?

Carson placed his hand on my back intuitively. "Are you sure you want to do this?"

I nodded slowly as I climbed off the bike, my eyes taking in the white exterior and red shutters. Nothing stirred inside me.

"We can knock on the door whenever you're ready," Carson said.

As much as I appreciated that, I knew I needed to do this now. Smiling at him, I headed up the front steps and knocked on the door. Carson's warmth pressed against my back, and I wondered if he'd ever know how much that meant to me.

A few seconds later, the red door swung open. An older man appeared, wearing dress pants and a wrinkled shirt. Heavy creases spread out from faded blue eyes that darted from me to Carson.

I drew in a shallow breath. "I'm Sa—"

"I know who you are," he said. "I was wondering when you'd come by."

A chill snaked down my back.

"Mr. Winchester," Carson said, inching forward so he was in front of me. "Samantha doesn't—"

"Remember anything?" he interrupted, his eyes never leaving my face. "That's what the detective has told us." A deep, unforgiving line appeared between his brows. "If you're here to see Cassie's mother, she's in bed and not taking visitors."

I had no idea who this man was, but he seemed too old to be Cassie's father. "I'm not here to see her mother. I was hoping that . . . I could see Cassie's room."

"And why would you want to do that?" He glanced at Carson, his nose twitching.

"I was hoping that it would help me remember her—what happened." I think I knew what was up with the look. "We aren't here to steal any of her stuff."

"I can stay outside," Carson suggested, voice flat. "It's no problem."

The old man huffed but stepped aside. "Not that I expected that either of you would steal her stuff. I don't imagine you remember which room is hers?"

Relieved, I stepped inside. "No. Sorry."

Carson sighed. "I do."

If that surprised Mr. Winchester, he didn't show it. "You have ten minutes, and then I must ask you to leave. Please be quiet."

Not wasting time, Carson wrapped his hand around mine and led me around the old man. We went up three flights of stairs and down a hall.

"Who was he?" I asked in a hushed voice.

"Cassie's grandfather. Not a very friendly man." He flashed a quick grin. "So don't take that welcome personally."

I glanced down at his hand around mine. "Where's her dad?"

"As far as I know, he wasn't in her life and never had been." Letting go of my hand, he stopped in front of a door that had three large daisies with pink petals drawn on it. "This is Cassie's grandfather's house. Her mom is pretty young, a good ten years younger than your parents. Between that and there being no daddy . . ."

"I bet that caused a scandal."

"Knowing you rich people? Probably," he said, and his jaw tensed. "You ready?"

I nodded.

Carson opened the door, letting me step inside first. A rush of cool air brought a peachy scent that tugged at me. I inhaled deeply, waiting for more but finding only a distant sensation.

Her room wasn't much different than mine, but as I walked over to her desk, running my fingers over her notebooks, I felt like I was walking inside a tomb. Shivers ran up and down my spine.

Carson remained by the door, silent and watching. I stopped in front of a stack of photos. Going through them, I kept waiting for a memory to spark. There were pictures of us together on a beach, at school, and at a ski resort. We wore matching outfits— pale pink. Some of the pictures were with our other friends. One I recognized from New Year's Eve because of the dress she wore.

She was in Del's lap. Both had huge, sloppy smiles on their faces.

Making a face, I showed it to Carson. "I have no idea who took this picture. Me? Trey?"

Carson's brows rose. "I don't know."

Her arm was around Del's neck, her check pressed against his. Del's hand was on her hip. "Awful comfy, these two," I murmured.

"Jealous?" he asked.

"No, not really." I sighed, putting the photos back on her desk. Beside her bed was a table painted bloodred. Interesting choice in color, but it was the music box that caught my attention. Walking over to it, I picked it up and turned to Carson. "I have one of these in my bedroom. It plays the same song."

"A lot of girls have music boxes, right?"

"Yeah, but it's identical." I set it down, weirded out by that. "Was I friends with Cassie when I was little?"

"No." He dragged his hand through his hair. "I mean, everyone grew up in the same circle, but you really didn't get close to her until you were, like, eleven or so."

Did we get matching music boxes then? Seemed like we'd be a little old for that. I picked up a stuffed unicorn that carried the scent of honeysuckle and then checked out her closet.

With each passing minute, my frustration mounted. I'd probably been in this bedroom a million times, and nothing about it was familiar. My hands curled into fists as I moved to the center of the room, staring at the red comforter that belonged to the best friend I also couldn't remember.

I threw the unicorn on the bed. Tears pricked my eyes. The swamping hole inside my head remained the same. Empty. Vast. All my memories were gone, stolen. It was like being violated, but there was no one to pin the crime on. My mind spun in circles.

"I don't remember a damn thing." My voice came out a dry, hoarse whisper.

"It's okay." He placed his hand on the small of my back. "It might take a little time."

A tremble ran through my body, and I hated it. Weak.

Helpless. Lost. I spun around, pushing the loose strands of hair out of my face. "What if I never remember? Do I live the rest of my life like this? One foot in a past I can't remember?"

His eyes widened slightly as he tilted his head forward. "I know this is hard for you to swallow right now, but if you never remember, you get to do something that most people never get to do."

"Like what?" I folded my arms. "Have a bunch of second firsts?"

"Yeah, *that*." Carson placed his hands on my upper arms, his eyes searching mine intently. "You get to start over. Experience all those things again. While everyone else is wishing for a do-over, you get to have one."

I wasn't ready to look at this as a glass half full. "And what about Cassie? I don't think she'll get to have any do-overs."

He dropped his hands, eyes downcast. "That's the hardest part to swallow."

We left before Cassie's grandfather could throw us out. I didn't want to go home yet, so Carson suggested a late lunch. He parked the bike across from a cemetery that was about the same size as the town. Tourists were everywhere, taking pictures of the old orphanage and the back of the Jennie Wade House, the home of the only civilian killed during the Battle of Gettysburg. As I followed Carson into a pub next to the orphanage, I almost wanted to join the tourists.

I felt like them, except I just happened to be sightseeing my own life.

Carson picked a booth in the back and handed me a menu. There was a curious look on his face as he watched me.

"What?" I asked.

He gave a slight shake of his head. "If someone had said a month ago that I'd be eating lunch with you, I would've told them to get off the crack."

I laughed, turning my attention to the menu. "I'm not sure if that's a good or bad thing."

"Neither, I guess. What I mean is that you never would've gone out with me like this."

"But we were best friends."

"When we were little," he said, tapping his fingers on the edge of the table. "We haven't been civil toward each other for years."

My cheeks heated as I remembered the things I'd learned that I had said to him. "I was such a bitch."

"You had your moments," he said lightly.

I peeked up at him through my lashes. "You know what I don't get? Why you're so nice to me now when I was such a jerk to you."

The low-hanging ceiling lamp glinted in his bright eyes. "Like I said, you had your moments."

"Good ones?"

He shrugged, and I didn't think I was going to get anything else out of him. Maybe I hadn't had any good moments, but then he let out a low breath. "When you weren't with Cassie and Mars was aligned with Jupiter, you could be like you used to be."

A faint smile pulled at my lips. "Wow. All that for me to be nice?"

Carson's grin was fast. Several seconds went by. "When my mom... when she passed away two years ago, you came to the funeral. Scott was there. Of course he was, but I didn't expect to see you there. Your father came, too, but you weren't with him or your brother. Afterward, when I was at home, you surprised me again."

"I did?" I whispered, watching him.

He nodded slowly. "There were a lot of people at our house. Mom had a lot of friends. She loved you, by the way." One side of his lips tipped up again as his gaze settled on the menu. "You visited her, you know? When hospice came in and when I wasn't home, you visited her. I don't think you wanted me to know that you did, so I never brought it up, but I know my mom appreciated that and I... I did, too. Anyway, after the funeral, I needed to get away to think."

"You went to the tree house?" I asked, remembering what he'd said before.

"Yep," he replied quietly. "I wasn't in there for more than twenty minutes, and then you kind of came out of nowhere. Climbed up into that damn house. You didn't say anything, but you sat down beside me and..."

"And what?" I felt as if I was hearing about someone else's history, and I was fascinated.

He leaned back, running the palm of his hand over his jaw. "You just hugged me. You know, like, for a while. You never said anything and finally you left. We've never talked about it. Sometimes I wonder if it really happened."

My heart tripped up, and relief eased some of the tense muscles in my shoulders. It was nice to hear that I had some redeemable moments. "I'm sorry about your mother, Carson."

He nodded again. "Anyway, like I said, you had your moments."

Realizing that was all I was going to get from him, I crossed my legs and looked at the menu again. "When this place was Spiritfield's, it had the best crab cheese fries ever. Scott and I used to fight over them."

Carson sucked in a sharp breath. "Sam?"

My mouth dropped open as I looked up. How had I known that? "I don't know why I said that."

He continued to stare at me, and pieces of what I'd said floated together in my brain. I could almost see us—my brother and me, much younger, sitting at a booth just like this, pulling apart a gooey mess of fries and cheese.

Excitement swept through me. I almost came out of my seat. "I remember eating here with Scott."

"It hasn't been called Spiritfield's for years, Sam."

I nodded eagerly, a wide smile pulling at my lips. "I don't remember anything else, but that's something right?"

"It's something." He smiled, but it didn't reach those eyes of his.

Before I could question it, the waitress appeared to take our orders, and buzzing on having one clear, nondisturbing memory, I didn't want to push my luck. For the first time in days, I felt as if I'd actually accomplished something. I threw myself into having lunch with Carson, laughing at his jokes and the stories he told me about when we were young, getting swept up in the crazy rush of feelings whenever our eyes would meet or our fingers would accidentally brush. I couldn't stop smiling, and when it came time to get back on the bike, he didn't need to pull my arms around him.

I did that without even thinking twice.

When we arrived at Carson's house, I realized I was reluctant to climb off the bike and go back home. It was like living two lives—the one the old Sammy existed in and the one that was taking place right now. That feeling, as Carson slid off the bike and turned to me, was confusing as hell.

Wordlessly, he unbuckled my chin strap and gently pulled my helmet off. His eyes were hooded, hidden under thick lashes, and unreadable. I wanted to thank him for going along with me today, to tell him that I had fun in spite of why we'd made the trip to Cassie's house, but any and all words died on my lips. There was a strange, powerful tension that crept over us, heady and warm, as he placed the helmet on the bike. I opened my mouth to say something again, but the strain built, stealing my breath, shocking me.

Carson placed his hands on my hips and easily lifted me off the bike, placing my feet on the ground, but he didn't just let go. His hands remained tight on my hips. An unknown need sprang alive, one I didn't fully understand. My skin felt tingly, hot. His steady breath teased the hair at my temple. My pulse jumped. What I was feeling was wrong. I knew that, because this should be happening with Del and not Carson. But what I was feeling was so startlingly real. Like a splash of vibrant color in a world that was a dark, drab gray.

Very slowly, Carson lifted his fingers and stepped back. He chest rose sharply, and when he spoke, his voice was rough and deep. "I've got to go."

Still speechless, I nodded.

His gaze dropped to my lips, and he took another step back. "I'll see you later, Sam."

In a daze, I started back to my house. Something ticked at the far corners of my thoughts. There'd been a moment, when his breath was warm against my skin, that it had felt right even though it was wrong. And more than that, it had felt *familiar*.

It happened in second period on Monday. I'd been busy pretending to pay attention when I was really thinking about Carson and what happened between us on Saturday. Had I imagined it? Had he felt it? Was it really even important considering everything that was going on?

A chorus of cell phones went off, one beep after another. Mr. Campbell stopped midlecture and sighed. "Turn off the phones, people."

No one listened. I glanced at Veronica as I dug out my own chirping phone. She was faster than me, pulling that cell out of her bag like a gunslinger.

Veronica's complexion turned a ghastly white under her tan. She lifted her head and turned to me, her eyes wide and wet.

A low murmur picked up, rolling like a wave through the

class. The text was from Lauren and just six words. Six words that should've changed everything, but there'd been a part of me that had been expecting it.

Maybe I already knew.

They found Cassie's body. She's dead.

chapter ten

The rest of the morning was a blur. Cassie was dead. That was all I could think about. She was dead. And there was a part of me that had been expecting it, waiting for it, even. Tendrils of fear curled around the lump of sorrow that had formed in my chest. It was tight, impossible to unravel.

Carson was subdued in bio, asking once if I was okay and then not saying too much the rest of the class. Del was waiting for me by my locker. He pulled my stiff, unyielding body into his arms and murmured something sympathetic in a choked voice.

I thought of the photo of them together—Cassie in his lap, his hand on her hip.

Cassie—the best friend I couldn't remember, the dead girl.

People were staring at us. I hated it.

I let Del lead me out of the school. No one stopped us. Every face we passed mirrored a mixture of shock and dismay. Everyone knew her, whether they wanted to or not. In a numb, detached way, I wondered if they grieved for her, or just for the fact that death didn't care about petty things like age.

"Don't you know? Fear and popularity go hand in hand," a soft, feminine voice whispered in my ear. "Let's rule with an iron fist."

I jerked around, gasping. My eyes darted around the pavilion. No one was there.

"Come on," Del said, eyeing me with concern. "We're getting out of here."

Following him around the school, I kept glancing over my shoulder. Had I really heard that voice, or had it been a memory wiggling free?

Maybe I was seriously going crazy. That was always a possibility—a likelihood.

There were several concrete benches on the patio behind the school between the football field and a smaller rec building. Everyone I knew was out there, sitting on the cold, hard surfaces.

Veronica, Candy, and Lauren took up one of the benches. Scott and Julie occupied another while Carson had one all to himself. I sat with Del, wholly aware of his hand around mine and the way Carson stiffened, focusing on the field behind us. I had to fight not to pull away from my boyfriend. He didn't deserve the cold shoulder, not from me.

"I can't believe she's dead." Veronica was the first to speak, sniffling daintily. "I mean, the longer she was missing, I knew it was going to end this way, but I hoped she'd be like Sammy."

That she'd just show up somewhere.

Lauren wiped under her eyes with two fingers as she clutched an oversize white purse to her chest. "It's just so horrible thinking about her being there. . . ."

"In the water," Candy whispered, shuddering as she continuously ran her fingers through her hair. "I don't think I can ever swim in that lake again."

Julie's brows arched as she glanced at a tight-lipped Scott. I wondered why they were even here. I knew they weren't close to Cassie or anyone else here. So what else didn't I know? Everything, it seemed.

"Did anyone say what kind of condition . . . she was in?" asked Veronica. "I wonder if the casket will be open."

Scott sat back, shaking his head. "She was in the lake. Who knows for how long? An open casket is probably going to be the last thing anyone is thinking of."

Veronica's eyes narrowed. "I'm just saying that Cassie wouldn't want anyone to see her unless she was . . ."

"The most beautiful girl in the room," I murmured.

Del's hand tightened around mine. "What did you say?"

I shivered. Again, I had no idea where those words had come from. Everyone was staring at me, waiting for an explanation. Shaking my head, I pulled my hand free.

"You said 'most beautiful girl in the room.'" Veronica stood, smoothing her hand down her dark jeans. "That's exactly what Cassie would've said. What *you* would've said. Have you . . . remembered something?"

Clasping my hands together, I fought the urge to start biting my nails. "No."

"Then why did you say that?" she demanded, eyes flashing.

"I don't know—sometimes these words just kind of come out." I glanced at Del, but he was staring at his hands.

"What? Like Tourette's?" Del laughed under his breath.

My cheeks heated with embarrassment and something far stronger. "It's not like Tourette's, asshole."

"What?" He looked up, his smile fading. "I know it's not. Come on, calm down." He reached for me, but I scooted across the bench. "Sam, it was just a question."

"A stupid question," Carson said, his jaw clenched tight.

Del's eyes narrowed into thin slits. "Why are you even here?"

"Good question," he muttered, but he leaned back, stretching out his legs and crossing his arms over his broad chest. Carson wasn't leaving anytime soon.

"Wait. Why isn't Trey here?" I asked.

Candy pulled out a nail file. "He didn't come to school today. I think he was sick or something."

"Do you think he knows?" Julie asked, wrapping her arms around my brother and pressing her cheek against his shoulder.

"Of course he does." Candy rolled her eyes, filing away at one of her nails. "Everyone knows."

Julie shot the girl a look like she wanted to punch her in the face. I wanted to punch someone, but mostly out of frustration. "You know what I find strange?" Julie said, closing her eyes.

"I guess we're going to find out," muttered Candy, swiping the file back and forth.

"Knock it off, Skittles," Carson said.

Candy flipped him off with a perfectly manicured middle finger.

"What do you find strange?" I asked, ignoring the two.

"Besides the fact that Cassie would've been anywhere near the lake this time of the year? She was a great swimmer." Julie opened her eyes, glancing at me. "The girl was part fish."

Veronica settled back down, on the edge of the bench closest to Del. "Well, I doubt she went there to go swimming."

"That's not what Julie means," I said, remembering the vision I had of falling. "If Cassie was in the lake, she should've been able to swim, right?"

Del cleared his throat. "There are some hellish rip currents and superdeep parts, but she knew that lake and which areas to avoid."

"Then maybe she was already . . . out of it before she hit the water." Or dead, but I couldn't quite say that.

"Well, you had to have been with her," Veronica said, snatching the file away from Candy and shoving it in her bag. "That's so annoying, not to mention unsanitary."

"How is that unsanitary? I'm just filing my nails."

"It's gross. Little bits of your nails are flying all over the place." Veronica shuddered as if that was more disturbing than a body in a lake. "I think there are pieces on me."

Smiling at the absurdity of it, I glanced up and caught Carson's eyes. They glimmered in the light. When I looked away, I realized Del was watching us. A pang of guilt flashed through me. "Did anyone see her that day?"

"Besides you?" said Veronica, and there was no mistaking her tone.

I sat back. "What are you trying to say, Veronica?"

"I'm not saying anything, *Sammy*." She pulled out an oversize pair of sunglasses and put them on. "She was obviously with you. You were walking down the road that leads to the lake."

"She knows that," Scott said, leaning forward. Contempt dripped from his voice. "But she has *amnesia*, if you haven't figured that out yet. I can probably give you a definition if you're still confused."

"You know, I'm with Del on this. What are you guys doing here?" Veronica raised her eyes.

"We're here because *someone* needs to be here for my sister," he shot back.

That surprised me . . . in a good way. From all accounts, Scott and I had been missing that twin-bond thing people talked about.

"I'm here for your sister, Scott." Del sounded offended. "I'll always be here for your sister."

Scott's lips thinned. "That is almost comical coming from you."

"Babe," Julie said, pulling on his arm.

"What the hell is that supposed to mean?" Del demanded.

"Del, if I were you, I'd just sit back and shut up." Carson stretched lazily, but he was coiled, ready. "That's my advice."

What in the world were they talking about?

"I saw her," Lauren's quiet voice intruded before Del could respond, and those softly spoken words silenced everyone.

My heart leaped in my throat. "You did?"

A pink flush stained Lauren's cheeks. "I did. It was around

seven at night. She stopped over and dropped off a purse she'd borrowed—my D&G. She was ... really irritated about something."

"You don't know what she was upset about?" I asked.

Lauren shook her head, eyes on the ground. "She wouldn't say. I think it had something to do with a guy. You all know how she got when she was having guy troubles."

"Okay." Del stood, shoving his hands through his hair. "Does it matter why she was upset? It doesn't change anything."

I stared up at him. "You're right—it doesn't change the fact that she's dead, but it might help us figure out what happened to her."

Del rubbed his jaw. "But her being upset over a guy or whatever doesn't have anything to do with what happened to you."

"How do you know?" Scott asked, and he had a point.

"It's not just what happened to me," I said. "It's what happened to Cassie, too. Any information—"

"So, what? You're going to play Nancy Drew?" Veronica asked, her eyes darting between Del and me.

If I didn't know better, I'd say that Veronica would agree with just about anything Del said. Striving for patience, I ignored her. "Do you remember anything else? Like what she was wearing?"

"She had that red dress on. The sweater one," Lauren answered.

Candy's chin jerked up. "The knockoff Prada?"

I would've rolled my eyes at the disdain in Candy's tone if not for the fact that every time I'd seen Cassie—or brought up a memory of her, if that was what the flashes were—she'd had on a red dress. That had to mean I wasn't taking a sharp left into crazy town—good news.

"Are you okay, Sam?" Carson asked.

Nodding, I let the conversation move on without me. Del eventually sat beside me again and snaked an arm around me. Leaning my head against his shoulder, I closed my eyes. My mind was spinning. The day we both had disappeared, Cassie had been mad. That alone didn't tell me anything, but the fact that she had actually been wearing the same dress I kept seeing her in was unnerving. And beyond that, grieving for someone I couldn't remember but who'd been an intricate part of my life was difficult. There were moments when I could almost taste the loss, when it could've consumed me and pulled me under. Then the sorrow would ease off and be replaced by confusion and the need to be away from all these people—to be alone.

Carson had pressed the tips of his fingers together, shielding his mouth when I opened my eyes again, drawing my attention right to his lips. Our eyes met for a flicker of a moment, and then he looked away. Del's arm tightened around me, and another, different kind of guilt surfaced. Feeling torn in different directions, I sat up, putting a little distance between us.

"Okay," Julie said, stretching her legs and standing. "I'm going to say what no one else seems willing to say."

"That you actually tolerate Scott?" Carson said blandly.

"Ha." Scott smirked.

"No," Julie sighed. "Do you think Cassie was . . . murdered?"

Our mismatched group fell silent. My heart rate picked up.

Murdered. It made sense. If Cassie was such a great swimmer, she wouldn't have drowned, and then there was me. Was it possible that I had witnessed what had happened to Cassie? And if so, did her murderer then try to deliver me to the same fate?

No. It could've been an accident. But then, what happened to me? Had we both had an accident? She died. And I survived.

I glanced up. Carson was watching me again. Stark concern deepened the hue of his eyes. I wondered if he had realized the same thing—if they all had. When I glanced over at the girls—my friends—there was something in their eyes that had nothing to do with concern for my well-being. For a minute, I didn't want to believe it, but there was no mistaking the shadow in their gazes.

Suspicion.

Mom was secluded in her bedroom when Scott dropped me off after school. Having the house to myself until he returned from baseball practice and Dad came home left me ample time to mull everything over.

Cassie was dead—most likely murdered. And I'd been there. The visions—fragmented memories—had to be clues to what happened. I just needed to piece them together.

Curling up on the window seat in the sunroom, I stared at the small garden and the main road beyond the small stone fence. My history textbook lay unopened by my feet. I chewed on my fingernail. Carson had seen me do it during bio, saying it was a habit that I'd always had. So it was an old part of me that had somehow stuck.

My thoughts went straight back to Cassie.

She'd been upset the day we disappeared, probably because of a boy. Trey—the on-and-off-again boyfriend who'd conveniently been sick the day her body was found? Had I gone to see her, pulling girl duty? But what had happened after that? What explained the visions of blood on the rocks, Cassie yelling at me, and then the feeling of falling?

And why had we met up at the state forest, of all places?

Those memories couldn't be hallucinations. I wasn't crazy, but the more I turned things over in my mind, the stranger I felt. Then there were the two notes. . . .

Sunlight reflected off the roof of a white car coming up the driveway, catching my attention. I straightened, dropping my hand as it came fully into view. It wasn't Dad's Bentley, and it was too soon for Scott to be back.

The car stopped in front of the house, by the gaudy fountain. A man stepped out, buttoning his blazer. Dark sunglasses hid his eyes, but I recognized the slicked-back dark hair and broad forehead.

Detective Ramirez was here.

"Shit," I muttered, jumping from the window seat. Hurrying through the maze of archways and rooms that never appeared to be in use, I rushed to get through the house before he woke up Mom. I opened the door, slightly out of breath. "Detective?"

He took off his sunglasses, sliding them into the breast pocket of his jacket. "Miss Franco, do you have a couple of minutes?"

Stepping aside, I glanced behind me. "Yeah, but my mom's asleep and Dad's at work."

"That's fine. I just have a few questions, off the record." He stepped in, eyes taking in the foyer and not missing a single detail. "A good place to sit?"

I doubted anything I said to a detective was off the record, but I didn't have anything to hide and I wanted to help him. Bringing him to the small sitting room, I sat on the couch while he took the recliner. "Is this about Cassie?" I asked, folding my hands.

Ramirez nodded. "I assume you've heard?"

"Yes. It was all over school today."

"And how are you holding up?"

How was I holding up? I almost wanted to laugh, but I figured that would be inappropriate. "Good, I guess."

His lips curved up on one side. "I wanted to go over a few things with you. See if it sparks anything. You okay with that?"

"Yes." I picked up the delicately embroidered pillow, placing it in my lap. "I want to be able to help."

"Good." There was that one-sided smile again. "Cassie was found a few yards down from the waterfalls in the lake, tangled up in . . ." He stopped as I felt the blood drain from my face. "Well, the details don't matter. Right now, we're not sure what the cause of death was, but from preliminary investigation, it doesn't appear to be a drowning."

"Cassie was a good swimmer." I squeezed the pillow. "That's what her—my friends said today."

He nodded slowly. "Her mother said that Cassie was an excellent swimmer who was also very well versed in the terrain of the state park and the trails up there."

"But we were up there at night," I said, frowning. "Del said I was with him until that evening."

"Yes, I talked to him while you were missing." He leaned forward, dropping his hands between his knees. "Do you have any idea why you two would go up there at night? As familiar as Cassie and you were with the terrain, it would've been dangerous. One slip..."

I swallowed hard. "I really don't know why, and I've been trying to figure it out all day. Lauren... Lauren Cummings said she was upset. Maybe we went up there for some girl time." *Girl time* sounded stupid even to me, but I was out of ideas.

"I've also spoken to Lauren, but from what I could gather, it wasn't like either of you spend time at the lake during the night—at least not this time of year." He paused, meeting my eyes. "Now, you said you had this... feeling of falling when we talked and that you had heard the water. Do you think it's possible that you were near the waterfalls?"

"I guess so, but I don't even know where the waterfall is... now. Or how to get to the lake."

His head tilted to the side as his gaze dropped for a moment. "Do you remember anything else? Even if it seems like a minor detail, it could be helpful. And you want to help, right?"

"Yes." Realizing I was holding the pillow like a shield, I shoved it aside. "I've told you about the rocks. I've seen those before, but they're covered in something that looks like blood, but I'm... I'm not really sure. I know that's not much."

"No. That's something." Ramirez smiled tightly. "Anything else?"

I lowered my eyes, chewing on my lip. Telling him about seeing Cassie would most likely make me sound like a lunatic.

"Samantha, *anything* would help."

Heavy footsteps thundered through the house, alerting me to my father's arrival. Detective Ramirez stood, twisting toward the open archway.

Dad came in like a furious storm, cheeks flushed with anger and narrowed eyes glinted at the detective. "What are you doing here?"

"It's okay, Dad. He just had a couple of questions."

"No. It is not okay." He placed his hands on his hips, pushing his suit jacket back. "Do I need to explain the law to you, Ramirez?"

"I'm well versed in the law, Mr. Franco," the detective replied blandly.

"Is that so?" His voice took on a hard, unyielding edge that I knew I had to have heard before. Probably when I'd driven that car into a tree. "You cannot talk to my daughter without one of her parents present or her lawyer. Ever."

"Sir, this isn't a formal investigation, and your daughter agreed to answer—"

"My daughter is just a teenager—she's only seventeen." Dad stepped forward, towering over the detective. "Did you tell her it was off the record? I'm sure you did. She doesn't know how these things work, but I do."

My brows rose. Knots formed in my stomach. Had I done something wrong by talking to the detective? As I chewed on my thumbnail, my gaze bounced between the two men. "Dad, I was—"

"Do not say another word, Samantha," he said, and his tone was like an icy breeze on my skin. "If you want to question my daughter, you do so with my permission and with fair warning. If not, the next time you even come within twenty yards of my house, you better have a warrant."

My mouth dropped opened. *A warrant?* Why would he need a warrant? I wasn't a suspect. Suspects got warrants. Panic clawed at my insides as I stood on shaky legs. Was I a suspect?

Detective Ramirez cleared his throat, and when he spoke, he was calm and unaffected by my father's orders. "I understand, Mr. Franco. Hopefully it doesn't come to that. I know my way out."

Dad folded his arms, and without another word, Detective Ramirez left. I sat back down, dizzy. "Dad, he was just asking questions. It wasn't a big deal."

He crossed the room, dropping down so that he was at eye level with me. "You don't understand how the police work, princess. You're a child, and with everything that has happened to you, it would be easy for them to confuse and manipulate you."

Indignant anger filled me. "I'm not stupid. Just because I can't remember anything doesn't make me a helpless child. He was just asking me questions about Cassie. I want to be able to help the police."

"I know." He sighed and then reached out, pulling my hand away from my mouth. "You're still a nail biter. Your mother hates that."

"Sorry," I mumbled, squeezing my knees with my hands.

He stood and walked to the mantel above the fireplace. His spine was unnaturally stiff. "I know you're not stupid, Samantha. You're a clever girl, but I don't want you talking to the police again, okay? Not without me around. Do you understand?"

"Why? What's the big deal? I don't have anything to hide."

He turned halfway around, smoothing a hand over his hair. "The big deal is that you were most likely the last person who saw Cassie—you were probably with her when . . . when whatever happened to her occurred."

"I know! And that's why I need to talk to the police."

"No. That's why you *can't* talk to the police!" He dropped his hand to his chest, and I was suddenly worried he was going to have a heart attack. My dad looked fit and trim, but I imagined he was under a lot of stress with work . . . and me. "The last thing you need to be doing is talking to the police. Right now, if it turns out that she was murdered, you're their number one suspect."

chapter eleven

uspect? Murderer? I'd been right about the looks I'd thought I'd seen in Veronica's and Candy's eyes. Suspicion. My heart was pounding as I paced my bedroom later that night on an empty stomach. The thought of food made me want to hurl, so I skipped dinner. *Suspect. Murderer.*

Those words were foreign to me. Not in the sense that I didn't understand what they meant, but because I couldn't associate their meanings with me. The words shot across all my nerves, like tiny shards of glass, fraying them, slicing them open.

Did my dad really think that was why Detective Ramirez was questioning me? Because the detective thought I'd killed Cassie? And did my friends think the same thing? They couldn't. It didn't make sense. I'd been hurt, too, obviously. Bad enough that everything that was me, all that I knew, was gone.

And I could never kill a person. Didn't they know that?

There was still a chance that what had happened had been

some kind of freakish accident. I knew enough to know there'd be an autopsy done to determine cause of death.

Stopping in front of the mirror in my closet, I swallowed the lump of fear that rose in my throat before it could consume me. My reflection stared back at me, cheeks pale against the cinnamon tone of my hair. With my face devoid of makeup, I looked a lot younger than I did in the photos. There was a skittish glint to my eyes, one I doubted the old Sammy sported.

"I would never hurt Cassie," I said, needing to hear someone, even if it was me, say it.

My reflection tilted her head, lips curving up in a mockery of a smile. "Liar."

Gasping, I stumbled back, tripping over the stupid teddy bear on the floor. I hit the side of the bed hip-first. Fresh pain exploded as my pulse pounded wildly.

There was no one in the mirror now.

Body shaking, I tucked my legs under me and stood. The movement jarred the bed and the table beside it. Already off-kilter from when Del had messed with it, the music box fell to the floor, uttering two weak, broken musical notes that sent chills dancing down my spine.

I picked up the box, turning it onto its side. An opening on the bottom had popped out when it fell, wide enough to fit half a deck of cards. The slot looked empty, and in a daze, I closed it and placed it back on the table.

A sick, twisting feeling built in the pit of my stomach as I turned around, pushing the long strands of hair out of my face.

Sharp tingles traveled down my back, and I was suddenly too hot and the room was too small.

My reflection had spoken back to me.

That was officially crazy sauce.

I started pacing again, avoiding my reflection just in case it decided to have another impromptu conversation. What just happened could not have been a memory, and there was no way I could explain it as anything other than a good ol'-fashioned delusion.

I'd imagined calling myself a liar after I said I couldn't hurt someone. Nice, really nice. Tucking my hair back, I dragged in a deep breath, but it got constricted in my chest. Needing to get out of the room and possibly even the house, I threw open the door and rushed out into the hallway.

Rounding the corner, I smacked right into a rock-hard body with enough force that the poor guy let out a grunt and hit the floor. Thrown off balance, I toppled down on him. In a second, I recognized the clean, citrusy scent.

Carson.

Our bodies were pressed together in all the wrong places. Or the right places, depending on how I wanted to look at it. Not that I thought it was right. It was definitely wrong, especially the way his chest felt incredibly muscled under mine, his stomach like steel. Heat zinged through my veins.

Carson's hand curved around my waist as his head lifted slightly. We were so close I could see the darker flecks of blue near his pupils. So close that his warmth breathed new life into the dark, empty spaces inside me. My gaze fell to his lips, and I wanted to know so, so badly how they felt. To taste his kiss. To let go of all the strings tethering me to the old Sammy and lose myself in him. Funny how all my worries about being insane suddenly went out the window.

Those lips spread into a crooked half smile. "Hey there, Sam...."

"Hey," I whispered. "Were you coming to see me?"

His smile spread into a full one, and my heart skipped a beat. One of his front teeth was chipped at the bottom. "I was actually here to see Scott, but..."

"Oh." I felt like the biggest dork ever. "Then you better get going."

"Yeah, I should." His gaze dropped to my mouth, and my stomach tightened. "But you're going to have to get off me first. No rush. Just saying."

My cheeks caught fire. "Good point."

"It is," he murmured.

I still hadn't moved. The apocalypse could be going down outside and I would remain right where I was. My body pressed against Carson, his hand tightening on my waist.

So caught up in whatever this was, neither of us heard my brother until he spoke. "Do I want to know what you guys are doing?"

Carson chuckled deeply, and I felt the sound in every cell. "We're just wrestling."

"Really," Scott replied drily.

I rolled off Carson and pushed to my feet. "I ran into

him—in the hallway and knocked him down." I felt the need to explain. "We weren't wrestling . . . or doing anything."

Scott's lips twitched as if he was fighting a grin. "It's all right, Sam. I'd rather see you rolling around with Carson out in the open than Del."

My jaw dropped. "That's not—"

"Hey!" Carson said, dropping his arm around my shoulder. "We have your brother's permission."

"Man, you must really hate Del," I said, ignoring the way the whole left side of my body was pressed against Carson's.

Scott rubbed the heel of his palm over his temple. "Yeah, well, I don't like him."

"Why?"

"Just don't," he replied, and then turned around, heading back into his bedroom.

I wiggled out from under Carson's arm. "Well, I'll see—"

"Hey." He caught my arm, stopping me. "Where were you heading in such a hurry?"

"I was just going to . . . take a walk."

"It's almost nine."

I shrugged, and my stomach took that moment to grumble. "Or get something to eat. Maybe some ice cream. I saw a carton of double chocolate earlier. I can't remember the last time I ate ice cream." I was rambling, but I couldn't stop. "Granted, I can't remember much of anything, so that doesn't say much. Yesterday I discovered I love hamburgers without tomatoes. No pickles, but extra bacon."

Carson's grin grew the longer I talked. "How about cheese?"

"I'm ambivalent toward cheese." I grinned. A few days ago, I had one of those moments where I couldn't stop talking with Del, and he'd been less than amused by it.

Carson let go of my arm. "So, back to the ice cream . . . you sure you saw some?"

"Yep."

"Mind company?"

My heart got all kinds of happy at that suggestion. "I thought you were here to see Scott."

"He can wait." Carson nudged me with his shoulder. "Can't he?"

I peeked at him, deciding that sharing some ice cream wasn't a cardinal sin and I could use the distraction. "Sure."

Carson followed me downstairs and through the rooms. It took me a couple of moments to find the bowls and silverware. Then I dug out the ice cream. He piled his bowl high with mound after mound of chocolate goodness. I added three large scoops to mine, and then we sat at the bar, facing each other.

"Where are the parents?" he asked, smashing the ice cream with the back of his spoon.

"I don't know where Dad is, but Mom's in bed." I leaned forward, lowering my voice. "I think that's all she does. Was she always like that?"

He glanced up as he took a bite. "I didn't see her often. She kind of has a problem with me being in the house, so I usually try to limit my visits."

I frowned. "Why?"

He smashed some more of his ice cream. "Your mom isn't

big on me hanging out in the house because of my dad." Pausing, he shrugged. "She probably thinks I'm going to steal some of her art."

I clenched the spoon so tightly I wouldn't have been surprised if it bent. "That's so messed up. Your dad is no different than mine. They just do different jobs. I don't get what the big deal is."

He had that look again—the one that made me feel as if I were a puzzle he couldn't even begin to figure out. "You know what I always thought was funny?"

"What?"

"From what Scott has said, your dad was very much like mine, before he met your mother. Didn't have a lot of money, came from the working class and whatnot, so I could never figure out how he ended up with your mom."

And that was a puzzle I couldn't figure out. "Me neither, because Mom comes from—"

"Old money, and they tend to stick together. Maybe he just swept her off her feet."

I started to grin at that, picturing my dad winning my mom over through all kinds of romantic gestures, but then I thought about how they were now. There was more romance between me and my hairbrush than between those two.

Carson took a huge bite of his ice cream. "This is good stuff."

Watching him dig in, I waited until most of my ice cream melted, and then I twirled my spoon around the bowl, turning it into something like pudding. When Carson laughed, I grinned at him. "I think I like it like this."

"Yeah, you did that as a kid. Drove your mom insane."

Chocolate slipped off my spoon, plopping into the bowl as I studied him. "Were we really best friends?"

He nodded. "Yeah, we were . . . inseparable for a long time."

As I'd done a thousand times since learning Carson was the answer to my security question, I tried to picture us doing things together—running, playing, getting into trouble. Sadly, like everything else, the memories just weren't there no matter how hard I tried. If I was being honest with myself, I think it was the *possibility* of those memories that I missed the most.

"You have that look on your face," he said, brushing his hair off his forehead with his free hand. "You're not happy about something. Bad company, eh?"

"No. Not at all," I assured him. "It just sucks not being able to remember anything. I think . . . I would've really liked those memories."

His eyes met mine for a moment. "I still have them, though. If you want, I can share the highlights with you."

A grin pulled at my lips. "I'd like that."

And so Carson did. He went through the greatest hits of our childhood while we finished our ice cream. Riding bikes, climbing trees, swimming, and making forts with branches—we'd done it all. It turned out I'd gotten Carson's arm broken, too. This time by jumping from one of the rocks on Devil's Den, taking him along with me. He'd missed an entire season of Little League.

Scott was right—Carson and I had been closer.

The whole time he talked about us, the skin around his eyes crinkled, and I was drawn into his steady gaze, infatuated with eyes that shone like lapis lazuli. Through it all, pressure built in my chest. Some of it was good, because it felt as if I were about to fly off my seat, but there was a tightness to it, tinged with sadness and shame.

"I really am sorry for being such a tool to you," I said again. The fact that I had been kind to his mom and then him after she had died didn't make up for everything else. "You didn't deserve the way... I ended up."

Carson opened his mouth but closed it. Several moments passed, and then he leaned forward, crossing his arms on the bar. "I'm going to be honest, okay? When you apologized before, I was like, whatever. Because it's hard to believe that you really mean it based on my... past experience with you."

I cringed and suddenly wished I hadn't eaten so much. Ice cream curdled in my stomach. "I understand—"

"No. You don't." He met my stare. "Because I get that you really do feel bad. A couple of weeks ago? I'm not so sure. But you do now. And that matters. Okay? The past is in the past. It's done. Let it die."

Seeing the sincerity in his eyes, hearing it in his voice, some of the pressure lessened. "Thank you," I whispered.

Carson nodded, and there was another stretch of silence between us.

"The detective stopped by after school," I told him, staring at the mess in my bowl. "Dad got pissed, practically kicked him out."

"Why?"

I shrugged. "He didn't like that Ramirez was asking me

questions without him being there . . . or a lawyer." I glanced up, drawing in a deep breath. "Dad thinks I'm their number one suspect."

His brows knitted. "What? Are you serious?"

"Yeah, since I was the last person to see her."

"But no one knows if you were," he argued, much to my relief. "Anyone could've been with you guys. And what happened to you two might not have been related. It could be a freak coincidence. An accident."

"That's what I'm hoping," I murmured, and then louder, "Anyway, who do you think would've been with us? I mean, if it wasn't an accident."

"You're wondering who could've been with you two who would have wanted to . . . hurt her? Or you?" He sat back, running a hand through his messy hair. "God, Sam, that's a messed-up thing to even consider."

"Tell me about it." I started nibbling on my thumb but found that the nail had already been chewed down. "It could've been me for all I know."

His brows shot up. "What? You? No. There's no way."

I made a face. "The old Sam sounded pretty capable of just about anything, and apparently Cassie and I had this weird friendship. Maybe we got into a fight and . . ."

"And what? You killed her?" He rolled his eyes, laughing. "There's no way. Yeah, you had a mean streak, but you wouldn't have hurt anyone. And that doesn't explain how you got hurt."

It didn't, and for once, the impossibility of something was

reassuring. I tucked my hair back. "Okay. If you had to pick someone, who would it be?"

He stared at me, dumbfounded. "Pick someone who is capable of killing? Jeez, I hope I don't know anyone who is."

"I know, but if you had to pick someone who would hurt Cassie, who would it be?"

Blinking, he looked away. "There's a huge list of people who were angry with her, but to kill her? I don't think so."

"Carson..."

He cursed under his breath as he faced me. "Okay. There's Trey. They had a shitty relationship. And then there are at least a hundred kids at school who probably fantasized about pushing her in front of a bus a time or two."

I wrinkled my nose. "Nice."

"Look, you don't remember her, Sam. Cassie was a ... I'll put in this way: she had very *few* good moments. She was terrible to kids who didn't come from money, didn't drive luxury cars or spend their summers on a yacht, which is freaking hilarious if you think about it, because she would have nothing if it weren't for her mom's father. Not only that, she was manipulative." He leaned forward, resting his elbows on the bar. "Every month, she would pick a new target—a kid she'd pretend to want to be friends with, because they had something she needed. She'd be nice to them, and the rest of you would go along with it, and then once she had what she wanted, she'd publicly shame them one way or another. Once, she had the entire school believing Sandy Richards was a lesbian."

Sandy was in my history class. Quiet girl. I liked her. "Who cares if she was a lesbian?"

"No one would, but Cassie made it sound like Sandy was obsessed with her and came on to her. Total bullshit, and I'm sure half the school knew that, but no one would go against Cassie." Sitting back, he folded his arms. "Because no one would go against you, and everyone knew if they messed with Cassie, they were messing with you."

The pressure was back, clamping down on my lungs. "Why do you think Cassie was like that?"

"Hell if I know, but she was . . . she was messed up." He turned his head and his jaw was working again. "Partied a little too hard sometimes . . . and she'd just start crying and flipping out for no reason. Trey used to say it was daddy issues, but who knows."

Daddy issues? I mulled that over, remembering that it appeared she had a father on the absentee list. Then I asked something I probably shouldn't have. "Why did I act the way I did?"

He blinked again and his eyes widened. "Jesus, Sam, I wish I knew, but I don't. Your parents were good to you. And so was Scott, and even though you changed when you started hanging out with Cassie, not everything can be blamed on her. You made those decisions."

"I know." I lowered my gaze. "Cassie and I were terrible together, huh?"

He blew out a long breath, and when I looked up, he was staring out the French doors. "It was weird, like two people coming together and bringing out the absolute worst in each other. If you guys had something on someone, you'd use it to your advantage. Ever the opportunists . . . and there were a lot of people with a lot of reasons not to like you. But hurt you? That's different."

Shame was back, burning through me like acid. I took one last spoonful of melted ice cream, wishing I'd kept my mouth shut. Carson glanced at me and then laughed softly.

"What?" I dropped the spoon in the bowl.

"You have ice cream on your chin."

"I do?" I wiped at my chin. "Did I get it?"

Shaking his head, he reached over the bar and smoothed his thumb under my bottom lip. My chest rose quickly and my breath caught. His thumb stayed just under the corner of my mouth, but his fingers spread underneath my chin. They were calloused against my softer skin, sending a shiver of pleasure through me. Our eyes locked, and I waited for him to remove his hand, because surely the tiny smidgen of ice cream was gone by now, but he didn't.

Instead, his thumb inched up, trailing across my bottom lip. I sucked in a breath, but like the one before, it got lost somewhere. A heady wave of warmth rolled through me.

I swallowed. "More ice cream?"

A lopsided grin stretched across his lips. "Sure."

Part of my brain just clicked off. Placing my hands on the edge of the bar, I leaned forward and stopped thinking about *everything* other than the electric feeling he created with the simplest touch. I wasn't quite sure what I was doing, but my body took the lead. My pulse thrummed, and my heart soared when his hand slid to my cheek.

This was wrong, but it also felt so incredibly right.

A throat cleared, and I jerked back, nearly falling off the stool. Much to my horror, Mom stood under a hanging fern, a full glass of red liquid in her hand. "It's late, Carson," she said, eyes and tone cold. "I think it's time that you head home."

Carson slid me a quick smile as he stood. "Sorry, Mrs. Franco, I didn't notice the time."

She nodded curtly.

He glanced at me over his shoulder. "See you at school, Sam."

My cheeks felt as if they were on fire as I stood. I wanted to walk him out, but he had already disappeared around the corner. Seconds later, a door opened and closed. I'd totally sucked up his time—he hadn't even visited Scott.

"What are you doing, Samantha?"

I took deep breath. "I was eating ice cream."

"Don't play coy with me."

"I'm not playing coy with you, Mom. I was eating ice cream with Carson. What's the big deal?" I turned my back to her and picked up our bowls, carrying them to the sink. "It's not like—"

"I'm not sure I even know you anymore," she said, voice tight as she set her glass on the bar. "Two weeks ago, we wouldn't be having this conversation."

"Yeah, and two weeks ago, I was a total bitch." Who apparently had an entire school full of enemies. "So if being a nicer person is a giant letdown to you, you're just going to have to deal."

"This isn't about you being nice." She followed me to the sink, knocking the bowls out of my hand. One hit the stainless steel and rolled to the side, the other split into two large chunks of ceramic. Stunned, I stared up at her. "You're going to ruin your life, getting involved with boys like that."

I backed up. "Mom, we were just talking."

"That's not what it looked like to me." Her cheeks were flushed the same color as her silk blouse. "Boys like him—"

"There isn't anything wrong with Carson!" I brushed past her, not wanting to argue. Not like I didn't have enough problems without getting into a verbal smackdown with her. "I'm tired—"

"Don't make the same mistake I did," she said in a low, barely audible voice, nostrils flared.

My eyes widened with shock. "What? What is that supposed to mean?"

"It doesn't matter." Her heels slapped off the hardwood floors. "I won't have you embarrassing yourself any further. It's bad enough—"

"It's bad enough *what*, Mom?" I whipped around. Screw the not-fighting part. Everything boiled up inside me, spilling over until all I felt—all I knew—was anger. "Am I still an embarrassment to you? Are all your friends *talking*? Except now they're talking about what happened to me—to Cassie? How terrible it must be for you."

Her eyes narrowed. "Are you sure you don't have your memories back? Because this sounds terribly familiar, Samantha."

"Does it? That's great." I tried to stomp past her, but damn she was quick, blocking me.

Regret turned the flecks of green in her eyes darker. "I'm sorry, sweetie. None of this is your fault. No matter what happened or what you might have done, none of this is your fault."

Shock rippled through me as my mom turned away. I heard her stop by the liquor cabinet, and I knew she was taking the bottle with her. In a daze, I left the kitchen and saw my dad standing there.

He looked away, eyes closed and brows furrowed. "Samantha—"

"She thinks I did it?" My voice was small, hoarse. "She thinks I did something to Cassie?"

"No." His eyes shot open wide. "No, she doesn't think anything like that. She's just tired, and all the stress has . . . has affected her. Your mom isn't . . ." He shook his head. "She doesn't think that."

Nice of him to try to convince me, but I didn't believe him. "Do you think I did?"

"No, baby, I don't think you had anything to do with what happened," he said, trying for a smile but failing. "It's late. Go upstairs. Things will be better tomorrow."

For a moment, all I could do was stare at him in icy disbelief. Tears built in the back of my throat, and when I could move, I flew past him. I wasn't sure what I was running from, but it didn't matter where I went. What Mom had said haunted me as I stripped off my clothes and changed with shaky hands.

I sat down on the bed, pulling my legs up to my chest. Resting my head against my knees, I dragged in deep breaths that did nothing to quell the rising panic. Carson might have believed I wasn't capable of such a thing, but what was I supposed to think when my own mother thought I was?

chapter twelve

 *M*rs. Messer had this thing with her glasses. She put them on when she started talking, took them off before she finished a sentence, and then nibbled on the temple piece. Within the first five minutes of our session on Wednesday, she'd already completed the cycle five times.

I slid down in the seat, smothering my yawn with my hand. She'd spent the better part of our time together checking over reports from my teachers.

She placed the papers in a folder and set it aside. "As expected, none of the teachers have any concerns. If anything, you're actually paying more attention in class now than before."

"Well, I guess that's one good thing."

Her smile was tight-lipped. "How's everything been at home?"

I schooled my features blank. "Everything's okay."

On went the glasses. "Your mother contacted me yesterday. She's concerned about how you're adjusting to everything."

Jerking up in my seat, I snapped my mouth closed. Mom hadn't spoken to me since the blowup on Monday night. And I was okay with that. "She called you?"

"Yes. She's worried that you're having a hard time connecting things from before the . . . incident with your life now." Off went the glasses. "Do you want to talk about it?"

My teeth ached from how hard I was clenching my jaw. "It's more like she's having a problem with the way I am now."

Mrs. Messer nibbled on the end piece. "Something to do with a boy . . . ?"

Heat swept over my cheeks. "I was eating ice cream with a boy and she freaked out." I couldn't believe my mom had called her! Mom hadn't made good on calling an actual therapist, but telling the school counselor was bad enough. Gripping the arms on the chair, I took a deep breath. "I'm not the same person I was before the *incident*. And you know what? I think it's a good thing. I was a complete and utter bitch before."

Putting the glasses back on once again, her lips twitched as if she really wanted to smile. Not the fake, tight smiles she always gave me. "Well, if it makes you feel better, I did explain to her that she would see personality changes."

"I bet she took that well," I grumbled. "She thinks I'm . . ."

"She thinks what, Samantha?"

I started chewing on my thumbnail as my foot anxiously tapped the floor. The urge to spill my secrets came at me fast and hard, and I wanted to cave. "I don't know. She's embarrassed by me. I think she's always been."

"I'm sure that's not true," the counselor said, watching me. "Have you been able to recover any more memories?"

Focusing on the picture of the cherub-faced little boy in the photo on her desk, I gave a lopsided shrug. "Just bits and pieces, and they don't make much sense. There hasn't been a rush of memories, even though I've been doing like you've told me. I thought... I thought the news about Cassie would trigger *something*, but it hasn't."

"And how are you handling the news about Cassie? Do you still feel apathetic toward her?"

I hated it when she said things like that, even though I understood what she meant. My inability to recall the feelings surrounding my relationship with Cassie did make it hard to share in the grief everyone felt over her sudden death. "I'm trying to remember her."

"That's not what I meant," she said.

Returning to my thumbnail, I refused to answer. "Can I ask you a question?"

Mrs. Messer nodded.

"Do people who start to get their memories back see... weird things?"

Her eyes blinked slowly behind her glasses. "What kind of weird things?"

I shrugged again. "I don't know. Like just seeing weird stuff or hearing voices?"

She took off the glasses, folding them this time. "Some memories can come back in the form of voices or images that may seem strange. If you could give me an example..."

I waited for her to put the glasses back on or to chew on them, but when she did neither, I knew I'd thrown her off her game. Not good. Just from her lack of fiddling with her glasses, I guessed hearing and seeing weird things wasn't normal.

When I didn't elaborate, she moved on, but I knew she'd come back to it again, probably on Friday. "Cassie's funeral is on Monday. That may be a hard... event for you—"

"Or maybe it will help me remember something."

"Maybe," she agreed, scribbling something down on her pad.

My session was over, and I had to hurry to my locker so I wouldn't be late. The first thing I saw when I opened the metal door was a note, written on yellow paper, folded in a triangle. Looking around before I opened it, I made sure no one was lingering nearby.

These notes baffled me—hell, they frightened me. If it had been me... if I'd done something to Cassie and somehow hurt myself in the process, what explained these notes? What was worse? Being responsible for Cassie's death or the possibility that the culprit was still out there? The same person who was stalking me with a never-ending supply of legal notepaper?

I didn't have an answer. Sighing, I unfolded the note.

You know why she was at the lake.

Part of me wanted to laugh as I folded up the note, adding it to the other one in my bag, but a familiar unease coated my throat. Obviously I didn't know why she was at the lake. Whoever was leaving these things needed to get a little clearer about my situation, which brought up bigger questions.

Who was leaving these notes, and how much did they know? Closing my locker, I turned as Del rounded the corner and sauntered toward me. A little stab of guilt shot through me as I remembered how badly I'd wanted to kiss Carson.

Del wrapped his arm around my shoulders and kissed my cheek before pulling back, tugging lightly on my ponytail. "You look tired. Doing okay?"

I smoothed my hand over my hair self-consciously. "I really didn't put much into getting ready today...."

"It's okay." He wrapped his hand around mine as we started down the hall. "Everyone understands you've been through a lot, and with the news about Cassie, no one expects much."

My brow arched, but I didn't say anything. Stopping outside of my math class, he kissed me good-bye—this time on the lips. Not a bad kiss at all. It was warm and dry, soft. Even patient, but my toes still curled for all the wrong reasons.

Del pulled back, searching my eyes intently. "You sure you're just tired?"

Mysterious notes, the possibility that I might have had a hand in what happened to Cassie, and crazy thoughts aside, I had serious boy troubles. As if my life couldn't get more complicated, I was lusting after the wrong guy according to everyone else—my brother's *best friend*—while my boyfriend patiently waited for me to snap out of it.

I needed to figure out how I felt about Del if there was any hope for us because stringing him along wasn't fair. If I was no longer the girl who'd fallen in love with him, it wasn't right to keep up this . . . this charade.

Mulling over my options during my morning classes, I still had no idea what to do. I didn't know what it was that kept me *lingering*. Fear of letting go of one of the last things that linked me to my old life? My relationship with my old friends was practically nonexistent at this point, leaving Del as the last vestige of the old Sam. Unable to decide how I felt about that, I eventually pushed those thoughts away and focused on Cassie. The most recent note told me nothing, but it did point me in the right direction.

I needed to get to that lake.

Maybe seeing it would trigger a key memory—help me remember an important detail. Selfish as this was, the need to know what happened wasn't just for Cassie anymore. I needed to prove to myself that I wasn't the one responsible for what had happened. To her and to me.

A plan formed slowly in my mind, and before heading to my friends' table at lunch, I was already in the process of implementing it. I stopped at my brother's table. "Can I borrow your car after practice?"

His brows inched up his forehead. "I'm not sure about that."

I sat down, prepared to beg and plead. "I promise I won't let anything happen to your car. I just need to do something after school."

"What?" he asked, eyes narrowing.

"Something," I said. "*Please*, Scott."

Julie grinned at her brother. "I can't remember the last time I heard her say please, so you kind of have to let her."

"You're not helping." Scott sat back, eyes still trained on me. "Why don't you let Julie take you wherever you want to go?"

"I can't," she said quickly, then flushed. "Not that I don't want to, because I kind of do want to hang out, Sam."

"Okay." I still felt a little stung, even though I hadn't planned on bringing anyone with me, but she seemed as if she genuinely wanted to be friends again.

Looking relieved, she smiled. "I have to work at the theater after school. It's my shift today."

"Oh, crap, I forgot." Scott sighed. "Fine. I'll be home before five. You can borrow it then, and I swear, if anything happens to my baby, it's your ass."

Ecstatic, I jumped up and leaned across the table, hugging him. "You're the best."

My brother's jaw dropped. He shook his head, speechless, as I said good-bye to an equally shell-shocked Julie and headed to the back of the cafeteria. Only when I plopped my plate down beside Lauren did I realize Carson hadn't been at the table. During bio, he'd acted as if nothing had happened between us, and that was probably for the best. At least until I figured out what I was going to do with Del.

I felt better than I had in days. It was as if I finally had a purpose, something to investigate, instead of sitting around in a daze. I dug into what I thought was sliced ham.

"So, I saw you talking to Julie." Veronica picked at the label of her bottle of water. "Did you guys kiss and make up?"

"She was actually talking to her brother," Lauren said, her eyes nervously bouncing between us.

"I don't understand why your brother is with her," Candy said. "He's definitely dating down."

I bit down on the anger building inside me. "What's wrong with Julie? She's really nice, and my brother likes her."

"What's wrong with her?" Candy glanced across the table at Veronica. "Her father works at a cigar shop in town. And not like he owns and works there, but, like, works there for minimum-wage slave labor."

"He does?" I feigned shock. "Holy crap, I can't believe they let her attend school here."

"I know!" Candy nodded.

Lauren smothered her laugh with her hand.

"She was being sarcastic," Veronica explained, her cheeks flushed. "God, you're such an idiot."

"I'm not stupid." Candy folded her slender arms and then giggled. "Okay. I may not be the smartest cookie in the shed."

I stared at her. "It's the *sharpest tool* in the shed."

She shrugged. "Whatever."

"So is everyone excited about prom?" Lauren asked, striving to lessen the tension building at the table. "It's, like, less than a month from now. Daddy is getting me this champagne-colored—"

"Shut up," Veronica snapped. "No one cares about your damn dress."

"Hey! Don't talk to her like that." I clenched the fork. Good thing it was plastic, because I wanted to shove it into what I suspected were surgically enhanced lips. "Jesus."

Veronica's skin flushed an unpleasant shade of red under the tan. "Okay. You're being a bitch, Sammy."

"I am?" I put the fork down, dumbfounded. All the irritation bubbled up and spilled over. A rolling anger took hold. "I'm not making fun of someone because their parents aren't rich or because they don't wear size Gap Kids. That's what *you* are doing."

"Okay. I'm just going to have to be up-front with you." She twisted toward me, clasping her hands in her lap. With her collared blouse over her gray sweater, she looked like she was ready to give a sermon. "I understand that you've had some problems—"

"You mean not having any memories?" I shot back.

"Whatever. But that's no excuse for how you've been behaving. If you keep dressing like you're a homeless chick and—"

"What's wrong with how I'm dressed?" I was wearing jeans and a shirt, for crying out loud. Most of my clothes at home were way too nice to wear to school, and seriously? Why would I want to wear a damn dress or skirt every day?

She gave me a *duh* look. "And if you keep talking to people like *them*"—*them* had to be anyone with a median household income under six figures, I assumed—"you're going to turn into a bottom-feeder. And we're going to have serious problems."

Our little spat was drawing the attention of the kids closest to us, and I could've just shut up then or got up and walked away, but I couldn't. I was so tired of . . . of *everything*—the looks, the snide comments, and how Veronica and Candy acted as if my memory wasn't the only thing I was lacking. And maybe it was more than that—the frustration of not knowing anything, of being confused all the time.

Either way, I was so done with these bitches.

"You know what? We already have problems," I said.

Veronica's eyes narrowed. "Is that so?"

"If getting my memories back means becoming a huge bitch like you? Yeah, I think I'll pass on that."

Some of the kids around us stopped eating. Others choked on whatever was in their mouths. My entire body burned with anger, and I wanted to say more than that, but I grabbed my tray and stood.

"Don't ever think about sitting here again," Veronica said, her chest rising rapidly.

"Fine with me," I tossed back.

Drawing in a deep breath, she swirled in her seat. "You're going to regret this."

"Already do, honey." I didn't wait for her response. Edging around the table, I made my way to the front of the cafeteria. Eyes were on me, and I didn't care. A weight lifted off my chest. I felt free—free of having to fit in with people I couldn't relate to anymore. Adrenaline put an extra kick in my step as I dumped my tray. Part of me wanted to run back there and kidnap Lauren. She was the only decent one among them.

On the way out, I glanced over to my brother's table. They were too far away to have heard us, but the whispers flying around the cafeteria had already reached them. Julie caught my eye and grinned before she rested her chin on my brother's shoulder.

With some time to spare before lunch ended, I headed for my locker. Rounding the corner, I came to a complete standstill.

Carson was leaning against a locker across from the library, his back to me. A pretty brunette smiled up at him as he handed her a backpack that must've belonged to her. All I could hear beyond the irrational buzzing in my ears was the deep, husky laugh that curled my toes *in the right way* as he slipped the bag over her shoulder.

A pang hit me right in the chest, splintering my heart. I had no right to that pain—no right to the fire building inside me, but I wanted to bum-rush the two and force them to have at least five feet between them.

And there was no way in holy hell I would do such a thing. Maybe the old Sammy would've, but then again, the old Sammy didn't like Carson on most days.

I took a step back, and it was suddenly like watching two actors on a black-and-white television, except the girl in front of him . . . it was *me.* I was on the tip of my toes, in his face. At first I thought I was kissing him because I was *that* close, but then I heard myself speak—this lifeless gray version of me.

"I saw you," I sneered. "I saw you with Dianna. I know what you did."

Carson threw up his hands, laughing grimly. "As always, you're sticking your stuck-up nose where it doesn't belong. You have no clue what you saw, Sam."

Laughing, I tossed my hair over the shoulder. "Oh, we'll end you, Carson. You just—"

Whatever else I'd said was lost to me. I'd stumbled into a locker, and the rattling sound sucked me out of the vision. All I knew was that the girl who was *really* in front of him was

Dianna, but the reason behind the confrontation with Carson was unknown. Who was the "we"? And what had I seen him do with Dianna that could've been used as a threat?

Carson looked over his shoulder, brows knitting when he saw me. "Sam?"

Backing up, I shook my head in confusion. Switching from a memory—or possibly a hallucination—to what was really happening had my mind spinning to catch up. That, and my reaction to seeing him with a girl. "I'm sorry. I . . . I didn't mean to interrupt."

"Wait," Carson said, stopping me. "Is everything okay?"

I nodded. "Yeah—sure, I'm okay."

His eyes narrowed, and then he turned to Dianna. "Can you hold on a sec?"

"Sure," she said, pulling out her cell and suddenly becoming very interested in it.

He crossed the distance between us, reaching out as if he would touch me but stopping before he made contact. "Sam, what happened?" he asked in a low voice. "You're bleeding."

"What?" I looked down. The sleeve of my sweater was pushed up to my elbow, revealing two jagged scratches that beaded tiny drops of blood. A dull ache radiated from my arm. "I must've . . . scratched myself."

He took my hand, swallowing. "How could you not know if you did that, Sam? That's . . ."

Messed up? I pulled my hand free. "I have to go."

"Sam—"

"She's waiting for you," I whispered, backing off. "I'll talk to you later."

His jaw clenched as he gave me a sidelong glance. "Okay. There *will be* a later."

I wasn't sure what that meant, but I nodded. Forcing a smile that felt wobbly, I turned around and headed to the nearest bathroom. Heaviness pressed down on my chest, spreading to my shoulders. The back of my throat burned as I dropped my bag near the sink and turned on the water.

How had I done that to myself without even noticing or feeling it until now? And when had I done it? Swallowing hard, I felt my stomach roll as I shoved my arm under the faucet. The raw skin stung, adding to the already overwhelming pressure of unshed tears. Water ran red until it turned a faint pink against the porcelain basin.

Lifting my chin, I stared into my own frightened eyes. My heart threw itself against my rib cage. What would Mrs. Messer say about scratching yourself so deep that the skin tore? Probably the same thing she'd say about talking reflections. A strangled laugh escaped my lips. I doubt either of those fell in the normal range of coping mechanisms.

I took a breath, but it got stuck. There was most definitely something wrong with me. Crazy wrong.

When Scott returned home after baseball practice, I took my purse and my hastily scribbled directions down to the garage. I had a couple of hours before the sun set, so I managed to avoid most of Scott's questions. I felt bad for being short with him, especially because he was letting me borrow his car, but I didn't have much time.

It took me a little over forty minutes to reach Michaux State Forest and to find the summerhouse. Common sense told me that if I was going to start anywhere, it would be there.

Easing the car down the gravel road, I leaned over the steering wheel as a two-story log cabin came into view. Two garage doors were under the raised porch, and the entire front of the house was nothing but windows. A patch of land had been cleared around the front, and trees choked the back of the house. Parking the car, I clenched the keys in my hand and climbed out.

Shivering, I inhaled the scent of pine and rich soil. Something else lingered behind the scent—wet, familiar.

Most of the houses I passed on the way up had screened-in porches, but this house had a tiered deck. My sneakers crunched over gravel and tiny broken branches as I headed toward the steps. I tried to picture summers here, walking this very same path dozens of time.

The stairs groaned under each step, echoing and causing me to wince. A large, empty ceramic flowerpot sat in the corner. I went up the second set of stairs, to the main deck that appeared to wrap around the whole house.

As expected, the front door was locked. I crept along the railing of the porch. There was a can full of cigarette butts that looked newish. Mom and Dad claimed that the home hadn't been opened since last September, but I doubted the butts would've retained their color that long.

Had someone been here? Did I smoke?

Shaking my head, I moved toward the back of the house, and there was the sound of something rushing, peaceful. It sparked the unrest inside me, stirring the abyss where my memories existed. The sound...

Water.

Excitement bubbled. I knew that sound—*the lake.* Hurrying down the back steps, I half slid down the sloping hill that met the heavy wooded area. The ground was covered with small rocks and fallen branches, and despite the fact that I had no conscious memory of the layout here, I navigated the area with ease. Maybe I had been back this way before? There was no other way to explain it. Anyone without some knowledge of the woods behind the house would probably break his or her neck wandering around at night. Pushing bare, low-hanging branches out of the way, I headed toward the source of the sound.

Up ahead, there was a boat docked. *Angel.* Recognizing the boat from one of the photos on my wall, I stepped on the dock, caught off guard when it bobbed under my feet. My gaze drifted beyond the boat, and I sucked in a sharp breath.

The lake was a deep, glossy blue and larger than I'd expected. The surface dipped and rolled gently in the breeze, holding a lifetime worth of secrets in its depths. It went on as far as I could see, curving around a bend. I lifted my gaze and couldn't find anywhere nearby that would explain my memory of falling. There were just trees with tiny buds and boats docked all around the lake.

Shoving my hands into the pockets of my hoodie, I trekked

across the man-made beach, following the shoreline. Detective Ramirez had mentioned a waterfall, which seemed to be the likeliest place for someone to take a fall.

I rubbed my sleeve over the scratches on my arm, trying not to think about how they'd gotten there. The sand was eventually replaced by mud that formed a weathered trail. Trees began to crowd the edges of the lake, and the farther I went, the louder the sound of rushing water became. I inched around a large oak and came to a standstill.

Water spilled over a rocky cliff, slamming into the lake twenty feet below. Frothy white water bubbled over sharp, jagged rocks jutting out of the lake. As I lifted my gaze, vertigo swept over me. I reached out blindly, placing my hand on the tree for support.

Around a hundred feet above the waterfalls was a cliff. It wasn't a smooth descent from there. Large rocks protruded from the side of the mountain, rising up between thick bushes and smaller trees. A stream of water snaked its way down the hill.

I had a hard time believing someone would've made that fall. There were too many bone-breaking obstacles in the way. But if someone was pushed . . . he or she would've cleared the hill. My eyes moved down the horrific drop. The person would've ended up in the lake below.

An unnerving sense of rightness settled deep in my bones. Pushed—Cassie had to have been pushed. And me? Did I take the same fall? I shuddered as I recalled the memory of falling . . . and falling. That had to be it.

Seeing the cliff didn't spark any memories in me, but I knew—*I just knew* this was where it all had gone down. There had to be another way to get up there. The climb was too steep, and I doubted I would've made it. I needed someone who knew his or her way around here, who could get me up there. Maybe Scott? Carson? My belly warmed at the latter. He might know his way around, but running to him didn't make sense, especially after seeing him with Dianna—

Snap!

I froze. What was that sound? Straining, I held my breath and listened. Birds chirped and the branches above swayed, but those weren't what I'd heard.

Snap! Another twig snapped, followed a few more seconds by the distinct sound of someone walking. The tiny hairs on the back of my neck rose, and my heart leaped into my throat.

It came again, closer.

Spinning, I scanned the trees. It could be anyone—someone out walking or jogging. I strained to listen but heard nothing. Not even natural sounds. The whole forest had fallen deathly quiet.

A blur of black darted behind a tree up ahead. Catching it out of the corners of my eyes, I noticed that it was tall and definitely not bear-shaped.

"Hello?" I called out, my fingers clenching the car keys.

There was no response, and I couldn't see whatever or whoever it was. Willing my heart to slow down, I started back toward the summerhouse. I'd made it about five feet before I heard a crunching sound behind me. I whirled around, eyeing the gloom that was falling between the trees.

The shape shot between two trees. The shape was male—dressed in black. A cap was pulled down, hiding his face. Hope sparked, but it was quick extinguished by dread. It couldn't be Carson. He wouldn't hide behind trees, and he would've answered when I called out.

A normal person would've answered when I called out.

Icy fingers of anxiety trailed down my spine. My chest compressed as I took a step back. "Hello?"

Nothing.

Throat dry, I turned around and picked up my pace. It could be anyone—it could be whoever was responsible for what had happened to Cassie and me. Not wanting to take any chances, I glanced over my shoulder. I saw nothing at first, and then . . . he was several feet behind me, off the trail, moving in quick, ground-eating strides.

I stopped.

He halted.

I took a step forward . . . and his step matched mine.

This . . . this wasn't good. Warning bells went off. Instinct kicked in, and I took off. Over the sounds of my feet slapping on the ground and my thundering heart, I heard him crashing through bushes. Coming after me, chasing me . . .

I darted through the trees, kicking up dirt and small stones. Fear caught my breath as I pushed at the branches ripping at my hair. The edge of my sneaker caught on an exposed root, and I spilled forward, my knees and palms taking the brunt of the fall. Rocks ripped open my hands, tearing the denim and then the skin on my knees. I yelped in response to the sharp pain.

My vision dimmed. The color of the fallen leaves and muddy

brown faded into gray. *Not now. Please, God, not now.* It was too late—I was sucked into the vision.

I was crawling on the ground, one hand in front of the other. No. Not the ground—a rocky, slippery hill. Pebbles and clumps of dirt broke free, pelting my face. I was numb, moving only on instinct. Nothing hurt. I clawed my way up, and my fingers slipped. Grasping wildly at rocks, roots, anything I could get my hands on, I slid down several feet, losing whatever ground I'd gained. My hands were gray, but red streaked the backs of them, caking my fingers. Nails cracked open.

Gasping in air, I blinked and color returned to the world. I looked over my shoulder. Two legs encased in black jeans stood a few feet behind me. Terror punched me in the gut. Scrambling over the ground, I ignored the pain and ran.

It felt as if an eternity had passed before the boats came into view and my feet hit the sand. I didn't dare look back as I rushed toward the woods separating the lake from our house. My breath pawed at my chest as I shot free of the tangled branches and darted around the porch.

I cried out when I saw Scott's car. Kicking up gravel, I slid around the hood and finally looked behind me.

No one was there.

Turning around, I scanned the thick trees. He could be hidden anywhere, waiting to jump out and do . . . do what? Finish what he'd started? But why? Who was he? I reached for the handle and the door opened. Had I locked the car when I left? I couldn't remember.

Climbing in, I quickly pressed the button on the side to lock all the doors. I slumped in the seat, dragging in deep breaths that shook my entire body. I was nauseated and dizzy—adrenaline had me feeling as if I'd had one too many energy drinks.

I opened my eyes and put shaky hands on the steering wheel as I glanced at the passenger seat. A piece of yellow paper folded into a triangle was resting on it. My heart took another painful jump.

That hadn't been in the car before.

Hands trembling, I reached over and picked up the piece of paper, quickly unfolding it. There was just one sentence, written in the same childish handwriting that was becoming as familiar as my own.

You know who killed Cassie.

I threw the note in my purse and started the car. Peeling out of the gravel driveway, I maneuvered the car down the narrow road, the back of my neck tingling.

Keeping my breaths long and even, I pulled out onto the main highway. I couldn't afford to think of what had just happened. Time to freak out would come later, when I wasn't behind the wheel of my brother's car. I reached for the volume on the radio, wanting to drown out my thoughts, when I glanced up.

All I saw was the dark shape of *him* in the backseat, a brief glimpse in the rearview mirror. The world tilted, pitching me to and fro behind the steering wheel.

Oh my god.

He is in my car.

Terror rolled through me like thunder through the sky, dark and threatening, stealing my breath. Everything happened so fast. I thought about stopping, jumping out of the car and running, or slamming on the brakes. But I didn't know what I did. Panic seeped from my pores, coating my skin. My brain was firing useless signals. There was a blast of a horn that sounded like it was miles away, and I couldn't breathe.

He's in my car.

A scream rose from the depths of my body as the darkness moved toward me, and then *this* sound—metal crunching, ripping apart—cut off my scream. Knocked to the side in one heartbeat, I was jerked back in the next, slamming my head off the steering wheel. Fierce, blinding, paralyzing pain stabbed at my skull. Glass shattered, picking at my skin.

And then there was nothing.

chapter thirteen

An annoyingly persistent beeping sound thrust me into a world where my skin felt too tight, too dry. And every—*every*—part of my body ached as if I'd gone one-on-one with a truck. My eyes opened into thin slits, and the lights were too harsh. I moaned, immediately closing them. I wished I could disappear back into the darkness.

"Sam?" The bed dipped beside me. "Sam, are you awake?"

The sound of my brother's voice dragged me back, forcing my eyes to open. His face loomed over mine, blocking some of the light. Dark shadows blossomed under his eyes. His hair was a mess, sticking up every which way.

He smiled weakly. "Do you remember me?"

"Yeah," I croaked, wincing. I tried lifting my arm, but something tugged on my hand painfully. Tubes. There were tubes everywhere, connecting to that damn beeping machine. I wet my lips. "What . . . what happened?"

"You were in a car accident." He dragged his hand through

his hair. "Dad's out in the hall, talking to the doctors. The police think you lost control on the highway."

I struggled to sit up, too weak to really lift my head. "What about the other driver? Are they okay?"

"Don't try to sit up. I got it." Scott grabbed an extra pillow off the chair and then gently slid his fingers under my head, lifting slowly as he got the pillow under me. "The other driver was clipped. They're fine."

My head protested the movement, as did most of my body. "Your car . . . oh my god, I'm sorry."

Scott settled back down, rolling his eyes as he fixed the thin hospital blanket. "I don't care about the stupid car. It's already taken care of. I'll get a rental in the morning." His eyes lifted, meeting mine. "How are you feeling?"

"Like I was in a car accident," I said, lifting my free hand once I figured out that one wasn't hooked up to anything. I touched my head gingerly. There was a bandage on my forehead. "How . . . bad is it?"

"Nothing too serious. Not like you need your brain anyway, right?"

I laughed and then groaned. "Ow."

"You got a lot of bruises and probably will hurt for a while, but you'll survive."

"That's good." I closed my eyes, wanting to move but knowing it wouldn't be a good idea. Something waited on the fringes of my thoughts. Something I couldn't quite grasp. A quick peek through the window told me that night had fully fallen. "How long have I been here?"

He glanced over my shoulder, sighing. "It's close to five in morning. You've slept this entire time."

Oh god.

"I think I heard the doc saying he was going to keep you through today for observation after everything . . . else." He smiled again, but there was an edge to it. Wariness. "So you get out of school the rest of the week. Way to go."

I wanted to laugh and joke, but his smile nagged at me. "You've been here this whole time?"

Scott nodded. "Del the Dick stopped by before they ended visiting hours. So did Julie." He paused, a real grin tugging at his lips. "And after I texted Carson, he was here in under ten minutes. Was not happy when they wouldn't let him stay."

"Carson," I murmured.

"Yeah, he . . . was really worried, sis. He and I are going to have to talk about that." A troubled look eroded the teasing grin. "Sam, the EMTs and police said you were talking when they arrived on the scene. Something about—"

Dad entered the room, looking every inch the poster child for country club member of the month. Not a single piece of his hair was out of place. He came right to the other side of the bed, smiling down at me.

"How are you feeling, princess?" he asked, brushing the hair off my bandaged forehead.

"Okay." I glanced at my suddenly quiet brother. "Where's Mom?"

Dad's smile faltered. "She was here earlier, but she's at home . . . resting."

I blinked back the tears that sprang to my eyes. Mom hadn't stayed. I was in the hospital, hooked up to machines, and my mom was at home *resting*. I hurt all over, and my mom wasn't even here. And I wanted her—suddenly needed her—to tell me I was okay.

Maybe she couldn't look at me anymore, believing that I'd had something to do with Cassie's death—it all came rushing back then.

Going to the cabin, finding the lake and the cliff above the waterfalls, then the man chasing me, the note . . . the car—my heart started pounding, and the machine matched the beats.

I struggled again to sit up, but Scott and Dad kept me still. "You don't understand," I gasped, head throbbing. "There was someone in the car. He was in the backseat. Did they get him?"

Dad pushed down on my shoulders lightly, clearing his throat. "Samantha, there was no one in the car."

My forehead ached. "No. You don't understand. He was following me in the woods, and he put this note in my car—"

"What were you doing up at the summerhouse?" My dad's eyes met mine.

I glanced at Scott, swallowing. Who cared why I was there? Didn't they understand? "I thought if I went up there . . . I'd remember what happened." My throat felt like paper. Each sound was like a dry whisper. "Dad, he was chasing me. And then he was in the car. That's why I wrecked."

"Who is he?" Scott asked.

"Scott," my father warned.

My brother's face darkened. "Sam, who was following you?"

"I don't know who he was." I pressed the palm of my hand to my brow. "I didn't get a good look at his face, but he's been leaving me notes." Recognition flickered in his eyes. "I put the note in my bag—where is my bag?"

Then Scott looked at our dad, who shook his head. "What?" I demanded.

"Sweetie, you should get some rest." Dad grabbed my hand, pulling it away from my face. "You're getting yourself worked up."

I pulled my arm away. Something tightened in my chest. "Is my bag still in the car?"

"No," Scott answered, looking away. "Your bag was in your bedroom. You didn't take it with you."

"What?" My head swam in confusion. That made no sense. "That's not right. I brought it with me, and I put the note in it."

Scott shook his head, his voice sad. "Sam, we had to get your bag because you didn't have ID on you when the police got to the scene. You didn't take it with you."

I felt cold as I stared at him, but I started to sweat. "But there was a guy in the car. . . ."

"There was no one in the car." Dad placed his hand over mine.

No. No. No. "He was in the backseat. And he was following me. I didn't—" A sour-faced nurse came in, not saying a word as she went to the tubes hooked up to the IV. There was a needle in her hand. Panic curled around my insides. "What is she doing? Dad?"

"She's just giving you some pain medication." He patted my hand. "It's okay."

I watched her press down on the needle. Fluid bubbled in the IV. She left without looking at me or saying a word. I thought nurses were supposed to be nice. "Dad..."

"You need to rest."

I didn't want to rest. I wanted them to believe me. Turning my head, I met my brother's troubled eyes. "Scott, someone was following me when I was at the cabin. And someone had been there. There were fresh cigarette butts and—"

"Honey, that was from me." Dad thrust a hand over his head. "Sometimes I go up there to smoke. Your mother doesn't know. I quit years ago, but with everything recently..."

I stared at him. "But... but someone was in the car. He scared me and that's why I lost control."

Scott's eyes cast down. "Sam, the car doors were locked when the police got there." He said his next words slowly, carefully. "He couldn't have locked the car doors after he left the car. The computer in the car was fried. They had to cut the car door open to get you out."

Oh man, his car.

"The insurance company is already—"

I cut my dad off. "There was someone in the car." My voice rose, cracking. All of it had been too real to be a hallucination. And I had a vision—a memory of crawling. How could I have a vision inside of a hallucination? "I didn't imagine it! I'm not making it up."

Dad sat back, looking helpless. "I know you're not making it up, sweetie. I don't doubt that you believe someone was in the car."

I sucked in a sharp breath, understanding what he wasn't saying. "I'm not crazy."

He made a strange noise, and he looked like he was about to crack—like he was about to crumble into a thousand pieces. "I know, baby. You're not crazy."

And I knew right then, when he looked away and a muscle popped in his jaw, that he didn't believe what he was saying.

The doctors let me out of the hospital that evening with a prescription for pain meds and orders to take it easy over the next couple of days. If it hadn't been for what had put me in the hospital a couple of weeks ago, they probably wouldn't have even kept me that long.

Red roses from Del had been placed on my desk in my bedroom, filling the room with the crisp, fresh scent. A smaller basket of bright pink peonies peeked out from behind the vase. They were from Veronica and the girls.

My purse was on the chair in front of my desk: house keys, wallet, and phone tucked inside. I dumped everything out on the seat. No note.

I felt sick.

How could I have hallucinated *all* of that? My skin felt numb, thoughts muted. The painkillers were still kicking around in my system. Dragging my feet, I went into the bathroom. Bandage off, the purplish bruise seeped out from my hairline, spreading over my left temple. There were tiny scratches on my arms from the glass. Nothing as bad as what I'd done to myself earlier on Wednesday.

A lump rose in my throat, and I swallowed it down. My palms were raw. Changing slowly into a tank top and sleep shorts, I saw that my knees hadn't fared much better. At least the whole falling-down part was real.

In a daze, I brushed my teeth twice and then crawled into bed. There I stayed, forcing my eyes closed. Mom visited me once. She didn't say much, but her manicured nails were chewed down to their beds.

"I'm glad you're okay," she said, moving to the door.

I said nothing.

"I . . . I love you, honey."

There was nothing for me to say. The words were on the tip of my tongue. Fighting or not, memories or no memories, I still loved her, but nothing came out. She stared at me with weary, sad eyes and then left.

She thought I was capable of killing someone. No leaps of imagination were required to assume she also thought I was crazy.

Scott stopped in just before ten, but I didn't speak to him, either. I pretended to sleep, and then I did sleep. Sleeping didn't require thinking. Thinking led to questioning my mental state.

Sometime later, something soft caressed my nose. The scent reminded me of spring and early summer. I pried my eyes open. One of Del's roses was right in my face, but the tan fingers around the glistening stem didn't belong to my boyfriend.

Carson's cocky grin went up a notch. "Wakey, wakey, eggs and bakey."

"Are you really here?"

He lowered the rose. "Yeah, I'm here. Why would you ask that?"

Explaining that I was experiencing vivid hallucinations probably wasn't the route to go. I blinked the sleep out of my eyes, and once my brain caught up with the fact that he was really here, there was a fluttering in my chest. I decided to go with, "What are you doing here?"

He leaned against the headboard, stretching out his long legs. Shoes were off, revealing plaid socks. "I wanted to see you. You gave us all a scare, Sam. Again."

"Sorry," I mumbled, sitting up. A wave of dizziness rolled through me as I clutched the comforter to my neck. Glancing at the clock, I saw that it was only a little past ten in the morning. "Skipping school?"

"Yep." He laid the rose on his thigh and then folded his arms behind his head.

"How did you get in here?"

The cocky grin was back, and I had trouble keeping my eyes on anything other than his totally kissable lips. "Dad is working in the game room, installing new floors. I waited until your mom left and snuck in."

I stared at him.

A bit of indecision crawled into his deep azure eyes. "Scott knows I'm here."

I didn't have any words for the rush that was building in me, swelling with each breath I took. Emotions swirled and whipped like soaring birds, thrilling, hopeful, and so, so confusing.

"I ... can leave if you want me to."

"No," I said quickly. "No. You don't have to leave. I'm just surprised."

His eyes met and held mine. "Your parents wouldn't let anyone see you." He paused, looking away. Some of the casualness leaked out of his posture, tightening his biceps. "Scott's worried."

My fist dug into the comforter with disappointment. "So that's why you're here? Because my brother's worried?"

Carson's head snapped in my direction. His brows were low, expression serious. "Sam, I'm here because *I* was worried."

"Oh." My cheeks flushed as I lowered my gaze to his lips— *damn it.* "I'm okay."

"Are you?" The serious look was still there as he searched my face intently.

I nodded.

Slowly, he lowered his arms and reached out, carefully running his fingers over the nasty bruise on my forehead. "What happened?"

The brief butterfly touch sent shivers over my skin. "I had a car accident."

His look turned droll as he placed his arms back behind his head. "I got that much."

I bit my dry lip as I glanced at the seat. The contents of my purse were still there. No note. No guy in the backseat. And there was a good chance there had been no man in the woods.

Throat dry, I peeked at him. "Stay?"

Carson arched a brow. "Not going anywhere."

My mind was confused by how happy that made my heart and body. Nodding, I threw off the comforter, climbed off the bed, and headed into my bathroom. I brushed my teeth and washed my face quickly. When I walked out of the bathroom, Carson was where I'd left him. I grabbed a bottle of water off the desk and took two aspirins instead of the pain meds. I started to ask if he wanted anything to drink, but he had an energy drink on the floor beside the bed.

His eyes followed me back to the bed, and just then I realized I was only wearing a pair of tiny sleep shorts and a thin tank top. I had a feeling the old Sammy would've slowed down or swayed her hips, but I hurried to the bed and slipped under the quilt instead of the covers, flushing from head to toe.

Carson chuckled.

"Shut up," I muttered.

He twisted onto his side, facing me, eyes sparkling with mischief. "What? I like the look."

I rolled my eyes and snuggled down. "You're here to talk about my pajamas?"

"No, but it's not a bad conversation starter." Carson scooted down so that he was stretched out beside me. With just the patchwork quilt between us, it felt so strange to be lying in bed beside him. Strange but good. "You going to tell me what happened?"

"Did my brother tell you anything?"

Carson smiled faintly. "No."

The urge was there, like it had been with Mrs. Messer on Wednesday. I wanted—needed—to tell someone, and there was the level of explicit trust with Carson. And he was here because he *cared*. Del could've snuck in if he was really concerned. That wasn't fair, and I knew it, but it was the truth.

Carson was here.

Here even after I spent a good five or six years being a tool to him. He'd already seen the worst of me. My faults were exposed to him like live wire.

I drew in a shallow breath. "I think I'm crazy."

chapter fourteen

*I*t seemed as if Carson was expecting me to say a lot of things, but that wasn't one of them. His eyes narrowed. "You're not crazy."

The sincerity in his voice brought a lump to my throat. "You don't understand what's been happening to me."

"Then tell me," he said, eyes locked on mine.

And so I did. I told him everything—the notes, everything that had happened at the lake and then in the car. I even told him about my mom's suspicion and—the worst thing of all— the hallucinations. When I finished, so much pressure lifted off me. Nothing was fixed or better, but I felt as if I could finally breathe for the first time since I came to, walking that lonely, unfamiliar road. I expected him to pat me on the head and then run from the house.

Carson did neither.

"You're not crazy," he said vehemently.

"I'm not?" Tears that had been building finally spilled over, coursing down my cheeks. "I really can't tell the difference between what's real and what's not real anymore."

He inched closer, chasing the tears away with his thumb. "Look, there's got to be an explanation for a lot of these things. You said Scott saw the first note, right? And I saw you with the yellow piece of paper in bio that one day. Those notes existed."

"But what about the one in the car? I didn't even have my purse with me, and I would have sworn that it was there."

"Look, I'm not ruling out stress. When my . . . when my mom died, my dad thought he did so many things that he didn't do. Once he left the car running and blamed me for it. He even wrote notes, like to-do lists, and then forgot he did it." He caught another tear, wiping it away. "And you said the guy was kind of like a black blur?"

I nodded, sniffling.

"In class that one day you were drawing a dark figure. I think what's happening is your subconscious is pushing through. The guy in the woods and in the car—it could be a memory." A muscle popped in his jaw, but his eyes, so vividly blue they looked violet, were still incredibly soft. "You don't know what happened to you. Someone could've been chasing you. The hallucinations could all be memories."

"My reflection talking to me is a memory?" I blushed even though I'd told him about it.

"Like I said, some of it's probably stress, and that's nothing to be embarrassed about," he said gently. "You've been through a lot, Sam. And you're putting a lot of pressure on yourself to remember so you can help find out what happened to Cassie." He paused, cupping my cheek. "Please. Please stop crying."

His softly spoken plea reached down inside me, clamping around my heart. I nodded, doing my best to stop my tears. It was hard, given how freaking perfect he was being about all of this.

"Thank you," I finally said when the tears subsided, and he pulled his hand back. "I mean it. I don't feel so . . . so crazy right now."

A small grin tugged at his lips. "I'm happy to hear it."

My chest fluttered again, and I rolled onto my back, taking deep, steady breaths. I'd told him about the vision with Dianna, and I wanted to know what that was about, but I knew better than to push it right now.

Carson also flipped onto his back. Several moments passed between us; the silence was soothing, not at all awkward. "You really think going up on the cliff would help?"

"Yeah," I sighed, wiping my palms over my damp cheeks. "I think it might. Mrs. Messer keeps suggesting that I visit familiar places."

"I can go with you," he offered. "I know the layout pretty well. You used to know your way around there, too."

I used to know a lot of things. Turning my head toward him, I smiled. "If you can . . . that would be great."

"Would Del the Dick get mad?" One dark eyebrow arched mockingly.

Good question. I gave a lopsided shrug. "I don't think so, but you shouldn't call him that."

Carson chuckled. "Do you care if he gets mad?"

My immediate response was on the tip of my tongue, but I squelched it and changed the subject. "I doubt my parents will let me out of the house this weekend, but maybe after school..."

"Whenever you want, just let me know."

"I will." I looked at him again, my eyes crawling across the broad cheekbones and parted lips. Part of me knew then that I would never grow tired of looking at him, but it was so much, much more than that. Carson made me feel normal—sane. That was worth more than anything I could ever say or do to repay him. "Thank you for coming by. I really mean it."

He smiled again, revealing that chipped tooth, and my breath caught. "It's no problem. I'm surprised you haven't kicked me out yet."

"Really? You shouldn't be. I like you," I said, flushing. "I probably shouldn't admit that, but I do. I like you, and I can't figure out why I didn't see it before."

There wasn't surprise in his expression, just curiosity as he watched me. He rolled back onto his side. His knee pressed against my thigh, separated only by the quilt. His proximity made the bed seem much, much smaller.

"It's weird," he finally said. "There're parts of you I recognize. Your... boldness is familiar. The way you just say whatever you're thinking."

Right now I was thinking about how crazy it was that my entire leg was tingling and how nothing in this world could make me look away. Our faces were only inches apart. The space was sweet and torturous. None of these sensations occurred when I was with Del. That had to mean something.

"And then there's this whole different side that's new." His lips tipped up on one side. "The funny thing is, this new version of Sam reminds me of how you were when we were kids."

My gaze dipped to his lips. They were so full, so soft-looking. "Is that a good thing?"

Carson's smile faded. "It's different."

"Oh." I met his eyes again, wondering if I could just will him to kiss me and if I should even want that, all things considered. "That doesn't sound good."

"Different is good." He drew in a stuttered breath and looked away.

When I realized I was still staring at his profile, I forced my eyes to the little stars on the ceiling.

"You were my first kiss," he said quietly.

I nearly jumped from the shock, and from the fact that I oh-so-liked the sound of that. "I was? Was it good? Were you my first kiss?" *Please say yes, please say yes.*

Carson tipped his head back, shoulders shaking in a silent laugh. "We were ten, so I'm hoping I was your first kiss."

Ten? My shoulders deflated. Way too young to mean anything.

"We were playing spin the bottle or something lame like that," he added, tipping his chin down so he was looking at me. "Your parents caught us. Your mom flipped out, but your dad laughed."

I frowned. "I can imagine."

We sat there for a while in silence, and once again it wasn't silence filled with pity and discomfort. Just two people who were able to sit—or lie—side by side in peace. It was perfect.

"Should I leave?" Carson asked, his breath dancing over my forehead.

I shook my head. "I don't want you to . . . yet."

He seemed to understand and didn't push it. A few minutes later, he shifted, and before I could feel the cold bite of disappointment, he lifted his arm and waited. My heart pounded off my ribs as I realized what he was offering. Dizzy and breathless, I scooted toward him and slowly placed my cheek on his chest. There was a heavy, tense pause, and then he wrapped his arm around me, curving his fingers over my shoulder.

I didn't know what to do with my hands, but he smelled like citrus and soap—a scent unique to him. Eventually, I folded my hands against his side, and he jerked a little. Worried that I'd done something wrong, I lifted my chin and my breath stalled again.

Carson was looking at me, and our mouths were only an inch or two apart. Sooty lashes hid his eyes, but I felt them, their power. And the need in them, as if it were my own—*it was my own.*

And suddenly it didn't matter that everyone believed I didn't know who I was anymore, because with him—with Carson—I knew who I *wanted* to be, and that was all that mattered.

He made a low sound in the back of his throat and moved toward me, pressing his forehead against mine. My hand seemed to know what to do. I placed it on his cheek, my thumb smoothing over the skin below his lip, and he shuddered at the slight touch. It felt as if I'd never done this before, even if Del claimed we'd done *everything* before.

This was my first—that I remembered—with Carson, and that felt right.

My thumb found his lower lip, and the sharp edge of his teeth grazed my skin. The act was strangely intimate, rough and sensual. My eyes fluttered close, and I waited for my second first kiss. . . .

Carson wrapped his hand around mine, gently pulling it back.

Not what I was waiting for. *Damn it.* I opened my eyes, confused. "Why?"

"Why? *Why* is your favorite word now, isn't it?" Humor laced his words, not annoyance or frustration. "You're still such a freaking terror."

When Scott had said that before, it hadn't sounded like a good thing, but Carson made it sound endearing, fun. I smiled. "I want you to kiss me."

Heat flared in his eyes, and something inside me knew how to respond to that. The edge of the quilt slipped a little, and I pressed forward, our chests touching. Everywhere our bodies met, my skin warmed in a way that felt completely new.

A sudden deepening of his eyes occurred, and his jaw tensed. "Sam . . ."

"Carson?"

Carson closed his eyes briefly. And then he rolled over me, supporting his weight with one arm so quickly that the air left my lungs in a harsh rush. He stared down at me, eyes a mosaic of every blue possible. "You shouldn't be asking me that."

There was barely an inch separating us, and I had trouble focusing my thoughts. "I know."

He reached down, brushing the thick strands of hair off my cheek. His fingers lingered against my skin, sliding down to my jaw. Staring at his lips, I needed to know how they felt. How they tasted. I inhaled sharply, bringing my chest against his once more. A dizzy rush of sensations cascaded through me, and again, I was struck by the sense of how right this was.

Carson lowered his head, and my heart stuttered. He pressed his lips against my forehead, then my temple, a sweeping brush along my cheek, and then he placed a wickedly chaste kiss on the corner of my lips. He spoke into the warm space between our lips. "You're not mine to kiss, Sam."

I felt the extreme urge to pout, and Carson must've sensed it, because he laughed softly and cupped my cheek. His body lowered onto mine in a way that said it was completely at odds with what was coming out of his mouth. Wishing the quilt wasn't between us, I shifted under him. His eyes closed, and the hand beside my head pushed into the mattress as his jaw worked. I moved my hips again, and then gasped at the raw shiver that whipped through me.

Carson dropped his forehead to mine again. "Sam, you're really making it hard to be a good guy."

I placed the tips of my fingers on his cheek, and his lashes swept up. "What if I don't want you to be the good guy?"

"I want to be the good guy with you." He took another breath. "You deserve that."

Oh.

"I don't like Del," he admitted, staring straight into my eyes. "He's a dick, and you've *always* deserved better than him, but I'm not that kind of guy. At least, I'm trying to not be with you."

"But I'm not his."

His brows rose as he pulled back. His fingers found the silver chain around my neck. I caught my breath when the back of his knuckles brushed over my collarbone as he held the Tiffany's heart between us. "This says differently."

chapter fifteen

Spring had greeted us with a brief rain shower on the morning of Cassie's funeral, but then the dark clouds parted an hour before and the sun shone, casting light over the large funeral home. School hadn't been canceled, but it might as well have been, as it seemed the entire student body was there, shuffling up the walkway that separated the old part of the cemetery from the new. Everyone was dressed in black. Some wore slacks while others had dug out black party dresses.

The service... it was what I'd expected, but worse. There were so many tears, even from those I figured Cassie would have never been nice to. I had to squelch the urge to get up and run several times. It was hard to breathe in there. Hard to even think with the remembrances and the songs played. But with Del keeping his hand clamped tightly around mine, and my parents behind me watching like hawks, I didn't dare move.

For the hundredth time, I closed my dry eyes and dragged in a ragged breath. The sorrow for the girl I couldn't remember built in my chest, but it wouldn't break free. Just like I couldn't break free.

I looked at the well-manicured fingers curled around mine, and in the middle of all this sadness, I felt guilt. Guilt for not being able to shed a tear—for holding this boy's hand when I'd begged another to kiss me a few days ago. My life was a mess, but as my eyes were drawn to the casket's polished mahogany, I knew that my life—as screwed up as it was—had to be better than no life.

Tulips surrounded the coffin, and a picture rested in a bed of baby's breath. I hadn't gone up during the visitation, but I could see the photo from here.

It was of us.

We were sitting on a bench at school, backs against each other, cheesing it up for the camera. It was the first time I'd seen the picture, and we looked younger in it, our smiles real, connected somehow.

"I took that picture," Del whispered in my ear, catching me staring at it.

Nodding, I slipped my hand free. Scanning the front of the church, I caught sight of Cassie's mom. The only reason I knew it was her was because she was sobbing, clutching a picture frame to her chest during the entire service. My heart broke for her.

Even with the tears, Cate Winchester was beautiful. Young. Her light brown hair was cut in a fashionable bob, accenting high cheekbones and a graceful neck. Some of Cassie's features were there—the lips and the slender frame.

There was a moment of silence as the pastor returned to

the podium. The back of my neck tingled. I twisted around in the pew, and my gaze slid to the back row. My eyes locked with Detective Ramirez's dark eyes.

"Samantha," my mother hissed, drawing my attention. She looked mortified. "Turn around."

Scott rolled his eyes.

Biting my lip, I whipped around and faced the front. Del dropped a heavy hand on my knee and squeezed, causing me to jump. Veronica shot me a look over the rim of her sunglasses, and then her gaze dropped. Her plump lips thinned, and she stiffly turned away.

I took a deep breath and lowered my head in prayer. Familiar words resonated through the church. Del's hand crept up my thigh, and my body locked up. Not just because it was completely inappropriate on about a thousand different levels, but because somewhere over the long weekend, I'd made up my mind that the two of us needed to have a serious talk.

Without any warning, my vision dulled, turning gray. The church, coffin, Del's creeping hand—everything—broke away, leaving just Cassie and me.

She plopped down on a bed—her bed. "Stop bitching. You're lucky to have a dad who wants to be in your life."

I rolled my eyes, sitting on the edge of the bed as I stared down at my toes. A jar of red nail polish was in my hand. Everything else lacked life and vibrancy. I looked over my shoulder. "You can have him."

"Really?" She rolled onto her side, flipping her long hair over her slender shoulder. "I'll take him. And that supercute sweater you're wearing. Oh, while we're at it, can I also have Del?"

Annoyance flashed and grew in me like a weed. "You don't even try to hide the fact that you always want what I have. And you aren't getting my sweater."

Grinning shamelessly, she watched me with catlike interest. "But I can have Del? Awesome."

My eyes narrowed as I twisted the lid back on the polish. Standing, I placed it on her bedside table and picked up the music box. "You'd like that, wouldn't you?"

She sprang from the bed and grabbed the music box out of my hands. Holding it close to her chest, she smirked. "You don't really want him, but you won't let him go."

For a moment, I thought she was going to clunk me over the head with the box. "I'm out of here," I said.

Cassie laughed. "Don't be pissy, Sammy. It brings out the lines around your mouth. Wouldn't want to age yourself prematurely."

"Don't be a bitch," I retorted, heading for the door.

She dashed in front of me, grasping my arms. Her eyes, greener than mine, filled with regret. "Don't be mad at me, Sammy. I wasn't being serious. You know that, right?"

I shifted my weight from one foot to the other. Part of me wanted to push her away. She thought I didn't have my suspicions—that I didn't know. But the other part of me, well, it felt bad for her. After all, I understood Cassie better than anyone else. Knew why she did the things she did, even to me—her best friend.

"Please?" She bounced on her heels.

Forcing a smile, I nodded. "Yeah, I'm not mad at you."

Cassie let out a squeal and wrapped her arms around me. "You know, when we're old and ugly, we're still going to be best friends, right?"

I laughed. "If we don't kill each other before then."

Feeling the blood drain from my face, I was abruptly pulled out of the memory when Del's hand slipped between my thighs. Sucking in a sharp breath, I grabbed his wrist, stopping him from going any further.

He shot me an innocent grin.

Disgusted, I tossed his hand back into his lap. My hands were shaking as I tucked my hair back, focusing on the pew ahead.

"What's your deal?" Del asked in a hushed voice.

"Besides you fondling me *during a funeral?*" I hissed back. "I remembered something."

He drew back slightly, eyes growing wide. "What?"

Veronica was staring at us, so I lowered my voice even more, but I was sure she overheard me. "I was talking with Cassie in her bedroom."

Del's brows rose. "Nothing much, then."

It wasn't to him, but it was the first time I'd remember anything normal about Cassie. But what had I been suspicious about, and what did I know about Cassie that explained her behavior? *The plot thickens.* My lips twisted and then my stomach dipped as I remembered the last thing I had said to her.

If we don't kill each other before then.

After the service, everyone piled out in the parking lot. The graveside service was family only.

I scanned the crowds, looking for my parents.

Mom stood by the Bentley, lips pursed as she pointedly stared out into the cemetery at my dad. He was talking to Cassie's grandfather, who looked just as forlorn as he had when Carson and I had visited. Shaking the older man's hand, Dad then turned to Ms. Winchester. His lips moved into a sad, sympathetic smile, and then Ms. Winchester's face crumpled, and she burst into tears once more.

I had to look away.

My gaze landed on Mom once again. It struck me as odd— and rude—that Mom hadn't offered her condolences. Glancing over my shoulder, I thought I saw Carson's familiar dark head, but he wasn't in the crowd.

Del dropped his arm over my shoulder. "You ready?"

I watched my brother's eyes narrow as he studied Del's arm. Was I really ready? No. But Del and I needed to talk. "Yeah, I'm ready."

In more ways than one.

Turned out, I didn't get a lot of one-on-one time with my boyfriend. A huge group of kids had gone back to his parents' "farm" after the services. The farm was really just this barn that had been decked out into some sort of playboy clubhouse.

The bottom floor was full of overstuffed couches around a TV screen that was the size of a Hummer. There was a bar where I assumed the stables used to be, and it was in full use right now. Upstairs, the loft had been divided into three guest rooms.

They were also in use.

Sex, drinking, and death seemed to go hand in hand. Maybe

it was the way people dealt with death. Losing yourself when faced with something so final was appealing.

Except I'd already lost myself.

A kid bumped into me, and I moved farther into the corner. All of this might have been my thing months ago, but now I wanted nothing more than to disappear into the walls. Everything was too loud—the music, the conversation, the laughter.

Scott was nowhere to be found, having disappeared with Julie and Carson.

Carson.

I'd fallen asleep with him beside me on Friday, and when I woke up later, he was gone.

We hadn't talked since.

Clutching the red plastic cup to my chest, I pressed against the wall, scanning the crowd while trying to get my heart to slow down.

"There you are," Del called out, shuffling past a couple who seemed to be in a contest to see who could kiss the longest without coming up for air. "I've been looking everywhere for you."

I eyed the bottle of Jack in his hand. The barn wasn't so big that you could lose someone. "I've been here."

Del leaned in, giving my cheek a sloppy kiss that reeked of alcohol. "Why are you standing in the corner by yourself? Veronica and Candy are right there."

Veronica and Candy were on one of the couches, surrounded by girls I didn't recognize. Lauren didn't come, opting to go home after the funeral. I couldn't blame her.

"You look so lonely over here," Del said, dropping an arm over my shoulders as he leaned in. He caught a piece of my hair with his free hand, twirling it around his finger. "Your friends miss you, Sammy."

I wanted to miss them—really I did—but the only one I could even tolerate now was Lauren, and she wasn't even here. I looked up at Del, taking in the straight teeth, the square jaw and aristocratic nose. Everything about him was perfect, from the strategically placed highlights in his carefully styled hair to the tips of his shoes. I could see what I'd been attracted to. Who wouldn't have been? But nothing stirred in my chest.

"Come on," he said, swaying into me. "Let's go somewhere private."

Private? My heart flopped over heavily as my gaze drifted up to the lofts. We needed to talk, but not in one of those rooms and not when he was obviously drunk. "I want to stay down here."

He took a swig out of the bottle and then frowned. "But . . . you're not doing anything down here. You're just leaning up against a wall like . . ."

"Like what?" I dipped out from underneath his arm and placed my cup on the table next to us.

Del turned his head to the side, his jaw working. "I don't know. It's just not you. I'd usually have to pull you away from everyone for some quality time."

Irritation built inside me, and my eyes burned. "If you haven't noticed, I've changed."

He gave a dry laugh and took another drink. "Yeah, I've noticed."

Guilt washed over the annoyance, because *I* had changed—not Del. Blaming him for it wasn't right. I shifted my weight. "Del, I'm sorry."

He finished off the rest of his bottle and then tossed it into an overflowing trash can. "I'm not mad. This is just hard. You're a totally different person, and no matter how much you try, I know you're not feeling it."

My brows inched up. *Whoa.* Okay, maybe it was time for the conversation. And it might be easier than I'd realized. He already knew things weren't the same. I stepped forward, stopping when we were inches from touching. "I really am trying hard, but—"

"We just need to try harder. I know."

Oh. No, not where I was going with that. "Del—"

"Sammy, I still love you even though you . . . aren't acting right." He placed his hands on my shoulders, drawing me against his chest as he supported his weight against the wall. Glassy eyes met mine. "We're meant to be together. And we've faced harder things than this."

The music pounded in my ears as I stared up at him. "We have? I thought we had a perfect relationship, Del."

He stared at me. "We did—we do!"

"Then what did we face?"

His mouth opened and closed. "Sammy, let's not focus on that. Tell me what I need to do to make this work, and I'll do it."

"No. I want you to tell me, because I have this feeling . . ."

"Oh, she has a feeling!" Veronica's voice trilled over the music and conversation, followed by her giggling. "This reminds me of something."

Turning around, I saw Veronica standing a few feet away. She wobbled to the side. Someone turned the music down. My eyes found the source. Candy. Dread poured into me, locking up my muscles.

"You had *a feeling* during the funeral, didn't you?" Veronica's voice rang loud with false interest.

Everyone stopped. Dozens of eyes were on us, and the barn suddenly seemed too small. I stepped back and met the wall. Del had inched to the side, eyes downcast. A look crossed his face, tightening the features. At first I thought it was concern, but then I realized it was embarrassment.

I was alone.

"So, tell us what the feelings are like?" Candy joined in, flipping the icy sheet of blond hair over her shoulder. "Is it like psychics on those shows?"

A girl laughed. Others snickered.

I folded my arms around me, wanting to crawl into a hole. "I don't think so."

"It's not?" Veronica leaned against the back of a couch, her catlike eyes narrowed. "So, what's it like, then?"

A slow anger built inside me. Why were they doing this? Yes, we'd obviously grown apart, but to put me on the spot like this? "I really don't want to talk about this."

"Why not?" Candy whined, but her eyes sparked with maliciousness. "Everyone is dying to know what it's like not having any clue who you are. And, wow, being the last person to see Cassie alive. What's that like?"

"Knock it off," Del said, finally speaking up. He'd found

another bottle, clenching it tightly in his hand. "You're embarrassing her."

Or was I embarrassing him?

Candy rolled her eyes, and a dark-haired boy strolled up behind her, wrapping his arms around her tiny waist. Trey. I almost didn't recognize him. He whispered something in her ear while he met my eyes. He grinned. Candy giggled, pressing back into him.

Veronica's lips pursed. "What happened at the funeral?"

My head snapped in her direction. "I'm not talking about that here. Sorry."

"Don't be such a bitch, Sammy. Everyone wants to know what it's like." She turned around, raising her voice. "Right?"

Voices cheered and people chattered all around me. Their eyes bore into me as they pressed forward. I was falling again, but not from a cliff. I'd been at the top of the social ladder, above them, but now I was tumbling off it, hitting every single rung on the way down. Bruised and shaken, I felt the pressure build in my chest.

Who knew how many of them had waited for this day to come? And could I blame them? No. I'd probably terrorized half these kids. I searched the sea of faces for my brother—for Carson. My gaze skipped over one and darted back. Heart stopping, I thought I saw Cassie's face—smiling at me. Happy. Thrilled.

I couldn't catch my breath.

Veronica's smile grew. "Okay. You don't want to talk about that. Understandable. But you know what I heard?"

"No," I think I whispered.

"When you wrecked your brother's car—Mike Billows said

you kept talking about someone being in the car with you, but there wasn't anyone there." Her voice rose. "He said you were crazy—'Insanity Sam,' I think he said."

Crazy. Insanity Sam. The words bounced around in my skull. For a moment, the faces around me blurred out of focus. I was crazy. No one had been in the car. And how did she know? I looked at Del, but he was still staring at the floor. A second later, I remembered who Mike Billows was: a kid in my bio class who volunteered with the fire department.

"Seeing things?" Candy said, feigning sympathy. "That must really suck."

Trey smacked her hip. "Be nice."

She giggled.

"Or maybe," Veronica continued, "you've always been crazy, and we just didn't know it." I wanted to throw myself at her, but I couldn't move. "You *sure* you don't remember the last time you saw Cassie . . . alive?"

I sucked in a sharp breath. Some of the faces lost their smiles. They were glancing at one another, no longer sure if watching my fall from grace was funny and entertaining.

A tall blonde pushed through the crowd, knocking kids out of the way. Julie took one look at Veronica and sneered. "Are you drunk or just a dumb bitch?"

"Excuse me?" Veronica shot back, lip curling. "You can't possibly be talking to me."

Julie got right up in her face. "You're right, there are a few dumb bitches here. But I'm talking to you. So what's your problem?"

Music suddenly blasted the air, drowning out whatever the two girls were saying, but it looked heated. I owed Julie—owed her big-time. But I had to get out of here. The dark brown walls of the barn were spinning. Nausea rose sharply.

Del reached for me. "Sammy—"

I pushed away from him, plowing through the closest group now fixated on the girl fight about to go down.

"Hey!" snapped a girl. "Watch where you're going."

"Sorry," I murmured, keeping my eyes on the floor.

Another body blocked me. I stepped to the side. Too hot—I was too hot. Bodies were everywhere, pressing into me, suffocating me. Too much perfume—too many sounds. My heart slammed off my ribs; my lungs squeezed. I needed to get outside, get fresh air. The pressure increased and settled on my chest, cutting off the oxygen. Thoughts swam; the walls tilted.

Did you kill her? a voice whispered.

I whirled around. "Who . . . who said that?"

The boy closest to me arched his brows, muttering something under his breath, and turned away.

Did you kill Cassie? the voice said from behind me.

Spinning around, I tried to breathe. Faces blurred. My vision darkened at the corners. Tremors ran up my legs. I was going to pass out here, in front of everyone. How lame . . .

A strong hand found mine in the mess of people and squeezed gently. That scent—*his* scent—surrounded me. I inhaled deeply, expanding my lungs. I lifted my head, and my eyes met startling blue eyes.

Carson looked grim. "You want to get out of here?"

chapter sixteen

In Carson's father's old red pickup truck, which smelled faintly of cigars, I pressed back into the seat and continued breathing deeply, hands clasped against my stomach. My pulse had finally started to slow down.

"If I had known what was going on, I would've come inside sooner," Carson said quietly.

I swallowed. "It's not your . . . your problem, and it's okay."

"It shouldn't be your problem, and it's not okay." He reached over, gently pulling my hands free. "Are you all right?"

"I'm fine." I let out a shaky breath. "I think I was having a panic attack. I thought I heard . . ."

"Heard what?" His hand smoothed over mine, then folded over it.

When he was touching me like that, I'd probably admit just about anything. I turned my head toward him. A fine current of electricity shimmed between us. "I thought someone asked me if I'd killed Cassie, but I was . . . hearing things." Forcing a weak laugh,

I looked out the window. Kids streamed out the barn doors. Del was among them. "Or maybe some of them do think I killed her."

"They don't think that."

I shot him a dull look. "It's not like I'm a fan favorite here—then or now."

His lips twitched. "Well, if they do think it, then they're idiots." He let go of my hand and started the truck. It rumbled to life. "So, want me to take you home? Or do you want me to go get Scott for you?"

"Actually, do you have plans? I was wondering if you'd like to do something with me today."

He arched a brow. "The answer is yes and always, probably for a very long time, too." His gaze dropped to my lips. "But unless you've kicked Del the Dick to the curb, I'm going to have to refuse."

My cheeks burned, and my stomach warmed at his teasing. "Um, that's not what I'm asking, but good to know."

"Hmm. It wasn't?" Carson's lips spread into a half grin. "So what were you asking?"

Images of us together occupied my mind for a couple more seconds. "I was wondering if you would take me up to the cliff."

"I can do that." Carson shifted the gears. His hand brushed along my thigh, and I jerked at the contact. "But you probably want to change first."

The images were still there, in a lot more detail than before. Us kissing. Touching. Talking.

Carson slid me a look. A knowing, smug grin split his lips. "Sam."

I blinked. "Change of clothes. Got it."

He chuckled as he shifted gears again, grazing my leg with the side of his hand. I doubted it was accidental. Then he threw his arm over the back of my seat and turned his head toward me. Because I was staring at him, the movement put us within kissing distance. My heart leaped into my throat. For a moment, I thought he was going to say "screw the good-guy thing" and go for it. A second later I realized he was backing up.

Awkward.

Carson met my eyes and winked. I let out the breath I was holding, so aware of him that I felt as if I'd climb out of my skin at any second. And he knew it. That smug half grin was on his face the whole way to my house.

I snuck in and quickly changed into hiking-appropriate clothing. The house seemed empty, but I didn't stick around to find out, doubtful that either of my parents would've been down with me hanging out with Carson.

We stopped at his house, and he changed out of his dress clothes. Returning in under two minutes, he'd thrown on a pair of jeans and a light sweater.

The trip to the state forest was bumpy. The truck rocked, and my phone slipped out of my fingers, falling to the floorboard. Reaching down, my hand knocked into something soft, and I grabbed it with my phone.

It was a hat—the black baseball cap I'd seen him wear before.

An image of the man in the woods flashed before me. He'd

been wearing a black cap, but that . . . that was only a memory or a stress-induced hallucination. It couldn't be . . .

"Your hat?" I said hoarsely.

Carson glanced at me, brows raised. "Yeah, had it for years."

I put it on the dashboard, quickly dismissing the irrational fear. As we drove up the narrow dirt road, I glanced at him. "I tried to talk to Del before Veronica turned on me."

He gave me a sidelong glance. "Sam, I don't want to be the reason why you leave him."

"You're not," I said honestly. "Things aren't the same between Del and me, and that has nothing to do with you."

"Okay." One of his fingers tapped on the steering wheel. "Has he told you anything about your relationship?"

I shook my head. "Other than our relationship was perfect? No."

Carson let out a choked laugh. "He said that? Wow."

"What?" My interest was immediately piqued.

"Your relationship was far from perfect." Turning onto a gravelly, bumpy road put us right into direct sunlight. He reached over, grabbed the baseball cap, and slid it on. "You guys were like Cassie and Trey, fighting all the time."

"Are you serious?"

"Yep." He squinted, making a sharp right. "You guys didn't break up like Trey and Cassie did all the time, but you two fought like crazy."

I slumped back against the seat. Del had lied to me, and I'd believed him—believed in this perfect, fairy-tale romance.

Feeling stupid, I glared out the window. There were more than enough signs that things weren't perfect. The looks the girls gave me, the times Del had slipped up.

"You doing okay over there?" he asked.

My hands balled into fists. "I'm pissed! It's bad enough that I don't remember anything, but lying to me? He took advantage of me. I feel like an idiot."

"You're not an idiot, Sam."

Pressing my lips together, I shook my head. Maybe I wasn't stupid, but I'd been incredibly naive. How many more people were lying to me? And about what? About things that were far more serious than the status of my relationship with Del, no doubt. My chest ached at all the possibilities. What if I was a murderous teenage brat and all the signs had been there? And no one wanted to tell me?

We came to a stop at a dead end blocked off with a chain and a weathered sign that marked the property private.

Carson killed the engine and sat back, looking at me. "There's a trail that actually leads straight from your parents' house to the cliff. I only know from helping Dad do stuff around the summer home. You could've made it at night, though."

Looking around and seeing nothing but thick wilderness, it was hard to imagine wandering around here at night and not getting eaten by a bear. "Who owns it?"

"The state, I guess. Not really sure, but you and Scott used to hang out up here a lot when you were younger." He paused. "I would tag along when your parents let me. You used to love to stand on the edge of the cliff. Freaked me and Scott out."

I smiled faintly. "So this place meant something to me?"

"I think so."

Reaching for the handle to open the door, I drew in a deep breath. "Ready?"

"Can you wait a sec?" Carson asked, pulling off the cap. He ran a hand through his hair, then tossed the hat onto the dashboard. "There's something I need to tell you."

Dismay stirred inside me, and my heart dropped all the way to my toes. Nothing good came from statements like that. Letting go of the handle, I twisted toward him. "What?"

He stared straight ahead, eyes narrowed and jaw clenched. "I haven't been completely honest with you about some things."

I opened my mouth, but nothing came out except a ragged breath. The ache was back in my chest, but different this time. It was centered over my heart, raw and worried like an overexposed wound. Part of me didn't want to know what he hadn't been truthful about, but I couldn't—wouldn't—run from this. Squaring my shoulders, I braced myself for whatever he was about to say.

"Okay," I finally said. "Tell me."

His gaze slid toward me. "Remember when I told you that you were my first kiss?" When I nodded, he let out a long breath. "Well, you were also my last kiss."

I cocked my head to the side, unsure I heard him correctly. Out of everything I was expecting him to say, that wasn't even near the bottom of the list. "Come again?"

Carson's lips twitched into a tiny half smile that quickly faded. "I saw you the night you disappeared."

Forcing myself to not climb across the seat and throttle him, I gripped my knees as anger pricked at my skin. "Why didn't you tell me?"

"It's complicated. And I know . . . I know that's not a good-enough excuse. I told the police, so I'm surprised that they never told you." He looked away, working the muscle in his jaw. "But what happened between us . . ."

I sucked in a sharp breath. *Between us* could mean only a few things. If he'd lied to me about *that* . . . well, the pressure building in my throat and behind my eyes said enough. "What happened?"

"I was hanging around with Scott, watching a movie down in the basement. It was close to ten when I left. The house was completely dark. I don't even think your dad was home. I headed out the back way, through the sunroom, just in case your mom was roaming around. I didn't see you at first." His forehead creased as he ran the tips of his fingers down his face. "I heard you—you were sitting on one of those damn window seats, crying. I should've turned and went in the other direction, but I couldn't walk away. Not when you were crying."

My fingers loosened around my knees as some of the tension eased off. Carson wasn't the kind of guy who could walk away from a crying girl. Recalling what I did know about that night, I felt a sour taste in my mouth. "I was with Del until nine."

Carson nodded slowly. "I asked if you were okay, and you got up and turned on the light. You weren't wearing that . . . necklace. So I figured you had a big blowup with him."

"He said I took it off to shower after . . . uh . . ."

He arched a brow. "Unless crying is something you typically do after having sex, I have a feeling that's not why you took it off."

Mortification turned my entire body red. That was so not the conversation I wanted to have with Carson. "Okay, good point. Moving on."

"Well, you acted like you normally did. Got in my face, and we started arguing, but it was different." He leaned his head back against the seat, closing his eyes. "As pissy as you were being with me, you were *still* crying. And I'd never seen you like that. I don't even know what I was thinking, but I grabbed you to . . . comfort you or something, and you just came at me."

"I came at you?"

One side of his lips curved up. "You kissed me. No warning whatsoever. You just laid one on me."

Oh dear god. I slumped against the seat. Not only was I a mean girl, but I'd also molested Carson. Nice.

"I was kind of shocked at first . . . and then I kissed you back." He sighed again. "It was all pretty intense—angry, actually. Kind of hot, too. Then you got a text message, pushed me away, and stormed off. That was the last time I saw you."

Having no idea how to respond to any of that, I stared at him. Being upset had to have something to do with Del and then my phone going off. . . . Cassie? My thoughts lingered on that for a moment and then flipped right back to the fact that I had kissed Carson—really kissed Carson.

"Why didn't you tell me this before?" I asked quietly.

He tilted his head toward me, meeting my stare with

crystalline eyes. "Don't take this the wrong way, but I'm not proud of it. Even though you didn't have that damn necklace on, as far as I knew, you were still with Del. And I'm not big on making out with another guy's girlfriend. I know I have a reputation—maybe you don't remember it."

"I've heard," I muttered.

Carson snorted. "And you were upset. Shit, that's, like, taking advantage of you. My mom would've knocked me upside the head if she were alive."

I smiled faintly at that, but then I thought of Candy and Trey. Had they been messing around before Cassie and Trey broke up? Possibly not very important now, but something about that nagged me.

"Are you pissed at me?" he asked quietly.

Good question. I wasn't sure how I was supposed to feel. Del had lied to me. My friends had lied to me. And now Carson had. Part of me could understand why Carson had felt he had to lie to me, but it didn't make it okay. I looked away, putting my thumb to my mouth and gently chewed at the nail. "I don't know."

Several moments passed, and then Carson reached out, pulling my hand away from my mouth. "You should really stop doing it."

My face flushed. "Yeah, I guess . . . it's a nervous habit."

"You used to do it as a kid."

"So you've said." His hand was still around mine, the warmth of his fingers pleasant in spite of the lie. "So I kissed you?"

"Yeah."

I nodded slowly. "And you kissed me back?"

"Yep."

Sending him a sidelong look, I raised my brows. "Well, did you like it even though you weren't proud of it?"

A smile pulled at his lips, and a wicked glint darkened his eyes to midnight blue. "Oh, yeah, I enjoyed it."

I felt my lips responding to his smile. "Well, that helps me not to be too mad at you." I pulled my hand free and reached for the door handle. "You ready now?"

Carson nodded, and we climbed out of the truck. He went to the chain, lifting the rusted metal high enough that I could easily dip under it. He moved in front of me, and I followed, mulling over what I'd discovered. Truth be told, I really didn't know how I felt about his lying to me. And that wasn't even the most important part of what he'd told me.

Why had I been crying after leaving Del's?

Del had lied about our relationship—that much was certain. But about what, exactly? Had we broken up? Is that why I'd taken his necklace off? And most important, did our breakup have anything to do with Cassie?

Once again, the picture of Cassie and Del floated to the surface of my mind. But this time it was different. Feelings were tied to the image. Anger. Disappointment. I knew there was more, just out of reach, waiting for me to put two and two together.

Cassie.

Del.

I stopped beside a prickly bush as a wave of foreign emotions crashed over me. Cassie and Del...

Having realized I'd stopped, Carson backtracked. "Hey, you doing okay?"

"Yeah, I just...I don't know." How could I explain what I was feeling—thinking? I tipped my head back. Deep blue sky broke through the branches. "Do you think Cassie and Del had something going on?"

"I really don't know," he said, leaning against a tree. "I wouldn't put it past either of them."

"Why was I friends with someone like that? How could I date someone like Del?" Before he could answer, I'd figured it out. The revelation wasn't new or anything, but it still stung like a wasp. "Because I was just like them."

Carson pushed off the tree and took my hand, threading his fingers through mine. "You really weren't. Not always, and you aren't anymore. That's got to mean something."

I glanced at him. "Second chances, right?"

He nodded and then started walking again, keeping his hand secured around mine. I tried not to put much thought in it.

The path we walked wasn't much of a path at all. It was an uneven stretch of land that continued uphill until the two of us were forced to break contact lest we lose our footing. Pieces of dirt and small rocks kicked up, rolling down the hill behind us. Finally we cleared the trees and crossed a grassy patch.

Breaking away from Carson, I slowly moved to the edge of the cliff. Wind, cold and wet, whipped my hair back. Tips of trees guarded the waterfall below, and like I'd suspected, the fall was rocky and sheer.

I waited for vertigo to slam into me, but as I stood at the

edge, I realized the height didn't bother me. In fact, there was something thrilling about being up so high. "I think I still have a bit of an adrenaline junkie in me," I said.

Carson's laugh was strained. "That's kind of good to hear, but do you think you could move back from the edge a little?"

He'd stayed near the trees, and I wondered if he was afraid of heights. "Do you think if we fell from here, I could've survived it?"

"It's possible. Crazier things have happened. Or she could've jumped."

Turning around, I stared at him. That wasn't something I'd considered.

Carson eyes flinted away from mine, narrowing on the empty space beyond the tips of trees. "It's just a possibility," he said quietly. "People do insane shit like that all the time."

But everything I knew about Cassie told me she wouldn't have done that. Not alone . . . I swallowed, unable to wrap my head around the budding idea forming there.

"Feeling . . . or remembering anything?" he asked.

I shook my head, disappointed. Nothing was coming to the surface besides more questions and confusion. Walking back toward the cluster of trees to the right, I started chewing on my nail. Large pines reached around the boulders jutting out of the ground, and beyond the rocks was nothing but the fall—the fall I had to have taken.

"Lucky to be alive" was an understatement.

Time passed in silence. Carson remained on the other side, letting me stay here as long as it took. I leaned against a tree, eyes narrowed on the edge of the cliff. I was ready to give up, tell him we should head back, but then a cold shiver danced down my spine. It was the only warning.

This wasn't like the visions I'd been having. There was no gray film, and I didn't see anything. I just felt it—heard my own thoughts as if the past had been layered under the present, but now was resurfacing.

In a blink of an eye, Carson was in front of me, his expression pinched with concern. "What is it?"

My mouth worked at a reply as my heart sped up. "I shouldn't have been here."

"That night?" he asked.

Nodding, I turned to the tree, running my hand along the rough bark. Touching the tree made me feel like one of those psychics on those TV shows Candy had been talking about, but I just knew I'd been here—right here. "I think ... I was hiding behind these trees. It's like I wasn't supposed to be here, but I was. I know that doesn't make sense."

"It's okay." Carson followed me around the tree.

I closed my eyes, but I couldn't *see* anything. "She wanted me here—Cassie. She wanted me to see them together."

"See who, Sam?"

I shook my head in frustration as I opened my eyes. "I don't know, but I think I knew she wanted me to see them—to know. And I know it was a guy—a guy she wanted me to see her with."

Carson took a step back, inhaling sharply. Our eyes met, and the cold feeling was now working its way up my spine now.

He reached out, taking my hand. "Sam, do you know who she was with?"

"No, but I think I have an idea."

The look on his face said he was thinking the same thing I was, and it was terrible—heartbreaking in a way that made me soul-sick and dizzy. Things clicked into place, one tiny disturbing clue after another.

"Del," I whispered.

chapter seventeen

We're meant to be together.

Wasn't that what Del had said? And from the glimpses of his world and my own, there was a lot of expectation revolving around our relationship.

Enough to kill for, so an affair would remain hidden? *Second- or third-generation rich kids, like royalty...*

So many times I'd tried to bring up Cassie, and he'd grown visibly uncomfortable and refused to talk about her. The most recent memory of Cassie asking if she could have Del resurfaced and lingered. Had they been sleeping together, and she wanted me to know? Lured both of us to the cliff, and Del, not knowing I was there, had pushed Cassie?

I felt sick.

The ride back to Carson's house was tense and silent. Both of us were wrapped up in dark thoughts. He parked the truck in the driveway and killed the engine. Facing me, his eyes were somber, lips drawn tight. "I can't believe it. As much as I dislike him, I can't picture him doing something like that."

I didn't want to believe it, either. "Maybe it was an accident."

He ran his hand through his hair. "Okay. If it was an accident, what about you? Did he accidentally push Cassie and then you?"

"I don't know," I whispered around my poor nail. And Cassie falling really didn't make sense the more I thought about it. The very first memory I'd had was of blood on the rocks—the flat sandy-colored rocks that covered the cliff.

"And Del doesn't have the balls to do something like that," Carson said, mostly to himself.

I made a face, but then my heart skipped a beat. "Did I have the balls to do something like that?"

Carson laughed, and then his eyes widened. "You're being serious? You think you pushed her because of Del?" Disbelief colored his tone. "Sam, you're not a murderer. Not now and not then."

"But what if I was mad? What if Del left and I confronted Cassie? And things got out of hand?" The more I thought about it, the more I wanted to vomit. "We were kind of explosive together, right? Maybe *I* accidentally pushed her."

"You didn't do that, Sam." He grabbed my wrist, tugging my hand away from my mouth. "You're not that kind of person. You never were. And besides, it wouldn't explain what happened to you. You push her and then change your mind and jump? It wasn't you."

"That's a good point."

He sighed, letting go of my wrist. "You don't believe it. Why? Because you've been seeing things—because a bunch of stupid kids are saying stuff they don't have any idea about? That doesn't make you crazy, a freak, or a murderer. You're a good person. Don't ever question that."

My chest swelled at his words, and tears filled my eyes. Without thinking, I leaned across the gearshift and placed a brief kiss on his cheek. Carson stiffened for a second before turning his head, bringing his lips oh-so-close. A tremble ran through his body.

"Thank you," I whispered, probably for the hundredth time.

He nodded, throat working as he swallowed hard. "I mean it, Sam. I'm not saying it to just make you feel better."

Each word he spoke caused his lips to graze my cheek, sending a shiver through me. Reluctantly, I pulled back. "I know."

A faint smile appeared. "Can you do me a favor?"

"Anything."

"I really don't think Del could've done something like that, but be careful." His eyes locked on to mine. "Please."

"I will." I didn't want him to worry, but talking with Del was something I had to do. And the faint smile was still on Carson's face, but it never reached his eyes. He was worried, and he had good reason to be. If it hadn't been me, then whoever the killer was had to be worried that I'd get my memories back.

Later that evening, after I'd changed into a pair of comfy sweats and a cropped hoodie that I'd found in the closet, I sat on my bed and took the Tiffany's necklace off. Holding it up so that the ceiling light reflected off the white-gold design, I tried to remember the first time I took it off.

Nothing came to me—no feelings, thoughts. I sighed, laying the necklace on the comforter.

Footsteps in the hall drew my attention. I looked up, seeing the shadow of the body first before the person reached the open door. It wasn't someone I'd expected.

Del.

My breath caught as he stopped in the doorway and leaned against the frame. I had no idea where my parents were, and I was pretty sure Scott was in the basement. "How did you get in here?" I asked.

His brows slanted. "The front door was unlocked."

"And you just let yourself in?" Coldness had crept into my voice without my meaning it to be there.

"Yeah." Confusion was etched across his face as he inched into my bedroom. He was wearing the same dark slacks and button-down shirt he'd donned for the funeral. "Since when has that been . . . the necklace?" He stopped just shy of the bed. "You took it off?"

Scooping it up, I ignored my nervousness. "I was just looking at it."

His eyes flashed, not nearly as glassy as they'd been at the barn, but the scent of alcohol was still wafting from him. "I left the party."

"Oh?" I held the heart tightly, the metal biting into the fleshly part of my palm.

"You're pissed. I know." He sat on the edge of the bed, twisting his midsection so he was facing me. His eyes were glued on my hand. "Veronica and Candy were just messing with you."

My brows rose. "*Messing* with me? And you just..." I trailed off. What he did or didn't do wasn't the problem here or what was even important. "Del—"

"I didn't do anything. I know. And I should've made them stop." He took a breath, rubbing the heel of his hand over his jaw. "I'm sorry. I don't like seeing you embarrassed and hurt."

I blew out a tired breath as I studied him. I couldn't help but see him and Cassie together, but could he have been responsible for all this? My instinct told me no, but how could I really trust that? And that wasn't even the reason for why this needed to end.

Letting out a sigh, he sprawled across my bed, on his side. "Don't you like the necklace, Sammy? If not, I can buy you a new one—something better ... with sapphires? They're your favorite stone. Well, they were...."

My fingers loosened around the necklace. "I don't need a new necklace."

He looked up at me, his eyes full of uncertainty. "Then tell me what I need to do to make you happy. I can take you to that restaurant in Philly that does the sushi the way you like it. Or we can spend the weekend at the Poconos. I'm sure your parents will be okay with that."

I winced. There wasn't anything he could do. Lies about our relationship and my suspicions aside, this was coming. I knew days ago that I needed to end things with him. I just didn't feel what I should when we were together. My breath didn't catch.

There wasn't a soft flutter in my chest. My stomach didn't get tipsy just hearing his name. Those were all things that I felt for another boy . . . and that was just wrong.

Del must've seen it in my eyes because he sat up, searching my face intently. "We can make this work."

"I don't think we can," I said softly.

He looked away, shaking his head slightly. "Is it because of what happened today?"

"N-no, not . . . not really," I stuttered. Had I done this before? If so, did I suck as badly at it then as I did now? "I'm sorry. I really am. I just don't—"

"We can work on this." He turned to me again, eyes so dark they almost looked black. "You just need more time."

I met his stare. "Time isn't going to change anything. I don't feel that way for you. We'd make good friends, but—"

"I don't want to be friends with you." He jerked back, eyes widening. "I can't believe you're doing this after everything."

This hurt more than I had expected. I wrapped my fingers around his wrist and turned his hand over.

"Don't," he whispered. "Sammy, don't do this. . . ."

Wetness gathered in my eyes as I placed my hand over his, pressing the necklace into his open palm. The moment my hand touched his, I shuddered. The memory came on so quickly it left me spinning. A dull gray film dropped over my eyes.

"Don't you dare act like this is my fault!" I screamed.

"I'm not acting like anything! Jesus." He flopped back on his bed, grabbing the remote control. "I don't know why you're making such a big deal out of this. You had fun while you were doing it."

Tears clouded my eyes as I looked down. Humiliation didn't even cover it as I thumbed through the photos on his phone. Pictures all linked to text messages he'd sent Trey, who in turn had sent them to everyone.

I sat on the edge of the bed. I was so stupid, so freaking stupid. I wanted to die.

He nudged me in the back with his bare foot. "Don't be upset with me over this, okay?"

Don't be upset? *Everyone had seen these pictures. No wonder Veronica looked like she'd scored the entire spring Prada line this morning. And I bet Cassie was just thrilled. In that moment I hated them all.*

Muttering under his breath, Del sat and wrapped his arms around my waist. "Look, all the guys think it's hot as hell. They're jealous of me."

I stiffened. All the guys *... The entire baseball team had been sending these pictures back and forth. Mortification squeezed my chest, stealing my breath. My brother had seen me doing ... doing this? So had Carson?*

I shrugged off his embrace and stood. "Don't touch me."

Del rolled his eyes. "Whatever."

"I can't believe you did that." I threw his cell phone. It hit the hardwood floor, bounced once, and then cracked. A sick sense of justice filled me when the screen went gray.

Del shot off the bed, grabbing his phone. "Damn it, Sammy! Do you have any idea how much this cost me?"

"Do you know how much that embarrassed me?" I fingered the heart at the end of the necklace. "Or do you even care?"

He looked up, eyes narrowed. Tossing the phone aside, he stalked toward me. "You shouldn't have done that."

Swallowing, I backed up. "I hate you," I whispered.

"No, you don't." He grabbed my hand, squeezing so that the heart dug

*into my palm. I winced. "And don't pull your little 'I'm going to break up
with you' bullshit. You know you're not. So just get over it."*

I was sucked out of the memory because I couldn't breathe.
Del's arms were around me, holding me tight against his chest. I
could feel his heart pounding as fast as mine.

"Sammy, say something," he said. "Damn it, are you okay?"

Hot rage swelled inside me. The mysterious pictures my
mom had referenced had been explained. My voice came out a
broken whisper. "Don't touch me."

He stilled against me. "Sammy..."

The anger warmed me from inside, sharp and explosive.
"Don't touch me!" I screamed, breaking free of his suddenly lax
hold. Jumping from the bed, I backed away from him, my chest
rising and falling unsteadily. "You took pictures of me doing *that*
to you?"

Del's mouth dropped open as shock flitted across his face.
"You remember?"

"How could you?" I demanded, the humiliation washing
over me as if it had happened yesterday. Everyone had seen those
pictures. *Everyone.* "How could I've been okay with that? What the
hell was wrong with me? I can't believe I stayed with you. Jesus."

"Do you remember everything?" He stood, taking a step
toward me.

"Don't come near me!" I took another step back, hitting the
wall. "I don't need to remember anything else. That was enough."

Relief shone in his eyes so quickly that I thought I'd imagined it. A keen sense of wariness was there now. "Sammy, you
forgave me for that."

I laughed harshly. "Then I'm an idiot, because from what I remember, I wasn't happy about it."

He dragged a hand through his hair, tugging at the ends. "It wasn't my fault. Trey got ahold of my phone and saw the pictures. He sent them to himself, and then it just went crazy from there."

"Like that's supposed to make it better?" I strove to keep myself from kicking him right between the legs. "Did I know you took those pictures, Del? And don't you dare lie to me!"

Del looked away, and that told me everything. Disgust rolled through me, and I clung to it. Better than the self-loathing lurking underneath it. How could I have stayed with him after such a betrayal? And I had a feeling that he was right—I had forgiven him.

I wanted to hurl.

"Get out of here," I said, voice shaking.

His head whipped back to me. "You're overreacting. You just need to calm down. We can—"

"There's no 'we' in anything! This whole 'I'm breaking up with you' bullshit is for real this time." Del took another step forward, and I screamed, "Get out!"

"Sammy, I'm sorry. It was wrong what I did. I get that. But we can talk about this."

A wicked sense of déjà vu hit me. How many times had we been in this same position? He'd do something. I'd get mad. We'd fight. Rinse and repeat. But this time was different—I was different.

"Please leave," I said, much calmer.

He opened his mouth, but footsteps pounded through

the hallway. A second later, Scott rushed the doorway, cheeks flushed. He glanced at Del and then me.

"What the hell is going on in here?" he demanded.

Annoyance crossed Del's features. "This isn't any of your business."

My brother stepped into the room, his hands closing into fists. "Are you serious?" He glanced at me, eyes bright and furious. "Why were you yelling, Sam?"

"I want him to leave," I said, folding my arms.

A grim smile appeared on Scott's face. "Then you'd better be leaving, Del."

Anger replaced the annoyance, and I was reminded of the rage behind the desperation in my first memory of him. I knew being turned down wasn't something Del was accustomed to.

"Don't do this, Sammy," he said with that same look.

I didn't understand why he even wanted to make this work, but it didn't matter. I wasn't backing down. Even before the memory resurfaced I had my mind made up. This just cemented my decision. "Please leave."

Del took one step toward me, and that was it.

My brother shot across the room, moving like a streak of lightning. There was a brief second when I wasn't sure what he was going to do, and then I saw him cock back his arm. His fist crashed into Del's face, and the boy went down like a sack of potatoes, smacking on the floor with a heavy thud.

Scott lowered his fist. "You have no idea how long I've wanted to do that."

chapter eighteen

I'd waited downstairs while Scott revived Del and then got him out of the house. It turned out Scott had been in the basement the entire time, and he'd locked the front door behind him when he'd come home. Meaning Del had lied again and most likely had a key. First thing on my to-do list was to get it back from him.

Scott advised me to leave that up to him.

"Are you going to tell me what happened?" he asked, grabbing a bag of frozen peas out of the freezer.

I sat down at the bar, feeling my cheeks burn. "I remembered something."

"Something big enough for you to kick his ass to the curb." He plopped the bag down on his red knuckles and winced. "Do tell."

"Well, I was already going to break up with him before I remembered."

He sat across from me, brows raised. "Does this have anything to do with Car?"

"No!" My cheeks burned even brighter.

"Okay." A grin appeared on his lips. "So what's the deal?"

Chewing on my pinkie nail, I shrugged. "Things aren't the same between us. So I'd decided to call things off. When I gave him back the necklace, I remembered...something that had happened."

His brows inched up his forehead.

I sighed. "He took... *pictures.*"

Scott scrunched up his face, as if he was about to vomit on me. "Those pictures..."

There went any hope that he hadn't seen them or heard about them. I dropped my head on the counter and sighed. "It's so embarrassing. I had no idea! I mean, I didn't know he'd taken them at all, and supposedly Trey found them and sent them, but still."

Scott cursed. "You didn't know he took them?"

"No," I moaned.

Another explosive curse caused me to jump a little. "I asked you about those pictures, Sam, because I was pissed. You acted like it was no big deal. If I'd known, I would've knocked him the hell out a lot sooner."

I raised my arms helplessly, keeping my face planted on the counter. "Yeah, well, apparently I got over it."

Several seconds passed before he spoke. "I think I'm going to bust his other eye."

As much as that made me all warm and fuzzy inside, I lifted my head. "You can't. Just leave him alone. It's over with—we're over." I covered my face with my hands. "Man, how can I show my face?"

"Sam, that happened, like, seven months ago."

"So? I just remembered it." I groaned again. "This is horrible."

"Everyone has forgotten about it, considering everything else," he said gently.

"Yeah, because they think I *killed* Cassie or I'm crazy." I dropped my hands. Scott watched me, appearing to be caught between amusement and sympathy. I scowled at him and then saw how badly his knuckles were swelling under the bag. "Does it hurt?"

He shrugged. "Worth it."

"Thank you," I said, shifting on the stool. "I know I was a shitty sister—"

"Stop." He waved his uninjured hand, staring at the bag. "Back to the whole everyone-thinking-you-killed-Cassie thing. Julie told me what the girls were saying at the party today. You know they're just being dumb. No one thinks that."

I gave him a bland look. He changed the subject to what Carson and I had done when we left the barn. When I told him about going up to the cliff to see if it would spark my memory, he looked as if he wanted to knock the bag of peas upside my head.

"The cliff is dangerous," he grumbled, standing. Taking the bag to the trash can, he turned back. "You shouldn't be up there."

I frowned. "Why not? It might help me remember."

He threw the peas away and slowly opened his fist. "Why do you need to remember? It's not going to change anything. Cassie will still be dead."

"I know that," I said, unsure why he was so against it. "But I need to know what happened. It probably wasn't an accident, and she deserves justice."

Scott rolled his eyes. "Cassie deserved a lot of things."

My mouth dropped open. "Scott! That's not cool."

He returned the look I gave him earlier. "*You* don't remember her. *You* have no clue how messed up she was. And *you* were fine until you started hanging out with her. Sorry if I'm not all torn up." He paused, exhaling roughly. "Okay, that wasn't right." He lifted his eyes to the ceiling. "Sorry, Cassie, wherever you are."

I slid off the stool. "I need to know the truth. It's, like, closure. I can't move on until then."

His eyes met mine for a few seconds, and then he raised his brows, not in a mocking way but more out of concern. "What if the truth isn't to your liking, Sam? What if it only makes everything worse?"

That was the million-dollar question. The feeling of having done something wrong resurfaced, wrapping itself around my insides, tightening until I was sure I was going to have some epic ulcers soon.

"Then I'll have to deal with it," I said finally, sitting back down. "But I need to know. Good or bad."

Scott looked away, his teeth sinking into his bottom lip. I could tell this conversation upset him, and I knew he was worried that all my poking around would eventually stir up something that I wouldn't be able to deal with. I sought to change the subject.

"So Dad's not home?" I asked, and he shook his head. "He's never really home, is he?"

"He's probably at the office. He stays there a lot." He dropped into the seat next to me and rested his chin on his good hand. "Comes home late."

"And Mom is always in bed?" I twisted toward him.

"She's pretty much hiding in her bedroom, but yes."

"Has it always been like this?"

Scott's brows rose as he seemed to think the question over. "For the last five or so years it has been. They barely even speak to each other or stay in the same room longer than a few minutes."

I lowered my gaze. "Why are they still together?"

"You want a serious answer to that?" When I nodded, he laughed under his breath. "Before this happened to you, you knew why."

"I did?"

He nodded. "Mom's not going to divorce Dad because of what people would say, unless staying married to him was worse somehow. Dad knows that, and he'll never leave Mom, because, well, she owns him."

I frowned. "Owns him?"

"He has nothing without Mom." He laughed, but it was dry. "All our money is on her side, and I'm sure there was a nasty little prenup that means she gets everything if they divorce and he keeps what he had when he entered the marriage, which wasn't much."

"But Dad works." I shook my head. "Even if they divorced, he'd have all the money from that."

Scott smirked. "You're forgetting one important little factoid about that. Dad works for Mom's side of the family. If they get a divorce he'll be out, and our grandfather has enough pull to make it very difficult for him to get another job at that kind of level in a funding firm."

"Damn," I whispered.

"Yep. I'd rather be homeless and living in a box if I were him, but Dad likes his lifestyle. He didn't give a shit about what other people thought when we were younger, but now . . . he knows Mom does, so he'll put up with anything to keep her."

I sat back. "Oh."

After that, Scott and I parted ways. I went back upstairs and closed the door behind me. Exhausted from everything that had happened in the last twenty-four hours, I just wanted to sleep. My brain was still slowly turning over all that I'd learned, and even with the memory of the pictures resurfacing, I knew there was still more to my relationship with Del. That there had to be a good reason why I'd stayed with him after something like that. I could think of a few people who could give me brutal insight on our relationship, but outside of them, those who'd actually talk to me about it was limited.

Had Del and I been on the same path as our parents? Marrying because it was expected and for money? That didn't make sense, because both of us would have access to our own funds.

I headed into the bathroom and picked up my toothbrush, catching sight of my reflection in the mirror. Dark smudges had blossomed under my eyes. As I spurted a dab of toothpaste on the toothbrush, I looked away for a second, maybe two.

Cassie stared back at me, with mirroring shadows under her eyes.

Gasping, I jerked back. The darkness under her eyes spread across otherwise flawless cheeks, following the path of her veins, as if someone had injected her with ink. I couldn't look away as she opened her mouth in a silent scream that raised the tiny hairs all over my body.

Not real. This can't be real. I squeezed my eyes shut, counted to ten, and then reopened them. The image in the mirror was my own.

Breathing heavily, I planted my hands on the sink and dipped my head, dizzy and nauseated. Several moments passed before I felt sure I wasn't going to vomit.

I tossed the toothbrush into the basin and left the bathroom, shaken to the core. Pulling back the covers, I started to climb in when I saw the edge of something yellow sticking out from underneath the music box on the nightstand.

Heart tumbling over itself, I sat down and reached over, picking up the box. A yellow piece of paper folded into a triangle stared back at me. A huge part of me wanted to put the box back down and cover it completely.

Instead, with my breath caught in my chest, I picked up the note and then set the music box down. My fingers were numb as I unfolded it, revealing the childish scribble.

Don't let <u>him</u> know you remember anything.

Don't let him know you remember anything?

Let who know? The question kept me up most of the night even though I was exhausted. And there was still a bigger question—who was leaving the notes and why?

When morning came, I could barely pull myself out of bed and take a shower. The ride to school with Carson and Scott was quiet, but I figured that wouldn't last long.

And I was right.

Whispers and long looks greeted me the moment I stepped through the double doors. News of my accident and subsequent barn-party fail had reached those who hadn't been at the party. Everyone seemed to know about the guy in the backseat who couldn't have possibly been there.

When I headed to my locker, I spotted Del at the end of the hall. He looked as if he'd gone toe-to-toe with a professional boxer and lost.

His entire left eye was swollen shut, the skin covered with a purplish-blue bruise that looked painful. He was getting a lot of stares, too.

Keeping my head down, I quickly grabbed my morning books and hurried in the opposite direction.

I didn't make it.

"Sammy," Del called out, not too far behind me.

With my heart in my throat, I kept walking. The last thing I needed was a scene. People had enough reasons to talk about me.

"Damn it," he grunted, catching up to me by the stairwell. Grabbing my arm, he pulled me to a stop. "Are you just going to ignore me?"

I turned around, sucking in a sharp breath. Up close, the black eye was worse, but there was something glinting in his one good eye. Something that chilled my insides, made me want to run.

"We need to talk," he said, voice low.

I shook my head. "There's nothing to talk about."

He leaned in, his head inches from mine. There was a minty scent on his breath. "You at least owe me a chance to explain, especially after what your brother did."

Any feelings of dread I had were quickly replaced by irritation, and I tore my arm free, not caring what people thought. I *owed* him? "I don't owe you anything, Del."

He exhaled. "I know you're mad, and I get that, but all I want to do is talk to you. You can't just break up with me and have that be it. You don't get to make a call like that without giving me the chance to fix it."

My mouth gaped as I took a step back, hitting the edge of a glass case full of plaques and metals. "Look, I'm sorry. Maybe Scott shouldn't have hit you, but this is my choice. I don't need your permission."

His jaw popped out. "That's not what I meant. I know you don't need my permission. You're twisting what I'm saying."

Across from us, a few kids had their phones out, texting away. My heart sank a little, knowing that by the beginning of first period, this would be all over the damn school. "Del, I don't want to talk about this. Maybe later—"

"Later? You promise?" He grabbed ahold of my hand again.

"Tell me you promise, and I'll believe you. Okay? Because out of everyone, I have your back, Sammy. You just don't realize that."

I opened my mouth, but nothing came out. The desperation he threw off covered my skin like a slimy, dirty substance. Why was he so frantic to salvage this relationship? It wasn't great before, and it sure as hell wasn't something worth fighting for now that I'd lost my memories.

"Is everything okay here?" Mrs. Messer's voice came out of nowhere. "Samantha?"

Del dropped my hand, and I turned, swallowing. "Yeah, everything is fine."

Her dark eyes settled on him. "And you?"

He nodded, taking a step back. "Everything is great."

"Then I suggest you get to class," she responded coolly.

With him facing me, Del's one-sided smile looked wrong with the black eye. "*Later.*"

I said nothing as he pivoted and stalked off. The icky feeling was still coating my skin, seeping through. Clenching the strap on my bag, I shuddered.

"Is everything really okay, Samantha?" Mrs. Messer asked softly, coming to stop beside me.

Nodding, I worked to keep my voice level. "Yes. We were just talking."

Her gaze didn't miss anything. "Is the condition of his face something I should be concerned about?"

"No," I said, shaking my head. "I have to go."

Mrs. Messer nodded. "I'll see you tomorrow morning."

There was no escaping our meetings, but it was better than the alternative—an honest-to-God real psychiatrist. Hurrying to homeroom, I slid into my seat seconds before the bell rang. The first two classes weren't bad. It was the next class, English, that I was dreading.

Veronica was waiting for me when I walked in and headed for where I'd been sitting since I returned to school. She stuck out one thin arm, blocking me. "You can't sit here."

For a moment I entertained the idea of grabbing her by her overprocessed hair and dragging her to the floor. "Why?" I demanded.

She twisted her lips into a frigid smile that was oddly familiar. Candy snickered from her seat. "Mr. Dase?" Candy raised her voice, waving her arm back and forth. "Mr. Dase?"

The teacher looked up from the stack of paper on his desk and let out a loud sigh. "Yes, Candy?"

"Can you make Sammy sit somewhere else?" she implored. "We don't feel comfortable sitting here with her."

Fire scorched my cheeks as a dozen or so faces turned to me. One stood out the most—Goth Boy. I expected him to look pleased that I was getting paid back for the years of abuse I'd put him through. Instead, his almond-shaped eyes just looked sad behind the spikes of black hair.

Mr. Dase raised his brows. "Why don't you feel comfortable, Candy?"

"It's okay," I said, hating the way my voice trembled as I headed to an open seat in the back. "I can sit back here."

Satisfied with the resolution, he went back to shuffling his papers, but out of the corner of my eyes, I saw Veronica shoot Candy a pointed look.

"Mr. Dase," Candy whined, waving her arm again.

Taking my seat, I gripped the edges of my desk.

"Yes?" Mr. Dase sighed.

Candy sat up straight, pushing her chest out and arching her back. "I don't like that she's sitting behind me." Her voice dropped to a stage whisper. "You do know she was the last person to see Cassie alive, right?"

My knuckles ached from how tight my grip was on the desk. Okay. That was it. There was a good chance I would hurt one or both of them.

Our teacher's expression remained bland. "I am sure you're perfectly safe where you are."

He then moved on to roll call, and that quieted Candy down, but the damage was already done. Stewing with anger and embarrassment, I had no idea what was covered in class. When the bell rang, I had to force myself to walk out of the class without confronting them. Their laughter followed me through most of my classes.

In bio, I figured Candy would keep quiet without Veronica being there, and I wondered if that had been me once—calling the shots like Veronica. Making the other girls do terrible, mean things out of spite and boredom.

I was now a strong believer in karma.

My crappy day got a little better when Carson came into

class. The smile on my face wasn't forced or weak. It was big and stupid—real.

He didn't smile back as he sat beside me, and I felt the happy little feeling deflate. "Why did Scott give Del a black eye? He won't tell me why."

"Oh." Not what I'd expected. Glancing up at the front of the class, I could tell that Candy was trying to listen. Squeezing my pen to keep myself from turning it into a weapon of mass destruction, I kept my voice low. "Del didn't really do anything."

"He didn't?" His voice was dangerously soft. "Because I'm thinking the worst here, and if so, he'll have a matching eye by the end of the day."

My eyes widened. "No—no, nothing like that. I broke up with him, and then I had this memory about something he did. We kind of got into it after that, and he wouldn't leave. Scott sort of took care of that."

"What do you mean, he wouldn't leave?" Anger shone from his blue eyes, along with a fierce protectiveness that had me wanting to smile like an idiot.

"It's not a big deal, really. Everything is fine now." With the exception of Del thinking he could somehow renegotiate our relationship status.

Carson didn't look too convinced, but he scooted closer, pressing his knee against mine. "What did you remember?"

"Uh, it's really embarrassing."

"I can deal." He grinned.

My lips twitched. "I'm sure you can, but I'm not confident that I can." I watched him as he waited, sighing when I realized he wasn't going to let it drop. "I'm sure you already know. It has to do with...photos on a phone."

One brow arched, and then he leaned back as he figured it out. "Would this be something that happened around seven months ago?"

I nodded as my entire face turned warm. "Yeah, well, I had no idea he'd taken those photos when...it was happening." Focusing on the back of Candy's head, I continued almost painfully. "I don't know why I forgave him when it happened. I can't even wrap my head around it. It's disgusting."

"So you weren't okay with it?"

"Not from what I do remember. I was pretty pissed." I peeked at him from underneath my lashes. "So...you saw them?"

He watched me for a ridiculously long time. A brief, indiscernible emotion flickered across his face. "I saw them."

"Great." I tucked a strand of my hair back, searching for a much-needed change in subject. "I got another note last night, after Del left."

"What did it say?" He sounded relieved by the topic change, too.

I pulled the note out, showing him. Again, another unclear expression appeared as he read it. "It would be nice to know who 'him' is," he said, folding it and handing it back over. "Who do you think is leaving these notes?"

"I don't know," I whispered, shoving the note back into my bag. "It would have to be someone who has access to my house. That really limits the whole pool of suspects."

Carson agreed, and we didn't have any more time left to

discuss potential candidates. Class started, and we had to examine cell growth in plants under a shared microscope. Tingles shot up my arm every time our hands brushed when we exchanged slides.

After class, he walked to my locker with me, waiting until I was ready to head to the cafeteria. I wasn't sure if he was keeping an eye out for Del or if he had been as unwilling as I'd been to leave bio.

As we neared the doors and crowded room, I stopped. "I'll be there in a few minutes."

"Okay." He looked reluctant to head in, but I smiled and then he nodded, went around me, and disappeared.

I waited for the one person I'd hoped would be up-front with me, ignoring the looks of those passing by me. I spied Julie up ahead. Her long skirt flowed around her ankles as she strode down the hall. Her lips spread into a smile when she saw me, but it quickly faded when I grabbed her arm.

"Hey," she said, glancing around. "What's up?"

"Can we talk somewhere private?"

Julie's ponytail bobbed as she nodded. "We could go to the computer lab. No one is in there during lunch."

Perfect. I followed her down the hall, past the library, and into the cold, silent lab. She dropped her bag in a chair. "What's going on?"

I took a deep breath and then said something I should've said days, if not weeks, ago. "Not to be all twelve-step program on you, but first off, I'm sorry for whatever I might have done or said to you." I felt the heat creeping across my cheeks. "It wasn't right for a multitude of reasons, and I have this feeling that you were probably the only true friend I had and I screwed that up." Julie hesitated. "Sam, I could take up an entire week listing all the shit you've pulled, but seriously? You're not the same. When Scott first told me you... you changed, I didn't believe him, but I saw that it was true the day you sat at the table, and it's still true. In the way you talk, how you carry yourself and look at people. You remind me of how you used to be, and that's good enough of an apology. Anyway, it's in the past. I'm over it."

Tears rushed to my eyes. It wasn't much of a forgiveness speech, but it was close, and I'd take it. "Okay. I want to ask you something, and I want you to be honest."

Taking ahold of her ponytail, she started twisting the end around her fingers. "All right."

"I remembered something last night, about Del and me. He'd taken these photos of me—"

"The ones where you were giving him a blow job like a porn star?"

I grimaced. "Yeah, thanks, but I hadn't known he was taking them. I must've heard about them after the fact and blown up."

"You didn't know?" She leaned against the edge of the desk, eyes narrowed. "What an ass."

"My thoughts exactly." I propped myself against the table beside her. "But I forgave him, and I don't know why I would have. I was hoping you could tell me... what I was like when I dated Del."

"Oh, wow." Julie blinked. "Honestly?"

I nodded.

She gave a short laugh. "I'm not even sure if you really loved him or if you two were sort of expected to be together. Your families are, like, the richest in the county. You both were popular and good-looking. It was assumed you two would get together. . . . Well, either you or Cassie when her mother moved back, but I don't think anyone really thought that until she got older."

"Did she want to date Del?"

"She wanted everything that you had, if you ask me." She continued winding the hair around her hand. "It was freaky, honestly, how much she tried to be like you. I always thought she was two seconds from going *Single White Female* on your ass. So did Scott."

"So you think I was with Del only because everyone expected us to be together?" My brain rebelled against the idea. All the reasons she'd listed were so damn shallow it was pathetic.

"I think so." She twisted toward me, tilting her head to the side. "When we were younger, in middle school, you had the biggest crush on Carson."

My stomach tightened at his name.

"You two hung out so much, but then Cassie came into the picture," she said, almost sadly. "And then Del."

Shame and guilt swirled in my stomach, and I lowered my chin. "I don't understand where I went wrong. How I could just dump people and be okay with what Del did?"

"I don't think you were ever okay with it. You acted like you were." She sighed. "But I knew better. You were embarrassed when the pics started getting sent around. And it pissed me off so much that you acted like it was okay. It was so passive, and I wanted to hit you. Seriously."

"You probably should have."

Jules laughed. "I'll keep that in mind."

I smiled. "It couldn't have just been Cassie and Del that changed me."

"I don't think it was." She pushed way from the table. "I think your mom had a lot to do with it. She hated our friendship because I'm not in a country club or whatever." She rolled her eyes. "And God knows she hates that Scott loves me. Your dad seems cool with it, or at least he's good at pretending that he is. Anyway, you became just like your mom. I really don't know how Scott turned out so different." She let go of her ponytail, flinging it over her shoulder as she grabbed her bag. "You acted like your parents, Sam. They'd do anything to make themselves look good. Even if it meant lying to save face, which is what you did when the pics went live. You acted just like them, and I'm sure that if your mom thought she could get away with killing me and stashing my body somewhere to ensure her son was no longer dating a commoner, she would."

I wanted to laugh, but I wasn't sure if she was joking or not.

chapter nineteen

Mom was waiting for me when I got home after
school, crystal wine goblet in hand. From the
displeased twist of her lips, I knew this wasn't
going to be good. Going to the small sitting room, I dropped my
bag on the couch and flopped down.

She followed. "Del's mother called me this afternoon."

Picking up a magazine, I pretended to have no idea what she
was talking about. "Did you guys have a nice chat?"

"Not really," she said, sitting in the leather chair. "She told
me that Scott hit him? And that you broke up with him? I assured
her that all this must be a misunderstanding."

I made a face. "Are you not even curious why Scott hit him?"
I watched her sip from her glass and felt a surge of anger. "He
wouldn't leave. That was after I tried to break up with him and
found out about *those* pictures, Mom."

Her hand trembled as she set the glass down on the small
table beside her. "Samantha . . ."

Twisting toward her, I wanted her to understand where I was coming from. Maybe I wanted her to see me for who I was now. "Mom, I didn't know he took those pictures. And I wasn't okay with it."

She blinked, smoothing her linen pants with a hand. "That's good to know. I'd hate to believe that you were okay with something so . . . trashy."

Trashy wasn't the only word I would have gone for. *Disgusting. Violating.* "Then you have to understand why I can't be with him."

"Honey, what he did was wrong, but he made a mistake. Everyone does."

Shocked into silence, I stared at her.

Running her fingers along the gold bangles circling her wrists, she sat straight and stiff in the seat. "Your father—he's made mistakes. And we wouldn't have been married for so long if neither of us learned how to forgive."

Gradually, I came out of my stupor. "Del took pictures of me giving him a blow—"

"I understand that, Samantha." Her nose wrinkled. "But this incident happened so long ago. And I'm sure he feels terrible about it. He *has* to feel terrible about it."

"I really don't care if he feels terrible," I admitted, and wondered if I should feel bad for that. "I can't believe you'd ever be okay with me being with him after that."

My mom sighed. "I'm not okay with the fact that he did that, Samantha, but he's young and he's a male. God knows this won't be the last stupid choice he makes in his life."

"It will be the last stupid choice he makes that involves me!"

She ignored that. "You have every reason to be upset with him. I don't blame you for that, but I think you should talk with him. His mom and I were saying that after...well, after everything, both of you could use some time to get reacquainted without all these outside influences confusing you."

I thought there was a good chance that when I had left school that day, I had veered straight into crazy land. Part of me wanted to laugh at the absurdity of my mom defending Del for doing something so vile, but the other part of me, the huge part, was stuck somewhere between being ticked off and being disturbed.

"Outside influences confusing me?" I said finally.

She nodded. "Well, with Cassie and your memory, it's understandable that it would take some time before you—"

"Why do you want me to be with Del so badly?" I cut her off. "I don't get it. Is this normal? Do moms usually get this involved?"

Something flashed in her eyes, gone too quickly before I could name it. "It's important to your father and me that you are involved with someone who can take care of you and is of your same...stature."

There was more to it. I knew it, but like everything else, it was too far out of reach. Uncertain if it even mattered, I let it drop. "Mom, I'm not getting back with Del. I'm pretty much disgusted with him on a cellular level."

Picking up her glass, she watched me over the rim. "You haven't been spending any time with your friends."

"My friends are assholes."

"Samantha!" she exclaimed, staring at me as if I'd brandished a knife.

I fought a smile. "It's true. And you can forget about me patching things up with them, too."

"I think you're exaggerating." She finished off her glass and smiled. It didn't crack the cool beauty of her face. "You always had a tendency to do that."

"They're calling me Insanity Sam and insinuating that I had something to do with what happened to Cassie." Mom flinched. Maybe I should've softened the blow of my social downfall. Too late now. "So, yeah, I'm not exaggerating."

She opened her mouth but seemed to think twice before speaking. I studied her in this rare moment when she actually appeared to be thinking something instead of drinking and being disappointed with me.

I stiffened.

As soon as the last thought had formed, I felt that wave of familiarity and a surge of distress. At once I knew I'd been in this position before with her. Not wanting her to be disappointed and not knowing how to make that happen or if I even could make it happen.

Stupid tears burned the back of my eyes, and I cast my gaze down. Her free hand was closed in a fist. Her knuckles were white. My throat tightened. "I know you're disappointed—"

"No, honey, I'm not." She rose and sat beside me, but I still didn't look up, because I wasn't sure if she was lying.

And like a piece of a puzzle clicking together, I suddenly knew her disappointment wasn't directed just at me, but at herself, too. It was something that I must've known before that night on the cliff.

"Honey, I just want the best for you. That's all." She paused, brushing a sheet of my hair back from my face. "And you're heading down a path I'm not sure is going to be best for you. Breaking up with Del, alienating your friends..."

I shook my head. "Those were the right decisions, Mom."

She hesitated. "And you've been hanging out with Carson a lot, haven't you?"

My head jerked up, and she quickly removed her hand. "So?"

"His father is cleaning your father's office for extra money, Samantha. Not exactly dating material."

"Well, I'm not dating his father, now, am I?" I snapped. This whole argument was ridiculous. "I'm not even dating Carson."

"But you like him."

"Yes. I do like him, Mom. I don't get why you have such a problem with that. You married Dad!" Her eyes widened. I had her. "He didn't have money."

"Your father was at Yale when I met him. That was different."

"How so?" I demanded. "He still didn't have money, and Carson is going to Penn State."

She didn't answer immediately, and when she did, it was not what I'd expected. "Your father...he swept me off my feet, Samantha." A far-off look came to her eyes, and the mask she wore slipped away. I could almost imagine what she must've been like when she met my dad. "We met on accident, at a party, and he wasn't like any guy I was used to. And because of where he went to college, I assumed...well, I assumed he was like me. My father wasn't happy when the truth came out, and maybe I should've..."

Maybe she should've listened to her father? Mom didn't say

that, but I knew that was what she was thinking, and I wasn't sure how to really respond to that.

Taking a small breath, she shook her head. "You deserve someone who can give you the world, someone who can stand on his own. Do you understand me?"

I think I did. "But money doesn't give you the world, Mom. Not everything."

She opened her mouth, but a door creaked somewhere in the house. My father's footsteps were heavy and quick. Mom turned to the door, and the moment he entered, his dark brows furrowed and jaw clenched, I knew this was bad.

"What is it, Steven?" Mom asked, standing, once more cool and aloof as ever.

Dad glanced at her and then me. His hair looked as if he'd run his fingers through it a lot, like it had been the day he walked into the hospital room. "Joanna, I don't want you to panic. Everything is going to be okay. This is just procedure."

She folded her thin arms across her chest. "That isn't a very reassuring opening statement."

"We need to take Samantha down to the police station," he said, his gaze darting back to me, and he smiled. My throat dried. "Detective Ramirez has questions, and Lincoln is already there waiting."

The buzzing in my ears canceled out whatever my mom said. Lincoln was the family lawyer.

I swallowed hard as I stood on weak legs. "Dad," I croaked.

He was in front of me, clasping my shoulders gently. "It's okay. They just want to ask you questions."

"But they've already asked me questions, over and over. And they never made me go down *there* before." I peered over his shoulder. Mom had drifted off to the side, her fingers pressed against each of her temples.

"I don't want her going in there alone," Mom said, surprising me. "I will go—"

"No." Dad's shoulders squared. "Stay here. I will handle this."

"But why do I have to go there?" I asked.

Again, he tried to smile. "Because that's how they do things by the book, honey. It's better if we seem as if we have nothing to hide."

"We don't have anything to hide." Before, when Ramirez had been here, my father hadn't been the least bit willing to discuss anything with the detective. Something had changed.

The interrogation room was nothing like what I'd seen on all the television shows. There wasn't a one-way glass mirror, just a really small room with four walls devoid of any decorations and a table with three chairs.

Thomas Lincoln, lawyer extraordinaire, sat beside me. Detective Ramirez studied us from across the table. There was a notepad in front of him and a pen he kept twitching in his hand. I couldn't stop staring at it. In front of my lawyer was the warrant for the search that was taking place right now. Cops were combing the house, messing with my mom's fine china.

She was probably stroking out right now.

I knew I was close to doing the same, especially when Dad

stayed outside the room. He was allowed in, but Lincoln strongly advised against it.

All I could think about were those notes, but they were in my bag, which was with me. How in the world could I explain them if they decided to search that? Oh yeah, I have no idea who's leaving these notes, but they're weird, right? Yeah, not good.

"Are you going to read Samantha her rights?" Lincoln asked, leaning back in his chair.

Ramirez tapped the pen off the pad. "I only have a few questions, and unless Miss Franco admits to anything, I don't see the need for that."

Hope sparked in my chest.

"Oh, I see. You just wanted her out of the house so it could be searched," Lincoln said. "Then, if you find something, she's already here."

My hope crashed and burned a fiery death.

The detective ignored that, turning his dark, tired eyes on me. I doubted they had a lot of teenage murder suspects around here. It had to be getting to him. "Before I get to some questions that I have, has there been anything that you've remembered or discovered since the last time we talked?"

Telling Ramirez that my friends and ex-boyfriend were asshats probably wasn't what he was looking for. "Nothing," I said, telling only a half lie. Anything that I'd remembered wasn't concrete and hardly made any sense. "But I've been trying. I've gone to Cassie's house and—"

Lincoln touched my arm. "Samantha, you don't have to tell him that."

I sat back and folded my arms.

Ramirez glanced at the lawyer, his nostrils flaring as if he smelled something bad. "Miss Franco, you can finish."

"I suggest you don't," Lincoln said.

Confused, I glanced between the two men. "It's not a big deal. I went to Cassie's house once, and I even went to the lake and the cliff." Lincoln stiffened beside me, but seriously, I hadn't done anything wrong by going to those places. "I was hoping they'd spark some kind of memory, but they didn't."

"Why did you think they would?" Ramirez asked.

"My guidance counselor told me I should surround myself with familiar things, but it hasn't been working."

"Interesting," he murmured. "Did you go there alone?"

I locked up. "I went to the lake by myself."

"And that's when you had the car accident?" When I nodded, he scribbled something down. "And the other times? Were you alone?"

The need to lie, to protect Carson, seemed irrational, but I didn't want to bring his name up. However, Cassie's grandfather had been there. "My friend went with me to Cassie's house and back to the cliff."

"And who was that?"

I chewed on my nail. "Carson Ortiz."

He nodded, and I couldn't figure out what that meant. "Anything else you'd like to tell me?"

I glanced at Lincoln, who looked as if he wanted to duct-tape my mouth shut. "No."

"Okay." Ramirez's smile lacked warmth. "There are a couple

of things I wanted to know and get your opinion on, and then once my officers get back, you'll be free to go home, all right?"

Stomach full of nerves, I nodded.

"We got the autopsy report back from the state coroner's office on Cassie." He noted my shudder and continued. "The toxicology report showed that she was taking antidepressants and had phentermine in her system."

"Phentermine?" I asked.

"Diet pills," Lincoln explained, readjusting the button clasped over his potbelly. "Besides the fact that most teenagers don't know that term, my client is suffering from dissociative amnesia, as you're well aware of. I'm not sure what you're getting at here."

"I understand that, but I was hoping that maybe some of this rings a bell for her," Ramirez answered, and something about his tone said he wasn't entirely convinced about my amnesia. I was right. "I've been doing some checking in on this . . . this disorder. It appears that people can actually fake it—"

My mouth dropped open. "I'm not faking it!"

Lincoln squeezed my arm in warning. "Detective Ramirez, we agreed to come down and answer these questions, but if you're going to make insinuations regarding Samantha's medical condition—a condition that can be verified by several doctors—then this interview is over."

"I wasn't suggesting that *she* was faking, but that the condition *can* be faked," he said. I called bull on that, but whatever. "Asking those questions can't hurt," he went on. "Not when we're dealing with a girl's murder."

I straightened. "So she was definitely murdered? It wasn't an accident?"

A strange look shot across the detective's face. He leaned forward, putting on elbow on the table, pen still in his hand. "No. It wasn't an accident. The autopsy has proved otherwise."

The room shifted to the left, and I squeezed my eyes shut. Each breath I took hurt. *Murdered.* No more swaying back and forth on what could've happened to her. She had been murdered. "I want to know what happened." My voice came out tiny, hoarse.

The hand around my arm spasmed. "Samantha, I'm not sure you want to know."

I opened my eyes, and both men were staring at me. There was a part of me that was squeamish, didn't want to know, but I pushed it down, all the way down. "I need to know."

There was a pause. "The autopsy showed that there wasn't any water in the lungs. She didn't drown."

A little bit of relief snaked through me. Drowning was horrific. "Then what happened?"

"Results showed that Cassie most likely died due to blunt force trauma to the skull." Ramirez started tapping his pen, his gaze analytical and trained on my face. "She was dead before she ended up in that lake."

"But she could've fallen, right?" I glanced at Lincoln. He looked apoplectic, red cheeks and all.

Ramirez's pen froze. "The crime scene investigation team has been out there. There is no way someone would have cleared the hill and hit the lake below without her jumping, being pushed hard . . . or thrown. And it is very unlikely that she fell down the hill and somehow rolled off the cliff above the waterfall."

"That's what I thought." My voice rasped. *Damn.* Who knew being right could suck so bad?

"Samantha," Lincoln interjected, "I must insist that you don't speak."

The detective was on that like a pack of dogs on a three-legged cat. "What do you mean, that's what you thought?"

Lincoln huffed. "Don't answer that."

I ignored him. "It's just, when I went there, I thought it would be difficult to fall from there and hit the lake without . . . being pushed. And I must've fallen, because I've had this . . . memory of climbing up something."

"I thought you didn't remember anything?" The detective's voice was sharp.

I gritted my teeth, realizing how that looked. "It's not a clear memory, more like fragments and just a feeling. I don't even know if it's real."

He watched me for a few moments. "This memory of climbing? Do you think it involves the cliff?"

"I think so." I lowered my eyes. "I don't really remember anything else." That made sense, that is. I lifted my lashes, meeting his acute stare. "I really wish I did. There is no one else who wants to know what happened that night more than me."

"Besides her mother," he corrected, sitting back. His dark gaze went to the lawyer. "Obviously, both of you girls were on the cliff. We've established that. One of you lived. One of you died. The question remains, was there a third person, Miss Franco?"

I let out the breath I didn't realize I was holding. "I don't know."

When I got home, my room was a mess. Knowing that strangers had combed through my undies creeped me out. I felt violated. Nothing had been spared in the investigation. Not even my bed. What did they think I'd hide in there? My laptop was also gone. Forensics. According to Ramirez I'd have it back in a week.

I really hoped I didn't have a porn addiction I'd forgotten about.

It took me the better part of the evening to clean my room. Mostly because my mother's constant hovering slowed things down. Pale and stricken, she left me alone only to return with a cold-cut sandwich for me. The act surprised me and it also scared me. I could see that she didn't seem concerned about how all this would make her look to her uppity friends.

Worried, but this time it was for me.

That didn't make me feel any better, because I knew I had a reason to be worried. My interrogation—er, questioning—went downhill quickly after Ramirez asked who the third person was. He kept asking the same questions in different ways, trying to trip me up. It became clear that he believed I was faking or I wasn't telling him everything.

Lincoln broke out the lawyer guns. He wanted evidence. Detective Ramirez laid it out plainly. I was the last person to be with her. My "memory loss" was my only defense, the only thing "getting in the way of justice." Any evidence the police had was circumstantial, but people had been convicted on far less. Lincoln told me and my dad afterward that it would never get to that point. I wanted to believe him, but my paranoia was hitting epic levels.

One of you lived. One of you died.

Pacing the length of my bedroom well into the late hours, I was a nervous, sweaty mess by the time I slid between the covers, pulling them over my head like a child. There, in the safety and isolation of my blanket cocoon, I reasoned things out.

Cassie had been murdered. Skull crushed before she was sent over the cliff. Or maybe on the way down. Either way, she'd been pushed. There was little to no evidence supporting that she'd jumped. It was obvious the police didn't believe it was a suicide. No water in the lungs. One of two things happened: I'd hit her with something and then pushed her and then somehow fallen off the cliff myself, or there had been another person there who was responsible for everything. Hit Cassie with something, pushed her off the cliff, and then did the same to me—or at least tried. Or she could've hit her head on the way down.

One of you lived. One of you died.

I somehow felt closer to Cassie than I ever had before. We were still joined by the secret of that night, a memory I couldn't reach.

At some point I dozed off, and I dreamed of the cliff, of Cassie and a third person who kept staying out of my direct line of sight, hiding his or her identity from me. I woke up, my skin sticky with cold sweat and the covers twisted around my hips. Tears clung to my lashes.

Minutes passed, and I kept my eyes squeezed shut. I tried

counting to one hundred, but I only made it to twenty before tiny bumps spread across my skin. A shiver of awareness alerted me to something unnatural in the room.

My breath slowly leaked out of my lips as my muscles locked up. Someone was in the room with me. Every cell in my body knew this. Too afraid to open my eyes, I remained perfectly still.

An icy breath moved over my brow, down my cheek.

I swallowed, and my eyes popped open against my will and a scream came tearing out of my throat. I wasn't alone.

chapter twenty

$\mathcal{S}$wathed in darkness, he leaned over me. All I could see was his chest, but I could feel his breath. I couldn't move, couldn't stop screaming as he pulled away. *Get up! Hit him! Get away!* My brain kept spewing out commands, but my body wouldn't obey.

He was still there, a cold hand moving along my neck, over my pounding pulse. "Samantha," he said roughly, voice somewhat familiar. "This shouldn't have happened."

Then the lights turned on, blinding me in their startling intensity, and I could move. I jackknifed up, my mouth open, bloodcurdling sounds still coming from me. Arms were suddenly around me, and my shrieks pitched even higher.

"Shh, Sam, it's okay. Everything is okay. Shh, it's all right."

I struggled to recognize the voice and the arms around me. All I kept seeing was the man above me; I felt his cold breath and chilly fingers above my pulse. I couldn't stop shaking, no matter how soothing the words being whispered in my ear were.

More voices finally broke through—my dad—Mom. It was Scott holding me, trying to snap me out of it.

"What's going on?" Dad demanded, a black pistol in his hand.

Mom sat beside Scott, placing a hand on my back. "Samantha, baby, talk to us."

It took several tries to form a coherent sentence. "He was in my bedroom, standing over me! I woke up, and he was there."

"Who?" Scott asked, pulling back so that his eyes met mine. "Who, Sam?"

Dad rushed to the bedroom windows, fiddling with the locks while I focused on my brother's face.

"I don't know, but it was him. It was *him*."

Scott's brows knitted as he glanced over my shoulder. "Was it Del?"

"Don't be ridiculous," Mom snapped, patting my back. "He wouldn't come in here and scare her like that."

I twisted out of Scott's arms. "I couldn't see his face, but he must've gone out the windows or something."

His face pale, my dad lowered the pistol. "Oh, Samantha . . ."

"What?" My voice pitched. "He was in here! He was standing over my bed, touching me."

Mom stood, pulling the knot on her silk robe tighter. Her eyes met my father's. "There's no more waiting, Steven. She needs to see a doctor."

I sat back, fingers digging into my comforter. What were they talking about? Who cared about a damn doctor? There had been a man in my bedroom.

"She's fine. She just had a nightmare." Scott rushed to my defense. "There's no reason to bring out the straitjacket."

"What?" I shrieked. *Straitjacket?* My pulse sped up.

"Scott," Mom said, sighing, "go to your room."

He ignored her.

Dad sat down on the other side, catching my hand in his free one. "Baby, the windows and the balcony door are locked from the inside. The alarm is set. It didn't go off."

"No. No! There was someone in my room." I pulled my hand free, scooting back from him. "You have to believe me. I was awake. He was standing over me."

He shook his head. A sad, tired look pierced his eyes. "There wasn't anyone in your room. You were dreaming or—"

"Or I'm seeing things? Like the guy in the backseat?" I yelled. Terror dissipated, replaced by rage. "Is that what you think?"

Mom wiped at her face. It was the first time I'd seen her cry, but the tears only infuriated me. "You've had a stressful night, sweetie. We're not judging you, but you need—"

"I don't need help!" Okay, maybe I did, but I scrambled under Scott's arm. He grabbed for me, but I was quick when I wanted to be. Maybe some of the things I had been seeing weren't real, but this . . . this had been real.

"I think you should sit down," Dad suggested as he rose. "We can talk about things in the morning."

Ignoring him, I grabbed my bag out from under my desk and dumped it onto my bed. Among the books, school papers, and pens, four yellow notes fell onto the bed. All of them except the one I'd found in the car.

"What are you doing?" Scott asked, eyes bugging out as he saw the notes.

I had the most horrible thought then. What if Scott was leaving those notes? I looked at him, really looked at him. He hated Cassie, but . . . but no way. I dismissed the notion.

I spread the notes across the bed. "There! See! I've been getting these damn notes on and off. Someone has been trying to talk to me, to warn me."

Mom stepped forward, peering over my shoulder. She clamped a hand over her mouth and whipped around. Her shoulders shook.

"What the . . . ?" Dad picked up one of the notes—the one that read *Don't look back. You won't like what you find.* "Jesus."

"See!" I almost clapped and jumped. The notes were my only way of proving that I wasn't a hundred percent insane. "They're proof that someone knows what happened. Maybe whoever is leaving those notes is the person who was with us that night."

My father's fingers curled around the note, damaging the already crinkled paper. "Why didn't you come to me when you first got one of these?"

"I . . ." My gaze darted to Scott. He ran a hand through his disheveled hair and lowered his chin.

Dad swung around, a vein pulsing across his temple. "You knew about this? You knew this was happening and you didn't tell me?"

"It's not his fault," I defended him. "And really, that's not the issue here. Someone has been sneaking in here, leaving me notes on my bed, in my locker at school, in my book bag."

"I'm calling the doctor in the morning," Mom said, rubbing the skin around her neck until it was pink. "That is the end of it."

I threw up my hands. "Call the doctor! Fine! But can we focus on the important stuff?"

Scott looked up, pressing his lips together. "I should've told you when you first showed me the note, but I just . . . didn't want to upset you. I'm sorry."

Dread snaked down my spine. "What are you saying?"

"The notes, they're all from the same kind of paper and they're in your handwriting. From when you were a kid," he said, glancing at Mom. "You've been writing the notes, Sam."

Denial rushed over me. "No. No way. I'm not writing those notes."

"Wait here." He rose, heading out of the bedroom.

Turning to Dad, I pleaded with him. "It's not me, Dad. I'm not that crazy. There's no way it's me leaving those notes! I would remember writing them."

Dad smiled weakly. "I know. You're not crazy."

But I saw the truth in his eyes. I sat in a daze of disbelief until Scott returned with a folded-up piece of green construction paper. "This is a birthday card you made for me on our seventh birthday." He sat beside me, unfolding it. "See?" He pointed at a stick-figure drawing of a girl with long hair. "That is you and this is me." He pointed to a stick boy with freckles.

Man, I had no talent.

Scott let out a shaky breath as he picked up a note and spread it out above the birthday message. "Look, Sam."

I saw it immediately, and my world crumbled a little more. I opened my mouth, but nothing came out. The childish scrawl on the card and the note were the same, down to the identical, fat *D*.

My handwriting.

"No," I whispered. Tears blurred my vision as I lifted my head. "No. I don't understand. I don't remember writing any of them. It doesn't make sense."

Scott folded the card, and when he lifted his head, he looked so young. "I'm sorry."

"Stop saying that!" I cried. "Please stop. I'm not . . . I'm not crazy."

Rushing toward me, Mom clasped my cheeks with her hands. Her eyes were clear of sleep and alcohol. "We know, honey. It's just the stress from everything. We're going to get you help."

My eyes shifted over her shoulder to my dad. "Do you think I'm crazy?" My voice broke.

"No." He looked away. A muscle popped in his jaw. "Never, baby, never."

Tears streamed down my face. Someone, I don't know who, hugged me, but I was numb. Numb. Numb. Numb. Their faces blurred. It was official. Seeing things, hearing voices, writing notes to myself and not remembering . . . I *was* crazy.

I got up and went to school the next morning, pretending as if I wasn't one step away from full-blown schizophrenia. Dad had still been home. Over a cup of coffee, he told me that he was picking me up after fifth period.

Not even ten hours later and they'd already found me an appointment with a real shrink.

Scott didn't say anything when I climbed into the car, but he stopped halfway between our house and Carson's. "I'm sorry. I should've told you before, but..."

"It's okay." My voice was flat as I stared out the window. I was still so numb inside, cold and lifeless. "I should be the one apologizing. It's not your fault your sister's a lunatic."

"You're not a lunatic." He grabbed my hand and squeezed. "It's going to be okay."

I nodded but didn't respond. Honestly, it wasn't going to be okay.

Scott let go, and we made the short trip to Carson's house. My heart hurt just thinking about how Carson would look at me if he really knew the truth. They talked about a game that had been on last night while I stared out the window, trying to keep my eyes dry.

Suddenly, Carson propped his chin on the seat above my shoulder. Capturing a piece of my hair between his fingers, he tugged gently. "You're awful quiet this morning."

Scott glanced at me. There was a silent message in his stare, but I had no idea what it meant. I forced at faint smile. "I'm fine. Just sleepy."

Carson accepted that and moved on, but his eyes lingered on my face when we parted ways.

I spent the better part of the morning destroying what was left of my fingernails on my right hand. A giant clock hung over my head. Ticking down the minutes until I either lost my mind completely, was arrested for the murder of my best friend, or was eventually silenced by the individual who was really responsible for the murder before I could learn his or her true identity.

Needless to say, I wasn't kidding myself with any happy endings.

Had I been trying to warn myself when I wrote those notes? I flipped back and forth between being guilty and innocent. In each scenario, I was still bonkers.

Making matters worse, Detective Ramirez and another deputy returned to school, questioning kids once more. Veronica and Candy both were singled out in English class. In bio, Carson confirmed he'd been questioned in the previous period.

"It's definitely a murder investigation." His head was bent low, so only I could hear what he was saying. "The questions they were asking were obvious. Like if I knew anyone who wanted to do her harm. They even asked about you—if you had any enemies."

Knowing that someone was asking those sorts of questions made me feel overexposed, as if I'd been slit open and laid bare for all to see.

"They talked to me last night," I admitted, clenching my pen.

"I got that feeling. They asked about the trip we made to Cassie's house and the cliff."

"Sorry." Unable to look at him, I focused on my textbook. "I didn't want to get you involved."

"It's okay." Under the table, his hand found my empty one. Threading his fingers through mine, he squeezed. "I'm not upset that you told them that we went there. It's not like we were doing anything wrong."

Aware of his hand around mine and the pleasant tingle that shot up my arm, I wondered if he'd still hold my hand if he knew the truth. Or would he call me Insanity Sam like everyone else? My eyes burned.

As the teacher started the lecture, Carson shifted his hand, tracing his thumb over my palm in a silent alphabet. As if I weren't distracted enough. I jumped a few times, scraping the legs of my chair on the floor, especially when his fingers reached the center of my hand. Carson would chuckle softly, and the two kids in front of our table kept turning around, glancing at us.

By the end of class, my cheeks were rosy and my nerves were stretched tight for several reasons—one of them being the fact that Carson was still holding my hand.

Out in the hallway, he pulled me against the wall and lowered his head so that we were eye level. "I want to see you after practice."

My heart did a little happy dance, but I shook my head. "I don't know . . . if we should."

His lips curved up on one side. "I'm asking to hang out. That's all, Sam."

I flushed. "I know, but . . ."

"But what?" His lopsided grin spread. "Or do you want to play the field now that you're single? Keep your options open?"

Rolling my eyes, I laughed. "That's not it."

"Good." He stepped forward. Our shoes touched. People were watching, and I couldn't care less when my eyes locked with his. "I'd be sort of disappointed. So, meet me at eight. The tree house clandestine enough for you?"

I knew I should tell him no. "Okay."

My therapist was an old man who smelled of pipe tobacco and wore thick, square glasses that I think were supposed to be hipster. He had a head full of silvery hair and a beard I couldn't stop staring at. Awards and certificates lined the walls. Photos of him hunting, holding a deer by its antlers, and deep-sea fishing off a yacht were mixed among them.

He asked very few questions, all designed to get me to talk about how I felt, what I worried about, and more important, what I'd felt before I "remembered" things or "found a note" left to me.

He'd write in his little notebook, and I seriously doubted they were notes from the way his pen moved. I think he was doodling.

The session lasted exactly thirty-three minutes.

I left his office and climbed into my father's car, clutching slips of paper to my chest. My dad didn't speed off, throwing distance between the car and the shrink's office, as I knew Mom would have. He watched me closely instead. "What did Dr. O'Connell have to say?"

"I don't have schizophrenia. Good news."

He arched a brow.

I sighed, handing him my prescription for Buspar. "He said I have severe anxiety disorder plus post-traumatic stress or something. The pills should take effect in about two weeks. This one"—I waved another prescription around—"is called Ativan. I'm supposed to use it in case I have a panic attack or whatever, which he thinks is what is happening when I . . . see the shadow guy."

"Shadow guy?"

"Yeah, that's what I've nicknamed the guy I see but isn't really there." I paused, recalling what the therapist said about him. "He thinks the shadow guy could be stress-induced hallucinations or memories of that night, that I'm shielding myself from seeing his face."

And see, that was the kicker. If the shadow guy was a product of my lost memories, taking these pills could hinder what I'd remember from that night. I was caught between wanting to take them so I'd feel normal and not wanting to because they'd cut off my only avenue to remembering what happened that night.

"Okay." He took that piece of paper from me. "And how long will that take to work once you . . ."

"Once I start seeing or hearing things?" I felt bad when he flinched and looked away. "About thirty minutes and I'll be high as kite and happily sedated."

"Samantha . . ."

"It's okay." But it really wasn't. I swallowed the hard lump in my throat, hating the idea of having to take pills. "The doc didn't say how long I'd need to be on them."

"What did he say about the notes?"

A fine drizzle covered the windshield before I answered. "He said it was probably my subconscious trying to make contact with me." My laugh was dry. The therapist had asked how I'd felt before I found a note, if didn't remember what I was doing before then. And I realized that each time I'd found a note, I'd had a dizzy spell or a brief flash of memory. During those times was when I'd supposedly written the notes to myself. He'd said that I could've actually remembered everything during those moments but was still blocking them out.

I sighed. "It's like I have an alien living in my body. He said that may or may not stop with the medication."

He gripped the steering wheel. "And the memories?"

I shrugged. "They could keep coming back or stop completely, but the pills might affect them."

Dad nodded, stuffing the papers into the front pocket of his suit jacket. "I'll drop you off at home and get them filled for you."

"Thank you." I buckled myself in. "Dad—"

"It's nothing to be ashamed of, honey. Okay? I don't want you to feel like there's something wrong with you."

"There *is* something wrong with me," I said drily. "Remember—hallucinations, panic attacks, blah, blah?"

"You know what I mean." He started the car, carefully angling it out of the parking spot. "I just want you to get better."

"Me too."

He glanced at me, and my heart ached at the sadness dulling his eyes. Stopped at the edge of the parking lot, he reached out and palmed my cheek. "I just wish..."

"Wish what, Dad?"

A weak smile flitted across his lips as he removed his hand and pulled out onto the road. "I just wish you didn't have to go through any of this."

Tipping my head back against the seat, I closed my eyes, listening to the rain smack off the roof. "I know."

chapter twenty-one

Ten minutes till eight, I placed the prescription bottles unopened in my medicine cabinet and grabbed my hoodie. I was supposed to take the Buspar with dinner, but I had no idea what it would do to me, and I wanted to talk to Carson without being doped up. Before whatever it was we had going on could go any further, I had to tell him the truth.

I slipped out through the basement, letting Scott know that I was going to meet up with Carson. He'd cover for me in case our parents came looking.

I shoved my hands into the center pocket of my hoodie and followed the thin slice of moonlight that seemed to lead right up to the edge of the lawn. From there, I stayed on the trail, busying myself with how I was going to tell Carson I was crazy.

When I saw the tree house, Carson stuck his head out the opening to the observation deck. A baseball cap was on his head, pulled backward. "Come on up."

In spite of what was going on, I grinned as I climbed up the wooden planks. He grabbed my hand through the opening when I reached the top, hauling me up. "Thanks," I said, looking around the square room built for kids much, much younger than us.

A thick blanket had been spread out, and I crawled over to it, sitting down. He sat beside me, stretching out his legs. "Nice touch," I whispered.

Looking proud of himself, he grinned. "I thought it would make it a little more comfortable."

I clasped my hands together, throat dry. How did I start this? There wasn't a manual on these kinds of things.

Carson nudged me with his shoulder. "I wanted to ask you something."

"Okay." My fingers dug into my palms.

"I did have an ulterior motive for luring you out here, away from your brother."

My heart thumped heavily. "You did?"

He nodded. "Do you know what's happening in three weeks?"

"Um, the end of April?"

"Yeah, that and prom."

I stared at him.

With his eyes on my face, he laughed. "You look a little shocked by that."

"I just . . . haven't thought of prom."

"I figured as much." He scooted over, and his entire leg pressed against mine. "I know a lot is going on, and going to the prom might seem stupid, but I think it's what you need."

"It is?"

"Yes, and there's something else you need."

There were a lot of things that I needed. My eyes searched his face, and for the hundredth time, I wanted to kick myself for not seeing him before for who he was. "What?"

Carson tucked my hair behind my ear, his hand lingering against my cheek for the briefest second. "You need me to take you to the dance."

I opened my mouth, but there were no words. A sudden rush of images of being invited to dances in the past flashed in rapid succession. Hide-and-seek invites, a card stuck in roses, a large banner spread across the baseball diamond. All of them intricate setups, but for some reason, Carson inviting me to the tree house to ask me pulled at my heartstrings.

Carson lowered his chin. "Usually, I can figure people out by the looks on their faces, but I have no clue what you're thinking. Good idea? Bad. Terrible?"

I stared to laugh, but it was choked off as reality came crashing back. "It's a wonderful idea, but I can't go with you."

"I'll admit. I'm kind of confused." He leaned back, resting his hands on his knees. "You think it's a wonderful idea, but you can't go with me?"

"Yes. No." I shook my head. "You don't understand."

He gave me a small, thin smile. "Yeah, I don't. Care to explain?"

"Trust me, you don't want to go to the dance with me."

"Why don't you let me be the judge of that, Sam? Wait." Understanding colored his tone. "Is it because of the police investigating Cassie's . . . murder? And you think you did it."

"Car—"

"You did not kill Cassie, Sam. Okay? Get that through that thick—albeit cute—skull of yours. You're not a murderer."

"It's not just that. I'm . . . I'm sort of messed up."

He stared at me. "Aren't we all?"

"No, not like this." I lowered my eyes, fidgeting. "I'm really messed up, Carson."

There was a heavy sigh. "You're stressed out and—"

"I had to see a therapist today!" I said, probably a little louder than I should have. Tucking my legs against my chest, I forced my voice lower. "Last night . . . last night I woke up and I thought there was someone in my room. I thought he was touching me. And no one was there, Carson."

"Okay." His voice was gruff. "It could be stress. Or it could be a memory. You've said that some of the memories were like they were really happening, right?"

I laughed, and it was the wrong thing to do, because it sounded all kinds of wrong. "That's not all. Those notes I'd been finding? They're in my handwriting. I've been writing notes to myself and not even remembering it."

"Sam—"

"Please don't say something to make me feel better about all this." I fought to swallow the tears, clearing my throat twice. "I left school early today to meet with a shrink. I'm going to be on meds. So I know something is wrong with me—more than just stress."

After my speech, silence descended between us. I was doing

everything to keep from crying, because out of everyone, what he thought of me had come to mean so much. Prom was definitely out of the question. Who wanted to take Insanity Sam? Our friendship might also go down the drain. Hell, I was surprised he was still sitting here.

"Okay," he said finally. "I'm going to say something, and I'm only going to say it once, and then this is done."

I lifted my wet lashes. *Here it comes.* Preparing for what I was sure would be probably the nicest rejection in the history of mankind, I nodded and got ready to bolt through the tree house opening.

"I know you didn't have anything to do with Cassie," he said. "And you have got to stop living your life as if you did."

I blinked, waiting for the rest.

He spread his hands along my cheeks. "I don't care if you have to see a shrink or go on medication, Sam. I'm being serious. That doesn't change that I've always thought you are an amazing person."

Through bleary eyes, I searched his face for signs that he was joking. "How can you say that—"

"When you wouldn't give me the time of day for years?" He laughed. "Remember, Sam, you had your moments. And those moments outshone everything else."

"You're perfect," I whispered, blinking back tears.

Carson snorted. "I'm far from perfect."

I didn't believe that.

"So is it a yes or no?" he asked, moving his hands down my

cheeks, so that his thumbs curved along my bottom lip, sending a shiver through me, lessening the very real fact that I was a hundred percent certifiable. "Will you go to prom with me?"

I laughed at the absurdity of it. It was official. I was crazy—crazy in the way of seeing things, leaving myself notes, and tomorrow I'd be sitting in the therapist's office instead of my last period. And Carson still wanted me to go to prom with him.

Another thing was official. I was in love with Carson.

A wide, beautiful smile parted his lips, exposing the one chipped tooth that I found so, so charming. "I'm going to be honest. If you're going to say no, it's about to get really awkward up in here."

The swelling in my chest returned, but in a good way. Pulling back, I grasped his wrists. A horrible thought occurred. What if I had been crazy before the incident with Cassie but had hidden it well? Going to prom seemed like a bad idea, but if I was crazy then, I was crazy now. And if I hadn't done this to Cassie, what else would I be cheating myself out of experiencing?

"Sam . . ."

Letting go of his wrists, my arms went around his neck. Carson didn't hesitate. His arms went around my waist, holding me just as tightly.

"I'll take that as a yes?" He laughed, pressing his face into my hair.

I squeezed my eyes shut, hoping I was making the right decision. "Yes, I'll go with you."

* * *

In the car the following morning I turned to Scott and asked probably one of the strangest questions I could ever ask my brother. "Can you take me dress shopping?"

He choked on a piece of chocolate-frosted Pop-Tart. Part of it fell between the seat and center console of the car he'd been renting. "What?"

I flushed. "I need to get a dress for prom, and I don't have any friends."

Digging for the missing Pop-Tart piece, he glanced up at me. "You . . . you have friends, Sam."

"No, I don't." Swatting his hand away, I managed to scoop out the piece and toss it back in its wrapper. "Everyone at school calls me Insanity Sam."

"Not everyone." He stuck the pastry in his mouth so he could back out of the garage, then returned to holding it. "Okay. Who's taking you? If you say Del, I might thump your ass."

I made a face. "Carson asked me."

He spat out another piece. "And you actually said yes?"

"Yeah. I like him. A lot."

Scott tossed the rest of his breakfast out the car window. "Man, wow, back into the twilight zone." He slid me a sidelong look. His eyes glimmered. "He's a much better choice than Del."

"So you're not going to thump Carson's ass, then?"

"I don't know. I think I have to, just a little bit. Being your brother and all."

"Of course," I agreed, grinning.

He rolled his eyes. "Julie will go with you. She was actually planning to go soon."

Fiddling with the strap on my bag, I stared out the window, lips pursed. "I don't want you to make her do that. It would be embarrassing."

"I wouldn't make her. I'll ask her in class to see if she's game." He paused. "I promise if she isn't, I won't push it. Okay?"

"All right."

We coasted to a stop outside Carson's house. I leaned forward, eager to see him. The front door swung open, and there he was, in all his wet-haired glory. He looked magnificent in just jeans and a plain shirt.

Scott cleared his throat. "Did you . . . did you take your meds yet?"

Distracted from my blatant ogling, I faced my brother. "Yeah, I took my first one today."

"Do you feel the same?"

I'd taken the pill over an hour ago, and I wasn't feeling any different. "Yeah."

Scott dropped the conversation the moment Carson opened the back door. He slid in, dropping his bag on the seat beside him. Twisting around in my seat, I peeked over the headrest.

"Hey," Carson said, grinning.

My smile spread. "Hey."

A groan came from the driver. "This is going to suck."

Carson and I grinned at each other.

"Not for me," he said.

chapter twenty-two

Things were sort of okay over the next week. There hadn't been any more visits from Detective Ramirez, and my meetings with Mrs. Messer stopped since I began seeing Dr. O'Connell.

I kind of missed her and her glasses, though.

The pills seemed to be working faster than expected. No hallucinations or random notes. However, I did find my stash of legal notepad in the office at home while looking for some paper clips. Seeing the pad of paper kind of hit home for me. That night was bad, full of tears and frustration.

But even with the pills and how things had calmed down around me, there was this growing unrest within me, usually worse at night, when I lay awake, counting the neon-green stars to make sure there were still fifty-six on the ceiling. It was like a lull in the storm, right before chaos reigned supreme.

Each night, after practice, Carson came over to "watch TV" with Scott, which really was just a front to hang out with me without freaking my parents out. It seemed to be working, and those one to two hours a night had become the thing I looked forward to the most every day. We'd sit side by side on the couch, pretending to watch TV while Scott pretended that he wasn't watching us like a hawk. Carson had gotten creative in ways to *accidentally* touch me, a brush of his hand or leg. By the time he left, I wanted to crawl in his lap and kiss him.

And he hadn't tried to kiss me. We hadn't even come close since the day he visited me after the accident. I had a feeling that he didn't want to rush things because of everything that I'd been through, and I wasn't offended by that.

Prom became everyone's focus at school. Even Veronica and Candy had turned their slur campaigns toward their prom court competition instead of me. With each passing day, I faded into the background, and I loved it.

Del got to me after classes on Friday, while I switched out books, following up on the promise I hadn't kept.

The shiner had faded to just a very faint blue under his eye, but he looked like crap. "We need to talk."

I was so getting tired of hearing those words. Grabbing my trig book, I shoved it into my bag. "No, we don't." I spun around and headed toward the back entrance.

He was right beside me, dogged as ever. "People were talking in practice yesterday."

I could only imagine about what. Pushing open the door, I took the pavilion steps two at a time. Scott would be waiting to take me home before heading back for practice.

"Don't you even want to know?" he asked, anger sharpening his words.

"Not really."

He shot in front of me, blocking my path between two cars. "What is with you? You're acting like we weren't together for almost four years, Sammy. Four years and you can't even give me the time of day?"

There was a good chance that the pills might be kicking in ahead of schedule, because I wasn't angry. I wasn't even sad. Looking up at him, I felt nothing but general disappointment. Maybe it wasn't the pills—just a sign that I was moving on from this.

Kind of like how everyone seemed to be moving on from Cassie.

I shouldered my backpack and squinted. "I'm sorry. I know we spent a long time together—"

"But since you can't remember it, you don't care? Well, I do. I remember it and I care."

"That's not what I was going to say." I sighed, glancing over his shoulder. If Scott caught Del blocking me like this, he'd end up with another black eye. "I know you care about that time, and believe it or not, so do I."

"Good." He sounded hopeful. "At least that's a common ground."

"Not in that way. I care about you, and maybe one day I'll forgive you for those pictures, but even if I did, we aren't getting back together."

He reached for my hand, but I pulled away. Hurt flickered

across his face, but behind that was stubbornness and something darker and stronger than I cared to see. At least I knew the pills didn't totally squash my emotional compass.

"Can't we just go somewhere and talk?"

My mouth dried. "You have practice."

"Screw practice. Our relationship is more important than a damn practice."

"I'm not more important. Baseball means a lot to you."

"That's not true." He looked as if I'd hit him upside the head with a concrete block, as if he couldn't believe I'd disagree. "We need to talk this out."

Apprehension was growing rapidly, and it made me impatient to get away from him. "I need you to understand this, Del. We aren't getting back together. Not now. Not a week from—"

"It's true, then? What I heard in practice yesterday? That you're going to prom with Carson?"

I wasn't answering that question, because I knew it would be like opening Pandora's box and letting out a slew of angry problems. So I stepped around him and picked up my pace. Just a few more rows of cars, and I'd be free of Del. Just a few more steps...

"Damn it, Sammy!"

The anger in his voice caused me to jump, but I didn't look back. He'd turn my going to the dance with Carson into my choosing someone else over him. And Carson had nothing to do with Del. They weren't even in the same league.

Why was Del so determined to patch things? Another mystery I couldn't solve or even begin to understand. During lunch this past week, Veronica had been all but sitting in his lap. It was obvious she liked him and was more than willing to take their friendship to the next level. A much better choice than me for several reasons.

I jogged down a row, passing a dusty red Jeep, when something darted along my peripheral vision. My heart stuttered unevenly, and chills skittered up and down my spine. A loud buzzing filled my ears.

No. It's not real.

Again, on the other side of me, the figure moved, matching my steps. Air froze in my throat. Stress-induced hallucinations—panic attacks. That was what Dr. O'Connell had called them. If I got too upset, I'd start seeing things.

That was all it was. Not real. Not there.

Keeping my eyes trained on the sleek black sedan Scott had rented, I dug around in my bag for the bottle of emergency pills. I didn't have anything to swallow the pill down with, but I had to make do. My heart was pounding way too fast, my vision now darkening at the corners.

Not real. Not real. Not real.

A hand clamped down on my arm, spinning me around. My scream got stuck in my throat, and the bottle of pills hit the gravel. Raising my arm, I prepared to strike.

"Hey!" Scott blocked my arm. "Calm down there, ninja."

I pressed my hand over my thumping heart. "Jeez, you scared the crap out of me."

"I can see." He frowned, dropping down and grabbing my bottle. He handed it to me. "I called your name a couple of times. Didn't you hear me?"

"No." Shaken, I unscrewed the lid and dug out one tiny pill. "I didn't hear you, but I thought . . ."

"Here." He offered me his water. "You thought what?"

I downed the pill, wincing at the burn as it slid down my throat. "I thought I saw the shadow guy."

Scott placed his arm around my shoulders, steering me toward the car. "I think that may have been me, Sam. I was walking a few cars down, alongside you."

Great. Even with the pills I still couldn't figure out the difference between fact and fake.

"I was worried," he continued, digging the keys out of his pocket. "I saw Del down at the entrance. He looked pissed."

Not wanting to get into that, I didn't respond and waited for Scott to unlock the door. Still struggling to control my breathing, I dropped into the front seat and squeezed my eyes shut, waiting for the blissful stupor to do its job, to make me feel normal again.

To help me forget that not everything was perfect, that Cassie was still dead and I was still a suspect, and that growing feeling that something bad—something terrible—was waiting around the corner.

On Saturday, Julie arrived at my house. Not to hang out with Scott—although there was a lot of tongue action the first three minutes of her visit—but to go dress shopping with me.

A mass of knots had formed in my stomach, and I seriously considered taking one of the panic-attack pills, but I managed to convince myself I didn't need it. I was tongue-tied and unsure of how to act around Julie, so a whole lot of awkwardness ensued.

Julie drove a rusty sedan that should have been laid to rest about a hundred thousand miles ago. Fumbling with the seat belt, I inhaled the scent of freesia and stale fast food.

It was kind of a homey combination.

"Okay," she said, easing the car around Carson's father's work truck. "We have two options. We can shop in town or head into the city."

"It's up to you. I'm fine either way." Dad had given me his credit card, but I doubted he would have eagerly handed it over if he knew who my date was. Right now, they thought I was going stag. I was going to have to ease them into the truth.

Her lips pursed. "Well, the city is going to give us more options, but most likely be out of my price range. So we can do both if you want?" She glanced at me. "Or I can window-shop with you."

"No. We can stay in town. I'm sure I'll find something here."

Julie stared at me as if I'd just admitted to being abducted by aliens. "Are . . . you sure?"

"Yeah, I'm totally okay with that." I started to chew on my pinkie nail on my left hand. "Is that bad?"

"No." She blinked and then fiddled with the radio station. "It's just that you could splurge on a dress and get a really nice one."

But she couldn't, and that didn't seem fair. I shrugged. "A dress is a dress, right?"

She slammed on the brakes at the end of our road, pitching me forward. My eyes widened, expecting to see an animal or something in the middle of the road, but there was nothing. She slowly turned to me. "You are seriously freaking me out."

Uh-oh.

"I don't mean that in a bad way," she hastily added. "It's just that you are so, so different. Even the Sam I knew when we were friends would've demanded that we go to one of the designer shops in the city if she had gotten ahold of her dad's card. Even if it was just for the fun of it."

"Should we do that?" I would, if that was what she wanted. Deep down, I wanted her to actually have fun doing this, and maybe—just maybe—this could be the start of a friendship. Big hopes, I knew, but that was all I wanted: for her to like me.

Shaking her head, she laughed. "No. Staying in town works. Maybe we could get something to eat afterward?"

Optimism thrummed through me, and I nodded. "Sure."

The town was packed with tourists when we parked behind a strip of old homes converted into various stores: gift shops, bakeries, and thrift stores. Slipping on a pair of sunglasses I'd found in my bedroom earlier, I stepped out of the car.

People were snapping pictures of historical houses and the plaques that seemed to be every ten feet in town. The one closest to us was dedicated to an unnamed fallen solider. My heart sort of tripped over that.

"That sucks," I said.

"What?" She turned to see what I was staring at. "The monument?"

"The whole dying and no one even knowing who you are— being laid to rest without a name . . . or a history." I pressed my lips together. "I guess it's like that with Cassie. She's dead and no one knows why. There's no reason—just that she's dead. The end."

Julie placed her hand on my arm and squeezed. "The police will figure it out. They always do one way or another. She'll get justice."

My stomach pitched, and I forced a smile. "Yeah, they always do. At least on TV, right?"

She nodded, squeezed my arm once more, and sighed. "Okay. There's this secondhand store down the street that sells these vintage dresses—not Civil War–era vintage."

I laughed, letting go of Cassie and everything for the time being. "I hope not. I doubt showing up in a ball gown would be cool."

"Scott would be pissed. He'd never figure out how to take it off."

"Ew," I moaned.

Looping her arm through mine, she giggled. "There's this dress I've seen in there, and I've been kind of saving up for it." Her eyes lit up with excitement and the kind of love only the perfect dress could bring, and now I understood why it was such a big deal. "It's, like, this 1920s-style flapper dress with beads. Super flirty and just so cute. I hope they still have it."

"I don't know what to get," I admitted. "Or what I like, to be honest."

"Well, the evil Sammy"—she flashed me a grin—"would choose something that showed as much boobs and legs as humanly possible."

"Great." The bell rang over the door as we stepped into the store, which was a maze of racks. "What about the lovable Sam?"

Julie glanced over her shoulder with a frown. "Hmm, good

question. Since you were, like, eleven, I'd go with your boobs not hanging out, and actually . . . actually, you didn't wear a lot of dresses then. You were a jeans-and-shirt kind of girl."

"That's so helpful." I grinned, following her toward the back, where dresses hung on the walls and filled the racks. A few other girls were there. "So, what dress are you in love with?"

Reaching up on the tips of her toes, she grabbed for a dress shoved behind several long, billowy dresses. I fell in love with what she pulled out instantly. Silvery and shimmery, it was as if a thousand stars had been sewn into the dress, and when she held it up, the overhead light made them sparkle.

Darting to my side, she grinned. "I totally hid it behind the other dresses."

"I can see why. It's beautiful."

"Isn't it?" She looked like she wanted to make out with the dress. "The only thing is, if I do buy this, I won't have enough in time to buy shoes. And I don't have anything in my closet that would do this baby justice."

I ran my fingers over the intricate beads. "I think I have a pair of silver heels that would go with this dress, actually. They're really strappy." Julie's eyes nearly crossed with awe. "And the heels are, like, four inches, but if you want to borrow them, have at it."

"I think I love you," she replied.

Smiling, I shrugged. "Your affection is easily won."

"When it involves killer shoes? Yes." She clutched the dress to her chest and squealed. "I've tried it on so many times I think the owner of the shop is going to start charging me. Oh! I'm thinking about wearing this wig I kept from last year's school play. It's this short bob thing that would work perfectly."

She was in plays? "Yeah, it would go with the whole flapper thing."

"And not to mention I think Scott would love it." Her eyes glimmered with mischief. "It's like he's cheating on me with me."

I laughed out loud at that and returned to thumbing through the racks. Gravitating toward the longer dresses, I went through several black and red ones before my fingers stopped on one that was such a pale shade of green it reminded me of sea foam. Unhooking the dress, I held it up.

The material was supple, and there was a tight band of the same color under the breast. The top, with its neckline, reminded me of the famous Marilyn Monroe dress on the grate. I couldn't stop touching it.

"Oh, that would look perfect with your hair and complexion," Julie commented.

My smile was tentative. "You think so?"

"Yes. You should definitely try it on."

Taking the dress to the counter, I waited for the cashier to let me into the small changing rooms in the back. My back was to the window, and all of a sudden, I got this peculiar sensation . . . like if I turned around, someone would be standing right there.

I ignored it, watching the plump lady behind the counter finish ringing up a duo of giggling girls.

The feeling persisted. I rubbed the back of my burning neck as my heart rate pitched. Realizing I hadn't brought any of my pills with me, I focused on maintaining a slow, steady rhythm while Julie poked around the vintage clutches.

After what felt like forever, the lady led me back to the changing rooms and the feeling of being watched lessened until it completely vanished. Feeling good about taking control of my own mind, I stripped in the tiny stall and slipped the dress on over my head.

Twisting to the side, the material moved against my bare skin like satin. The hem swooshed around my ankles and the back dipped low . . . as did the front. Standing on the tips of my toes, I imagined the look on Carson's face.

My cheeks flushed.

"Let me see!" Jules banged on the door.

Opening the door, I stepped out and turned around. "What do you think?"

"Wow," Julie breathed, fixing the material on my shoulder. "It looks great. And it really shows off the girls."

Boy did it ever. "Too much?"

"Not at all." She peered over my shoulder. "I can't see anything looking down. Your date will probably be disappointed, but it definitely draws the eyes."

I laughed, doubting Carson would be too disappointed. What would he say? Something ridiculously sexy, I was sure. And would he finally kiss me? God, I hoped so.

"You should wear your hair up." Julie scooped up the long strands, twisting the mess off my shoulders. "Shows off your neck."

Sold on the dress, I quickly changed and checked out with

Julie. I thought the dress was a little pricey, but I believed Dad would be pleasantly surprised that I didn't break the bank.

We placed our dresses in the car and then headed to a diner down the street. As we waited for our meals, Julie chatted about her summer plans and how Scott was taking her skydiving after graduation. It would be a first for both of them. Apparently I'd done it already, but I didn't remember. Julie invited me, and the old spark of interest was fueled once more.

Near the end of our lunch date, Julie sat back and folded her arms. "So, you're really going to prom with Carson?"

I finished off the rest of my cheeseburger, nodding. "Why is that so shocking?"

She gave me a *duh* look. "Do you like him, or are you just going with him because you don't want Del anymore?"

Part of me was irritated by her question, but I kind of understood what she was getting at. My attraction to Carson *was* a shock. I was the only one not surprised by it. "I like him, Julie. I *really*, really like him. And I can't figure out why I didn't see it before."

"I can give you a few good ideas," she offered cheerfully.

"I'll pass." I sat back, grinning. "But seriously, I think he's freaking perfect."

Julie laughed as she propped her elbows on the table. "You really do like him! Look at your cheeks. They're red with love!"

"Shut up." I tossed my balled-up napkin at her.

She smiled. "I think it's great, though. Don't tell your brother I said this, but Carson's hot. He's got that whole Latin-lover thing going for him."

"Oh, jeez." Placing my hands against my red cheeks, I giggled.

"Seriously, though? Carson really is a great guy. That boy's a keeper." She sat back, grabbing the check. "And there's another benefit of going with him."

My mind went straight into X-rated territory. "Details?"

Mischief filled her eyes as she tilted her head to the side, sending long, straight blond strands over her shoulder. "The expression on your parents' faces when you break the news."

A sound rose from my throat, equal parts laugh and groan. "Mom's going to—"

"Flip the hell out," Julie finished for me. Sympathy crossed her face when she saw my look. "Don't worry. She'll get over it. Eventually. It only took, like, a year for her to warm up to me."

"That's really reassuring." I slapped the credit card down on the table. "But you know what? I really don't care. Carson's... he's worth them stroking out."

"Just—"

A slight shadow fell over our table. I turned, and my smile froze on my face. I almost didn't recognize the short, sleek brunette hairdo and the perfect face marred by exhaustion and sorrow I couldn't begin to fathom.

"Ms. Winchester," Julie said, straightening. Her eyes bounced to me, her gaze wary. "How...how are you?"

Her dull blue eyes slid from Julie to me. "I'm doing great, considering my daughter was murdered."

My brain emptied. Struck mute by her sudden appearance, I couldn't do anything but stare. Cassie's mom. My best friend's mom. Face pale, Julie shifted. I wanted to turn away, close my eyes in desperation. My mouth just wouldn't work. And I knew I needed to say something. I had to.

Finally, my brain kicked on and my voice came out choked and hoarse. "Ms. Winchester, I am so, so sorry about Cassie."

Grief darkened her blue eyes, but something darker and stronger churned behind that. "You are? Both of you?"

"Yes, ma'am," Julie agreed. "It's terrible...."

Ms. Winchester smiled tightly. Her lower lip trembled from the effort. "You looked very sorry when you were shopping for dresses."

The feeling of being watched had been because of *her*—Cassie's mom? What was she doing, peeping at us while we shopped? She continued before I could really digest it.

"Did you two have fun? Enjoy making plans for prom?" Her eyes fixed on me. "I assume you're going with Del."

My mouth opened, but Julie cut in. "Actually," she said, "Sam and Del aren't together."

Ms. Winchester didn't look surprised. "Sam? Tell me, *Sam*, how is that you're out here, buying prom dresses, while my daughter lies cold in her grave?"

"I—"

"You're just like him," she said, eyes glistening. "I told her to have nothing to do with you, but she didn't listen."

I flinched. "Like who? Who am I like?"

Cassie's grandfather appeared suddenly, grabbing Ms. Winchester's arm. "That's enough. You're making a scene."

"I don't care," she spat back, wrenching her arm free. And

she was making scene. Everyone in the cozy diner was staring. Locals. Tourists. No doubt this would be all over school by Monday. I wanted to fade into the cushion at the same time I wanted her to answer my question.

Julie started to stand. "I think we should go, Sam."

I rose on weak legs. "Ms. Winchester, if I remembered anything, I swear I'd tell—"

"How can you not remember?"

"I don't—"

Her hand snaked out, connecting with my cheek. The smack reverberated through the diner, and the sting was fiery hot. Eyes watering, I put a hand to my cheek, stunned.

Tears ran down Cassie's mom's face unchecked. "My baby had problems, but she didn't deserve that. You were her best friend, her only *real* friend. And she's dead and you're shopping for prom dresses. How can you live with yourself?"

chapter twenty-three

*L*iving was hard, but I was alive and that had to count for something. Right now, it was harder than normal. When I got home and my mom saw my freshly slapped cheek, she went through the roof like a rocket.

"We should file a police report, Steven." She followed my father around the kitchen island. Little pieces of hair stood out from her twist like a dozen tiny fingers lining her temples. "How dare that woman hit our daughter?"

Dad grimaced. "I think contacting the police isn't the best course of action right now."

"I have to agree, considering it was the mom of the girl they think I killed who smacked me."

"Samantha!" Mom whirled toward me, face aghast.

"What?" I threw my hands up. "It's true."

Her eyes narrowed. "Have you been taking your medication?"

"Yes," I grumbled, sitting down on the stool. A step outside the kitchen, Scott was eavesdropping. Not as if it was necessary.

Anyone within five miles of our house could hear Mom. He made a face at me when our gazes met.

Dad leaned against the bar, lowering his head so we were eye to eye. "Are you hurt?"

I shook my head. "No. I'm just surprised."

"Your entire cheek is bloodred." Mom placed her cool hand against it. "Hitting our daughter is unacceptable."

Pushing off the counter, Dad placed his hand on Mom's lower back, but she quickly stepped away. "I think it's best if we let this just die down," he said, dropping his hand to his side.

A snowball's chance in hell right there. Mom looked as if she wanted to lie down and die first, but Dad eventually got her calm. Surprisingly, Mom wasn't drinking, which meant this was the perfect opportunity to really make her go crazy.

"So." I drew the word out obnoxiously, earning a look from Mom. "I got a dress today for prom."

"Oh." Mom blinked and a faint smile appeared. "Did you? In town?"

"Yes. It's a really pretty vintage dress from this thrift store. It's in my room."

"Thrift store?" she repeated slowly.

From the other room, Scott choked on his laugh. I kept my eyes focused on our parents.

"How much damage did you do on the Black?" Dad asked, referencing his credit card. I dug into my pocket and handed over the receipt. His brows shot up. "Honey, our daughter is perfect."

She peered over his shoulders. "That's all? I have to see the dress."

Taking a deep breath, I slapped my hands down on my thighs. "And I have a date."

Excitement lit her usually serious hazel eyes. "Did you and Del make up?"

There was another strangled sound from the other room, and I was two seconds from body-slamming Scott. "Uh, no . . . we didn't make up."

"Then who are you going to prom with, princess?"

I glanced at Dad. "I'm going with Carson."

Mom sucked in a sharp breath and stared at me. It was almost as if I'd admitted to being part of a terrorist cell. "Samantha . . ."

"Don't." I stood, prepared to do battle. "I want to go to prom with him, and I'm going. He's a good guy and there's not a thing that's wrong with him. And I swear to God, if the fact that his dad works for us is mentioned, I will lose my shit."

"Samantha!" she snapped. "Language."

Choosing the moment to make himself known, Scott strolled into the kitchen, clapping. "Hear! Hear! I second and third that."

Mom folded her arms. "Scott, go to your room."

He sat in the stool I was standing beside. "Carson is a really good guy. Better than Del the Dick."

"Scott!" She was nearing stroke territory.

"Honey, I think . . . this is a good thing," said Dad. When she started to protest, he gave her a meaningful look. "Let Samantha make her own choices. Just like you did."

"That's not the same," she argued.

"If I remember correctly, your father didn't think much of me, because I didn't come from the right side of town." He smiled, but something moved across his face. A quick grimace twisted his lips. "And Carson is a good boy. We've never had a problem with him."

I bounced back on my heels. "Then it's settled."

Mom opened her mouth, but Dad jumped in. "It's not like they're getting married, for god's sake. They're just going to prom. That's all."

Suddenly, as I stared at my father, I understood what he wasn't saying. Maybe it was because somewhere deep inside me I knew how he worked, what he truly believed. His acceptance of Carson wasn't because he was that different from Mom, but because he saw this thing with Carson as temporary. I knew that if I announced that it was far more than temporary, he'd be joining Mom on the rocket blasting through the roof. No matter what his background was.

"Enough talk about my sister's dating habits," Scott said, drawing my attention. "Julie was telling me that Cassie's mom was saying some crazy stuff."

Back to that. I groaned. "Yeah, she kept saying that I was like 'him,' and I think she believes I know what happened, but I'm pretending not to."

"Him?" Mom frowned, messing with those damn bangles.

"I don't know." I sat back down, shoulders slumping. "But she did say she warned Cassie to stay away from me."

Scott rolled his eyes as he started rearranging the pears and apples in the fruit bowl. "That's funny, because everyone needed to be warned to stay away from Cassie."

Brushing his hands aside, Mom fixed the fruit back to

the way she had them. "I really do think we should report this, Steven. The poor woman is obviously unstable."

Dad shook his head, distracted. "We don't need to involve the police."

"But she's making outlandish—"

"No police!" He slammed his hand down on the bar, causing all of us to jump. Exhaling roughly, he shook his head. "I'll talk to Lincoln and give him a heads-up, if that makes you feel better."

Mom stared at him, her cheeks heightened with color. "Yes. That would," she said, her words clipped.

I glanced at Scott, who shrugged. An argument was definitely brewing, and I wanted to make a clean exit before it really got going. Watching them glare at each other and knowing that I was partially the cause of it sucked. Unnoticed by them, Scott and I slipped off the stools and out of the kitchen. The moment we rounded the corner, their voices went up.

"What do you think about them fighting?" I asked as we headed toward the basement.

Scott tossed an apple up in the air and caught it. "Who knows?" Throwing and catching the apple again, he looked at me. "But they took the Carson news surprisingly well."

"Yeah," I muttered, but I was distracted by how Dad had reacted to the idea of police. It had been the first time I'd seen him lose his cool, but I had a feeling I just didn't remember all the other times.

Two Saturdays later, I stared at the bottle of pills for panic attacks. A nest of butterflies had taken up residency in my stomach and now stirred, sending warring darts of panic and excitement through me. Dr. O'Connell had said the hallucinations and memories were most likely triggered by anxiety.

And going to prom with a boy I had seriously fallen for had my nerves stretched thin.

Turning the bottle of pills over, I swallowed. Taking one of these would ensure that I didn't freak out, but I'd be numb to everything: the first time Carson took my hand, danced with me, or—hopefully—kissed me. I wanted to *feel* it all, not just coast through it. And I was doing fine. No notes. No hallucinations. No memories. I didn't need these pills.

Decision made, I placed the bottle back in the medicine cabinet and closed the door. My reflection suddenly stared back at me. I'd spent the better part of the afternoon and evening doing my hair and makeup so that it would look perfect.

Brown, smoky eye shadow covered my lids, accentuating the green flecks. Opting for a faint shimmer instead of blush, my cheekbones looked higher, more defined. A glossy coat on my lips gave them that ready-to-be-kissed look. As Julie had suggested, I'd had my hair done with her earlier in the day. Curled into thick ringlets, my hair was twisted up by the stylist and artfully arranged. A few tendrils hung loose, framing my face.

A throat cleared, and I turned. Mom stood in the doorway of my bathroom and smiled a little. "You look beautiful, honey."

"You think?" I ran my hands down the sides of the dress.

She nodded. "You really do."

I smiled back at her. "Thank you."

Mom turned her head, but I saw the wetness gathering in her eyes. "Your date is waiting downstairs, getting interrogated by your father as we speak."

My eyes widened, and the butterflies took flight, trying to claw their way out. "He's here?"

She backed up, letting me slip past her. I grabbed my clutch and made it to the door before she stopped me. "Carson looks very nice, Samantha."

Surprised, I glanced over my shoulder. There were no words. Hell was having a snowball fight.

"Have fun," she said. "You deserve it."

"I will." I blinked back tears. No way was I ruining all this makeup. "Thank you."

Mom ushered me out of the room. Nerves taking over, I almost didn't go down the staircase, but she whispered words of encouragement and down I went, feeling like one of those girls in the cheesy teen movies.

Dad had Carson cornered in the sitting room off the foyer, and I grinned. Both of them had their backs turned, but what I could see of Carson in a tux so far, I liked.

I liked a lot.

Carson must have heard my heels clacking on the floors, because he turned around, a small, plastic box in hand. Our gazes locked, and the look in his eyes curled my toes. Then his gaze dropped and the naked approval in his expression had me wishing we were alone.

But we weren't.

Dad cleared his throat. "You look lovely, princess."

"Wow," Carson murmured, his eyes drifting slowly back to my face, leaving scorching heat behind. "Sam..."

"Hey," I said, my gaze dropping to the box. "For me?"

Carson swallowed as I moved to his side. His fingers shook slightly as he slipped a beautiful lily corsage that must've cost a small fortune out of the box and onto my wrist. I lifted my lashes, and found him staring back at me, his eyes an intense cobalt.

"You look beautiful," he said.

I flushed. "Thank you. So do you." And he did. The tux fit his broad shoulders and looked good against his sunbaked complexion. Magnificent.

Surprising me again, Mom actually wanted to take pictures. We posed for a couple of shots, and the small of my back tingled from the slight pressure of his hand. Through the whole process, I felt as if I were floating.

We escaped after Dad gave my cheek a quick kiss and Carson another hard look. Stepping out into the early-evening spring air, Carson found my hand and squeezed. "I'm not sure I want to go to prom."

"What?" I let him lead me over to his father's truck. "You don't want to go?"

He opened the door for me. "I'm not sure I want to share you with anyone."

I laughed. "I'm all yours."

"I'm going to hold you to that." He waited until I climbed in and then bent, kissing me softly on my cheek. "I'm really, really going to hold you to that."

A fine shiver danced over my skin as I watched him close the door. He flashed me a quick, almost wicked grin before he jogged around the front of the truck. Once behind the wheel, he turned to me.

"I can't believe you're actually here," he admitted, the tops of his cheeks flushed. "That *you* are with *me*."

A good kind of burn moved up my throat. "I can't believe it took me this long to be here with you."

chapter twenty-four

We met Scott and Julie at the Cashtown Inn for dinner. Reservations for the place had to have been hard to come by, but Dad had apparently pulled some favors and got the four of us a table in the packed dining room. Over a candlelight dinner, everything that had been going on faded into the background.

I hadn't laughed so hard in so long, and I don't think I'd ever felt this *good* before, sharing a way-too-fancy meal with my brother and his girlfriend, Carson's hand around mine under the table.

And none of the other kids at the inn said or did anything that indicated there'd be any problems. If anything, most seemed shocked when Carson and I headed out, hand in hand.

"You ready to do some dancing?" Julie asked, looking sexy in her shimmery dress and bob.

I nodded, grinning up at Carson. "How about you?"

He moved behind me, wrapping his arms around my waist.

Lowering his cheek to mine, he smiled. "I'm going wherever you are."

Scott glared at us. "I'm not sure I like this."

"Oh, shut up." Julie grabbed his arm, tugging him toward the car. "It's time to party." Grumbling, Scott let her pull him away. She looked over her shoulder, mouthing "Hot" before she smacked my brother's butt.

I laughed, leaning into Carson. He made a sound that caused a deep flutter in my chest, and his arms tightened around me. "If we don't leave right now for the dance," he said, his lips brushing my ear, "I'm pretty sure we're not going to make it."

My cheeks were flushed the entire way to the hotel holding our senior prom. With my arm wrapped securely in his, we headed through the back entrance, following the steady beat of music and laughter to the ballroom.

I tightened my grip on his arms once we stepped inside. Chandeliers hung from the ceiling, casting the only light over the pack of moving bodies. Lilies adorned the small round tables; what looked like garlands of roses decorated the stage under the banner. Small bushes and indoor trees were decorated with twinkling lights. The place was beautiful, surreal.

Almost immediately, friends greeted Carson. I smiled, loving the ease with which Carson dealt with people, the casualness and open friendship. People gravitated to him and, through him, to me. Several shocked looks greeted us, but I didn't care. There wasn't anything that could ruin this.

Julie and Scott reappeared, and before Carson and I could

share one dance, she tugged me onto the floor. "Dance!" she demanded, throwing her arms up in the air.

Laughing, I obliged and learned that I wasn't a bad dancer. Catching the beat easily, I moved to the music, losing myself in the fast rhythm. A sense of familiarity crept over me and, with it, a twinge of guilt, but I shook it off in favor of just enjoying the moment.

When the song ended, we headed back to where we'd left the guys. I bumped into a small brunette in a black dress. "Sorry!" I yelled over the music.

She turned around, eyes widening with surprise. "Sammy? You came?"

"Lauren, you look great." And she did. The dress fit her lithe body perfectly.

I expected her to hurl an insult in my direction, but she gave me a quick hug. "You do, too. Who did you come with?"

"Carson Ortiz." Pride shot through me. I came with *him*.

She blinked, but her smile didn't falter. "That's really awesome." Someone called her name, and she glanced away briefly before turning back to me. "Maybe we can get together soon? Catch a movie?"

"I'd like that," I said truthfully.

"Great!" She gave me another hug. "See you around."

Smiling, I headed back to Carson. I caught a quick glimpse of Candy grinding on Trey in a dark corner. Both looked a little tipsy. Ignoring them, I slipped my arm around Carson's waist from behind. "Dance?"

He turned, leaving his group of friends without another

word. We moved onto the dance floor, finding an empty spot. Then he slid an arm around my waist and pulled me against his chest. Our bodies molded together as I wrapped my arms around his neck.

"I'm glad you persuaded me to go," I said.

Carson smiled. "Not as happy as me."

Loving how he seemed to always know the right thing to say, I rested my cheek on his shoulder and closed my eyes. For most of the song, we stayed like that, lost in the slow melody and each other's arms. I couldn't remember any other dances that I'd attended, but it didn't matter. This was my favorite, with him, when I felt as if I weren't tied to a past I couldn't remember.

"I have to tell you something," he said, turning his head so his jaw grazed my cheek.

I lifted my head, meeting his gaze. "What?"

"I don't want this to end tonight."

My chest swelled. "What is 'this'?"

Carson grinned, and I realized we'd stopped moving even though others danced around us. "You. Me. Together beyond tonight. As in I'll take you to lunch tomorrow. Keep you around for dinner if you behave."

Feeling light, I laughed. "If I behave?"

"Mmm-hmm." He pressed his forehead against mine, his lips coming so intoxicatingly close. "And if you're really good, I expect to see you after practice on Monday. Then maybe a movie on Tuesday."

My eyes drifted shut. "What about Wednesday and going on forward?"

"That depends on if you're good or bad."

"What happens if I'm bad?"

"Good question." His hands slid to my hips and a wealth of heat followed the movement. "We'd have to work out some kind of punitive system. Bad could be good."

I started to smile. "Then what's good?"

"Good is good." He moved his lips over my cheek, and my breath caught. "See, I was kind of full of it a few seconds ago. You can behave or misbehave. I want a Wednesday, Thursday, and Friday with you. Several of them, back to back and so on."

A flash of guilt threatened to ruin the moment like an uninvited guest, trying to dig its claws in, but I opened my eyes. "Are you asking me to be your girlfriend?"

"So it would seem." His eyes glimmered.

"Well, I like the sound of that. Have for probably longer than I should admit."

His lips parted, and his mouth lowered to mine. Air got hitched in my throat, and my pulse thrummed. This was it. He was going to kiss me. Finally. Every cell in my body waited in sweet anticipation because I knew that even though I didn't remember all my other kisses, this one would so blow them out of the water.

Out of nowhere, Scott bumped into us. "I think there's a rule about space between partners. Don't make me enforce it."

Julie hung her head in shame. "You're *so* embarrassing."

I scowled at my brother, but Carson chuckled. "Way to kill the mood, bro."

"That's what I'm here for." He grinned cheekily, spinning Julie away from us.

Carson sighed. "Your brother..."

"Is a lovable idiot?" Mood ruined, I glanced around and cleared my throat. "I think I need to..."

He kissed my cheek. "I'll get us something to drink."

Reluctantly, I pulled free and headed toward the entrance. Our conversation had left me in a heady daze. My heart was doing little backflips, and I wanted to go find Julie and tell her that Carson and I were dating. There was definitely a squeal building up, demanding to be shared. Right now, it was a first for me and I floated as if I were walking on balloons.

I pushed on the bathroom door, and right away I wished I'd gone anywhere but there.

At the sink, Veronica grabbed a sheet of brown paper towel and scrubbed under her eyes, furiously wiping at the mascara. I started to hightail my butt out of there, but girl code demanded that I at least check on her.

Cursing myself under my breath, I let the bathroom door shut behind me. "Veronica, are you okay?"

Her lashes lifted. "What does it look like? I'm fantastic."

And that was why I hated girl code. Shaking my head, I turned back for the door. There had to be other bathrooms around.

"I thought he actually liked me," she said, voice cracking. "Wasn't I stupid? I bet that just makes you so freaking happy."

With a sinking feeling, I faced her. "Del?"

"Who else?" She laughed as she dabbed at the pink skin under her eyes. "He finally dumped you, and I had my chance. There wasn't even Cassie to get in the way."

I thought about correcting who broke up with whom but decided against it. "Seeing you cry doesn't make me happy."

She threw the towel on the floor and spun around, gripping the edge of the sink. The intricate curls atop her head bounced off her tear-stained cheeks. "All he's done is talk about you. About how you guys were just taking a break—that you two will get back together. I'm so sick of it!"

I was dumbfounded. "We're not getting back together."

"You should try telling him that." Veronica threw up her hands. Nails painted to match her bloodred dress. Dizziness crept up on me. "Not that it matters. He told me that your mothers are planning a trip for you to the Poconos to patch things up."

My mouth dropped. Oh my god, I was going to strangle that woman. And here I thought she'd been making progress tonight. *Ugh.* "Del and I aren't going on any trip."

Veronica started to laugh, but then it choked off. She sniffed. "You're not."

"He's all yours if you want him, but seriously, do you want him?"

She stared at me as if I'd suggested we go kick some puppies in the street. "Everyone wants him."

"No, not everyone does." Again, I started to turn but stopped. "You deserve better than some guy who spends his time talking about someone else."

Snatching another paper towel, she blotted her face. "Why are you being nice to me?"

Good question. "Why not?"

She sniffed again, turning back to the mirror. "Whatever."

I left the bathroom then and nearly plowed into Candy and a gaggle of girls. Oh, for the love of God...

Candy popped her hand on her hip. "How far have you fallen? Dating the help?"

"How desperate are *you*?" I shot back. "Dating your dead friend's ex-boyfriend?"

Her eyes shot wide and then narrowed, but I pushed past the girls. They followed me back into the ballroom, talking crap the entire way. I deserved a medal for not turning around and hitting one of them.

"Are you going to cry?" Candy crooned.

"What?" I frowned but kept going. Almost to the ballroom... *almost.*

"Or are you going to freak out and need to see your therapist?"

I spun around. "Why don't you try acting like a real friend and go check the bathroom instead of following me around like a pathetic puppy?"

Candy cocked her head to the side. "What's that supposed to mean?"

"Your friend—Veronica? She could use you right now. She's in the bathroom. Not having a very good time."

Her nose scrunched up as if I'd just asked her to figure out the square root of three. "You're probably seeing things again,

319

huh? Veronica is having a great time. She's going to be voted prom queen."

I gave up at that point. "Whatever."

"Insanity Sam!" Candy trilled, earning a few chuckles.

I rolled my eyes. "Clever, real clever."

She bobbed her head at me like an ostrich and then turned on her heel, teetering away. A few girls were left, and I met their stares. Something in my eyes must've reminded them of the old Sammy because they scattered like cockroaches.

Refusing to let any of them ruin my one night of normalcy, I entered the ballroom and searched for Carson. Spotting him with my brother and a few other baseball players, I headed in his direction.

A tall, slender body suddenly appeared in front of me, dressed in red. In an instant, the dancing bodies, the music, and the dazzling lights all disappeared. The world turned gray.

Cassie was in front of me.

Her pretty dress was ragged and hung limply from her ghastly pale arms. A dark oily substance seeped down her face. I took a step forward. The side of her head . . . it was shaped wrong, sunken in.

Cracked. Shattered.

Bile rose in my throat. "Cassie," I whispered.

And I realized then she wasn't really standing. Her arms and legs sort of waved in a lazy rhythm, as if something carried her body. Part of me recognized what I was seeing—Cassie floating in the lake, which explained the doll-like vacancy in her eyes.

Another form appeared between us, scrambling through the air . . . or over the boulders. Moonlight reflected off the slender body. Wind blew back long strands as she screamed out, "Cassie!"

My heart stuttered. It was me—me staring down at Cassie's body.

From the darkness, someone appeared, reaching out to the gray version of me. I turned, horror and disbelief etched into my face. My face contorted as I stood, taking a step back.

The other person was taller, broader. Frustration boiled in me. I couldn't see his face!

He reached for me, and I could taste the panic pulsating off both of us. My foot slipped on the rock; my arms flailed as I tried to keep my balance, to grab for something—for him. A silent scream parted my lips as my body bent in half.

And then I tumbled over backward—gone, falling as the dark void reached up and pulled me down. Gone.

I jerked out of the vision when a body bumped into mine. Dazed, I twisted around.

A face leered into mine. "What are you doing? Move out of the way, freak."

Barely hearing the words, I stumbled toward the doors. Horrible as it sounded, excitement pulsed through me. It hadn't been just Cassie and me. Someone else had been there with us.

And then a different scenario crept into my thoughts. The other person might not have pushed Cassie. I'd been the one on the edge of the cliff, screaming her name. He could've been there, witnessed it all. But that didn't make sense. If there had been a third person and he had seen me, why hadn't he gone to the police?

He would've, unless he had something to hide.

I had to talk to Carson.

Pulling my cell out of the clutch, I sent Carson a quick text, telling him I was going outside for some air just in case he started looking for me. Leaving the ballroom behind, I stepped into the dimly lit hallway that led to the back parking lot. My heels clicked on the floor, a steady echo that kept me company. I placed my hand on the cooled glass of the door, stopping when goose bumps spread across my flesh. The tiny hairs on the back of my neck rose.

I looked over my shoulder, scanning the empty hall. No one was there, but I couldn't shake the feeling of being watched. It swirled inside me, like dark ink spilled into water. Pushing open the door, I stepped out into the night air and refused to look behind me.

Ignore the feelings—they aren't real. The memories were, but everything else was just me freaking myself out . . . or trying to communicate with myself, which was odd and downright insane-sounding.

I clicked across the parking lot while every nerve seemed to be firing at once. *Look back. You'll see him. He's there. Waiting and watching.* My heart started racing as fast as it had when Carson had come so very close to kissing me while we danced. Only not as pleasant.

My cell phone chirped loudly from inside my clutch, causing me to jump and almost eat asphalt. Placing my hand over my slamming heart, I let out a shaky laugh. Scared to death by a text message. *Jeez.* Stopping beside a large tree, I dug out my cell. Carson's name flashed across my screen.

Then I heard it, the equal, measured steps—heavy and foreboding, sending my pulse racing. Ice formed tight balls inside my stomach. *It's not real. It's not real. One. Two. Three.* The footsteps were closer. The back of my neck burned with awareness.

I couldn't breathe.

Fingers shaking, I ran them across the screen of my cell, opening Carson's text. B THERE IN A SEC. My lungs spasmed, working again. Carson was coming. I was okay. I would be—

The loose strands of hair on the back of my neck stirred. Warmth moved over my skin.

A hand circled my bare arm, and my heart lurched into my throat. I started to scream, but another hand clamped down on my mouth, smothering the sound.

"Don't scream," he said.

chapter twenty-five

The second I recognized the voice, anger replaced the terror. I slammed my elbow back into Del's stomach with everything I had in me. Pain radiated down my arm, but with a startled grunt, he let go.

I whirled around, ready to use my clutch as a deadly weapon. "What is wrong with you?"

He clutched his stomach, eyes wide. "Jesus, Sammy, that wasn't necessary."

I wanted to hit him again. "It wasn't? You snuck up on me and put your hand over my mouth! Jesus, I thought you were going to . . ."

Straightening, he met my stare. "Do what? You had to have heard me walk up behind you. I wasn't being exactly stealth about it."

"But . . ." But I thought he hadn't been real, just another auditory hallucination. Now I wanted to hit Dr. O'Connell. What if Del had been some kind of psycho? And I just stood there, telling myself he wasn't real? I shook my head. "It doesn't matter. What do you want?"

He looked wounded. "I just wanted to talk with you. You did promise, by the way."

I slipped my phone back into the clutch. "I didn't promise anything, and you're here with Veronica—"

"I don't care about Veronica!" A vein pulsed along his temple, and I took a weary step back. "I only came with her because you've been avoiding me, not giving me a chance to talk to you."

Weeks later and he still wanted to fix things? Sad . . . and even a bit disturbing. I searched over his shoulder for Carson, but the parking lot appeared empty.

"Did you really come here with Carson?" Del asked. "Like, as a date?"

My eyes shot back to him. Upon closer inspection, I saw that his cheeks were ruddy. Temper or alcohol? "Yes. He asked me and I said yes."

Del shook his head as he ran his tongue along the front of his teeth. "So you're dating Carson now?"

Our newly labeled relationship seemed too fragile to blast to the entire world, but before I could say anything, the immediate lack of response hit a sore spot with him. He cursed. "Carson of all people? His dad works for your dad, Sammy. He's below a bottom-feeder."

"He's not a bottom-feeder!" I took a step forward, hands shaking. "And I don't care that his dad works for mine. It doesn't matter. Money doesn't buy taste, personality, or common decency."

His eyes narrowed. "Are you saying *Carson* is better than me?"

I didn't want to stoop to that level, but ugly anger turned me inside out. "Yes, he is better than you."

"You know what? I wouldn't have *wasted* almost four years with you if I'd known what a complete and utter loser you were going to turn into." He took another step, towering over me. His own fury rolled off him in dark, murky waves. "I would've stood by you, too. While everyone is calling you Insanity Sam, I've backed you up, protected you! I've kept my mouth shut."

"Kept your mouth shut about what?"

"What? You can't figure it out? I know, Sammy," he sneered. "You can forget loyalty. You screwed that up. And you're nothing without me."

I recoiled, stung by the venom lacing his words. And what was I supposed to know that he knew? Before I could demand answers, another voice, cold and hard, intruded.

"See, that's where you're wrong," Carson said from behind him, startling both of us. "She's actually about a thousand times better without you."

Del spun around. "Why? Because she's screwing—"

Carson's fist slammed into Del's jaw. There was a fleshy sound, and then Del's head jerked back. He folded like a deck of cards, hitting the ground and rolling onto his side, clutching his jaw.

"You know, I was sort of jealous when I found out Scott got to give you that black eye," Carson said, shaking his right hand. "But then I told myself to be patient. You'd give us another reason to knock the living shit out of you."

"What an odd thing to be patient for," I mumbled.

He ignored me. "Listen to me clearly, Del. Don't talk to her. Don't even look at her again. If you do, you can trust that a busted jaw isn't anything close to what I will do to you. Got that?"

Del grunted something in reply that suspiciously sounded like a string of four-letter words.

Coming to my side, Carson leaned in, his lips brushing across my cheek as he spoke. "I think we should get out of here before I hit him again."

I glanced over his shoulder. Del was picking himself up off the ground, leaning against a car for support. My hand found Carson's and squeezed. "I think you're right."

Part of me wasn't surprised that the night ended with fists being thrown. On the way home, I told Carson about the memory I had but kept Del's cryptic words to myself because I didn't know what they meant. Like me, he seemed excited about this development. At first.

"This is a good thing. Maybe you're starting to remember everything. . . ." He trailed off, focusing on the road.

I studied him in the darkness of the truck cab. "What's wrong?"

He shook his head, and several moments passed. "You remembering what happened is dangerous. I don't like to think that whoever was responsible is someone close to you, but if that person knew you were starting to piece together that night . . ."

I swallowed, looking away. My memories were dangerous,

but they were also the key to the truth. I shook my head as if I could shake off the fear starting to cling to my skin.

"And that's not all," he admitted after a few minutes.

"It's not?"

Carson gave a slight smile. "I hate myself for even thinking this, because I know how important getting your memories back is, but if you get your memories back—"

"Will I be like I am now or like the old Sammy?" I finished for him, chagrined. "I don't know, Carson. I like to think that, if anything, I've gotten a second chance at a personality improvement, and that won't go away."

He chuckled. "That's good to hear."

I bit my lip. "Will you still like me if I remember everything?"

His brows furrowed as he glanced at me. "Sam, I liked you before you lost your memories. You just didn't see that."

"I see it now," I whispered. "And I'll still see it, no matter what I remember."

He flashed the smile that warmed me to the core as he pulled onto the road leading to our homes. I took a deep breath. "I don't want to go home yet."

The smile sort of froze on his lips, and even in the darkness, I could see the blue of his eyes deepening, becoming the color of a summer sky. "It's my dad's weekend off. He's visiting his brother in Pittsburgh."

Empty house? I swallowed again, but for a different reason. "Do you . . . want to hang out a little while longer?"

"Do you really need me to answer that?"

I gave a nervous laugh as my fingers started working on the

beads sewn into my clutch. He parked the truck in his driveway. "Sit still."

"Okay," I said, curious.

Flashing me a quick grin, he hopped out of the truck and came around to my side, opening the door. Then he offered his hand with a bow. Just like that, most of my nervousness vanished as I placed my hand in his.

"I can't remember the last time you were in my house," he said as he unlocked the front door. "At least six years or so."

"I spent a lot of time here, right?"

"Practically every day," he said quietly.

Memories of our childhood together were locked away from me, but knowing that we shared that time calmed the rest of my anxiousness.

Carson's house was dark and quiet. With his hand wrapped around mine, he guided me through the living room. I bumped into the back of a couch and then a small desk, sending several sheets of paper fluttering to the floor.

He led me to his bedroom, and my heart rate picked up. Letting go of my hand, he turned on a small lamp beside the bed. It wasn't much light, but I could make out a small desk in the corner, a dresser with a bunch of clothes folded atop it. For a guy's bedroom, it seemed awfully clean. I placed my clutch on his desk.

Carson shrugged out of his tux jacket and his shoes and socks, draping the jacket over the back of his chair. Not sure what to do, I took off my shoes and sighed with relief. My poor toes were killing me.

Turning off the lamp, he moved back to me and stopped short. "We didn't get enough dances."

"No, we didn't."

He snaked an arm around my waist, lifting me up so my feet were on top of his bare ones. I laughed as he started to sway, moving both of us in a silent rhythm. "Is this making up for it?"

"Yes." I smiled, resting my head on his shoulder. "I like this better."

"Why? Because Scott's not here to be a douche?"

I laughed. "One of the reasons."

His hand squeezed mine. "Did I tell you how beautiful you looked tonight?"

My smile grew to epic proportions. "You did, but you can tell me again if you want."

Carson's laugh rumbled through me, and his other hand pressed on the small of my back, bringing us closer together. Our chests met, as did our hips and every other place. A flush started to spread down my throat.

"You look beautiful," he whispered in my ear, his hand moving up my spine to rest at the nape of my neck.

I lifted my head, pulling back so I could see his face. With only the light of the moon flowing in through the window above his bed, he almost didn't look real to me. Slowly, I reached up and placed my palm on his cheek. "Thank you," I whispered.

He didn't smile, but his eyes took on a hooded, lazy quality that tightened my stomach muscles. The longing in his stare matched what I felt inside, increased the yearning until I could hardly stand the intensity.

"Are you finally going to kiss me?" I asked, dizzy with anticipation, want, and a thousand other things.

One side of his mouth tipped up. "Maybe."

I leaned in, breathing the same air as him. "I'm not sure I like the sound of that."

"Me neither," he teased, his chest rising unsteadily against mine. Letting go of my hand, he cupped my cheek, running his thumb along my jaw. My hand fluttered to his chest, and his heart was pounding as fast as mine.

And when his head lowered, the sheer look of passion in his eyes stole my breath. His mouth moved against my forehead, trailing a path down along my cheek. I shivered against him, my eyes drifting close. And finally his lips brushed mine questioningly, once and then twice. My lips parted in response, and the velvety, supple kiss deepened. His tongue moved against mine, as if he wanted to capture my very essence with a simple kiss.

He made a deep sound in the back of his throat, and my fingers dug into his crisp shirt. Everything fell away, and there was just him and me, the way he kissed, the way he held me against him, as if I was something precious and invaluable to him.

And then we were moving. His legs hit the edge of his bed, and he folded down, cradling me close to him. My knees were on either side of his hips, sinking into the mattress. Our kisses didn't stop. Not once, not even when his fingers moved to the straps on my dress, slipping under them.

He paused, and when he spoke, his voice was thick. "You okay with this?"

"Yes." I nodded, too, just in case the one word wasn't enough.

Carson's lips pressed against mine once more, and with shaky fingers, I undid the buttons on his shirt, pushing the sides over his shoulders. His skin was hot under my fingers, taut and smooth. My hands slid over his chest, down the ropy muscles of his stomach. Years of playing baseball had done him well.

All this felt like the first time for me, and I had a deep sense of gratitude for that because I wouldn't have wanted to share this moment with anyone else. His lips left mine, traveling over my chin, down my throat.

"Samantha." He said my name over and over again like it was a prayer or a curse. I wasn't sure which it was, but every time he spoke, my heart turned over in a heady way.

A shudder rocked his body as I pressed a kiss to his forehead. In that moment, I knew he'd been waiting, wanting this for far longer than I could have ever imagined. A giddy rush followed, and I felt heavy and light in his arms, safe and cherished. I wanted to laugh, to slow down, to speed up, and to never, ever stop. My head was spinning when his fingers slid down my arms, bringing the straps along with them. His fingers found the tiny zipper on the back of my dress, slowing inching it down to my hips.

Carson eased me onto my back, raining kisses over my cheek, lips, throat, and shoulders. His hand drifted down my stomach and lower, lingering until I thought I'd come out of my skin. He curved a hand around my thigh, hooking my leg around his waist, and we moved against each other until we were breathless, covered in each other, drowning together.

Perfect—we were perfect together. There wasn't a moment

of hesitation or doubt. No nagging voice in the back of my head, and Carson had given me plenty of chances to pull the brakes, even before he stopped to grab protection.

"Are you sure?" he whispered against my lips.

"Yes." The next words sort of just came right out of me in a breathless rush. "I love you."

Carson stilled. I wasn't sure he breathed in those following seconds, and maybe tomorrow I would kick myself in the face for saying those three words, but right now, I didn't want to take them back, even if they were too much, too soon.

He closed his eyes and let out a long breath. "Say it again."

"I love you." My voice was louder, stronger. "I love you."

Another second passed and then he brushed his lips across mine. "I didn't think I'd ever hear you say those words."

I pressed my palm to his cheek. "I did."

He opened his eyes, and they locked on to mine. "I've loved you as long as I've known you, Sam. Just as much as I love you right now."

The infinite tenderness in his bright eyes brought tears to my own. I held them back, fearing he wouldn't understand they weren't sad tears. His body shook, and I wasn't sure if it was out of relief or anticipation, and then I wasn't really thinking anymore... or maybe I was thinking so much I couldn't pinpoint one thought or one sensation. Part of me worried that the meds that had built up in my system would somehow dull everything, but they didn't. It was so much, and it was all new to me, fresh and thrilling.

When things did slow down, my heart was still racing,

my breath sawing in and out in a pleasant daze. Muscles weak, thoughts like big bowls of jelly, I smiled up at him.

He gave me a lopsided grin. His dark hair was damp against his forehead, curling slightly. "You okay?"

"Perfect," I breathed.

Carson kissed me and then rolled onto his back, wiggling an arm around me and pulling me against his side so that my head rested on his chest. Each breath he took was ragged against my flushed cheek. "What do I have to do to persuade you to stay here?"

I giggled. "Not sure my parents would appreciate that come morning, but I can stay..." I paused, for the first time feeling uncertainty creep over me. "I mean, if you do really want me to stay for a little while longer."

He turned his head toward me. "Sam, I don't want you to leave. Ever. And I know you don't want to leave."

The stupid but wonderful swelling was back in my chest, and I could've floated right off that bed. "Okay."

His throat worked as he watched me. "I wasn't just saying shit before, Sam. I do love you—I have loved you. I hope you—"

"I meant it," I said, tangling my fingers in his. "And I think ...I think I felt this way before but never admitted it."

Carson's lips tipped up at the corners. We stayed in each other's arms, talking about nothing important, laughing quietly, stopping to kiss and pausing to touch, losing ourselves for a little while longer and letting time slip by. I must've dozed off, because I knew I was dreaming. It had that hazy quality to it, almost real but not quite.

I was waiting outside the library at school, my head tipped back. Satisfaction poured off me, dampening the jealousy that simmered in my belly whenever I saw him even looking at Cassie after that party.

I had him and I was going to ruin him.

Footsteps sounded, and I opened my eyes, already smiling with anticipation. Carson stepped out, saying something to Dianna.

I bolted off the wall, stepping directly in front of him. "We need to talk."

His bright blue eyes sharpened with wariness. He glanced at Dianna. "I'll see you later."

The girl nodded and quickly darted off. I smirked, cocking my head to the side. "How are you, Carson?"

"What do you want, Sam?" He started walking. "I've got things to do, and even though I'm sure this is going to be interesting, I don't have time."

My eyes narrowed at him. Jealousy was there, but so was anger. How could he always be so dismissive of me? Every guy in this damn school wanted me. Everyone but him.

"I know something," I said.

He stopped just before the doors and rolled his eyes. "And . . . ?"

"I know you're paying Dianna."

"Yep, for sex. You got me."

I pressed my lips together, pissed that he wasn't at all intimidated by me. Probably had to do with the fact that I'd spent the better part of my life running around shirtless with him and my brother. "I doubt you need to pay anyone for sex. Although I'm surprised you actually got with Cassie without her paying you."

His eyes settled on me, steady and consuming. I loved and hated his eyes. "Is this what you wanted to talk about? The fact that I hooked up with Cassie months ago?"

"No." My hands balled into fists. Jealousy was a bitch, but so was I. And I knew what I was about to do was so wrong, but I didn't care. I just didn't care. "But it has to do with the fact that you're paying the daughter of your history teacher. Hmm . . ." I tapped my chin. "I wonder what for. Wait. Don't you share that class with Cassie?"

Carson folded his arms. "Yeah, I do."

"And she said that you're failing that class. So I wonder what you could possibly be paying Dianna for."

"Gee, I don't know, but I'm sure you're going to tell me."

Anger flushed my skin, sharpening my tongue. "I know you're paying Dianna to get her little hands on her daddy's tests and she's helping you cheat."

He stared at me a long second, then laughed. "Okay. You got me. What are you going to do, Nancy Drew?"

My hands itched to slap him. "Cassie knows, and you know how terrible she is with keeping a secret."

His jaw worked.

"I'm sure a little birdie will put it in the principal's ears soon enough, and then you know what will happen." I grinned then, loving the way his attention was completely on me—bad attention, but I had it. I had him. "They take cheating seriously around these parts. So does Penn State, I hear."

Carson's lips thinned. "Jesus, Sam . . ."

I pushed open the door, stepping out into the brisk March air. "You can kiss that scholarship good-bye. Shame."

"You're such a . . ."

"What? A bitch?" I glanced over my shoulder, meeting his eyes. "Ouch."

"No. You're not a bitch." He followed me outside, eyes sheltered. "It's sad, actually, when I think about how you used to be."

Not what I'd been angling for, and beneath the anger, hurt waited.
"I'm not sad."

His lips twitched into a mocking smile. "Yeah, you are. Do your worst,
Sam. And you'll regret it."

Jerking up, I clutched the blankets to my chest. Pressure
clamped down on my throat, on my chest. The dark, poster-
covered walls of Carson's bedroom shifted unsteadily.

It wasn't a dream. Oh god, no, it was a memory. I knew it
in my bones, in every cell. Carson had been paying Dianna to do
his essays, to fix his exams for the one class he was failing. And
somehow I'd found out—I'd told Cassie and I'd threatened to
expose him, ruin his baseball scholarship and his life.

Do your worst . . . and you'll regret it.

Sickness rose in my throat. Had he . . . could he have been the
third person on the cliff? My entire body went cold. It couldn't be.
Oh my god . . .

Out of everyone, he had a reason to shut us up. Suddenly,
I remembered the sense of wariness in his gaze when he saw me
the first day back home, the way he didn't really have anything
good to say about Cassie, how he knew the cliff just as well as I
did, and how adamant he was that I hadn't been the one to hurt
Cassie. The notes I was leaving myself—*Don't let him know you
remember anything.* Had my subconscious been trying to warn me?

To warn me to not let Carson know?

chapter twenty-six

eart pounding, my stomach rolled. I'd just given myself to him, told him that I loved him, and...I couldn't even finish that thought. I needed to get out of here, to think this through, because it couldn't be him—anyone but him.

Carson stirred beside me, slowly sitting up. "What is it, Sam?"

"I have to go." My voice came out in a hoarse whisper.

"Okay." He yawned, running the palm of his hand over his forehead. "Let me walk you back. It's late."

"No. You don't have to." I threw off the cover and found my dress in a pile.

Carson sat up, swinging his legs off the edge of the bed. "It's not a big deal. I don't want you to..." He trailed off, watching me tug the dress on over my head. Grinning, he reached for me.

I jumped back, tripping over his shoes. I caught myself on the wall.

His grin faded. "Are you okay, Sam?"

"Yeah." Panic pawed at me as I managed to get the zipper halfway up my back. "It's late. I just need to get back."

He didn't look entirely convinced now that he was wide awake. Worry furrowed his brows as I searched for my shoes, finally giving up when I couldn't find them in the dark. Grabbing my clutch off his desk, I backed up toward the door.

"I'll... I'll see you later." Emotion clogged my throat, but I couldn't let myself think about what had happened between us and what he could've done without breaking down.

He stood, and it was a lot to keep my eyes trained on his face. "Wait. Why are you freaking out? Sam?"

Unable to say anything without bursting into tears, I reached for the door and blindly stumbled out in the narrow hallway. Bumping into shadowed objects, I ignored the flashes of pain and rushed to the front door. I winced at the whining sound the door made and slipped outside, closing it behind me.

I dragged in gulps of air. Sharp pebbles dug into my feet, and then blades of cool grass cushioned my steps. *Was it Carson? Had it always been him?* A splinter hit my heart, and then another. *Carson.*

My thoughts swam, going from the moment I saw him in my bedroom, up until the last, soul-burning kiss he'd given me before I fell asleep. Hurrying across the trimmed field, I balled my hand over my mouth to stifle my cry. It couldn't be him. I trusted him beyond a doubt, and he'd been so kind toward me, even though I'd been sure I didn't deserve it. Doubt blossomed under the confusion, trying to take hold, but those words...

Those words—they had to be a warning.

"Sam!"

A strangled sob escaped me. I couldn't face him, couldn't even look at him without giving myself some time to reason this through.

Carson caught up to me before I even reached the halfway point. Catching my arm, he spun me around. He was bare from the waist up, pants not even buttoned in his haste to reach me.

"What's going on, Sam?" he demanded, eyes wide and dilated.

I tried to wrestle my arm free. "Please, just let me go. Please."

He held on. "What's wrong? Did we go too fast? Just talk to me, Sam."

My breath caught as my eyes met his, and another crack pierced my heart. "Did you do it?"

"Did I do what?" He reached with his free hand, brushing back my hair. "Talk to me, Sam. Help me understand what's going on. Whatever it is, it'll be okay."

The tenderness in his voice caused my chest to squeeze. How could he be like this after what he'd done? It made all this incredibly surreal. "I...I remembered something."

Confusion poured from him, so sincere I started to doubt myself. "Okay. What?"

"It was about you," I said, my pulse pounding. "I knew you were paying Dianna—cheating on your history exams. I must've told Cassie, and I...I threatened you at school, when you were leaving the library. You told me that if I told anyone, I'd regret it."

Carson dropped my arm and took a step back. "Sam..."

I trembled at the weight of his one word. "I told you I was going to tell the principal."

"You ... you think ...?" He dragged a hand through his hair. "You think it was me because of that?"

"There was a third person there, and you ... you had reason...."

He stared at me, pain—not anger—contorting his face, and my conviction started to waver even more.

"I can't believe you," he said, stunned.

"Me?" I wrapped my arms around myself, shivering.

"Yes! You! My god, I thought ... I thought you'd changed, but that's the old Sammy. Jumping from one messed-up assumption to another, making everything about you!" He stepped forward, eyes flashing in the thin slice of moonlight. "What the fuck, Sam?"

"But I saw you with her, you were giving her money, and I threatened you. I told Cassie! We were planning to go to the principal." Even as those words left my mouth, I had a second to realize how truly bitchtastic I'd been. Sure, cheating was wrong, but jeez.

Carson stared at me, then laughed grimly. "You have no clue what you saw."

"Then tell me because I really don't want to believe this!"

He flinched, and again, I was hit with another pang of doubt. He was angry with me, but not in the way I thought he'd be, and there was too much hurt behind his words, in his eyes.

"You saw me paying Dianna. That did happen. But I was paying her to *tutor* me in history."

My arms fell to my sides. "What?" I choked out.

"Yeah, that's what I was paying her for—still am. My dad has been working overtime for *your* father to get that money, cleaning his offices and doing all kinds of bitch work so I'll keep my scholarship."

I remembered what my mom had said. Guilt whipped through me with barb-tipped lashes. Oh my god, how could I be so . . . so wrong? "Why didn't you tell me when I accused you?"

"Why did I need to? Why did I owe you, of all people, the truth then? You wouldn't have believed me." He drew in a deep breath and cursed. "Jesus, Sam, you thought it was me? That I pushed Cassie off a cliff and then you?"

Tears built in my eyes as I pushed my wind-tossed hair out of my face. "But you said I'd regret it."

Carson jerked back from me as if I'd slapped him. And maybe a slap would've been better. Since the accident, Carson had been there for me and he hadn't doubted me once. And I had.

"As in one day, you'd regret the things that you've done. Not in the way you think—*wait*. You *really* think I meant I'd hurt you? Even after I told you how I felt?" When he saw the answer in my expression, he swore again. "I could never, *ever* hurt you. You could've gone to the principal or whoever, and I wouldn't have done a damn thing about it."

"Why didn't I go to the principal or Cassie?"

"I don't know." He took a breath, exhaling harshly. "I'd like to think you had a change of heart, but that's doubtful. You and Cassie disappeared that weekend."

And I knew then he was telling the truth, and I had acted impulsively when I came out of the memory. I couldn't see through the tears as I reached for him blindly. "Carson, I'm so—"

"You're sorry?" He dodged me, backing away as he shook his head. "Not as sorry as I am."

My heart cracked straight down the middle. "I'm so sorry. I'm just confused. I only remembered—"

"And you automatically assumed that I was capable of those things? Why? Because I seem likely to bribe, cheat, and murder someone? Then hang around you and *sleep* with you after I tried to kill you?" Pain lanced his words, as if I'd cut open a fresh wound. "Because the old Sammy would have believed those things, but I thought she was gone. Obviously, I was wrong."

"Carson—"

"No." He kept backing up, his jaw clenched tight. "No. You're still the same old Sammy. Just not as mean as you used to be, but she's still there. Stupid me to think any different."

Apologizing felt stupid and pointless. What I'd accused him of was terrible, but I couldn't stop. I needed him to know how awful I felt. Hurrying toward him, my foot caught on the gown and I stumbled forward.

Carson caught me by the arms before I could crash face-first into the hard ground. "Jesus, Sam," he said through clenched teeth.

I pressed my forehead against his bare chest, barely able to breathe past the tears. "I'm so, so sorry. I'm just so confused."

His hands fluttered around my arms and a second later, he wrapped me against him, burying his face in my hair. His embrace lasted only a few moments at most, and then he let go and stepped back.

"Go home, Sam." His voice was tight, choked. "Just go home."

Standing there, I watched him turn and jog away, disappearing into the shadows. An ache opened in my chest, rushing through me. I could've gone after him again, but I knew . . . I knew I'd lost him before I really even had him.

When I woke up the following morning, every part of my body ached for different reasons. Some of it was good. Most of it was bad. I didn't want to open my eyes or get out of bed, but I became aware of the fact that I wasn't alone.

My brother sat at the head of my bed, legs crossed at the ankles and the morning newspaper in his lap—the sports section.

Rubbing my hand over my swollen eyes, I scowled. "What are you doing in here?"

"Hmm . . . questions, questions. I have some of my own." He folded the newspaper and dropped it on the floor. "What happened last night?"

I stared at him, in no mood for brotherly caring-and-sharing time.

He raised his hand. "I'm curious. You left prom after only being there an hour. Carson took you home, apparently. Del looked like I'd punched him again, but I didn't." He paused, ticking each one off his finger. The ring finger was next. "I went running with Carson this morning, and all he would say is that you had some memories come back and then he wouldn't talk at all. Aaaaand..."

"There's more," I groaned, shoving my face into the pillow. Hearing Carson's name had my heart aching in a way I knew I'd never get over.

"And even though you and Carson left *way* before I did, you snuck back into the house *way* after I got home. Care to explain?"

"No." My voice was muffled by the pillow.

Scott stretched out beside me. "I don't want the dirty details. I'd like to keep my breakfast in my stomach, but as long as Carson has been secretly in love with you—"

I popped up, rising to my knees. Thick curls still left over from last night fell in my face. "Oh god." I covered my face with my hands. "Kill me now."

"What happened?" He pulled my hands away from my face. "It can't be that bad."

"It is. It really is." I flopped onto my back. "I was terrible before I lost my memory and I'm terrible afterward. I accused Carson of being the one who hurt Cassie and me."

"Oh, jeez, Sam, you're going to have to give me a better explanation than that."

I did, starting with the memory I had at prom and the one later that night, leaving out most of what had happened with Carson. According to my version of events, I fell asleep talking to him.

When I finished, Scott shook his head. "He'll get over it, Sam."

"No, he won't." Because seriously, who gets over being accused of murder?

"Yeah, he will. He understands you've been through a lot. You've just got to give him some time."

I raised my arms helplessly. "I'm such an idiot."

"I'm going to have to agree with that." Scott stood. "Look, go take a shower. Julie and I are going to see a movie. You should come with us."

A little bit of interest stirred, but I shook my head. I needed more time to wallow in my lameness. Scott left, and I lay there for a while, staring at the ceiling. How could I be so stupid? It was a talent, I decided.

By the time I got up, it was late in the afternoon. Scott was still at the movies with Julie, Mom had left to attend a charity fund-raising meeting or something, and I had no idea where Dad was or whether he was even home. I dragged myself into the shower. At some point, the tears mingled with the water, and even after I'd dried off and changed, my face was still damp.

I had to make it up to Carson, but I wasn't sure I could. No one could blame him for not getting over this.

Sitting down on my bed, I glanced at the music box. The tingling, burning sensation shot up my spine, and I was tossed headfirst into a memory.

I stomped down Del's driveway, face full of tears. How could he do this? How could she? I was her best friend, the only person who put up with her crap, and she'd slept with my boyfriend.

I hated her—hated him.

Del caught up to me. "Sammy, I'm sorry. It was a mistake. I was drunk. So was she."

"Is that supposed to make it okay?" I spun on him, hands shaking. "It doesn't! You slept with my best friend!"

He glanced over his shoulders anxiously. "Keep it down. My parents are going—"

"I don't care!" My voice was shrill. "Did you guys wait until I passed out? Did you have fun ringing in the New Year with her?"

"No! It wasn't like that. I swear."

I laughed harshly and reached up, my fingers curling around the necklace. With a vicious tug, the delicate chain gave and snapped. I flung it back at him. "We're over. For real this time."

Del's mouth dropped open. "You can't be serious."

Oh, I was completely serious. I didn't care what my parents thought or wanted. And it suddenly made sense why Cassie wanted to meet me at the summerhouse later tonight. She was going to fess up to sleeping with my boyfriend. Nice. "I'm so sick of her doing stuff like this!"

He reached for me, but I stepped out of the way. "Sammy, you need to calm down."

I shook my head. "I'm so going to kill her."

When I snapped out of the memory, I was standing in my bedroom, staring at my reflection. The girl's face in the mirror was devoid of any blood, hazel eyes diluted to the point her eyes almost looked black. A tremor ran through her body, and her chest rose sharply.

She was me.

Taking a step back, I placed my fingers against my mouth.

Del had cheated on me with Cassie. Was that why I'd been so drawn to the picture of them taken on New Year's Eve? Another part of my subconscious trying to wiggle itself free, demanding that I acknowledge what that photo had meant to me? Again, Del had lied to me. I hadn't taken the necklace off because I wanted to take a shower. I'd thrown it in his face. I'd grown a pair and broken up with him. That small triumph was lost in the shadow of everything else, though.

The anger simmered through my veins still, like a poison infecting bone and tissue with a sickness. When I'd said I was going to kill Cassie, I thought I'd meant it.

Cassie had wanted to meet at the lake house, and according to Carson, I'd gone home first. And the reason why I'd been crying and had kissed Carson kind of made sense now.

I laughed and then cringed at the high-pitched sound.

No wonder Del thought I owed him. And he'd been right. He *had* been protecting me. Only he knew how upset I'd been at Cassie the night she died. Del had known the truth. There probably hadn't been a third person on the cliff, not in the literal sense, but just another way my subconscious was trying to tell me that someone else knew the truth, knew what I'd done.

The notes didn't make sense, or how Cassie and I had ended up on the cliff, but did it matter now?

A floodgate of emotions broke open, ripping through me as if I were made of tissue paper. All those moments when I'd suspected everyone—Del, Scott, Carson—and when I'd entertained the idea that it had been a stranger danced before me.

My knees were knocking together, my breath coming out in

short rasps. It had to be me—it had always been me. I had reason to hurt Cassie, more than anyone else, and that anger—that terrible surge of raw destruction—was still in me. Would I have really killed her over *Del*?

God, I'd never hated myself more.

I spun around, tears blurring my vision as I grabbed the music box off the bedside table and threw the box straight at the mirror. A disjointed note squeaked from the box. Glass shattered in dozens of pieces, falling and falling. I was that mirror—that box—destroyed, broken into a bunch of jagged sections.

The box hit the floor. The little dancer in her tutu shattered, but the base remained. It made another weak sound, like a tiny mewl.

Light flashed behind my eyes, followed by a slicing pain shooting between my temples as if someone had shoved a screwdriver behind them. I doubled over, clutching my head, wondering whether I'd somehow been cut by a sadistic piece of glass.

And then it happened.

Dizziness swept through me like tumultuous waves crashing and eroding the shoreline. With each lap, a new memory popped free. Jumping from halfway up the grand stairs, into Scott's waiting arms, giggling as he yelled at me. Mom replaced him, holding me tight as the doctor checked my broken wrist, her soothing words lost in my tears. Another came of me sitting cross-legged in the tree house, across from an impish ten-year-old Carson.

"Truth or dare!" I yelled.

"Dare." He grinned. "I dare you to kiss me."

That was caught and swept away, replaced by the first time

I met Cassie. How I'd been so drawn to her, like I was looking into my own reflection. The two of us running away from the boys, giggling when we tripped, dressed up in her mother's shoes and jewelry. On and on they came, going back in time and then fast-forwarding to when we were fifteen, sitting in her bedroom.

"You're so lucky," she said softly. "You have everything."

I didn't understand that then, but I'd watched her slide a folded-up piece of parchment into the bottom of her music box, securing the hidden slot.

And then that was gone, lost in a rising tide of memories. My life—the things I'd done and said to people. In a rush, all of it had come back to me. The childhood spent trailing my brother and Carson around—*Carson*. An entire wealth of emotion brought me to my knees. The almost obsessive friendship that I'd had with Cassie and how it had swallowed my entire life. Memories of being introduced to Del at a company holiday party, practically shoved together by our parents, pricked at my skin and heart. So much pressure to be perfect, to be better than everyone else. Anger swirled like ticked-off wasps in my chest. I'd been so angry, so bitter under the facade. So desperate to run my own life that I turned into the person who struck out, hurting others to make myself feel better, to have some kind of control.

But I was mean . . . because I could be. Because no one dared to stop me. There was no real excuse for my behavior, for what I let Del do, for how I let Cassie run my life. I'd made so, so many bad mistakes, but that night . . .

I'd gone to the cabin, caught in a stormy mix of emotions. I'd just broken up with Del and kissed Carson, and my best friend was a traitorous bitch. Another text from her had led me up to the cliff. I'd thrown my phone at a nearby tree before picking it up and slipping it in the back pocket of my jeans. I'd been so angry, even more irritated by the fact that I had to find my way through the woods in the dark without killing myself. I hadn't known what I was going to do when I got my hands on her, but like with Del, our friendship was over. Stealing my clothes and jewelry was one thing, but my boyfriend? That was it. I was done with her.

What I saw when I neared the edge of the woods and the cliff came into view wasn't something I expected or could really comprehend, but most important, I remembered.

I saw the face of Cassie's killer.

chapter twenty-seven

*M*y heart thundered in my chest, pounding the blood through my veins so fast that my stomach lurched and my bedroom walls seemed to spin crazily.

I remembered *everything*.

I'd gone there because Cassie had wanted me there. She wanted me to see, and I saw. I *understood*. Why her mother had wanted her to stay away from me. Why Cassie went after Del and constantly pushed me—constantly *took* from me—why our friendship was a bitter, vengeful, sad little monster underneath its complex, shattering layers.

Most of all, as I struggled to my feet, sorrow coursed through me, tightening my throat, squeezing my heart until it splintered into a million messy pieces.

I could barely breathe, think around the raw hurt.

Cassie... poor Cassie...

I knew who killed her.

Shards of glass crunched under my flip-flops as I stumbled over to my desk, grabbed my cell phone, and pressed down on the contact. The phone rang. Once. Twice. Five times. Tears blurred my vision. He wasn't going to answer. Of course not. I'd accused him of terrible things, and now that I remembered what a wretched beast I'd been to him, he shouldn't have been the one I called, but I had to tell someone. I had to get the words out of my mouth because they made it real. They changed everything.

Carson's voice mail picked up.

I squeezed my eyes shut. "It's me. I remember everything. I know—I know who killed Cassie. I don't know what to do. Please—"

My bedroom door groaned as it swung open, and I lifted my gaze. My heart leaped into my throat as my fingers dug into the slim phone. The figure filled the door—the same figure I'd seen in all those memories, looking down on me as I lay on the cliff, touching and checking for a pulse. The shadow man who haunted my steps was real. Maybe not in the backseat of the car, but I knew without a doubt that he'd been in the woods, watching me, grabbing my purse and the note from the car after I'd wrecked. Had he left me for dead twice?

My heart ached at the betrayal.

"Dad?" I croaked, dizzy.

"Hang up the phone, Samantha."

Hanging up the phone would be bad. Standing there was stupid, but I was shell-shocked. I shook as Dad stalked toward me, sparing a brief glance at the broken mirror and music box. He pried the phone from my tight grasp and disconnected the call.

"Who did you call, Samantha?" he asked, placing the phone in his back pocket.

I backed up. "No one."

He grimaced. "Don't lie to me. I know you were on the phone with someone. Who was it?"

There was no way I'd tell him. I clamped my mouth shut, praying that Carson decided to listen to my message and knew to call the police. Long shot, considering he'd probably delete my message without listening to it, and even if he did, he'd call back and Dad had my phone.

"It was Carson, wasn't it? Why, princess, why did you have to involve him?" He rubbed his brow, sounding disappointed, as if I'd stayed out too late and broken curfew. "This . . . we will have to work through this. I can deal with him."

Fear spiked through me. "Deal with him?"

Dad shot me a dark look, and I shrank back. "I did not pull myself out of the gutters and become who I am today to lose it all. Sacrifices . . . they have to be made along the way."

Crazy—he sounded crazy. "Sacrifices? Was Cassie a sacrifice? Was I?"

"Samantha—"

"Why did you kill her? She was . . ."

"Kill her?" He shook his head. "You don't understand."

"I remember!" The pain and panic in my own voice shocked me. "I saw you. You pushed her away and—"

"And she slipped and fell! She hit her head on the damn

rocks! It was an accident, Samantha. I never meant for her to get hurt. She just wouldn't listen to me!" He stepped back, moving his hands over his head, tugging on the ends of his hair. "From the day you brought her home from school, I knew she was going to be a problem. And I did everything to keep you two apart."

Besides the few moments he'd mentioned not liking my friendship, I remembered now. How turned off he'd been by my new friend. Not allowing her to sleep over, arguing with Mom—poor, naive Mom—when she went behind him and let Cassie stay. How standoffish he'd been to Cassie over the years, outright avoiding her whenever she was in the house or any talk of her.

I was going to hurl.

"Sit down."

My body locked up, and my eyes darted around the room frantically.

"Sit down, Samantha." His voice brooked no room for argument, and I sat on the edge of my bed, trembling. "You need to listen to me. What happened to Cassie was an accident. You have to believe me, princess. I never wanted anyone to get hurt."

Tears spilled over my cheeks. Thoughts raced together dizzily, and terror shuttled through my body. I needed to find a way out of this, and even though he was my dad, Cassie deserved justice. God, she deserved so much more than what her life had become.

He moved toward me but stopped when I recoiled. "I especially never meant for you to get hurt. I didn't even know you were there until it was too late."

I lifted my gaze, seeing the face of a true stranger. A man

I never really knew, capable of leaving one daughter to die after he'd killed another. "She was my sister."

"Your *half* sister," he corrected vehemently. "One night, Samantha, one night with her mother doesn't make her your sister."

"But she was your daughter!"

He crouched in front of me, taking a deep breath. "You are my daughter. Cassie . . . Cassie was a mistake."

I shook my head, scooting back from him.

A dark, terrible look flickered in his eyes. "Cate and I had agreed to keep our affair a secret. She understood how much I faced losing if your mother ever found out. She'd divorce me, and I'd lose everything, Samantha—my marriage, my job, everything I've worked for!"

One horrifying puzzle piece clicked into another after another. The prenup—no doubt they had a clause involving cheating, leaving the one having the affair with nothing. And Dad had nothing without Mom and her money.

"I don't know how she discovered it," he continued, standing slowly. My thoughts went to the music box and its hidden slot. "But she did. She wanted me to acknowledge that I was her father, but you know that. You were at the cliff that night. You heard it all."

Cassie had begged him to love her—to be her father and give her everything that he'd given me while I'd hidden behind the tree, fixated on the drama unfolding. Thinking back, I hadn't been afraid. Just so damn angry that my dad had cheated—cheated like Del—and Cassie once again had been the center of it all. Part of me had even been relieved when Dad had refused, pleading with her to understand that he would never go public with the fact that he was her father.

She hadn't backed down, and maybe what happened had been an accident. The rocks had been slippery, and it'd been dark. Either way, I'd seen Dad push her, and she'd slipped. The rocks had run red with her blood, just like the very first memory I'd had. And the horror I'd felt then, seeing my dad kneel over her prone body, was now rushing through me again.

"She was dead," Dad said, watching my expression. "I checked. Her skull...she was dead, and I panicked."

I'd been rooted to my spot in shock. Not making my presence known until he'd picked up Cassie...Anger squashed some of the fear. "You threw her off the cliff like garbage and then covered your tracks!"

He flinched. "There was nothing I could do! It would just be better if everyone thought it was an accident. Which it was!" His feet crunched over glass as he moved to the side, blocking the door. "And then you came running out from behind those damn trees. I didn't know you were there, didn't expect that Cassie had planned for you to hear everything." His voice cracked. "And you slipped on the damp rocks and her..."

"Her blood," I whispered, remembering how I'd screamed her name and then the terror when my feet moved out from underneath me, the sky tumbling over, the ground reaching up to catch me.

"You fell over the edge." His voice was hoarse.

"And you left me there to die." The hurt ran so deep I thought I'd drown in it.

"No! No." He came forward fast, grasping my shoulders and giving me a little shake. "I climbed down the cliff and I checked. I swear, I didn't think you were breathing. I checked your pulse. I couldn't feel one, and you didn't seem like you were breathing, and there was so much blood. Baby, I thought you were dead."

I shuddered. The night I'd found out that I'd been writing the notes—the nightmare that had woken me up had been a memory of Dad. "You could've called the police! You could've done something!"

"I panicked!" he roared, his fingers digging into my shoulders. "I thought you were dead, too. And I just panicked!"

I tried to shake off his grasp. His touch made my skin crawl. He was my father—flesh and blood, but he'd *left* me in a panic. "There wasn't a single moment afterward that you didn't consider calling the police? Not once while I was missing?"

He looked me straight in the eye. "I took your phone, and I couldn't..."

"You..." It hit me then, and I cried out. It wasn't that he *couldn't* call the police after the panic had subsided. It was that he *wouldn't*. The deeds had already been done, and the risk had been too great. The truth of his affair would have come out, and he would've lost everything—and been charged with Cassie's accidental death.

Money was more important to him. A relationship with his own daughter hadn't been enough, and neither had been my life.

"I'm going to be sick," I whispered.

Dad fingers loosened. "I'm so sorry."

A tiny part of me believed him, because I could hear it in his voice. "What did you think when they found me?"

Lowering his gaze, he didn't answer.

My body shook as another sob rolled its way through me. "What would you've done if I'd remembered then?" I gasped, trying to shake his hands off. "What *are* you going to do?"

"I hoped you wouldn't remember, but then you started poking around, writing those notes, trying to figure out what happened." He looked so disappointed, as if I'd failed him somehow. "The day you went to the cliff, I followed you."

Competing levels of horror and fury battled inside me. My hands formed tight fists. "I thought I was crazy! And you just let me believe that."

"I couldn't tell you the truth. You have to understand that." Dad shook his head. "I wasn't in the car, baby. You had a panic attack or something, but I found the note and I did call the accident in."

Like that made it better, redeemed him somehow. He'd accidentally killed Cassie and then left me to die . . . all so he could keep up his pathetic lifestyle.

He cupped my cheek, and revulsion twisted my insides. "You're my baby girl, my princess."

Cassie had been his baby girl, too, and that had meant nothing to him. Movement flickered behind him. Over his shoulder, I caught a glimpse of the door inching open. A long, thin shadow spread across the floor. My breath caught as a denim-clad leg appeared, and then long, tanned fingers gripped the door.

Carson.

I focused on my father, swallowing hard. "Why did you give her the same music box if you didn't want her to know?"

Caught off guard by the question, he blinked. "It was so long ago when I gave it to Cate." A faint smile parted his lips. "I had the boxes made in Philly. They're unique. It was a stupid, sentimental thing to do." He laughed then, the sound broken and harsh. "How was I to know that you two would be friends one day? Cate left town. I never thought she'd be back. Those boxes..."

Moving silently behind us, Carson squeezed in between the door and my wall. His eyes were fixed on us, and I had no idea what he was planning. I wanted him to run because I knew my dad owned pistols. He could have one on him now.

If Carson got hurt in all this...

"I'm so sorry." Dad's hand moved from my cheek to my neck. "I never meant for any of this to happen."

Another shudder rocked me. "Please, don't—"

Carson stepped on a piece of glass. The crunch sounded like a shotgun blast. Dad whipped around, and everything happened so fast. I jumped up as Carson rushed forward, as if he was going to tackle my father, but Dad—he moved so quickly. Like lightning, really. He swiped something off the floor and met Carson.

There was a pain-filled yelp, and Carson staggered back. Blood spurted from his left shoulder as he hit the wall. A scream rose in my throat, spilling over. Dad yanked the piece of glass out of Carson and reared his arm back.

I didn't even think.

Rushing forward, I grabbed the heavy base of the broken music box, and with another scream that rose from a deep place within me, I brought it down on the back of my father's head.

The bloodied piece of glass fell from my father's hand as his legs buckled out from underneath him. He folded like a paper sack.

I stepped back, clutching the music box. "Dad?" I whispered.

He didn't move.

Had I . . . killed him? I edged around his body, reaching Carson. "Are you okay?"

Face pale and contorted, he nodded as he pressed his hand against the wound. "It's not deep. Thought . . . I was going to rescue you." He gave a dry, shocked laugh. "Holy crap, Sam, holy crap . . ."

I dropped the box on the floor and placed my hand over his. Blood seeped through his fingers, causing my stomach to roll. "I'm so, so sorry."

"Stop." He grasped my other hand as he pushed off the wall, pulling me toward the door. "None of this is your fault. We need to call the police, but let's . . . get out of here first."

Together, we rushed from the room and down the hall. My eyes were fastened to him the whole way. The wound didn't seem too bad, but the blood kept making its way down his gray shirt. Dad had been aiming for his throat, but Carson's reflexes had saved him. And he'd most likely saved me by showing up. I'd gladly spend the rest of my life thanking him.

At some point my brain had clicked off, and instinct had taken over. Get out. Call the police. Get Carson help. It was all

I could focus on. He leaned into me, letting go to pull a phone out of his pocket.

We reached the door downstairs, my heart pounding as my fingers circled the cold doorknob.

"Stop!"

We whirled around. Dad was coming down the stairs, and there was that pistol—in his hand and pointed right at us. Carson pushed me back against the door, shielding my body with his.

"No!" I screamed, struggling to knock Carson out of the way. "Dad, don't do this!"

He came across the foyer, his arm shaking. "None of this was supposed to happen! You have to believe me, princess. I never intended for Cassie to die. For you—"

The gun went off, and I screamed, wrapping my arms around Carson's waist. I expected him to slump down, to fall, and the terror of losing him was so real I could taste it on my tongue.

But he never fell. He only turned slightly, trying to force me away, and I didn't understand why. Confusion poured through me as I managed to move to the side.

Dad lay on the floor, facedown. A red spot on the center of his back quickly spread. Lifting my head, I saw my mother standing behind him, holding one of his hunting rifles.

I sat on the front porch steps for the longest time, numb after answering so many questions. I'd learned that Mom had come home from the meeting and gone for the gun when she heard me scream upstairs. I don't know what had been going through her head when she saw Dad pointing the gun at Carson and me, only that she'd reacted. She had immediately protected me. No questions asked. No hesitation.

People came and went, trying to talk to me, checking me over. The lights kept flashing. Blue. Red. Blue. So many voices crowded me. Activity was everywhere, even after they'd rushed Dad off to the hospital.

He had still been alive then, but now, I didn't know.

Pulling my knees up to my chest, I tried to make myself as small as possible. The police still had Mom separated from me. Carson had disappeared in a swarm of EMTs and police. Had they taken him to the hospital? Was he okay?

Out of the mass of people milling about, a familiar figure headed toward me, and I looked up, surprised that he was still here. Other than the bandaged shoulder, he looked fine.

"Just a scratch," he said, dropping down beside me. He wrapped his good arm around me. In a daze, I noted that Dad hadn't injured Carson's throwing arm and ruined his future. "I have to go to the hospital, but I needed to see you first. Took a little convincing . . ."

I leaned over and kissed him deeply. "Thank you."

He kissed my temple softly, whispering something in my ear that I couldn't hear. Voices rose suddenly, and Scott appeared in the chaos, his face pale with shock as he strode toward us before being cut off by the police and led over to where they were questioning our mother.

A tremble ran through my body, and I twisted toward Carson, burrowing my face against his chest. What was I supposed to tell Scott? How were any of us going to get over this?

What Dad had done, what he'd planned to do to Carson and me, was a bitter ash forming on my tongue.

If Dad made it out of surgery alive or not, I wasn't sure I really wanted to know.

Carson's hand ran the length of my spine, soothing in spite of the tremble that coursed through his arm. The tears wouldn't stop, but beneath the sorrow, there was some relief driving them. The truth was finally out there, and maybe this would bring Cassie's family some peace.

Maybe it would bring me the same peace one day.

He brushed the hair away from the side of my face. "It's okay. Everything is okay."

And it would be. Eventually.

epilogue

There was one thing that I knew was the same before Cassie died and now. I had no patience whatsoever.

Shifting my weight from one foot to the next, I watched the time count down on the microwave like a bird of prey. Even when the contents started popping in rapid succession it still wasn't fast enough.

I hated missing previews, even the ones shown on DVDs.

When the kernels slowed in their explosions, I whipped the bag out of the microwave and emptied the popcorn into a large bowl waiting on the counter. Cradling the buttery goodness against my chest, I spun around. Strands escaped my messy ponytail, falling along my cheeks.

Mom leaned against the kitchen bar with a bottle of water. She hadn't picked up a glass of alcohol since that night. I couldn't blame her, though, if she had indulged, but she had become a stronger person. The media had gone crazy with the story once it went live, and there was no way Mom could worry about what her friends said anymore. And I didn't think she really did.

A tentative smile pulled at her lips. The gray shadows under her eyes weren't as dark as they'd been the weeks following Dad's arrest. He'd survived the shooting, and we were told he'd plead guilty to manslaughter plus a slew of other charges once he went to court. I really didn't know how to feel about Dad. I don't think I'd ever know how to feel about him.

"Watching a movie?" Mom asked.

I nodded. "Yeah, it's about to start."

She stepped aside. "I don't want to keep you, then."

It had been a month since I'd remembered everything, since the day Mom had shot Dad, stopping him from silencing the truth forever. Things hadn't been perfect. Over the course of the following days, I had moments when I couldn't remember something clearly and frustration would lap at my sides and quickly turn into anger.

Or when I couldn't stop thinking about Cassie and the horrific details of the night she died. All she'd wanted was what I had—a real father. I wished I could have gone back in time knowing what I knew now and been a better friend.

Tomorrow would've been her eighteenth birthday. I planned on visiting her grave site . . . with Cassie's mom. Strange to do so after she'd smacked me, but a few days after everything had happened, I remembered the music box.

With Scott in tow, I'd gone to Cassie's house, and reluctantly, her mom had let me inside. As I suspected, Cassie had hidden something important in the music box. It was why she never wanted me touching it.

The music box housed her birth certificate.

Her mom had no idea how she'd gotten her hands on it, but seeing my father's name listed as hers had been what started it all. I didn't think Dad even knew he was on that birth certificate.

Holding the proof of who Cassie really was to me—to Scott and our whole family—had been harder than I ever thought it would be. There were so many what-ifs—what if Cassie had confided in me earlier on, what if Dad had just told the truth and accepted her. So many things would've been different.

I'd stopped taking my meds, but I still saw Dr. O'Connell once a week. I hadn't written myself any more notes, but I woke up many nights covered in sweat and screaming like a banshee. It would be a long time before I was normal, but Scott was there those nights, and so was Mom.

Setting the popcorn bowl aside, I went to my mother and wrapped my arms around her. "I love you."

Her posture was rigid as she hugged me back. Not the best hug, but we were working on it. Our relationship hadn't been great before everything happened, but I figured it could only get better.

"I love you, too." She brushed the loose strands off my forehead. "Get. Go have fun."

Smiling, I untangled my arms and grabbed the bowl. Her gaze drifted over me, but she didn't comment on my oversize sweatpants and shirt that had seen better days. Better—she was getting better.

I hurried through the rooms, hanging a right. I went down the stairs two at the time. Laughter and the low murmur of conversation rose up. Someone had paused the movie for me.

And I had a feeling I knew who.

Unable to stop the grin spreading across my lips, I moved around the sectional couch, stepped over a pair of long denim-clad legs, and plopped down.

Scott stretched over and snatched the bowl of popcorn away from me. "Thanks," he said. "You're the best."

Julie giggled as she grabbed a handful. "Not saying much, considering the company."

"Whatever." He tossed a few kernels at her.

Watching them waste perfectly good popcorn, I sank back and inhaled the scent that always sent my heart racing—citrus and soap.

The arm on the back of the couch behind me slipped off and wrapped around my shoulders. He pulled me against his side and lowered his head, his lips brushing the curve of my neck as he whispered, "Missed you."

Good pressure built in my chest as I tipped my head back and met eyes so blue they reminded me of electricity. "I was only gone five minutes."

"So?" Carson said, lowering his head. "Long enough."

"Cornball," Scott muttered.

Julie smacked him. "Shut up. You say cornier things when no one else is around. He just has the balls to say it in front of us."

I laughed.

"Whatever. I have balls," Scott argued. "You know exactly how big—"

"No one wants to know that, dude," Carson cut in, but his eyes were trained on me as if I was his entire world.

"Agreed," I said quietly, reaching up and threading my fingers through the hair curling around the nape of his neck. His eyes flared, and my belly warmed. "Kiss?"

"Kiss."

He brought his mouth to mine, and even though this kiss was sweet and had nothing on what he could do when we were alone, my breath still caught in my chest and my toes curled. Each time we kissed, it was like the first time, over and over again. Nothing compared to it.

I was pretty sure nothing ever would.

"Okay. If you guys are done making out, ready to watch the movie?" Scott asked, sounding only a little peeved.

Carson's lips spread into a grin against mine. He stole one more quick kiss before he pulled back. "Yeah, we're ready as ever."

Cheeks flushed, I snuggled closer to Carson, throwing an arm around his waist. His fingers curled around the loose strands of my hair. The movie clicked on and the previews started to roll.

Things weren't perfect. They were far, far from it, but they were getting there, and I wasn't looking back. Not when there were so many good things in the future.

acknowledgments

Writing acknowledgments is always harder than writing the actual book, because I know I'm going to forget someone important. But here I go. First off, a big thank-you to my agent Kevan Lyon. This was the first book of mine that she read and offered representation on. It also turned out to be the first novel she sold in January 2012. Without her, this book wouldn't have been possible. Another big thank-you to Emily Meehan for reading the book and missing her train stops. I think that last part helped get a yes when it came to accepting the manuscript. This book also wouldn't be what it is today without Laura Schreiber, Mary Ann Zissimos, and the wonderful team at Disney Hyperion, especially Tyler Nevins, who whipped out an awesomely creepy cover that I still want to cuddle with. Taryn Fagerness has also played in a key part in getting *Don't Look Back* sold into many, many territories outside the United States. Special thanks to Angela from Reading Angel for being one of the first people to read *Don't Look Back* and fall in love with Carson, along with Lesa Rodrigues. And a thanks to Molly McAdams for making me feel good about writing a book that is so different from what I typically write. Thank you to Stacey Morgan for being the awesome person that she is, even when I send her questionable images on Yahoo. Also, KP Simmons and the team at Inkslinger for doing their magic.

But most importantly, the biggest thank-you goes to the readers. Without you guys, none of this would be possible. Hell, it would be pointless. I can never thank you all enough for allowing me to take my overactive imagination and put it to good use.

New York Times #1 best-selling author **Jennifer L. Armentrout** lives in Martinsburg, West Virginia. Not all the rumors you've heard about her state are true. When she's not hard at work writing, she spends her time reading, working out, watching really bad zombie movies, pretending to write, and hanging out with her husband and her Jack Russell, Loki. Her dream of becoming an author started in algebra class, where she spent most of her time writing short stories . . . which explains her dismal grades in math. Jennifer writes young adult paranormal fiction, science fiction, fantasy, and contemporary romance. She is published by Spencer Hill Press, Entangled Brazen, Disney • Hyperion, and Harlequin Teen. She also writes adult and new adult romance under the name J. Lynn.

Visit her online at www.jenniferarmentrout.com.